Falcon's Dream

T.S. Mos

ISBN: 978-1-7336587-7-5

Chapter 1

"Falcon, give me your hand!" Abra's voice echoed around me as I stepped into the portal behind him. I extended my left hand, as my right was busy clutching the hilt of my sword, ThornSting, in a death grip. A warm, strong hand grasped mine. "And for Gods' and Goddess's sake, open your eyes, woman!"

At his insistence, I did open my eyes only to instantly regret it. Abra, my warlock mentor and sometimes travel companion, stood before me, slightly to my left, but nothing else I could see made sense. Ahead in the distance, a cool blue circle of light pulsed gently, and by concentrating on it I managed to regain some of my balance. The walls of the tunnel in which we stood were shimmering, moving, and eerily reflective. So much motion and light playing everywhere made my head spin. I fought to keep myself from releasing ThornSting so I could clutch Abra's arm with both hands. There I was, standing in a magical portal, surrounded by raw energy, and all I could think was that my mentor had just called me 'woman'! Some very female part of me that I usually kept hidden, bound in chains, and buried, was suddenly free and laughing in delight. How in the world could the utterance of a single word make an otherwise rational female want to curl her toes?

"Look at me, Falcon," Abra demanded my attention. I was finally able to pull my eyes away from the hypnotic effects of the portal. "Pay attention! Watch where you step and follow me."

"Why must I watch where I step?" I countered, "Doesn't a portal go from one place to another?"

"Indeed," he nodded, "but where it goes depends on our intent. If we're not clear on where we're going, we'll end up where the portal wants us.

And if you're not careful you could step through the portal itself and end up somewhere else entirely."

"How can I be clear on my intent if I've no idea where we're going?" Trying to be logical without resorting to whining, I challenged.

"You can't know where you're going because you've not yet been there," he offered. "I shall be clear on our intent for the both of us this trip."

"And I can step through the portal itself?" I asked, suddenly wanting nothing more than to return to Corhaven and hide beneath my bed. "You didn't tell me this would be dangerous!"

"For an experienced warlock portal travel is not dangerous and in fact it is the safest way for us to travel. You must learn to look, listen, follow directions, and be single-minded in your journeying."

"You might have told me that before we started this," I complained while hating myself for doing so. "Are you going to hold onto me all the way through the portal?"

"Yes," he replied, "as this is your first such journey, I am, as you say, going to hold onto you to ensure you and I will reach the same destination. In time and with practice this will not be necessary. Now please give me your right hand."

Loath to let go of my sword, I hesitated.

"Falcon, give me your right hand," Abra insisted. "Trust me, you'll have no immediate need of your blade."

With great reluctance, I let go of ThornSting to extend my right hand. Abra released my left hand to grasp my right, and though I still felt a bit vulnerable, I realized that to some extent, I did trust him.

"Come," he said firmly as a thought occurred to me.

"But Abra, where else would I…" I started to ask as he raised his hand to silence me.

"There is a time and a place for questions and answers," he offered, "and this is neither. Let us journey now and we shall discuss matters at another time." Turning to face the light at the end of the portal, Abra held my hand firmly as he began walking.

'*Fine!*' I thought, silently fuming. Trying to see where I was walking was far from easy as the illumination in the portal was erratic and sometimes diffuse. Though I wondered if it was possible to use an Earth Star, like my Scorch, in a portal, I held my tongue, making a mental note to ask my question when the time was ripe.

I took three steps, but when I put my left foot down for the fourth there was nothing solid to catch me. Yelping, I struggled to regain my balance even as Abra pulled me back onto solid ground.

"Did I not tell you to watch where you're stepping?" He admonished. I began to mount a defense even as I turned to inspect where I'd walked. There was nothing unusual about the portal behind me, no hole, no broken surface, nothing!

"Abra, how can I tell where not to step if I can't see anything to indicate I shouldn't step there?"

"Look again, Falcon," he said calmly, indicating where I should look with an outstretched index finger. "See that place just there? It's not as reflective as the rest of the portal. It's lustrous but not shiny. That's where the membrane of the portal is weak. Never step where you see such luster."

"That's almost impossible to see," I gasped, imagining myself tumbling through the membranes of countless portals repeatedly landing in extraordinary places.

"With practice you'll come to sense such spots even before you're close enough to see them," Abra explained as he turned back to the blue light at the end of the tunnel. "Come, Falcon, we're almost through the portal. And when we reach the mouth, just ahead, I want you to close your eyes, take a deep breath, and step out. Don't worry, I'll still have your hand."

"First I'm to open my eyes," I sighed, "then I'm to close them."

"Trust me, Falcon," he grinned, "you'll understand why very shortly indeed."

As we reached the mouth of the portal Abra reminded me once more to close my eyes. He guided me step by step until I felt a difference in the air. Wind swirled around me, whipping my hair into my face. A whistling scream rose before subsiding. My companion patted my hand as he leaned close.

"Open your eyes, Falcon," he raised his voice to be heard over the roaring of the wind, "but do not move. I have you. You're safe."

Slowly I opened my eyes to peer around. For a moment it seemed we were standing in the sky, but I glanced down to see solid, red, sandy rock beneath our feet. It took me a moment to grasp our situation, though I was left speechless when at last I did. I could only look into Abra's dark eyes and swallow silently. He gave me a reassuring nod, squeezing my hand in encouragement as he lifted his eyes to the distance.

When at last I gathered my courage to look, I found we were standing atop a towering spire of stone. Other spires of equally terrifying heights surrounded the one upon which we stood, their numbers marching off in all directions as far as the eye could see. Red, orange, blue, and violet lights flowed like a wild river through the narrow canyons between the monolithic stones. I knew instantly the colors were energies carried by the wind.

"Why are we here?" I called to Abra, brushing an errant strand of hair from my face.

"Because this is on the way to where we need to be," he answered, nearly shouting. "Now, jump when I say to do so."

"Jump?" I called out, aghast at the notion.

"Now!" Abra commanded. I barely caught sight of him leaping into the air before closing my eyes. I really had no need to jump as the force of the warlock doing so yanked me off my feet. Abra's hand was the only thing I could feel for a moment before solid ground was suddenly beneath my feet. My knees bent slightly upon impact, but I was able to keep my balance and not fall to the ground.

"You can look now, Falcon," he directed calmly, just as I realized the wind was no longer screaming around us. When I opened my eyes, a thrill and a wonder I had never experienced rose in my heart. What I was seeing was amazing, incredible, and entirely confusing. I realized upon further inspection that what I at first took to be the face of a cliff before us was the facade of a towering building perched atop a raised foundation. A smooth stone road lay before the ornately carved wooden double doors and wound away in both directions. I noticed that we were inside a stone fortress with the road curling around the inner walls. To our right, adjacent to the building, was a circular low wall inside which stood an oddly shaped tower adorned with strange creatures in dancing poses. I stood staring, completely entranced by the sight for a time, until I noticed people in strange garments coming and going around us, some casting curious glances at me as they passed.

"It is a fountain, Falcon," Abra said, nodding at the odd-looking structure, "and sometimes there is water flowing from the top of the tower to rain down on the dancing statues below."

"What is it for?" I gasped, imagining what such a shower might look like.

"It is for nothing," he offered, "or rather, it is for decoration, for the simple beauty of itself, for all to enjoy."

"I've never seen anything like it!"

"I should think not," he chuckled.

"Where are we, Abra?" I asked, looking at the people as they went about their business, some carrying bundles of what looked like cloth, some toting leather satchels, some holding the hands of children as they hurried them along.

"Not only where, Falcon," he leaned near my ear to whisper, "but when."

"When, what?" I wrinkled my brow, trying to grasp what he was telling me. "You said this portal isn't like the one Mala and Mara showed me, so this isn't the past?"

"Not now, Falcon," Abra took my hand once more as he led me toward the raised road, "now we need to get inside that building."

"What is this building?" I couldn't help but ask as we hurried toward it.

"It was once an exquisite castle built for the nobility of this realm," he explained in hushed tones, "but it was abandoned, or rather it will be, and it's now being inhabited by the poor."

"This was a royal castle," I wondered aloud as I looked at the smooth stone facade and the narrow windows covered with shimmering glass. "It looks nothing like any castle I've seen."

"Again, I would expect that would be the case," Abra nodded curtly as we approached the elaborately carved, heavy wooden doors, "as nothing like this was built in your time."

"My time," I protested as he pushed down the handle on the door and shoved its weight. When the heavy door swung silently inward Abra pulled me into the cool darkness.

"Be still, Falcon," he whispered. "We must not be discovered here. Let us be quick and quiet."

"What are we doing here?" I whispered back in confusion.

"We're retrieving something very important," he grinned as he tightened his grasp on my hand. "Follow me and keep to the wall."

Stealing as silently as possible, Abra and I moved along quickly, staying in the deeper shadows. Down the wide corridor, tall open doors spilled weak light across the floor. Distant voices rose and fell in muffled discussion. My companion put his index finger to his pursed lips as he waved me forward. At the end of the hall a series of shallow steps led down into even darker shadows and, to my consternation, Abra went down them swiftly, leaving me no choice but to follow. The darkness was so heavy I could see nothing around me, not even my hand before my face.

"Abra," I whispered as loudly as I dared, "where are you? I can't see anything!"

When a soft light appeared just ahead, I was delighted and relieved to see Abra's face. He lifted his hand as the ball of light he held stretched its illumination around us. We were in a smaller, but similarly designed, lower hall which doubled back on the one we'd just traversed.

"Come, it's not much further," he nodded, turning to lead the way beneath the light. His shadow moved before me as the glowing orb created a halo that allowed me to see the details of the structure of the hall. Unlike the upper hall which had rooms on only one side, this lower hall had shorter, but equally ornate, doors on both sides indicating rooms on either side. Sconces of swirled metal were mounted on the walls near each door, though no flames burned on the candles each held.

At last, Abra stopped near a door on the right, raising his hand. I drew up behind him silently, waiting as he opened the heavy door. It creaked slightly but not loudly enough that anyone would hear or be alarmed.

"Come," he whispered as he ducked into the room. I followed, gently closing the door behind me.

"What we seek is here," Abra announced, looking around the room. Lifting the ball of light above his head, he moved toward the far wall.

"Come Falcon," he called softly, glancing back over his shoulder at me. "I need your help."

"What do I do?" When I moved near, he took my left hand in his.

"Hold this so that I can see," he instructed as he placed the light ball in my palm. To my surprise, it did not burn but instead felt cool and tingling on my skin.

Turning toward the wall, the warlock began to touch the stone here and there with his palms, as if searching for something. When a 'click' echoed around the room he stepped back as a panel in the wall slid away revealing a rectangle of darkness. I bent down to hold the energy ball near the opening as my companion slipped his hands inside.

"Ah-hah!" He smiled, obviously having found what he was seeking. Drawing forth his prize of what appeared to be a cloth bundle, he stood and straightened. "We've found it!"

"What is it?" I whispered, barely daring to breathe.

"It is a talisman," he answered succinctly, as he opened the bundle to withdraw a beautifully curved two-ended stone blade. Its handle, between the two sharp ends, was intricately crafted and appeared to be bone. Two large red stones were set in the handle, one at the base of either blade.

"It's beautiful," I gasped, "but talisman for what? It looks like some strange sort of knife!"

"Look carefully, Falcon," Abra replied as he lifted the object closer to the ball of light. "It is a haladie, and one day it will be needed."

Suddenly, a cloud swirled around the blade, dark gore dripped from the tips and oozed from the wicked sharp edges. Two ugly creatures carved into the handle rose to writhe, their maws gaping as they held the stones in misshapen claws. A stench, which threatened to make me gag, rose from the knife.

"Oh," I gasped as I covered my nose with my free hand, "cover it back up, please! I don't want to see or smell it again."

Chuckling softly, Abra did as I asked. Soon the stench dissipated and the air returned to normal. As he tucked the covered blade into his belt, I raised an eyebrow in confusion.

"How is that knife, that haladie, a talisman?"

"I shall explain that in time," he nodded, carefully taking the light ball from me. "Now, let us make haste. Our time here must be very short."

Gently opening the door, Abra moved the light first left then right to make sure the hall was empty. Without a word, he made his way down the corridor, sprinting lithely up the steps as he extinguished the ball of light. Behind him, in the shadow of his cloak, I could not see how he made the light orb disappear, so I put yet another question to ask the warlock on my ever-increasing list. He did not hesitate or say a word, but made his way once more along the wall deep in the shadows until we reached the large double doors. As if shaking off the appearance of stealth, the warlock squared his shoulders, took a deep breath, and opened the doors to step purposefully out into the daylight. Without glancing about, he strode along the castle road before stepping down when it gently dropped to ground level to join the wider, more-traveled road. I struggled to keep up with him as he quickly made his way back to where the portal had deposited us.

"Come Falcon," he commanded as he raised his right arm, sweeping his hand from left to right in the air before us. Taking my hand in his, he pulled me forward as the portal appeared, shimmering, and reflecting silently as it spun. "Close your eyes," he reminded me. I did as I was instructed as the warlock drew me once more into the portal.

Chapter 2

A loud splash drew my attention to the river's edge below me. The body of the blackguard who had just murdered my mother and wounded my father was quickly disappearing beneath the waves. A bolt of lightning ripped across the sky, its reflection flashing on the silver leaf-shaped brooch at the murderer's throat. Aeon, my father's black mare, shook her massive head beside me, snorting restlessly. I pulled her lead to turn her around, intending to return to the home where my father lay bleeding, my mother's body cradled in his arms. I had to get back to help! The smell of acrid smoke reached my nose before I laid eyes on the burning cottage. Flames licked from beneath the thatched roof, around the open windows and quickly consumed the partially opened front door. I had to get back there to save my father! I began to run as fast as my legs would carry me, realizing as I did so I had dropped Aeon's lead. No matter how fast I ran the cottage remained distant. Just when I was about to reach the yard, the place would suddenly be far away again. I couldn't run any faster, but I was getting nowhere! Suddenly the thatch roof exploded, collapsing into the structure, and sending plumes of spark and ash into the sky. The flames were quickly destroying my home. I had to get there! I knew it was hopeless, but I had to get there. Deep down I knew how the situation would end, but I had to hope that if I could just get there, I could make things turn out differently. If I could get back to the cottage, maybe I could save my father. Once more I reached the edge of the yard, heat, and thick smoke a wall between me and the man I loved more than anything in the world. I would not be stopped! I would save him!

"Noooooo…," a choking sob escaped my lips.

My own cry woke me as the sound of rushing footsteps approaching brought me fully to my senses. I sat up in the narrow bed, blinking in confusion mingled with relief, to find myself in one of Deacon's guest rooms. The fire in the hearth had gone out, but the room was only slightly chilly. I was happy to be awake.

"Falcon," came the muffled voice of my mentor, Cornelius Welkin, "are you well? Falcon!" He pounded on the closed door in obvious panic.

"I'm fine, Cor," I responded. Tossing back the covers, I climbed out of bed and hurried across the room, my bare feet padding quietly on the smooth wooden floor. Feeling foolish as I opened the door, I added, "I'm all right."

"What was that scream?" My beloved white haired, white bearded guardian blinked frosty blue eyes at me.

"I'm sorry. It was," I faltered, "it was a nightmare, I guess. Though it felt real enough. In fact, I can still smell the wood smoke and taste salty tears on my lips. That's odd, isn't it?" Lifting a lock of my hair to my nose, I took a deep breath of the pungent scent and looked up at Cor.

"Well, I," he began, as he slipped one arm around my shoulder.

"What's going on? Who screamed?" Deacon thundered into the room followed by the three other wizards who'd arrived yesterday for last night's ceremony. Everyone started talking and gesturing at once.

"Please, please," Cor raised his voice to get their attention, "our dear Falcon's just awakened from a particularly vivid nightmare, it seems. 'Twas herself who screamed."

"Falcon, I'm so sorry," Finias stepped forward to pat me on the shoulder. "Would you like a nice cup of hot tea to settle your nerves?"

"That might be nice, yes," I nodded, "tea would be lovely. I'm so sorry to have awakened everyone. This is so embarrassing. I haven't had this nightmare in years."

"Do you remember the dream?" Declan, the Elemental Wizard of Earth interjected.

"I do, yes. I was dreaming of the day my parents," I paused, realizing that even talking about the newly refreshed pain might make me cry. "I dreamed of when my parents were murdered and my home was destroyed. That was so long ago! This is the first time I've dreamed about that in, well, I can't remember how long."

"Maybe it was an after-effect of last night's elixir?" Eban offered as he stroked his fingers down his red beard, a habit he performed whenever he was deep in thought.

At the mention of last night's elixir, I recalled the entire evening in great and wonderful detail. It had been the night of my initiation into the Order of Healers and, as was customary, I'd been given an elixir to prophesy before receiving my sapphire blue sash. It had been a long journey for me to become a healer and I'd done so mostly to honor the memory of my mother, Selene Sylvan, who had been a gifted, talented healer. My father, Arne Rose, had been the captain of King Stephen of Esling's guard and though I had adored my parents equally, down deep I had been closer to him. He was everything I wanted to be: a valiant and brave warrior, one of action and honor. My mother's skills had been amazing, so I was often surprised and delighted at how she could heal sickness, mend injuries, and help others, but that was not something I was drawn to naturally. She had tried to teach me about herbs, how to make poultices, and create tinctures. But such lessons had seemed like mere distractions to me, drawing my attention away from what I really wanted to do, which was to become a guard for the king like my father. My mother's gift had been passed down to her through her mother and her mother's mother, and she was considered a wise and cunning woman, as she could often see future events. But until she was taken from me it had not occurred to me that I might follow in her footsteps. Once the mystery of my parents' murder had been solved and, with the help of others, I'd rescued Prince Rowan and returned him to Esling, I began my studies in earnest. For the past few years, I'd spent three lunar cycles at a time with each elemental wizard, availing myself of their kindness and wisdom. All told, I'd been in the presence of each wizard for at least a full year and had completed their tests and challenges successfully. Last night, as the full moon washed over the valley, an eerie green energy stirred around Deacon's cottage, turning it into an 'in-between' place. The felinetrix, Malamara, in singular human form, streaks of white hair on both sides of her face, looked on as I was initiated into the Order of Healers. Having been given a proper kit of healing herbs, bandages, splints, and ointments, I was presented with the much-honored sapphire sash. The elixir, I recalled, had tasted tart at first, but it blossomed bitter and burned as it went down my throat. My head felt strange. The world tilted a little as images rushed into my mind. I saw King Rowan marry within the coming year, putting a Queen on the throne of Esling. I saw his queen would eventually bear him three children. And I clearly saw a battle approaching. As quickly as the elixir-born images arrived, they departed, leaving me feeling much better, clear-headed, and light-hearted.

"Well," Deacon cleared his throat to gain everyone's attention, "as it's clear that our Falcon is fine and as this room was not built to hold this many of us, I suggest we all adjourn to the main hall. Eban can stoke the fire and we'll put on the kettle. We can relax and have a chat, wait for our nerves to settle so we can all go back to sleep."

"I second that," Declan raised an index finger, "let's go get some tea or maybe something more potent."

"Again," I offered with a sheepish grin, "I didn't mean to wake everyone. I'm sorry I screamed in my sleep." It amused me greatly that I was still referred to as 'our Falcon,' as if I were their possession, but it was certainly true that the wizards and Deacon had warmly welcomed me into their hearts and lives.

"Don't you fret, Falcon," Cor patted my hand gently, "we all have bad dreams from time to time. Maybe it means nothing, but maybe the nightmare does have some portent. Perhaps if we discuss it in detail, we can glean the truth of the matter?"

"I suppose you may be right," I shrugged, "and this is certainly not the place to discuss things." The small room in which I slept whenever I was at Deacon's place was not much bigger than a cubbyhole. The bed, designed to sleep one, had been much more comfortable for me when I was younger, but I was still fond of it and refused the offer of a larger room with a bigger bed. The hearth in the far wall was cozy and did a good job warming the place, but it was not big enough for more than two people to gather around. There was a small table against the wall upon which sat a pitcher and wash basin. Beside the table stood a straight-backed chair one could use to don one's socks and shoes, but it was not so comfortable that anyone would choose to relax on its stiffly woven seat. A small window in the wall adjacent to the hearth allowed the morning sun to light and warm the room during the day but at night it became a dark rectangle as it was too low to allow in starlight.

As the wizards and Deacon filed out, a black and white cat slinked in around the door jamb, scratching itself as it entered. Languidly, Mala, now feline, crossed the room to wind herself around my bare ankles. This wouldn't be an issue were the cat Mara, as she was particularly careful around human flesh, but Mala's focus was more on her own pleasure and she wasn't above using my calf for a scratching post or giving me a little nip just to hear me squeal. Quickly, I bent down to scoop her up in my arms, and held her to my chest as I rubbed her ears. Her purring was instantaneous and loud.

"Come on, Mala," I addressed the cat as I would were she in her human form, "let's go out to the hearth and I'll get you some milk. I'm ready for some hot tea."

My thoughts went back to when I'd first met Mala, and Mara. My father, as he lay dying, had directed me to follow the river Loar, to ride his horse Aeon to my Aunt Grete's house in the village of Duhne. I'd taken ill, become afevered, and had wandered lost until Abra had crossed my path. The young man with dark curls and beautiful eyes had built me a fire, shared his food and mead, and his family had tended to my clothes. When he disappeared and I woke to find myself alone I was much improved, but still wandering without clear direction. Eventually I'd fallen asleep at the base of a tree where Cornelius Welkin, affectionately called Cor, found me and took me in.

Once I'd recovered fully from my journey, Cor had delivered me to Duhne, where we discovered that my Aunt Grete had already passed on, leaving me with no family, no home, and very little hope for my future. On the way back to Cor's place, Corhaven, we'd stopped in at Deacon's and I'd been introduced to the healer as well as his companion, Mala. Deacon's lovely woman had insisted I join her in the woods at the water's edge where she directed me to 'draw down the moon' in my hands. It was discovered that night that I was not, as expected, one of the moon's witches, but was, instead, a solar witch. When the full moon transitioned to waning, my companion in the forest disappeared after turning into a big black and white cat. Her other half, Mara, had appeared in feline form, live mouse squirming between her teeth, and shifted into human form even as Mala bounded off through the woods. I'd never heard of a felinetrix, let alone actually met one, so I was both surprised and fascinated. Over the years the three of us had grown quite close, though the two were only together in singular human form rarely and only for very short periods of time. They explained to me that they could be together, as two females in human form or one singular female, only in 'in-between' places and times, though I'd not had enough experience with either to recognize such easily. It had been the felinetrix that had gifted me with the knowledge of my birth, showing me how I'd been offered to the God of the Sun when the Goddess of the Moon refused to save me after a difficult birth. They had escorted me to a portal in the trees and had stood with me as I observed the circumstances of my arrival. The two had held my hands while I cried over what I'd seen. I'd come to think of them as sisters, though they were quick to remind me they were two different aspects of the same being, but sometimes it was just too hard for me to grasp that.

"Are you coming, Falcon?" Cor stood near the door, head cocked, raising one eyebrow at me.

"I am," I nodded, releasing the purring feline amidst the covers on my bed, "but I want to put some stockings on so my feet don't get cold."

"What kind of tea would you like?

"Peppermint, of course!" I added as I crossed the room, "Is there any other kind?"

"I'll get Finias right on it," my beloved mentor smiled. "He fancies himself quite an expert when it comes to the art of drinking tea."

"Oh, I know, I know," I assured him as I plucked my only slightly worn stockings from the pile of clothes I'd draped over the back of the chair. "A good deal of my education with him included the proper way to brew and serve tea, how to grind beans for coffee, and which cheese to pair with which fruit!"

"Yes, that's our Finias!"

"Go ahead, Cor, I'll be in shortly," I suggested as I perched on the bed's edge, crossing my left ankle on my right knee. "Mala and I will be right there." The black and white cat, now curled up comfortably on my blankets, blinked bright green eyes at me as if in agreement.

Once my feet were warmly covered, I took the too long, too large, woolen shirt down from the peg by the door and wrapped it around my shoulders. Long ago the felinetrix had provided me with a lovely cotton shift to sleep in and it was often enough, but Cor had sacrificed the heavy woolen shirt to me for additional warmth during fall. Come winter, I'd wear one of my cloaks over my shoulders for warmth if the fire in the hearth wasn't keeping the place warm, but that had not been necessary yet. As we were just approaching Samhain, the final harvest, and Autumn had been mild, I hadn't worn the overshirt much either, but knew it would soon come in handy. I slid my arms into the voluminous sleeves before folding the cuffs up my arms to keep them from covering my hands.

"Come on, Mala," I cooed as I picked the purring feline up once more, pressing her to my chest, "let's go."

In the main room of Deacon's spacious home, the windows were open to the night air and though it was refreshing, I instantly felt chilled. Snuggling Mala, enjoying her warmth and the softness of her fur, I made my way to the hearth where Eban was stirring the embers into flames.

"Here you go, Falcon," the ruddy-complected wizard beamed as he scooted a wooden stool in my direction, "draw that up to the hearth and get warm. Deacon keeps his place a little on the chilly side. He claims it's healthier to breathe fresh air at night, but I suspect it's just that he forgets to close his windows."

"Eban Kendall," Deacon chided from across the room, "you know very well that fresh air is best. And if I've forgotten to close the windows it's probably because you wizards have spiked my spring water again!"

"Now, now," Cor interjected as he hung a kettle of water on one of the iron hooks over the flames, "gentlemen, let's not come to fisticuffs. There's mead in the stone jar on the table, we've bread and sweet biscuits, tea, and anything else anyone could want. I think it would be of benefit to discuss Falcon's apprenticeship now that she's a member of the Order of Healers."

"Quite right, Cor," Deacon beamed as he put empty mugs on the long wooden table, "and I'm honored to have her as my apprentice."

"What exactly does an apprentice do?" I smiled, "I mean, sure, I understand I'll get to work with you, Deacon, but what are the details? How long does an apprenticeship last? What do I get to do? Will I stay here with you or am I to travel? Will you go with me or will I go alone?"

"That's many questions, Falcon," our host replied, "and we'll get to them all shortly, but for now, get yourself something to eat. You'll have hot tea as soon as the water's boiling and we'll relax and discuss all manner of things."

"Like your dream," Finias added as he dropped linen pouches filled with tea leaves into two of the empty mugs. "I think it would be good if we discussed your dream, for perhaps there's a message there you should know."

"Well, I guess that's all right," I shrugged as I released the cat onto the wooden floor. She immediately took two steps closer to the fire, walking a tight circle three times before sinking onto the stones of the hearth. Her purring resumed as she closed her eyes. "I mean, I can tell you what I dreamed but I'm not sure what good it will do."

"It's not just what you dreamed, Falcon," the kindly wizard of the Element of Water explained as he pulled a stool up to the hearth to sit down beside me. "It's what you felt in your dreams, how what you were seeing in your sleep made you feel and act."

"I see," I peered into the fire, willing the kettle to start singing, "but can we discuss my apprenticeship first? I'd like a little time to think about the nightmare, if that's all right."

"Of course, dear," Finias smiled, gently nodding, "oh look, the kettle's about to sing its merry song. I'll make tea." Rising from his stool, he remained in a stooped position as he carefully removed the pot from its iron hook over the fire, potholder in hand. The kettle whistled until Finias removed the cap, moved to the long wooden table, and poured the boiling water over the tea pouches. Declan, Eban, and Cor were sharing mead while Deacon used a long sharp blade to slice cheese.

"First off," our host offered as he crossed the room, a piece of cheese held delicately between the thumb and index finger of his left hand, "let me say that this will not be a traditional apprenticeship, Falcon." Deacon, wearing a tan tunic and dark brown breeches, took his seat in the rocking chair nearest the window, his traditional spot for reading.

"It's not?" I looked up as Finias handed me a steaming mug of tea from which the aroma of peppermint was already wafting.

"No, for you see you are already a member of the Order of Healers and as such you require no apprenticeship or further training. This will be more of an education in who your patients will be, where they are, their family situations, and that sort of thing."

"I see," I murmured, blowing the steam from my brew.

"Falcon," Cor interjected, "your mother Selene Sylvan was a healer and a seer. She knew instinctively when she was needed and where she should go to be of service. However, she was a Lunar Witch, one guided by the Goddess of the Moon. You, on the other hand, are a Solar Witch, guided by the God of the Sun, so your gifts may be quite different from your mother's."

"Being a crusty old druid and not a witch at all," Deacon picked up the story, "I have no such gift of guidance, but those in this realm tend to seek me out and come here for healing. I will always be delighted should you find the time to come help me, Falcon, but there are some folks around here who often cannot travel. I know where they live and will show you, introduce you to those who may be in need of your healing."

"And should your mother's gift be one of yours as well," Finias chimed in, "riding the realm will make that apparent. Once you get the lay of the land you may sense it when someone needs you."

"Oh!" Burning the tip of my tongue on the tea, I chuckled, "I see what you mean. So, there's no tests or time involved with this apprenticeship?"

"No tests, Falcon," Deacon brightened, accepting a tankard of ale from Finias, who had apparently assumed the responsibility of making sure everyone had a libation, "and no specific time required. You'll learn at your own rate and will know when it's time to make your own way."

"But in the meantime, I'll still live at Corhaven?"

"Of course," the dark-haired druid flashed pale green eyes at me, "though you're welcome to stay here whenever you need to. I know several families whose homes are within a few days' ride. They have small children, even one an infant, and are often in need of care, so if you'd like we can ride out after sunrise."

"That would be great!" Taking a long draught of the now cooling tea, I realized that Finias had added honey from the bee hives nearby. Besides using the golden sticky stuff for sweetening tea and food, we also used it in healing, as it was quite valuable in soothing rashes, burns, and even abrasions. The idea of riding the realm with Deacon was exciting, as I didn't get that much opportunity to be alone with him. He was still quite an enigma to me so I hoped my apprenticeship would afford us the time to get to know one another better.

"Now," Finias returned to the stool beside mine before the hearth, "not to annoy you, Falcon, but can we talk about your dream now?" His pale hair, pulled back and gathered at the nape of his neck, shone in the light of the fire. His blue eyes twinkled, but there was obvious concern on his face.

"All right." I sighed, staring absently into my nearly empty mug, "It was basically like a memory of what happened when my parents were murdered and my home was destroyed. I pushed the killer's body down the bank into the river, watching it bounce in the current as it was carried away. I tried to get back to my home as it burned, but it always seemed just beyond my reach."

"Go on," he encouraged softly, "please!"

"I don't know. I guess I knew what was happening, knew how it would end, but just kept feeling like if I could only get there, I could change things!"

"So, you felt…"

"Angry, terrified, desperate," I answered, "maybe more, but mostly angry."

"And you've never had this dream before? Never experienced a dream in just this manner?"

"Oh, after my parents were murdered, I dreamed of that night often. In fact, whenever my thoughts were idle, visions of the incident would play over and over again in my mind. I couldn't help but relive the pain and anguish whenever my mind wasn't focused elsewhere. But that's been some time ago and I've not dreamed of that night in years. In fact, I don't often think of it anymore. Is that odd?"

"Not at all, Falcon," Cor interrupted. "You're healing yourself, so it's only right that you'd release the memories of that painful time."

"Now I feel a little guilty," I admitted. "I feel like I've forgotten my parents, just wiped them from my mind and my heart."

"You've done no such thing," Declan rose from his seat on the bench near the table, drinking horn in hand. "Cor's right, Falcon. You are healing.

You're not meant to dwell on the pain of that loss. Here, have a draught of mead. It will help you sleep."

"So, do you think there's any message in my dream?" Raising my eyebrows in question, I accepted the drinking horn, offering him my empty mug in exchange. Sipping the oh-so-sweet yet strangely tart drink, I let the flavors bloom on my tongue before swallowing to let the fluid go down my throat.

"It's hard to say right now," Finias took my mug from Declan as he made his way around the table to the kitchen area, "but it's certainly something to think about. And if there is a message there, something you or any of us should know about, we'll know it in time."

"Yes, I suppose so," I shrugged.

"Here now," Declan smiled at me, "have one more sip young lady, then off to bed with you."

"Alright," I returned his smile as I lifted the drinking horn to my lips. Once more, I took a sip of the delicious mead, swallowing as I handed it back to the Wizard of the Element of Earth. "Thank you!"

"Good night, Falcon," he bowed before turning away.

"Good night, Falcon," Eban Kendall added.

"Yes, Falcon, good night," Cor crossed the room, embracing me as I rose from my seat. Though I loved all the wizards and Deacon too, my favorite place in the world was in Cor's embrace. It always felt warm, quiet, and so safe in his arms.

"Good night, Falcon," Finias rose from his stool to hug me with one arm once Cor had released me. "Do sleep well this time."

"Thank you Finias," I replied, softly patting his chest.

"Sweet dreams, Falcon," Deacon offered as I started away from the hearth, "and you and I shall travel when the sun rises. Should be a lovely day for a journey. Mara will have provisions packed for us."

"Where is Mara, anyway?" Peering around the spacious room, I suddenly felt guilty for not noticing she was absent.

"Oh, she's likely out beneath the moon on one of her gathering adventures," he responded with a shrug. "Who knows what we'll find she's brought home come dawn."

"Well then," I looked at each of the wizards as well as our host, "thanks to all of you and once more I'm sorry I woke everyone. I'll try not to let it happen again." Snugging the woolen overshirt around my waist to keep the warmth from the hearth in, I bent over to scoop up Mala, as she'd awakened to wind herself around my ankles. Additional wishes of good night and sweet dreams followed me down the narrow hallway as I snuggled the cat on my way back to my room. "This time, no dreams, right, Mala?" Whispering, I rubbed the purring feline's ears, "No dreams this time."

Chapter 3

One warm, insistent paw patted my lips. Drawing a deep breath, I awoke to find Mala curled up on my chest, her head tucked beneath my chin. Why she had her paw on my mouth, I couldn't imagine, but it was nice to wake up to her warm, soft, purring presence. The hearth was completely dark, not even embers remained, so the room was chilly. I hated the thought of crawling from beneath my cozy blankets while the warmth and weight of the cat was so soothing and comforting. I was tempted to close my eyes, to go back to sleep, but I knew Deacon and the wizards would be waiting for me. And, I had to admit, I was curious as to where Mara had been and what she might have brought back with her. Over the years she and Mala had supplied me with lovely garments, soft leather boots, which I promptly outgrew so they were replaced with even nicer ones, and an ornately decorated leather scabbard for my sword, ThornSting. I felt a moment's pang of guilt over looking forward to the felinetrix's gifts, as if I were entitled or expecting something from her, before recalling Deacon's words that it brought her pleasure to see to the needs of others. He'd assured me that all I needed to do was offer my thanks and use whatever she gave me in happiness and good health.

"I'm sorry, fuzzy one," I sighed as I gently removed the sleeping cat from my chest so I could sit up, "but I have things to do and I'll get nothing done with you holding me down." Mala shot me a look of feline disapproval as I put her down on the bed beside me. "You can stay here and go back to sleep if you like, but I need to get washed up and dressed."

The black and white cat blinked those bright green eyes in acknowledgment as she promptly began grooming herself. She licked her right paw before wiping it down the right side of her face, gently drawing it down the length of her long white whiskers. As she was doing her morning ablutions, it seemed I was dismissed and could tend to my own, so I threw my blankets aside as I swung my legs off the side of the bed. Shivering slightly, I forced myself up to tiptoe across the room to the basin on the table. I dipped my hands into the chilly water and splashed it onto my face. Gasping from the cold, I wet and wrung out a cloth to wash as quickly as I could. Patting my skin dry with a soft towel, I donned my tan breeches, ivory linen tunic, and dark brown vest. As I sat on the edge of the bed to put on my stockings and boots once more, I glanced at the back of the chair where my sapphire sash hung. I was so proud of that beautiful length of fabric. It meant the world to me now to be of service to the people of Esling. I had the teachings of the Elemental Wizards as well as what I remembered of my mother's teachings in my head and in my heart, and I had started my own 'book of remedies.' My parents had both been learned people, each knew how to read and write, and all the wizards, though especially Cor, had afforded me access to their personal libraries. My mother's sacred book of spells and cures had perished in the fire that destroyed our home so all the knowledge and insights handed down to her from her mother and her mother's mother had been lost. I could only recall seeing her gently turn the brittle, worn, and aged pages, but I had not been allowed to touch them myself. This made me a little sad, though I could understand her reasoning. As a child I was probably not especially careful or gentle. Still, I appreciated the opportunity to gather what wisdom I'd collected into a book and it had been the felinetrix who had brought me the leatherbound book of blank parchment pages and a charcoal pencil. She assured me that later, when the time was right, I'd copy over my entries using ink that would never fade, but for the time being it needed to be removable in case I made a mistake.

As I tied the sapphire blue sash around my waist, cinching the voluminous tunic nicely, I made mental note to gather my belongings as soon as I'd eaten and had tea. ThornSting lay atop the mantle above the fireplace secure in its brown leather scabbard. The Solar Sword, which I'd been gifted by the wizards, remained hanging in its shoulder scabbard at Corhaven, for it was endowed with elemental magic and I could will it to my hand if ever the need arose. My blanket, which would be neatly folded and rolled to be tied to the back of my saddle, was draped across the top of a cord tied to two pegs in the wall as it aired and freshened. What clothes I had were neatly folded into a leather saddlebag, though the bag itself was worn and discolored from its many uses. I brushed my long, wildly wavy blond hair, smoothing it as best I could, braided its length, and tied off the end with a leather thong. Cor had gifted me the precious hairbrush years ago when he'd bought it for me from the innkeeper's wife in Duhne, and though the bristles were a bit worn, it still worked well. I cherished that hairbrush and carefully returned it to the cloth in which I kept what precious personal items I owned. Briefly, I unwrapped my father's silver brooch to touch the intricate scrollwork surrounding the rose emblem before wrapping it securely and returning it to the cloth. A similar cloth, folded beneath, held King Rowan's brooch, a silver vined circle around an upright sword with a lightning bolt. My Earth Star, the shimmering gem Scorch, which Declan had gifted me with when I first began my quest to rescue Prince Rowan, vibrated gently beneath its silken protection. I'd had it out beside the fireplace to soak up the energy of the flames, but had wrapped it and returned it to the pile of my possessions before retiring the previous night.

"Come on, Mala," I picked up the cat who had completed her grooming ritual and now sat on the bed patiently waiting, "let's go get food!"

The smell of apples, maple syrup and spicy meat cooking reached my nose as I stepped into the hallway. I took a deep breath, suddenly ravenous, and hurried to the main room where the gentlemen were all busy. Finias was just taking the steaming kettle off the hook in the hearth as I entered. He glanced up at me with a smile.

"There she is! Good morning, Falcon."

"Good morn, Finias," I grinned. "Would that be my tea you're about to pour?"

"So it is," he nodded as he carefully made his way to the table where he lifted a mug, "and I expect you'll be wanting your usual peppermint?"

"Surprise me. I'm feeling adventurous today." Crossing the wooden floor in boots so soft they made no sound, I stepped into the cold room off the kitchen area and grabbed a pail of fresh milk. A rapid-moving stream ran underground beneath Deacon's place so the cold room had been opened to it for storing food as well as medicinal ingredients that needed to be kept cool. The fresh air always startled me, usually causing me to gasp, and this morning was no exception.

"Come on Mala," I cooed to the cat in my arms, "I'll pour you some milk to drink before you go outside to hunt or do whatever it is you do."

"Here, Falcon, let me do that," Mara offered brightly as I stepped out of the cool room. "You get your tea and some food. I'll tend to Mala." The felinetrix, in human form, wore a long vivid blue gown with a white satin sash around her neck. Her ebony hair, brushed smooth, hung down her back while the streak of white on the left side of her face drew my attention to her big, bright, green eyes. Her smile was always generous and kind.

"Thanks Mara," I replied as I handed her both the cat and the pail, "I guess I should be moving quickly this morning."

"Are you excited about your journey?" Cor asked as he put a platter of his magnificent Tomcakes on the table. Oats, apples, and honey, the crispy cakes were griddled in butter so the scent made my mouth water. When I'd first met the wizard, he'd told me about how he'd created the sweet treats for his horse Tom, also known as Old Tom, and though he'd taught me how to make them myself they were never quite as good as those he made. It had crossed my mind that maybe he'd added some magic to the cakes, magic I either lacked or had yet to learn.

"I am," I nodded, reaching for a warm Tomcake. "And I guess I'm a little nervous too. I'm not quite sure what to expect."

"Expect a pleasant journey, Falcon," Deacon chimed in, "for we shall take our time and go as the wind takes us."

"How long will we be gone?"

"That depends on what we encounter, I should think. But likely three or four days, perhaps more if the need is great."

Eban Kendall and Declan Terrene burst through the front door amidst much shared laughter. Their cheeks were bright from the cold and they smelled of brisk fresh air.

"Good morn, lass," Declan bowed when he caught sight of me. "We've just come from the paddock where we readied the mounts for your journey."

"Your beloved Aeon is saddled and ready to go," Eban added, "and I think she's a bit anxious to be on the road. Those hooves of hers are fairly dancing in anticipation."

"And we've saddled Nex for you, Deacon, old man," Declan beamed, "if you think you can handle the stallion."

"It's true that I often make my journeys on foot," the druid admitted, "but if Falcon's willing to share the steed with me, I think I can handle him."

"Of course, Deacon," I nodded exuberantly, "you know you're welcome to Nex. And he's a most gentle thing now that he's been so long away from his cruel previous owner."

"Very well," Cor interjected, "that's settled so let's all sit down and eat. We'll help the journeyers prepare afterwards. I've cooked up extra Tomcakes, there's fresh apples in the larder, and cheese and dried meat wrapped ready to go. We just need to gather your gear, collect your food, fill your water skins, and you'll be on your way."

"I'm going to miss you," I murmured, looking up from my steaming mug of tea. When I caught Cor's steely blue eyes, he offered me a sweet smile with a wink.

"Wish we could go with you," the white-haired wizard offered, "but we're nearing last harvest and there's work to be done before winter arrives."

"I understand," I shrugged. "It's nice to know we've someone to come home to!"

Deacon took the seat at the head of the long wooden table while the rest of us sat down on the wooden benches on either side. I was to the host's right while Cor sat directly across from me. Declan sat to my right while Eban took the seat beside Cor. Finias, always concerned for the needs and wants of others, made sure all had drink before taking his seat at the far end of the table. A platter piled high with sausages and sliced meat, which I couldn't immediately identify, graced the center of the table. Baskets of fresh bread, crocks of sweet cream butter, jams and jellies, as well as bowls of fresh apples, pears, and a few late-season berries were scattered about as well. The fire in the hearth merrily hissed and crackled as we all ate quietly. It was an odd thing, I suddenly realized, for the elemental wizards to be so focused on their food that they didn't speak. Granted, I was distracted by the thought of the impending journey, and it made sense if Deacon, too, was deep in thought about it, but the wizards? I couldn't imagine why they were so subdued.

I had just emptied my mug, placed it back on the table, and popped the last bite of Tomcake into my mouth when Mara appeared from one of the back rooms. Parting the cloth drapes that covered the doorway with one elegantly long, pale hand, she held the other hand behind her back as she entered with a smile.

"Falcon, my dear," she beamed, "in honor of your achievement and your first journey as Healer, I've gotten you a gift."

"Mara," I shook my head, blushing, "you didn't have to do that."

"Oh, but I did," she insisted, moving her hidden hand from behind her back. She presented me with a lovely pair of soft, tanned leather saddle bags. "You shall be needing this now as well as in the future. Besides the saddle bags you have are nearly falling apart!"

Standing, I lifted one leg over the bench beneath me before drawing the other across. Making my way to where the felinetrix stood, I couldn't stop staring at the offered saddle bags. They were so pretty! I could imagine them riding comfortably behind my saddle, stretched smoothly across Aeon's back.

"Mara," I gushed as she handed me the bags, "this is just so very thoughtful of you. I don't know what to say!"

"Mala and I want you to have them," she explained, "for we know you'll make good use of them."

"Thank you," whispering, almost choked with emotion, I repeated, "thank you. And thank Mala too. I'm going to miss you!"

With a smile, she threw her arms around my neck, drawing me into a warm embrace.

"We will miss you as well, Falcon, but you may see us on the road, of course."

In the past I'd come to understand that the rules which governed our world had no such hold on the felinetrix. Whereas we humans had to either walk, run, or ride from one place to another, the felinetrix could merely be there one minute and gone the next, whether in cat form or otherwise. She'd appeared to me, as I traveled, more than once over the years I'd known her, often at the behest of her beloved Deacon, so I'd not be surprised to see her over the course of the next few days.

"Thank you again," I murmured as Mara released me, smoothing the length of my braid down my back as I turned. "I'm grateful for the saddle bags."

"You're most welcome, Falcon," she added, "and I've much to put in them after you've stowed what you need inside. Besides your kit, I've more herbs picked fresh last night, and additional fabric for bandages and poultices."

"Thank you! I'll go get my things now." Turning toward the hallway, I was suddenly struck with a pang of regret that I'd be leaving the company of such good friends. Even though I was traveling with Deacon, and that would be fascinating I was sure, I was going to miss the wizards and Mara and Mala.

As I entered the room I'd slept in at Deacon's place since first I'd met the druid, I realized how much I'd grown, physically, mentally, maybe even emotionally. Certainly, having been in the company of such learned and magically powerful beings had helped me heal from the scars of my parents' murder, and they'd kept me challenged and busy as they trained me for the future, but I realized I missed Abra, the warlock who both vexed and intrigued me. It had been far too long since I'd seen him, and I suddenly feared that he'd be unable to find me were he to come looking while I was journeying. Long ago, he'd led me through a portal to a place of unimaginable beauty and mystery where he'd taken possession of a talisman he claimed we'd one day need. It had been so long now that I had to wonder if he'd been mistaken. Perhaps he'd returned to his native Aeriene, never to return to this world again. I hated not knowing, I realized as I began to pack for the journey.

"All right, Falcon," I sighed, pulling my folded clothes from the old, worn saddle bag, "time to stop dawdling and worrying about the warlock. You've places to go and people to see!"

With that, I shook off my heavy thoughts to refocus on the tasks at hand. Opening the window to empty the wash basin, I tossed out the used water before straightening the blankets and pillow on the bed. I put my clothing in the new saddle bags, stowed my cherished personal items gathered in the cloth bundle on top of them, and retrieved ThornSting from the mantle. Pulling my blanket down from the line, I shook it out with a snap and folded it carefully before tying it to go behind my saddle. I secured the leather scabbard belt around my waist to hang below the sapphire sash before sliding ThornSting into place on my left hip. Once everything else was gathered atop the bed, I slung the saddlebags over my shoulder, grabbed my bedroll, and headed for the door. With one last glance back over my shoulder, I bid a silent farewell to the room as I headed to the main hall.

Finias and Declan were busy tidying up the table while Eban was stoking the fire in the hearth. Cor and Mara were on the far side of the room, backs to me, preparing provisions for the journey, I realized, and only Deacon was missing. I stood there silently for a moment, just taking it all in, creating a memory, until Eban looked up from the hearth, dusting the dirt and wood bits from his hands.

He beamed, "Ready to go, Falcon?"

"I guess so," I shrugged, glancing at all the things I was holding, "at least I hope so."

"Come then," straightening, he drew near as he lifted the saddle bags from my shoulder, "I'll give this to Mara and Cor. They can put what you'll need inside. Let's go out to the paddock and I'll help you load the rest of your gear on Aeon. Deacon's already out there loading Nex."

"Go ahead, Falcon," Cor turned, taking the saddle bags from Eban, "Mara and I will be there shortly. Deacon has your water skin as well as his own."

"All right," I smiled as Eban hurried ahead to open the door for me, "let's go!"

"Here," he interjected, disappearing behind the open door only to reappear holding my cloak, "don't forget this. You'll surely be needing its warmth this time of year. Mornings can be especially chilly now."

"You're right," nodding, I accepted the heavy brown woolen hooded cape, tossing it over my shoulder, "I don't want to forget that!"

The morning was cool and clear. The sun, just cresting the horizon, had not yet begun to melt the frost off the grass and fallen leaves strewn about the yard. What was left of the garden stood in the field south of Deacon's place looking sad and forlorn. Pumpkins and gourds had been gathered and were cozying up to the fodder shocks upon which corn was drying. Eventually the stalks would be fed to the livestock, but for now they stood sentinel scattered in the field. After Eban and I hurried across the yard together he opened the paddock gate and bid me enter. As promised, Aeon stood saddled and bridled, her reins loosely tied to a wooden post. She shook her massive head and snorted at my approach.

"Looking forward to a little exercise, huh girl?" Running one hand down her sleek neck, I chuckled as I tossed my tied bedroll across her back and draped my cloak across the saddle. Accepting the filled water skin from Deacon, I hooked it to the saddle and checked Aeon's rigging before turning to watch the druid preparing Nex. My travel companion was dressed in a deep green tunic, black breeches, and black boots. His cloak, a woolen deep gray, hung from his broad shoulders tied loosely at the throat. His long dark hair was smoothed away from his face and gathered at the nape of his neck with a braided leather strip. Unlike Cor, who sported a long white beard, Deacon had only a scruff of hair along his jawline and above his upper lip. Though I'd never seen him shave or trim his facial hair, it never seemed to grow or appear in need of attention.

"Thanks Deacon," I patted Aeon's shoulder, "and I guess we're ready to go as soon as Cor and Mara get here with my saddlebags."

"You're welcome," he nodded. "I've Nex all loaded and ready to go."

"Here we are," Cor announced as he and Mara crossed the yard, "your bags are properly packed, food is carefully loaded, and you may find a surprise or two inside."

"Thank you so much, Cor," I smiled, accepting the saddle bags in my left hand. Wrapping my right arm around his neck, I hugged him tightly. He smelled of soap, cinnamon, and tobacco and I drew in his scent for strength and comfort. "And you'll be hearing from me from time to time, I'm sure." The wizard and I had developed the ability to communicate across vast distances using only our minds. Whether it was his magic, my magic, or a natural melding of the two, we never questioned, as it seemed a useful and wonderful gift, not to be examined too closely.

"You know I'm always here for you if you need me. I'm just a whisper away," patting my back reassuringly, he gave me one tight squeeze before releasing me. "If there's any way I or any of us wizards can help, you just let us know."

"Of course," I nodded, wiping an errant wisp of hair from my eye, I caught the beginning of a tear before it could roll down my cheek. With a sniff, I tossed the saddle bags across Aeon's back, shifted the bedroll over them, and tied everything down. I drew my cloak around my shoulders as I released the reins from the wooden post and gently turned the great beast around so she was heading toward the open gate. Declan and Finias stepped out of the cottage as Eban hurried across the yard to meet them. Mara gave me a quick, gentle hug before moving around me to do the same to Deacon. Cor waved and joined the other wizards while Mara followed, her rich blue robes stirring gently with her movement. As I tied my cloak at the throat, I looked over Aeon's saddle at my travel companion, eyebrows raised in question. With a sharp nod of his head, Deacon mounted Nex so I grabbed the saddle horn and swung myself up onto my steed's back. Once my boots were properly in the stirrups, I gathered the reins, gave Aeon a pat on the neck, and clucked to her as I nudged her gently with my heels.

"Come on, girl," I murmured, "let's go!"

No further prompting or direction was needed, as the huge black mare snorted to set off at a canter. ThornSting bounced comfortably on my hip, its tip softly brushing the horse's side repeatedly. The saddle bags thwapped on her rump as they settled into place. Nex appeared beside me on the left as the white stallion caught up with Aeon. Deacon smiled and turned his attention to the road ahead.

"Let's let the horses work off a little energy," he suggested, voice raised to be heard over the sound of heavy hooves pounding the earth, "then we can walk them and enjoy some conversation."

"Sounds good to me," I agreed, relaxing the reins in my hand so Aeon could set her own pace. As she felt the freedom, the mare lowered her head, kicked up her hooves, and broke into a gallop. I lowered myself in the saddle as we fairly flew over the ground, both horses challenging for the lead.

Chapter 4

Aeon galloped over the hard-packed dirt road, her hooves kicking up dust, until she reached the top of a ravine where I drew her to a halt. The sides of the wash-out were loose and crumbling, as it had been quite some time since the rains re-routed the stream that normally ran along the other side of the forest. Late summer had brought storms and heavy downpours had swelled the stream, causing it to break its banks to flood across the road. The ravine was not so very deep and I realized I could have probably let Aeon cross it without direction. But as I preferred to stay in the saddle and not be tossed onto the road on my backside, I pulled back slightly on the reins as I guided the mare down one side and back up the other. Deacon did the same on Nex and when we were safely across, we nudged the horses into a comfortable walk.

"So," Deacon crossed his hands on his saddlehorn, reins held loosely, as he looked at me, "have you recovered from last night's dream?"

"Yes, I think so," I sighed. "As troubling as it was, it was just a dream and I'm awake now."

"That's right, Falcon," he nodded. "That is exactly right."

"Where are we going first?"

"First, we'll be stopping by the Fulton's place. It's a little less than half a day's ride so we'll be there before midday. Earl and Corliss Fulton have two children, Audrey and Brice. Audrey is five years old, in a hurry to be six, and Brice is three, I believe. The family is generally healthy, but I stop in now and again to drop off supplies for treating sniffles and upset tummies."

"What does the father do?"

"He's a wheelwright," Deacon replied. "He has a woodworking shop behind the house and he makes and repairs wagon wheels. He also makes wooden furniture and his talent for creating beautiful pieces affords his family a comfortable life. They've always insisted on paying me for my time and supplies, though there are many folks who will offer me food or other things in exchange for my services. If those offering can afford it, I accept, but if they clearly cannot I will refuse payment."

"And how do you determine whether someone can afford to pay or not?"

"You look around," he shrugged, "and you'll be able to tell. It may take you some time and practice, but you'll understand."

"I will?"

"In fact, lass, with you being a witch, your instincts and insights will probably be keener than mine," he laughed robustly.

"I guess time will tell," I replied, abruptly changing the subject. "Can I ask you a question?"

"Of course, Falcon. Ask what you will."

"It's just that we've not had much time alone together, you and I, and I've always been curious but never had a chance to ask before. How is it you met Malamara?" Raising one eyebrow, I looked carefully at the druid's face, seeking reassurance that I'd not asked something too personal.

"Well," he glanced up at the morning sky as if the memories could be found there, "let's see. I guess I wasn't too much older than you are now. I'd been a member of the Order of Healers for over a year, probably closer to a year and a half, and there had been an outbreak of fevers in the kingdom. This was not Esling, by the way. I was trained and began serving in Vineta and did not move to Esling until much later."

"Vineta?"

"A land far away, lass," he smiled wistfully.

"Ah, I see. Did you meet the felinetrix there?"

"I did, yes." Nodding, he explained, "You see, I had been traveling the land for many weeks, doing what I could to help those afflicted with the fever. It was a particularly strong and persistent sickness, and many died despite my best efforts. Eventually I developed the fever myself and was forced to camp at the edge of a forest, almost too weak to keep my fire burning."

"You knew that sweating would help break the fever," I offered, imagining him wrapped in a blanket, wracked with chills, sitting cross-legged as close to the fire as he dared with sweat streaming down his face.

"I did, yes," Deacon brightened. "And I must have fallen asleep because I thought I was dreaming when I saw this beautiful woman cross the field before me, walking so smoothly as if floating through the fog. I was sure it was the fever and that I was imagining her. But she spoke very softly and comfortingly to me. She stoked the fire and made some sort of tea I'd never tasted before. When she bade me lie down next to the fire I did so and she put a cool, wet cloth on my forehead. Soon the chills passed, I slept deeply, and when I awoke, I found the fever had broken."

"And was she gone?"

"I fully expected to find myself alone," he admitted with a grin, "and when I first opened my eyes and sat up, it appeared I was. But I heard singing. A lovely, delicate, female voice wafted around me and when I made it to my feet, I saw her approaching from the forest. She was carrying my water skin and it was obviously full!"

"And was it Mala or Mara?" I asked excitedly, "Or was it the two as one?"

"It was Mala that morning. And behind her Mara was winding herself between the trees, stopping to scratch her neck and sharpen her claws on anything that caught her attention."

"So, you met Mala as a woman and Mara in her feline form that morning? Did you have any idea what she was? Or, I mean, did you know what they were? I mean, oh, you know what I mean. Had you ever heard of a felinetrix before?"

"I had indeed, Falcon, though I certainly never expected to meet one." Stretching his back, he ran his left hand through the length of his hair, "It seems to be warming up, this morning. I may have to take off this cloak."

"How did you know about the felinetrix? I'd never heard of such a thing. How did you?"

"Where I was born and raised, it was something of a legend, I guess you would say. A felinetrix was said to be a magical being, one sent to a practitioner of magic."

"Like a witch's familiar?"

"Yes," he nodded slightly as he untied the top of his cloak with one hand. "I guess it would be very much like a witch's familiar." Looping the reins of Nex's bridle loosely around his saddlehorn, Deacon shrugged the cloak from his shoulders, rolled it, and draped it behind his saddle. "I don't suppose your mother had a familiar, did she?"

"No," I sighed, "but again, I didn't know she was a witch until I met Cor and the other wizards. I knew she was a healer, one of the Cunning Folks, but I had no idea she was a witch. I guess I really didn't know what a witch was. Who am I kidding? I still can't say I fully understand that." With a laugh, I drew Aeon to a halt to lift my water skin from the saddle. Pulling the stopper out, I hefted the weight up to let the cool fresh fluid fill my mouth. After three swallows, I wiped a few errant drops from my chin as I replaced the stopper and returned the leather pouch to its place. Deacon was having a drink as well, I noticed.

"We'll be in the forest soon," he offered as he returned his water skin to his saddle, "and hopefully it will be a bit cooler in the shade. There's a stream deep in the woods where the horses can have a drink and we can take a break to eat."

"That sounds good," I admitted. "So, you knew what Mala was when you met her. That's remarkable. But, if a felinetrix is like a familiar, and familiars serve witches, wouldn't that make you a witch?"

"Believe me, Falcon, I asked the same thing of her," he smiled broadly, "but she never gave me a clear answer. I'm clearly not a witch, nothing more than a dusty old druid, but for some reason she has stayed with me. She comes and goes as she will, of course, in whatever form she chooses, but mostly she's by my side."

"Do you love her?" I blurted out without thinking as the rush of embarrassment went up my neck.

"I do," he smiled kindly at me. "Perhaps we're not a traditional couple, but yes, I do love her, them, and I know she loves me. Or they do."

"It is confusing even speaking of the felinetrix, isn't it?" I chuckled despite myself.

"It is, it is," he joined me in laughter.

The buzzing of an insect drew my attention, forcing me to look here and there for it. The sudden swishing of Aeon's long tail made it clear that she was the target of its attack and she pounded her back hooves uneasily on the ground in response. With a snort and a whinny, she shook her massive head as she shuddered.

"Looks like we might need to outrun some bugs, Deacon," I patted my mount's neck to calm her.

"Not a bad idea," he agreed, swatting some invisible attacker from in front of his face. "Let's ride!"

With that, he nudged Nex in the flanks, snapping the reins on his neck, and the white stallion sprang forward. Aeon needed no encouragement from me, bolting into a run. We raced along the hard-packed road, wind whipping through my hair, until the forest came into view ahead. Autumnal foliage crowned the woods on either side of the trail but deep green still decorated lower branches of the trees. The shadows in the forest appeared dark and deep, and with another snap of the reins Aeon dropped her head to increase her speed toward them. I lowered myself over her neck to hold on as we raced over the ground.

"Whoa Nex," Deacon called to his mount as he pulled back on the reins, "whoa, whoa, boy." The mouth of the forest lay just ahead.

"Hold up," I commanded Aeon. "I think that's enough speed for now. Surely, we've outdistanced the bugs."

"Come Falcon," my companion suggested, "let's enjoy the shade and recover our wits. We've a way to go before we reach the stream, but it's cool and quiet in the woods."

"Yes," I wiped perspiration from my hairline, "cool and quiet sounds good."

The road into the forest was clearly old and worn. The two side by side tracks were a clear indication that it was used often by wagons, but it was also convenient for Deacon and I to ride together. Aeon claimed the track on the right and Nex fell into step with her on the left. A slight breeze stirred my hair, cooling the perspiration on my forehead and upper lip. I loosened the collar of my tunic to let the air refresh me. Nearby birds perched in the trees, singing, or issuing warnings of our approach to their distant counterparts. Somewhere high in the forest canopy a crow cawed brightly before falling silent. The response from another echoed through the trees.

I smiled at Deacon, "I always wonder what they're saying to one another."

"Cor hasn't taught you bird talk yet?"

"No," I shook my head with a sigh, "oh, he's tried now and again, but I don't have the ear for it, apparently. He's tried to teach me to understand Vesta, but her tones are just too subtle. It all sounds the same to me."

"Perhaps in time," the druid suggested. "And in the meantime, wondering isn't such a bad thing, is it?"

"Not at all," I brightened, "in fact it's fun to imagine. Oh, look there! Squirrels chasing one another through the forest. It looks like they have such fun!" Ahead and just off the road on my side, three gray squirrels raced up and down the trunks of the trees, barking and chittering at each other. A sparrowhawk swooped down out of nowhere, gliding silently, before it disappeared chasing prey. The forest was teaming with wildlife, I realized.

"Yes, the squirrels are having fun now, but soon they'll be busy hiding food for the winter," he offered as he looked around the place. "Look how quickly the leaves are turning colors and there's already quite some fallen from the trees."

"Hard to believe that winter could be so close when it's so warm today," I admitted.

We rode on in silence, listening to the birds singing, watching for chipmunks and squirrels, just enjoying the day. The steady, rhythmic, clop, clop, clop of our mounts' hooves was comforting and, in my mind, I sang a little tune to the sound. I was just relaxing, taking in the surroundings, when I glanced across at my companion to find he was doing the same. The track wound around the base of an earthen mound covered in vines and brush. As we cleared the hill the forest grew thicker and darker. The trees seemed to huddle together, and the leaves were so thick no sunlight got through. A noticeable drop in the temperature felt good for a moment before a chill ran down my spine. With a start, I realized this place in the forest was silent. No birds sang or called. No scurrying creatures stirred the leaves on the ground. The air felt different.

"Deacon," I dared only above a whisper, "do you feel that? There's something strange here."

"Nemeton," he responded succinctly, raising his left hand to point south, "just through the trees off that way. It's a very powerful and sacred one."

"You've been there?" I gaped at the thought of the druid communing with the Goddess and God in such a place. I knew the wizards often did so in various nemetons scattered throughout the kingdom, but I had not considered Deacon might do so also. Personally, even though it had been years since my parents were murdered and the fiend responsible had been dealt with, I was still not speaking to Deity. Anger still smoldered in my heart, and I had yet to come to terms with how the Goddess and the God had been so irresponsible as to let my beautiful mother and my noble father perish so suddenly and so unjustly. In the back of my mind, I knew that one day I would forgive them, but I was still not ready for that.

"I've been there, yes." Deacon nodded thoughtfully before adding, "Would you like to go see it?"

"No thanks," I shook my head vehemently. "I make it a policy to stay away from such places since I was forcibly ejected from one Cor and I visited."

"Oh yes," he raised one index finger, "I do remember that now. I had forgotten, as that's been so long ago. So, you've not been in a nemeton since before your parents…"

"Were murdered," I finished his observation. "And no, I have not."

"I see," he quipped.

Though I expected him to try to convince me that my feelings were childish and that I should grow up and get past them, he said nothing further. I waited for him to chastise me for my attitude, but he did not. We rode on together, the creaking of leather saddles and the clopping of horses' hooves the only sound. After some time, the bird songs resumed and the darkness lifted. A rabbit darted across the road while a squirrel, snapping its tail angrily at us, barked from the lowest branch of an oak tree.

"Stream's just ahead, Falcon," Deacon startled me from my reverie. "I don't know about you but I'm ready for a stretch and a bite to eat."

"Yes," I agreed, "that does sound good. I'm sure the horses could use some fresh water, too."

The sound of fast running water reached me before the stream came into view. Either the sound or the smell must have reached my mount too, for she pricked up her ears, snorted, and picked up her pace. Nex was not about to be left behind so he trotted up beside us and soon we reached the edge of the wide stream that crossed the road. A wide wooden bridge spanned the creek, but the horses paid it little mind. Aeon went to one side while Nex went to the other and both were drinking before Deacon or I could dismount. I swung my leg over the saddle and lowered myself to the ground, dusting my hands off on the front of my breeches. From inside one of the saddlebags, I withdrew folded fabric squares and a cloth bag, grabbed my water skin, and paused to find the proper place to eat.

"Over there," Deacon pointed toward a small clearing where travelers must have once camped. There were fallen logs arranged in a rough circle and in the center of that was the blackened, ash-scattered remains of a fire. There were some fallen leaves atop the ashes so it was clear it had been some time since anyone used the place.

"Looks good," I nodded as I made my way to the clearing. "Should we tether the horses?"

"They're busy drinking and they'll probably just munch on what grass and leaves they can find," he replied as he carried his provisions into the clearing and chose a log upon which to sit. "We can keep an eye on them but I doubt they'll wander too far." With that he spread a cloth across a fallen log and sat down beside it. From fabric pouches he withdrew bread, cheese, some strips of dried meat, and some dark berries.

"Guess you're right," I shrugged as I chose my seat and did likewise. Cor and Mara had packed similar food into my saddlebags; there was bread, cheese, and meat, but as they knew well berries were not my favorite I was supplied with apples and pears. I broke a piece of bread from the loaf, ripped a chunk of cheese from the wedge, and took two small strips of meat from the pouch. Folding the cloths back up and stacking them neatly, I decided to save the fruit for another time.

We ate quietly, Deacon and I. The sound of the gurgling stream was soothing and the beauty of the forest surrounding us afforded much to enjoy. Aeon and Nex, having taken their fill of water, meandered slowly along the bank of the stream nuzzling aside the fallen leaves in search of tender grasses. A breeze rose out of nowhere, blowing the corner of Deacon's makeshift table cloth up and sending my stack of cloth pouches toppling to the ground. Relieved that nothing was spilled or ruined, I shoved the last of the dried meat into my mouth to regather everything. Had the wind not picked up so suddenly we might have tarried there to enjoy our surroundings a bit longer, but it was clear that we needed to be moving on. Tucking my pouches beneath my elbow, I rose to brush the dust and dirt from the back of my breeches. I hoisted the water skin's strap over my shoulder as I stepped over a fallen log to make my way down to where my mount stood grazing. When the provisions were once more in my lovely new saddlebags and the water skin was once more hanging from the saddle, I gathered Aeon's reins, pulled her head up, and turned her around. Deacon had put his gear away and was talking gently to Nex as he drew him back to the double-tracked road. The wind whistled through the trees as we mounted our horses, starting toward the wooden bridge.

The clop, clop, clop, of shoed hooves on the arch of the bridge sounded particularly loud and hollow as we crossed. I couldn't even imagine how it would have sounded had the wind not risen to howl around us.

"Come, Falcon," Deacon raised his voice to be heard over the din, "I think it's time we make haste." With that, he nudged his heels into Nex's sides and snapped the reins smartly. The white stallion instantly bolted ahead. There was no time for me to even reply, so I heeled Aeon's flanks and lowered myself over her neck. The mare did not like to follow another horse, I knew, but it was best to let Deacon and Nex take the lead to ride in a line when going so quickly. I kept a taut hand on the reins to keep my steed from overtaking her companion, but let her ride as closely to him as she dared.

When at last we reached the edge of the forest, the road winding ahead through open fields now mostly barren of crops, we found the wind still gusting around us. We stopped the horses long enough to don our cloaks as a chill accompanied a growing cloud cover.

"Is there rain coming?" I asked the druid as I secured my cloak at the throat and swept its length around me. Sometimes I could smell approaching rain on the air, but not with such wind.

"I don't think so," he shook his head, peering up at the sky, "but we might still want to push on. The Fulton's place isn't far ahead and if bad weather does move in, they'll probably let us take shelter overnight in their barn."

"And if there is no bad weather?"

"If this wind lays and the clouds move on," he explained, "so will we. If all's well with the Fultons we'll move on to the next place." He made no further comment, only gathered Nex's reins in one hand and nudged him forward. The stallion settled into a comfortably quick pace and I let Aeon catch up with him so Deacon and I were riding abreast. Gray clouds scuttled across the sky, hiding the sun before releasing it. One minute I was warm while the next I felt a chill. Lamenting the arrival of the wind while chastising myself for my foolishness, I clutched my cloak together over my chest and tried to pay attention to my surroundings. One day, I knew, I would be making this journey alone and though I'd been on this road before, I had not come this far on this branch of it. I needed to pay attention and look for landmarks to help me learn the way.

The hard-packed, dusty road began to climb gently. Ahead, and at the peak of the rise, a dog trotted into sight, wagging its tail, and barking loudly. I couldn't tell from the tone if the animal was warning us away or merely announcing our arrival, but Deacon smiled reassuringly at me.

"That's Samson," he nodded at the creature so distant as to appear little more than a shadow. "He's the Fulton's dog and though he sounds mean he's really quite friendly. A bit protective of the children, he is, as you might imagine. But I'm sure he'll take a shine to you."

"Would a piece of Tomcake help him understand that I'm a friend and not an enemy?"

"It might," he laughed, "but that won't be necessary. He'll sniff around you, get a feel for your energy, your disposition, and you two will be friends, I'm sure."

"I hope you're right," I sighed, not especially looking forward to this initial encounter. I'd not had a lot of experience with dogs, though I thought they were wonderful and certainly beautiful. None of the wizards kept a dog, nor had my parents and I had never considered asking for one myself, which now struck me as odd. "Oh well," I muttered under my breath, "let's see how this goes."

Chapter 5

By the time we reached the Fulton's cottage, Samson had danced around both horses, barked his delight, and taken his place ahead to proudly lead us. The black and gray shepherd sported large, pointed ears, a long narrow muzzle, and teeth that indicated he was more than capable of doing serious harm to anyone who might cross him. In fact, once we got close enough to experience it fully, we discovered the depth and intensity of his bark was enough to send all but the foolhardiest running for cover. Samson's long tongue lolled out of his mouth in something of a goofy smile when he wasn't barking, and though at first his jumping and noise startled my mount, Aeon must have quickly realized he posed no threat and was soon paying him no mind. The dog led us off the road, up a wide track that wound between sparse trees, and to his master's home. In the yard, he gave two loud barks, looked back at us tail wagging, and loped away to his water dish near the barn.

A tired and frazzled looking young woman stepped through the front door onto the narrow stoop. Her dark brown hair was braided and coiled on her head, and the wind blew errant wisps around her face. She wiped her hands on the skirt of her dress as she looked up at me with a curious expression on her face.

"Who," she began, as her gaze slid to Deacon and her smile broadened, "oh, Deacon! I'm so happy to see you. You've no idea how good it is you're here."

"Mrs. Fulton," the druid nodded as he swung himself out of the saddle, "this is my friend and fellow healer, Falcon Rose. She's accompanying me in my travels to learn the way and meet folks. Falcon, this is Mrs. Fulton."

Putting my weight on my left foot in the stirrup, I lifted my right leg and swung it from across my mount's back, to lightly jump down. Dusting my hands off on my breeches, I adjusted ThornSting on my hip and straightened the sapphire sash around my waist. When I stepped forward to offer the woman my hand, she gave me a perfunctory glance, shook my hand, and nodded as she stepped back. At first glance I had taken her to be older, as her skin was sallow and there were dark circles beneath what were obviously tired eyes, but as I drew near, I realized she was probably a few years younger than me. It crossed my mind that, having been in the presence of the Elemental Wizards, I had stepped outside the normal progression of the years of life. I'd not even been old enough to know my sacred name when my parents were murdered, and since that time I had been living with Cor at Corhaven or staying with Declan, Finias, or Eban in their respective homes learning what I could from them. That the rest of the world had been moving on steadily, as always it had and always it would, and that girls my age were marrying, becoming wives and mothers, establishing homes and families, simply dropped beneath my notice, so focused was I on other things. Yet here, looking into this obviously tired woman's eyes, I felt the weight she had already assumed and a pang of guilt ran through me that I might not be stepping into my own responsibility.

"I'm pleased to meet you, Mrs. Fulton," I offered politely, lowering my eyes. "If I can be of service!"

"Yes, yes," she responded absently, "Falcon, is it? I'm Corliss Fulton. No need to stand on formality. Call me Corliss, please."

"Yes Ma'am, call me Falcon," I smiled.

From within the cottage a forlorn wail rose and crescendoed before falling away into a few broken sobs.

"What's wrong with Brice?" Deacon interjected.

"I don't know," Corliss sighed heavily. "He started having nightmares sometime last week and he's gotten to the point where he's afraid to go to bed at night."

"And Audrey? Is she too experiencing nightmares?"

"I've not seen her struggling in her sleep, and she's not come crying to me in the middle of the night. But when I ask her if she's having nightmares, she goes silent. She does have a little sniffle, and I've been giving her the tonic you left for us sometime back, but otherwise I don't know. She's helping her father in his workshop now. I was hoping to get Brice down for a nap and keep things quiet enough for him to get some rest so I sent her off with Earl."

"Is your son feverish?" I blurted out, realizing only after the fact that I might be stepping into Deacon's territory.

"Aye," Corliss nodded as she turned to usher us toward the cottage, "he does sometimes feel a bit warm and perspiring, but not often. I've given him some tonic as well, just a wee dram, and it seems to help him get to sleep, but he still wakes screaming and crying."

"We'll tether the horses here for now, Falcon," Deacon took Aeon's reins from my hands, "and tend to them later, depending on whether or not we need to stay, yes?"

"Of course," I nodded, resting my left hand on my sword's hilt. "Yes, of course."

"Please do come in out of the wind," Corliss brightened as she neared the stoop, "and I'll put on some water for tea. Would you like some stew or some bread?"

"No, thank you." Shaking my head with a grin I added, "We've just eaten back at the river. We're fine, though I'd not say no to some fresh water."

"Come on in," she offered as she swung open the heavy wooden door. The darkness inside the cottage was profound compared to the bright daylight in the yard, even though clouds did still scutter by and sometimes eclipse the sun. A fire burned low in the hearth across the wide-plank wooden floor. Clusters of herbs and dried flowers hung from the heavy beams spanning the low ceiling. A wooden table, smooth, round, and pedestaled, commanded attention in the center of the room. There was a hand tatted lace cloth spread on its surface, and a basket of fruit in the center.

"What a lovely table," I gaped, trying hard to recall if I'd ever seen such wonderful craftsmanship. Most of the tables I had seen in my life were simple constructs of lumber, either long and rectangular or short and square.

"Thank you," she bustled into the room behind us to draw dark curtains away from the windows. The meager light that streamed in from outside did not fully illuminate the room, but it did help us see the place in greater detail. "My husband, Earl, made that for me for our first anniversary. He put a lot of time and effort into it, and believe me we've had some nice offers from folks wanting to buy it."

"Mum, mum, mum," came a soft cry from a still-darkened corner. It took me a minute to recognize the shape of a rocking chair there, the shadows were so deep and my eyes had not fully adjusted to the light in the place. The back of the chair tipped forward and back as its occupant jumped to the floor before pattering to his mother's skirts. Brice Fulton stretched his little arms up in desperation as his mother bent down to scoop him up easily. He clung to her, nuzzling his face into her neck.

"There, there, babe," Corliss murmured.

"Good morning, Brice," Deacon greeted the toddler gently, "do you remember me? It's your buddy Deacon. I'm happy to see you. Can you come see me?"

Whether he was being contrary or honest, the child looked up at the druid, said nothing and only shook his head.

"Oh well, that's all right. I'll just have a seat near the fire and wait for tea." My companion offered as he crossed the room.

"You do that, Deacon," Corliss smiled, shifting her son's weight onto her left hip, "and I'll put the water on."

"Can I help?" My voice sounded strange as it left my lips. I heard it and instantly wondered if anyone else did. What I asked was nothing special or even remarkable, but the way the words fairly danced through the air made it clear I had done something. Neither Corliss nor Deacon responded immediately, but the toddler, Brice, still clinging to his mother, stiffened in her embrace. He lifted his head as he turned to face me.

Brice Fulton was a small boy with feathery soft-brown hair surrounding his cherubic face. Big, bright blue eyes, fringed with long, delicate lashes, looked at me suspiciously, but suddenly it was as if he recognized me, though we had never met. A sweet smile spread beneath his tear-stained cheeks and he held one chubby index finger out to me. His mother, suddenly aware and startled at her son's reaction, stood stock still. She peered down at her son before lifting her eyes to mine. A look of wonder spread across her face.

"He's never reacted to a stranger this way," she shook her head slowly, "in fact, he's so shy that he often hides from family and people we know. I don't know what this means."

"Hello Brice," I spoke softly, using the same tone and manner of speech as Deacon, "I'm Falcon. It's nice to meet you." Having had almost no experience with small children, as an only child myself, I was acting entirely on instinct and trusting in the magick I had been assured I'd inherited from my mother.

Brice didn't say anything, but he continued to point one little index finger at me as he began straining one arm in my direction.

I looked at Corliss, merely blinking, and she nodded in response. Before I truly understood what was happening Brice Fulton was climbing into my embrace, wrapping his tiny arms around my neck, and laying his precious wee head against my collar bone. In that instant, I realized that I had never held a little one in my arms, never felt that warmth and weight against me, and I knew it was more than magical. He stilled against me, and I patted his back as I moved gently from one foot to another.

"Please," the child's mother whispered, "take the rocker. Perhaps he'll sleep."

Not fully understanding what was going on, I nodded silently as I walked softly across the room, turned, tightened the child against me, and took a seat in the rocking chair. It groaned comfortably as it accepted the weight and squeaked slightly as I moved ThornSting's hilt so the length of the sword lay beside my left leg. Brice's arms loosened and dropped as he rested his head against me, his little legs straddling my lap. He took a few long, deep, breaths as he relaxed further. I realized he had indeed fallen asleep.

"This is most interesting," Deacon observed in a low, quiet voice to not disturb the child. "He seemed drawn to you Falcon."

"I think I felt something between us," I whispered as loudly as I dared, "but I don't know what it was."

"I do," my companion smiled conspiratorially but said nothing else. Instead, he turned his attention to our hostess who was preparing tea. They spoke softly between themselves and eventually she did cross the room to hand me a tankard of fresh water. I accepted it with a smile, drinking deeply as I rocked the sleeping little one on my lap.

"If you'd be so kind as to hold Brice and let him sleep as long as he will," Corliss turned back to me though she'd started across the room, "it would free me to do some chores and start supper. You're both welcome to stay and eat with us, of course, and you can bed down in the barn for the night if you'd like."

I raised one eyebrow at Deacon who simply shot me a knowing glance.

"I'll be happy to let him sleep as long as he will," I patted Brice's back gently as he slept, "though I feel guilty sitting here doing nothing."

"Oh, you're doing much more than nothing, Falcon," she assured me with a sigh of relief, "so very much more."

So, as the day wore on, I sat in the rocking chair in the corner of the cottage, gently moving forward and back. Corliss and Deacon shared tea before they set about doing various chores. My companion disappeared outside and our hostess followed. I found myself alone with the sleeping Brice Fulton on my lap. I could not help but recall when my father's spirit had come to me as I wandered in a fever after my home had been destroyed. He had reminded me what to do to lower my fever. He'd told me that the baby my mother had been carrying was a son and that perhaps one day I might meet him yet on my journey. The Falcon I had been back then still firmly believed in what I'd been told. The Falcon I had become was considerably more doubtful, I knew well. Silence, but for the occasional crackle of an ember in the hearth, settled around us. The weight and warmth of the child relaxed me. The gentle movement of the rocking chair calmed me further. I felt my eyelids slowly close and my breathing grow deep and steady.

An impossibly tall woman towered over me, but I knew she was not really a woman. Her features suggested she was warm and nurturing, but she was not. When she turned her oh-so-black eyes to me I felt a shudder of ice pierce me to the core. She pointed one long, gnarled index finger at me as her lips, first crimson and fleshy, spread into a black and gaping maw. The keening that came from her throat made me want to cover my ears and hide myself. Her skeletal finger stretched toward me and, though I recoiled, she touched the center of my forehead. An icy cold spread over my face. I shuddered at the sensation as a parade of images began marching through my mind. Bears with sharp, blood-stained fangs swiped huge, sharply-clawed paws at me. Darkly dressed beings pounded by on phantom horses and I knew they were after me and my family. I cowered, wanting only safety and security. Fires raged and exploded in surrounding trees as thunder and lightning shook the timbers of the house and flashed in the windows, blinding me briefly. The finger on my forehead continued to spread cold throughout my body. I struggled to be free only to find my efforts in vain. A stench rose to my nostrils, making me want to wretch and cough, but I was frozen, rendered incapable of movement. My blood ran cold as my skin began to tingle and turn stiff. I had to escape! She was going to kill me! She was going to destroy me! She was going to eat me!

'*Cor!*' I called out in my mind. '*Cor help!*'

For what felt like an eternity there was only silence in response. I could still hear the black-eyed woman keening, her wails rippling through me, sending tiny sharply-taloned fingers like serpents into me to rip, shred, and consume me.

'*Falcon,*' Cor's voice echoed around me, encircling me as surely as his arms did in an embrace, '*I'm here. You're safe.*'

'*What or who was that?*' I shook my head, realizing as I did so that I was awake and the icy finger that had been on my forehead was gone.

'*That I do not yet know, lass,*' he admitted, '*but you're free now and you're safe.*'

'*Cor! I wasn't me! I mean, well, yes of course I was me, but it wasn't me dreaming! Brice was dreaming, having a nightmare like the ones he's been having of late. He shared his dream with me. What does that mean?*'

'*Perhaps the child knows that you can save him from his nightmare?*'

'*How can I do that?*'

'*Time will tell, dear Falcon,*' Cor's voice grew distant. '*Time will tell.*'

Even as the Elemental Wizard's voice disappeared, my thoughts shimmered into a strange clarity as the child on my lap suddenly let out a soft whimper. He wriggled his little legs and flailed his arms, as he struggled to awaken.

"Shh, there, there," I bounced him gently on my lap, patting his back, "it's all right, you're awake now. It's all right." When I placed my palm gently across his forehead, I could feel a cold spot in the center, a spot just the size of the nightmare woman's fingertip. I touched my own forehead, but there was nothing unusual there

Finally awake, Brice looked up at me with tear-filled blue eyes, as his expression shifted. He looked at me with a knowing well beyond his age. In that moment, I realized that I had indeed experienced the child's nightmare, that he had somehow shared it with me and in doing so released some of its power to terrify him. He had rested even though he had dreamed. I rose from the rocker, holding him close to my body, and stepped outside into the early afternoon sun. The wind had calmed considerably and the air felt fresher. Samson came trotting out of the barn and, taking instant notice of us, barked sharply several times before launching himself in our direction. Though I expected to have to turn to protect Brice from the great dog's excited pounce, I did not. To my surprise, the beast came to a halt just before us, wagged his tail excitedly, and licked the child's bare foot. Brice giggled, pulled his foot up behind him, and leaned over to touch Samson's warm muzzle.

"Sam," the child smiled in utter delight, "Samsam."

"Samsam," I parroted him with a chuckle, "yes, indeed, that's your Samsam."

"Falcon," Deacon called out as he exited the barn, Corliss beside him. "I see your buddy has awakened. Did he rest well?"

"Mum, mum, mum," Brice called out in a delighted laugh when he laid eyes on our hostess. Wriggling insistently, he slid from my arms, down my leg, and took off as fast as his little bare feet would carry him. Corliss bent over and caught him in open arms when he launched himself at her.

"Aww...," she cooed, "Brice, my baby, my sweet, sweet baby."

"Yes," I replied at last to Deacon's question, "I think he did indeed have a good rest. And he certainly seems to be in good spirits now!"

"That he does," my companion agreed, beaming at the mother and son so obviously happy. "I suppose that means we should be moving on. There are others ahead who will need our services."

"Are you sure you won't stay at least to eat with us," our hostess pulled her attention away from her son long enough to offer, "as I'd love to thank you for your time. Stay and have supper with us. I'm sure Earl would like a chance to visit with you and meet Falcon, not to mention Audrey."

"Um, Deacon," I interjected, "can I have a word?"

"Excuse me," he bowed slightly as he strode to where I stood. "What is it, Falcon?"

"I wasn't lying, Deacon," I explained, "I believe Brice did rest well, but I experienced his dream, or rather his nightmare. I think if there's enough time, I should make some sleeping elixir to leave here with Corliss."

"Are you sure?" He regarded me closely.

"Please, I won't take long. I have the herbs and other things I need," I pleaded. "Just give me a bit of time. I'll be as quick as I can then we can leave. Please?"

"Very well, Falcon," he agreed as he moved back to where Corliss and Brice stood. The two began speaking, so I took the opportunity to make haste to where the horses stood tethered. From inside one of the saddlebags, I withdrew my healer's kit, closed the flap, and patted my mount's neck as I made my way back toward the cottage. Both Aeon and Nex looked rested and comfortable, but if they were like me, they were anxious to be back on the road. I would have to make quick work of this elixir.

On a table near the hearth, I placed my mortar and pestle, withdrew the needed herbs from a folded leather pouch, and began grinding. The more I thought about it the more I realized that Corliss would better benefit from a sachet she could steep in water and administer to her son. It would, over time of course, lose some strength with each use, but hopefully she could refrain from using it often and thus make it last as long as possible. I ground the herbs with the pestle, always rotating it to the right. Scraping the mixture into the center of the mortar, I started again, always grinding to the right and counting each revolution of the pestle as I had been taught. A soft song popped into my head so I began to hum it as I worked. The words rose unbidden, and I gently and quietly intoned them into my work. The earth's energy, stored in the seeds from which the herbs grew, burned still in the leaves and stems I was grinding. I envisioned the tiny seeds splitting, sending tendrils of roots into the soil while shoots climbed up to break the ground and reach the fresh air beyond. Life force drove the tiny plants toward the sun, drinking in rain, and eventually unfurling leaves. Buds formed and opened before dropping seeds back onto the ground. My hands and my song began to capture that life force and I watched as tiny violet sparks appeared in the cup of the mortar. The sparks grew brighter and bigger as I worked. I do not know how long I was at my labor, but when our hostess, her son, and Deacon came into the room I was startled out of my reverie. Quickly I put my right hand over the mortar to hide the violet magic I had brought forth. My mentors, the Elemental Wizards, and Deacon himself had often reminded me that our work must be hidden. There was a time when healing was seen as magical and a blessing and those who practiced the healing arts were respected and welcomed. But times had changed and now people trusted more in their religions and religious leaders and they were taught to fear what they did not understand. There were rumors of healers being imprisoned or driven from their homes, though we hoped fervently that the rumors were exaggerations and would eventually be proven false.

"Falcon," Deacon looked me deeply in the eyes, "I do hope we've not disturbed your work. This is Earl Fulton and Brice's sister, Audrey." Behind the trio followed a vivacious and obviously happy little girl as well as a powerfully built, bearded man.

"I, um," I stammered, trying to gather my wits about me, "I mean, of course you've not disturbed me. I'm almost finished, in fact. Hello Mr. Fulton, I'm Falcon Rose. Audrey, it's nice to meet you."

At that, everyone started talking at once. Earl Fulton stepped from behind the crowd to offer me one powerfully muscled hand, which I shook with as much strength as I dared. From the size of his arms and hands I could only surmise that he could fell trees without an axe.

"Falcon Rose," he glanced at me before looking at what I'd been doing, "I'm grateful for your help with my son. Any member of the Order of Healers is always welcome under my roof."

"Thank you, sir," I replied, just as his daughter pushed around the others to present herself.

"I'm Audrey Fulton," she beamed, with blue eyes darker than her brother's and long locks more golden. "I'm six years old. How old are you?"

"Well, I'm," I faltered, not sure where her question was going, "I'm happy to meet you, Audrey. My, you're a very pretty little girl."

"Are you going to stay and eat with us?"

"I, um," Glancing up at Deacon I searched his eyes for an answer, "I don't think we are. You see there are others who need our help and we've a long way to go. I'm just going to finish up the makings for an elixir for you before Deacon and I will be on our way."

"Are you sure? Momma says we have plenty and that we must share with those less," she struggled for the proper word, her lovely brow furrowing as she did so, "less, um."

"Hush now, Audrey," Corliss interjected, pulling her daughter away from me, "that doesn't apply to Deacon and Falcon. We do share with those less fortunate, but not everyone is less fortunate. Deacon and Falcon are healers and we owe them our gratitude."

Audrey, obviously skeptical and slightly hurt that her mother had rebuffed her in front of strangers, merely shot me a look of disapproval as she turned on her heel and began to dance around her father. She skipped and sang, delighting in Earl's attention. I could see the two were very close and it reminded me of my relationship with my own father. As happy as I was for Audrey and Earl, I could not help but feel a slight twinge of jealousy.

Deacon, Earl, and Corliss began talking so I turned my attention back to my work. From inside my kit, I withdrew a linen pouch, filled it with a third of the herbal mixture, and tied it with a cord. I did so two more times to finish with a total of three elixir sachets, lining them up neatly on the table. Gathering my things and closing my kit, I brushed my hands off on my breeches and cleared my throat.

"Deacon," I interrupted the conversation, "I'm finished here. I've made three elixir pouches which can be stored in a stone jar if you have one, Corliss."

"I do, I'm sure," our hostess responded.

"Good," I nodded, "now I want to warn you that the elixir these pouches make is very powerful and you must not use much of it at one time. Boil water, fill a cup, steep a single pouch until you see a foam form on the top, then remove and let the pouch dry. Cool the elixir and put no more than three drops under Brice's tongue. The dose is similar with anyone in need of restful sleep. For the children three drops, no more. If you or your husband need it, five drops and not a drop more. Never use it more than once every few days, better yet, use it only once a week. You can store the cooled elixir in a separate covered crock for as long as you like but if it starts smelling strange you throw it out and do not use it."

"I understand," Corliss nodded, staring absently at the line of pouches on the table.

"Deacon and I will try to stop in again on our way back to check and see how Brice is doing," I added, "and if I need to tweak the pouches I'll do so. But remember, the elixir is very powerful so use it sparingly."

"Yes, yes," she nodded, wringing her hands together, "and are you sure you won't stay for supper or stay the night?"

"No, thank you," I smiled in genuine relief. "We appreciate the offer, but the day's moving on and we must be too."

"Can I get you anything for the road? Have you enough provisions? I baked fresh bread this morning," she insisted, "let me get you some to take with you."

"We have plenty," I admitted with a grin, "but I can't refuse bread that's fresh. We'd love a piece or two."

"Wonderful," she nodded, shoving a wisp of auburn hair behind her ear. "You get your things together and I'll bring it out to you. I'm so grateful for what you've done, both of you." Our hostess glanced pointedly at my companion before turning toward the wall lined with shelves full of all manner of jars, bottles, crocks, fabric covered bundles and more.

"Come on, Falcon," Deacon favored me with a grin, "we've work to do!"

Picking up my kit, I tucked it beneath one elbow and started for the door, "Yes, and far to go."

Samson met us at the door as we stepped out onto the stoop, and he joyfully escorted us to where the horses stood waiting. I patted his head and scratched under his ears, assuring him that he was a very good boy and that

I would see him again. As I tucked my kit back into my saddle bags, the shepherd wagged his tail, circling me. I gathered Aeon's reins and climbed into the saddle as the dog went to say farewell to my companion.

"Let's go," I turned my mount, snapped the reins, and urged her forward. Behind me, I heard Deacon tell Samson we would see him again soon, then Nex's nose was coming up beside me as the druid caught up. We turned onto the road, once more heading west.

Chapter 6

A short time later Deacon and I were once more on the road, Corliss's freshly baked bread wrapped and tucked into my saddlebags. Samson had escorted us a short way, barking and prancing around our mounts, though at some point he had left us to our own devices and returned to his home. The wind had died considerably, in fact it was little more than a breeze, and the afternoon air grew warm and humid. I removed my cloak and rolled the sleeves of my tunic up on my arms, noticing Deacon had done the same. We rode side by side in silence for a bit before he cleared his throat.

"Our next stop will be Jack Adler's," he explained. "Jack's getting up there in age. His wife passed on a few years back and the children are grown and long gone. He still farms a bit, makes enough to pay his stipend to the king, but his joints sometimes bother him and he injured his foot a while back so it still pains him from time to time."

"And what are you not telling me?" The druid's evasive manner was strangely uncharacteristic. It was obvious he was hiding something.

"Jack's a bit different," he admitted. "In fact, he can be downright surly. Sometimes he's right as rain, pleasant, and as easy-going as he ever was, but other times he's combative, short-tempered, and cross."

"I see," I nodded absently. "And you're telling me about this so reluctantly because…"

"To be honest, I'm not sure how we'll find him."

"So…" My impatience was growing as Deacon kept reluctantly dodging the issue.

"So, it might be best if I talk to Jack first," he shrugged slightly, "so I can get a read on his mood and state of well-being."

"You think I might make him uneasy or angry?"

"Not at all, lass! But he's never met you and, in truth, he's become something of a recluse these past few years. He doesn't always take kindly to visitors. In fact, I think he mostly tolerates me because I'll share a dram of his brandy with him."

"Oh." I considered the matter for a moment, "So you go find Mr. Adler and I'll wait with the horses. If you think it's safe for me to meet him you can call for me. Otherwise, I'll just let you see to your friend and we'll move on."

"If you don't mind," he smiled sheepishly. "I probably should have warned you about Jack before we even started on our journey, but…"

"It's fine," I assured him. "Let's do whatever is best for him."

"I do want to hear about Brice's dream, Falcon," Deacon smoothly changed the subject. "Perhaps we can discuss it over supper later."

"Of course," nodding absently, my thoughts went back to Corliss's bread wrapped securely in my saddle bag. My stomach grumbled in anticipation.

A short time later, and well before sundown, we reached a spot in the road where an almost completely overgrown path turned off to the north. When Deacon pulled Nex's reins to the side the stallion turned onto the path and began trampling tall weeds, snapping brushy twigs with his hooves. I turned Aeon and let the mare pick her way through the undergrowth as well. It was clear the path had not been used in some time and the fallen logs that lay across it clearly indicated no wagon had been down its length in years. Had Deacon not known about, and been looking for, the trail it is doubtful I would have even noticed it as we passed by.

"Jack's place is just back here," my companion offered, "and I'll warn you it's a little run down. Jack's not been able to do much in the way of maintenance for a while, but he does the best he can."

"I understand," I replied, raising my voice slightly so he could hear me from behind.

"Here we are," he halted his mount to swing down out of the saddle. Wrapping Nex's reins around a wooden post which might have once been part of a gate, he turned to look at me. "I'll see if I can find Jack and see how he's doing. I'll let you know what's what in a few minutes."

"Of course," I nodded, more interested in investigating the place from the elevation of Aeon's back. There were clumps of brush-choked trees scattered here and there. Two overgrown evergreens almost completely concealed the front door of the cottage whose details I could only guess at. Part of the thatched roof was visible, though what I could see was clearly in need of repair and appeared to be mostly held together by invading vines. Though weeds choked most of the yard, I could still see Michaelmas daisies peeking through the brush and orange coneflowers poked their heads up valiantly. Wild grapevines, their wide leaves still lushly green, wound themselves around what once was likely a clothesline post, and even from a distance I could see abundant fruit ripe for the picking. As neglected and sad as the place was, I could see that it once had been loved and well cared for. The place still felt alive and lived in.

The sound of distant voices roused me from my reverie. Though I listened closely, I could discern no words, but the tone of the conversation sounded genial. I was aware that Deacon had crossed the yard and ducked around the far corner of the house. I had heard him call Jack's name once or twice. And though I had not actually heard a response, it seemed likely my companion had found Jack Adler. I straightened my tunic, adjusted my sapphire blue sash, and waited patiently.

"Falcon," Deacon called out as he and another gentleman appeared from around the corner of the house. The pair started across the yard. "Falcon Rose! I have a friend for you to meet."

"Of course," I replied as I swung down out of the saddle to land lightly in a bunch of fallen leaves. Dusting my hands on the bottom of my tunic, I moved ThornSting further back on my left hip, once more fidgeted with the sapphire sash around my waist, and stepped forward around my mount's nose. Quickly, I slipped Aeon's reins around the post where Nex was tethered before turning my attention to the approaching men.

Deacon had warned me that Jack might be combative, that he was not always himself, and that he did not know what to expect. He had painted images of a disheveled, declining, disturbed, possibly even feral elder in my mind, I realized, and the man I saw walking beside him bore no resemblance to those images at all. I was completely unaware of my own expression as the pair drew near.

"Falcon Rose," my companion introduced me, "I'd like you to meet Jack Adler. Jack, this is my young friend and fellow healer, Falcon Rose."

"I'm," I faltered, still processing what I was seeing compared to what I'd imagined, "I am, um. I'm happy to meet you, Mr. Adler."

"I see the old druid warned you about me, eh?" Jack smiled brightly, his clear blue eyes regarding me with obvious intelligence. His dark brown hair, long and smoothed back from his forehead, was streaked with white and his beard, braided and coarse, matched his bushy eyebrows. He wore a simple brown knee-length tunic over linen trousers, and battered, short leather boots covered his feet. Around his waist he wore a narrow leather belt, the long end extending to the hem of his shirt.

"I," struggling for the proper response, I could only extend my hand mutely.

"It's alright, Falcon Rose," Jack offered graciously, shaking my hand politely. "He had every right to warn you about me, Miss. I admit I was a bit unwell for a time."

"You were?"

"Well, you see, my wife Grace passed on over three years ago," he explained, his tone softening with recall, "and it hit me hard. Our children were grown and had moved away long ago and it had been just the two of us for so long. When I lost her, I guess I lost a part of myself, probably the best part of myself."

"That's understandable, Jack," Deacon interjected.

"Understandable or not, it wasn't right. I darn near went mad with grief. Took to spending too much time by myself and making and drinking brandy. I started having bad dreams, couldn't eat, couldn't sleep, pretty much figured I was ready to die myself!"

"What happened?" I gaped in wonder, as it was clear the man standing before me was anything but ready to die.

"I met a friend," he grinned so beautifully that I couldn't help but respond in kind. "God and Goddess know when I first saw her, I thought I was dreaming or seeing an angel. I really didn't think she was real. But she walked right down that path yonder, just as easy as you please, and introduced herself to me."

"She didn't!" Deacon beamed.

"She did! Said her name's Emmeline and that she and her daughter just moved into the old millhouse up the valley a way. She was carryin' a jug and she had a bundle tucked under her arm. She helped me up from the grass where I'd been sittin' all miserable like, and took me into the house. You won't believe this, but this angel, this wonderful stranger, she sat me down at the table, gave me some kind of fruity potion and food from the bundle she'd brought. She cleaned and tidied my house, all the while humming and smiling at me."

"She sounds wonderful!" I exclaimed.

"Emmeline's an amazing woman," Jack nodded emphatically. "Now, why don't you two come on in and we'll have some tea or something stronger."

I shot Deacon a sidelong glance as our host herded us toward the front door of the cottage, now heavily shrouded in afternoon shade. He merely smiled gently, shrugging almost imperceptibly.

Inside the cozy cottage the shadows were heavy, though the remnants of a fire smoldered red in the hearth. A small square table stood to the left just below two nearly opaque glass windows and small, well-worn wooden chairs were at either end. To our right, a counter ran the length of the room and a water pail, ladle hooked to the side, stood at the far end. There were various jars, boxes, and dishes stacked along the counter while loops of grapevine hung from heavy beams overhead. An iron grate stood to the side near the hearth, awaiting the arrival of a kettle of water or pot of stew. The cottage smelled of age, herbs, food, and something oddly tart. I didn't recognize the scent.

"Can I get you something? Some tea or water? Maybe some of my brandy?" Jack offered cordially.

"Nothing for me," I replied without hesitation.

"I'll have a wee sip of brandy if you're having some, Jack," Deacon smiled as he pulled the chair from beneath the far end of the table to sit down.

When I noticed a rocking chair with a woven-cord seat in the corner behind the door I decided I would stay out of the way and let the men visit at their leisure. Curious as I was about the situation, I realized it would likely be best if I stayed out of things and simply listened. Jack was, after all, Deacon's friend and Deacon was here to check on him, see if there was anything he needed, so the polite thing to do would be to simply sit quietly.

"Of course, of course," our host beamed, "though it will be but a wee sip for both of us. My days of drinking 'til I could drink no more are over. I've promised Emmeline that I'd take care of myself."

"Does she come see you often?" The druid raised one eyebrow at Jack as he decanted a cask of brandy. "Have you been to her place?"

"She comes from time to time though I've not been to her place," Jack responded as he put two small wooden cups on the table, hefting the cask beneath one arm to pour. "She and her daughter Z come see me every three or four days or so. They're both so lovely. I'm sure you'd take a liking to them, Deacon."

"I'm sure I would," he nodded, picking up a cup and taking a tentative sip. "Fine wine, Jack!"

"Thank you. I think so too. Been saving this cask for some time and because it is so good, I'm making it last. You sure you won't join us, lass?" Jack raised a cup to me.

"No thank you," I smiled as I rocked gently in the comfortable chair, holding the tip of my sword up so it wouldn't drag across the floor. "You two just enjoy yourselves. I'll sit here and relax."

"As you wish," he shrugged as he pulled the second chair from beneath the table. As he sat down, he placed the cask on the corner of the table and picked up his cup. "Now where were we, my friend?"

"You were telling me more about Emmeline," Deacon responded, "and her daughter. Did you say her name is Z?"

"I did, I did," Jack chuckled. "Strange name, I know. I asked her if it was a nickname or if it stood for something else. She just looked at me with those beautiful big green eyes of hers and smiled a little, like it was a secret."

"That's an odd reaction, isn't it?"

"I thought so, until Emmeline explained that Z doesn't speak. She was struck down with some illness as a young child and though she recovered she's never spoken. She can read and write, and she can make gestures to let you know what she wants you to know, but she doesn't utter a word."

"My, that is a shame," Deacon shook his head, "and there's nothing that can be done for her?"

"Emmeline won't discuss it much," Jack stared forlornly into the darkness of his nearly empty cup. "I think it makes her sad, so I don't push the subject. Guess the woman's got a right to deal with things as she sees fit. Being a widow can't be easy, her bein' so young and all, and havin' a daughter that's so beautiful but probably isn't fit to be wed, well, she's got hardships enough. She's so wonderfully kind to me, though. And I enjoy their company. Though Z doesn't speak, Emmeline's a fine woman to sit and talk with. She's bright and funny, has a lovely smile and the prettiest voice when she hums or sings."

"Sounds like you're smitten, Jack Adler," Deacon raised his cup in a toast. "Good for you!"

"Oh, don't get me wrong," Jack shook his head slightly, "Emmeline's a fine woman and any man would be honored to have such as her for a wife, but Grace was the one and only love of my life. I enjoy Emmeline's company, but my Grace was my life. Emmeline's just my angel. She saved me from myself and from my grief, but that's all it will ever be."

"Are you sure?"

"Aye," our host put his cup to his lips, tossing back the remainder of his brandy, "I'm sure."

"Since Emmeline and," Deacon paused, "Z are new to the area, do you think Falcon and I should call on them? Maybe we could see if they've any need of healing supplies and such?"

"I don't know," Jack looked puzzled suddenly. "They both look healthy, but I suppose it would be the neighborly thing to do if you were to call on them, introduce yourselves, and see if you could be of service. I, I guess that might be a good idea!"

"And you say they just moved into…"

"The old millhouse up the valley," he offered. "You remember, used to be the Corbin place before Maurice and his wife moved away. It was standing empty for years. I used to get flour from the Corbins so Grace could bake the most delicious bread." Jack's expression grew sad and wistful at the same time, before he seemed to shake himself from his memories.

"I remember the Corbins. How far is the millhouse from here?"

"Oh, not far," Jack replied, "less than half a day's walk probably. If you go back to the road, you can follow it west until you come to the river. Ride along the river north and it will take you right to the Corbin place."

"Which is now Emmeline's place," Deacon quipped.

"Aye, that's right, Emmeline's place," our host seemed to draw into himself, as silence washed over him.

Sitting quietly, gently rocking back and forth in my chair, I had inspected my fingernails, smoothed the hem on my tunic, and played with the tip of my sapphire sash for as long as I could. Finally, I closed my eyes and hoped to appear as if resting or even sleeping. I could not help but eavesdrop on the conversation, which I found fascinating, but I wanted only to be invisible or elsewhere. At first my mind conjured images to match what I was hearing, but eventually my thoughts wandered back to Corhaven. I wondered what Cor and the other wizards might be doing. Suddenly a woman appeared before me, distant, but clearly detailed. She was pale, her silver hair gathered in curls atop her head, and she wore a delicate lace embroidered gown of ivory linen. Her skin was smooth, despite her age, and her hands were crossed primly before her. Her eyes, dark and piercing, held a pleading, and though her lips moved, I could not hear what she was saying. Over and over again she mouthed the same words. I felt like I could almost grasp what she was saying, when the CRACK of a loud ember brought me fully awake and alert. Startled as I was, when I brought the rocker to a sudden halt a woman's voice echoed through my mind.

'No angel! No angel!'

"Grace used to love..." Jack was saying as I opened my eyes, but he paused to look across the table at me. He did not finish his comment.

"Were you sleeping, lass?" Deacon looked over his shoulder as he smiled at me from his chair at the table.

"Sorry," I drew in a deep breath to hide a yawn, "no, but I think I was close. The ember popping startled me though."

"Can I get you something?" Jack stood, turning to address me. "I have stew, cheese, fruit, tea."

"No thank you," I shook my head politely. "I'm fine." As I sat quietly enjoying the comfort of the cottage and the company of the two men, I recalled the image of the woman who'd appeared to me and I knew without a doubt that it was Grace, Jack's departed wife. I wasn't entirely sure what she meant by '*No angel,*' but I knew it was her. I resolved to keep my mind open as to the meaning of her message. Looking up, I stifled a small yawn as I realized Deacon was speaking of our departure.

"As you seem in no need of our services, Jack, I guess we'd best be on our way," my companion addressed our host, pressing his hands on the table to hoist himself up. "We've others to see on our journey."

"I guess we should be going," gathering my wits, I chimed in as I rose from my rocker. I almost asked if we were going to the millhouse, but decided against it. I couldn't remember if I was supposed to have heard that part of the conversation or not. "Of course, Deacon. I'm ready when you are!"

"Are ye goin' to Emmeline's place to introduce yourselves?" Jack asked brightly, to my delight.

"We will, we will," Deacon assured him, "and I'll be sure to tell your friend that you suggested we drop by. I'm looking forward to meeting her. What did you say her last name is?"

"I, I," Jack paused, pinching his bottom lip between his thumb and first finger, "oh, wait. I didn't say, but it's Caulfield. Yes, I'd almost forgotten, but her name's Caulfield. Emmeline Caulfield."

"So now the Corbin mill is the Caulfield mill," the druid smiled as he stepped away from the table and slid his chair back under it. "We'll be happy to meet Mrs. Caulfield. Considering what she's done for you, Jack Adler, I can't wait to meet her and offer her thanks. You're nearly a new man!"

"I am, I am," our host nodded excitedly as he opened the front door for us, "and I have her and her daughter to thank for it. It's lovely having new friends."

"It is at that," Deacon agreed, stepping back to let me pass. I exited the cottage first.

"It's been nice meeting you, Mr. Adler," I turned, offering my hand.

"Please, call me Jack," he shook my hand firmly, "and it's been my pleasure to meet you, Falcon Rose. Do come back any time."

"We will," my companion interjected, slapping our host on the shoulder as he shook his hand, "and we'll see you again soon. Do take care, Jack!"

"And you as well, Deacon," he raised one hand in acknowledgment. "Travel safe, my friends!"

As I swung myself up into the saddle, gathered the reins, and turned Aeon around, I cast a glance at Jack Adler and for a moment I saw a sadness wash over him. For an instant he appeared hollow, gray, almost a husk of a man, but suddenly he looked up at me and his expression brightened. He smiled cheerfully and waved once more before turning back toward his front door.

"Come Falcon," Deacon called from astride Nex's back, "let's make our way back to the road."

"Coming!" I responded, nudging my mare forward. My thoughts were awhirl as we left the cottage. All I had heard about Jack's new friend and her daughter sounded wonderful, yet there was something amiss there that I couldn't quite figure out. Certainly, it was odd that Emmeline's daughter could not speak, and a bit unusual that she went by the name Z, but those things in themselves could be explained, I admitted. However, Grace, the woman whose image had appeared to me, was obviously upset about something. Hopefully the ride to the millhouse would give me time to consider everything and perhaps make some sense of it all.

Chapter 7

The day was waning and the sun was starting to sink toward the horizon, washing everything in a pink-gold haze, as we resumed our journey, heading west.

"Will we make it to the millhouse before dark?"

"That depends on whether or not the weather holds off," Deacon replied. "But it looks like there may be some rain heading in our direction. We may be in for a wet night."

"Should we turn back and stay at Jack's place?" The thought of sleeping in the forest in the pouring rain did not appeal to me at all. I was more than happy to return to Jack's cozy cottage.

"No, that won't be necessary. We'll reach the river and follow it north. Even if it does start raining, we'll make it to the millhouse and introduce ourselves to the Caulfields. And if we're not invited to stay there, we'll ask permission to shelter overnight in the barn or one of the storage buildings on the property if they're still standing."

"You think she'll allow us to stay?"

"I hope so!" He grinned at me as he added, "It is unfortunate that we'll be calling on her so late in the day, as that's not exactly polite, but surely she'll understand. And with any luck Jack's name will buy us some good will with the new mill owner."

"Yes" I nodded, "I hope so too. I'll just be happy if we can find cover before the rain starts."

"Come then, Falcon," the druid snapped Nex's reins, quickening the stallion's pace, "let's make for the river ahead!"

Without reply, I kicked Aeon in the flanks and lowered myself in the saddle. We galloped along the hardpacked earthen road in silence as the clouds gathered overhead. I started feeling anxious, like we were not moving fast enough, like something was closing in on us. When we topped a short rise, there below us appeared the river running under an arched wooden bridge. When we reached it, Deacon slowed Nex to cross the bridge, turning him onto a trail that ran along the western bank of the fast-running stream. I reined in Aeon as I turned her to follow. Once off the main road we lost the sun's light quickly as the forest's shadows swallowed the trail.

"We follow along the river and soon we'll see the grain-storage buildings and the millhouse beyond."

"Will what's left of the daylight be enough for us to find our way?"

"I think we can make it alright," he shrugged. "Once we get past the woods here there will be more daylight visible, though the clouds do seem to be getting heavier. And if it is dark when we arrive, we should see lights in the millhouse windows."

We rode the narrow trail, the river gurgling merrily on our right and the forest marching along on our left. After a league or so, the woods fell away leaving before us an open glade. The river curved around to the left farther north and, in the distance, I could just make out the silhouette of what had to be the millhouse. There were three buildings standing in the glade, one in the southwest, one in the center, and the third in the northeast corner.

"Wow, does all this land belong to the mill?" I marveled at the gently rolling, treeless land.

"It did when the Corbins worked it," Deacon replied, drawing Nex to a halt. "From the forest in the south and west to the river east and north, and some on the other side of the river beyond the mill, the land was all part of the Corbin place. There used to be sheep and goats in this pasture. This was once quite a successful enterprise."

"What happened to the Corbins?" I looked over the width and breadth of the pasture, imagining how it must have once appeared with flocks of sheep and goats scattered about. The buildings must have once been full to overflowing with grain awaiting the millwheel, while the road was surely busy with the wagons of neighboring farmers coming with their crops and leaving with the processed flour.

"I'm not really sure, to be honest," my companion admitted thoughtfully. "The place has been vacant for a few years now. There were rumors that Maurice and Anna, I think her name was, had saved up enough money to move away. I seem to recall their eldest son had moved to the coast somewhere and they were going to join him and his family there."

"So, they just made their money and left this place empty?"

"Everyone assumed they'd tired of it and that someone else would take over, as the mill did quite a good business," he explained. "It's surprising King Rowan never made a point of putting someone else onto the land to maintain the mill, but that never happened. The place has stood vacant for too long. It's good that Emmeline Caulfield and her daughter have taken up residence here."

"Doesn't look like there's any grain in the storage buildings," I nodded at the empty structure before us. It had a roof and three walls, but the walls stopped short of meeting the roof, leaving a gap big enough for the stored grain within to breathe. "At least there's nothing in this one."

"Let's check out the other two then we'll go introduce ourselves to the lady of the house and her daughter," Deacon suggested, clucking to Nex. When I bumped my heels against Aeon's sides she responded with a start and a snort. We made our way to the second storage building only to find it in much the same state as the first, empty and smelling of heat and dust. Without comment we turned and rode to the building closest to the millhouse. As the other two, the structure was a roof with three partial walls and one opening facing north. From where we sat astride our mounts, we could clearly make out the details of the millhouse standing at the edge of the river. No lights burned inside, nor did any woodsmoke rise from the chimney atop the slate roof. In fact, I noticed, nothing moved in the glade at all. No birds were singing, no small animals scrabbled through the high grass, there was only silence and the lively gurgling of the river. The place felt empty, devoid of all life.

"Deacon," I murmured uneasily, "do you feel that? Do you feel how uneasy this place is?"

"Well," he nodded almost imperceptibly in the waning light, "I guess maybe I do. Something does feel strange."

"There's no one in the millhouse," I offered. "Look, no lights and I don't smell any smoke from the chimney. The place looks dark."

"Maybe they're away visiting friends or family," he suggested. "Or maybe they've just not yet lit the lamps or candles. It's not quite past sundown yet, Falcon."

"Yes, I guess so. You're right. Maybe my imagination is just running away with me. I'm probably just tired and hungry."

"Come, lass," Deacon offered, "let's go knock on the door and see if we can get permission to shelter somewhere here. Those clouds are getting lower and darker. I think I can smell the rain on the air."

"Yes, as can I," I took a deep breath and did indeed smell and taste the coming rain. "Let's hurry!"

The millhouse sat on the bank of the river. A silhouette of the massive wheel rose behind and to the right of the structure. On the east end, massive doors stood ajar offering a glimpse into the darkness where the grain must have once been stored prior to grinding. There was no sign of life around. The windows were dark. The only noise I could hear was the rushing of the river. We drew our horses to a halt before tethering them to a couple of posts outside the stone arch- covered front doors. I could not help but glance at the place with a sense of unease.

"Are you all right, Falcon?" Deacon patted his mount's neck as he made his way to where I stood. "Something wrong?"

"No," I sighed, "not really. It just feels strange here. I'm sure it's my imagination. Let's go introduce ourselves and see if we can find a place to shelter before the rain starts."

"Yes," he nodded, taking my elbow in his hand, "let's do that."

In silence we walked up the wide stone steps and crossed a narrow landing to stand side by side before the massive wooden doors. A heavy iron knocker hung slightly askew, and it squealed painfully when Deacon lifted and banged it back down. The sound echoed inside, but there was no response. Moments ticked by before he lifted the knocker and tried once more. Again, there was no response, but the heavy door moaned as it swung slightly open. My right hand crept to the hilt of ThornSting as the hairs on the back of my neck rose. Raising one eyebrow in question, I glanced at my companion.

"Perhaps we should go in," he offered, his voice barely above a whisper.

"Um, are you sure?"

"Come on," he nodded, shoving the door further open with his elbow, "let's look around. Perhaps Emmeline and her daughter are in trouble and need our help. Maybe something's wrong."

"Oh, I hadn't considered that," I admitted. "If you think we should, let's look around!"

Inside the millhouse the darkness was heavy. What meager light was left of the day outside was not strong enough to illuminate the cavernous structure. The silence within was deafening, only adding to my discomfort.

"Mrs. Caulfield," Deacon called out as he stepped inside. "Emmeline? Z? Is anyone here?"

"Wait a minute," I snapped, index finger extended before me, though my companion would not likely see it. Turning away from the doorway, I hurried back down the steps to where Aeon stood tethered. The black mare snorted and shifted her weight from one hoof to another as I unwrapped the leather cord from the flap of the saddlebag. Sticking my hand down into the pouch, I felt around until I touched the familiar fabric covering the Earth Star. I pulled the gem out of the saddlebag before rushing back up the steps to where Deacon stood just inside the door.

"Here," I offered as I unwrapped Scorch, "this will give us some light to see by."

The kyanite laced gem glowed softly at first, but the light grew as it woke. I held it up in the palm of my left hand, my right hand once more secure on my sword's hilt. Deacon stepped aside to let me pass. A gasp escaped my lips when I beheld the room, for it was completely empty. Gaps in the roof let bits of the darkening sky seep in while empty window frames on the opposite side of the room allowed a breeze to waft by. The black chasm in the adjacent wall was once a hearth, though it was now little more than a crumbled pile of stones. Cobwebs dangling from the exposed rafters in the ceiling waved softly. Following a hunch, I lowered the Earth Star for a closer look at the wooden floor.

"Deacon," I whispered, "look at this! No one's been here for a very long time. The dust on the floor's not been disturbed. There's no footprints or signs of anyone or anything having been in here."

"You're right, lass," he replied, wandering a bit further into the place. "This is quite strange!"

"Could Jack have been mistaken about where Emmeline said she lived? Are there any other mills on this river?"

"I don't see how he could be mistaken," Deacon answered thoughtfully, "as this is the Corbin place, or at least it once was. It's possible that there are other mills on this river, but none that I'm aware of."

Suddenly a heavy moaning reverberated from beneath our feet. At first, I thought the place might be collapsing on itself, but the sound continued, growing louder and deeper.

"Um," I uttered in confusion, "what's that?"

"It sounds like," he paused before continuing, "the paddle wheel that turns the grindstones! I think the wheel is turning!"

"How's that possible? We didn't hear it when we first came in and now it's turning?"

"I admit, I don't understand it either." Deacon scanned the room once more as he turned to me. "I don't see any point in further investigation. There's obviously no one living here. Either we're mistaken, Jack was mistaken, or something strange is going on with Mrs. Caulfield and her daughter, assuming Jack didn't dream them."

"So, what now?" The heavy thundering noise surrounding us made it difficult to think. I had to raise my voice to be heard.

"Shall we stay here for the night? We could probably find rooms far enough away from the grindstone that the sound wouldn't bother us."

The thought of the great paddlewheel suddenly churning in the river and the grindstones coming to life on their own disturbed me greatly. I was fervently hoping Deacon was in jest.

"No," I shook my head adamantly, "if the rest of the place is in such bad shape as this any rooms we might find would be of little protection. The roof here is too rotten and full of holes. Besides, I don't like it. There's something not right here."

"One of the storage buildings?"

"Yes," I nodded in relief. "One of those will be fine."

Not wanting to spend any more time than was necessary in the crumbling hulk of the millhouse, I made for the open doors and took a deep, cleansing breath when I reached the landing beyond. A few light raindrops touched my hair and face as I quickly wrapped Scorch back in its cloth. I fairly leapt down the steps, trotting to where Aeon stood waiting. Tucking the Earth Star into a saddlebag, I hurriedly grabbed the reins before swinging myself up into the saddle. Deacon was only a few steps behind me as I turned my mount.

"Just a minute," I announced, a sudden notion hitting me. "I'll be right back."

I heeled the mare in the flanks and guided her to the eastern-most end of the building so I could see the paddle wheel on the river. Though the night was closing in, I could clearly make out the shape of the wheel sitting idly, its lower paddles submerged beneath the water. It took me a minute to recognize the massive wooden blocks between the spokes where the wheel was attached to the building's wall. The mill's paddle wheel had not moved in a very long time, I realized. With a growing sense of dread, I turned Aeon back and headed toward where Deacon sat waiting astride Nex.

"What was it?"

"The wheel's blocked from moving," I explained quickly, "so it can't drive the grindstone. That cannot be what we heard."

"I wonder…"

"Please," I interrupted him, "let's get to shelter. I just want to be away from here."

With that, I kicked Aeon in the flanks and headed away from the mill. The rain became heavier as I hurried across the open field, and I considered entering the storage building nearest the millhouse, but decided I would rather be soaked than to sleep that close to the place. Surely, I reasoned silently, we would not get too wet if we kept riding until we reached the barn furthest from the mill.

The light rain had turned heavier and the drops were splattering on my head trickling through my hair to my scalp. Aeon shook her massive head, her mane casting off rain in all directions, but she did not slow her stride. It was with great relief that I turned her and rode into the eastern-facing wide opening of the storage building. The mare trotted to a halt, snorting, and shaking off the rain. I wiped the moisture from my forehead and dried my hands off on the legs of my breeches. Swinging down out of the saddle, I led my mount to the far side of the structure and tethered her loosely, promising her the freedom to graze in the surrounding fields in the morning as soon as the rain passed. Deacon rode Nex inside and climbed down from the saddle, wiping the rain from his face and hair.

"We called that a bit close," he smiled as he led his horse to the wall near where Aeon stood. "Would have been nice if the rain held off a few more minutes."

"I'm just happy to be away from the mill," I grinned. "You think we can manage a fire?"

"I'm afraid not," he shook his head, "as this place is tinder dry. Between the dust and leftover grain bits a fire would be too dangerous."

"Oh well, at least the night is mild and we're out of the rain. I guess a fire's not really necessary," I shrugged as I lifted the saddlebags from Aeon's rump.

We removed our gear from the horses and set up a makeshift camp inside the grain storage building. I put my saddle against the wall and tossed Aeon's blanket on top of it, as it would serve as my pillow. Unrolling my blankets, I shook them out to spread them on the ground. Deacon did the same though the spot he chose to sleep was closer to the structure's opening. At the foot of our blankets, we stretched out a cloth and withdrew the food parcels from our bags. Eagerly I unwrapped the bread Corliss had given us and offered Deacon the first slice.

"Thank you, Falcon," he smiled as he took a piece of bread and held it to his nose. "Mrs. Fulton is an excellent baker. It's a pity we'll have no fire for tea or coffee."

"I might be able to help there," I grinned, tentative yet excited to be able to use my powers. "Just pour some water in your mug."

"What do you mean?" My companion looked at me curiously.

"I'll show you what Eban Kendall taught me," I replied, taking a piece of bread from the cloth before carefully folding it back up and placing it on the ground between us. "Let me get my mug too!"

Fishing through the things in my saddlebag, I finally came across the carved stone mug Cor had provided me for traveling years ago and placed it before me. I pulled the stopper from my water skin to fill the mug before returning the cork to the leather pouch. Deacon filled his mug, a stone vessel taller and wider than mine, and placed it on the ground beside mine.

"Now what?"

"Now watch!"

Taking a deep, cleansing breath, I focused my attention on the water inside Deacon's mug. I felt each tiny drop as well as the volume of the fluid as one. Holding out my right hand, I gathered the energy in the center of my body, imagining it hot, bright, and moving. I kept focusing, focusing, building the churning power at my core until it was almost more than I could control. I willed it up to my shoulder and down my right arm, through my wrist and out of my palm. The sensation of the energy flowing was amazing, in fact it was delightful, and it always made me want to do it again and again, though Eban had warned me against that. Once I could feel heat rising from Deacon's mug, I moved my palm to hover over my own drink as I let the energy continue to flow.

"There," I sighed at last with a smile, "that should be hot enough for tea or whatever you're drinking."

"Tea is fine, lass," he returned my smile as he picked up his stone cup. With a hiss, he put it back down. "The stone is hot!"

"Sorry about that," I shrugged, "I was aiming for the water only, but sometimes the energy goes a bit wide."

"That's alright," Deacon nodded as he tossed a pouch of tea into the hot water, "by the time the tea's brewed enough the mug should be just right. That's a handy bit of magic Eban taught you!"

"It is," I nodded excitedly, "and what's more it's really fun!"

"I'd say he taught you well," he laughed. "And now, while the tea is brewing, will you tell me what you experienced with Brice?"

"Of course." As I put peppermint tea into my mug and watched the cloth sachet sink, I added, "Though there's not much to tell."

Briefly I described the dream I'd had, which I believed Brice was having as he slept on my lap, and how the woman who was not a woman touched me on the forehead and how the chill moved through me before the violent images ensued. As clearly as I could, I explained the emotions I had felt as the horrors paraded through my mind.

"What do you think it means, Falcon?" Deacon asked softly.

"Could the Fultons have an enemy?" I asked. "I mean, could they have someone who would wish to do them harm?"

"No," he shook his head, "I don't think so. They're good people! They're generous and kind. I can't imagine they would ever cross anyone enough to create an enemy."

"What about their land, their business, their home? Could someone want that enough to assault one of their children through dreams?"

"I don't believe so. Earl Fulton makes a comfortable living with his hands, but that's nothing someone else could take from him. Their land is not vast nor particularly fertile, being so close to the forest there's not much garden space. And you've seen their home. It's comfortable but nothing anyone else would covet. Why do you ask such questions?"

"It just seems strange to me that a boy Brice's age would be capable of having such a nightmare. The images felt intentionally cruel, like they were intended to frighten him for some reason."

"I see what you mean," Deacon nodded, absently running one thumb along the edge of his jaw. "A boy Brice's age shouldn't even be aware of some of the things you described."

"Yes, I agree. The nightmare didn't feel like something a little boy that age would experience. If his parents have no enemies, I can't even guess what's going on."

"Perhaps it's just a phase he's going through," my companion suggested hopefully, "and he'll outgrow it soon. At least the Fultons have the sleep elixir pouches now. Surely those will help."

"I hope so," sighing, I picked up my tea and blew steam from the top before taking a tentative sip. "Let's eat and get some rest. I don't know about you, but I'm tired."

"Yes," he raised his mug in a toast, "here's to supper and a good night's rest!"

Chapter 8

I had no idea how long I had been sleeping when I was startled awake. At first, I did not even know what had awakened me, but I soon heard a voice echoing around me. Distant and indistinct, someone was stridently calling my name. Struggling to throw off my woolen blanket, I sat upright to glance around the storage building. The rain had stopped and the moon and stars lit the glade. Deacon slept silently on his right side with his right hand curled beneath his chin. Aeon and Nex stood quietly across the way, their tails swishing softly from time to time.

"Falcon," the distant voice beckoned, though I couldn't tell if it was male or female.

'Cor! Can you hear this?'

No response came from my beloved wizard. I knew it was late or possibly even very early morning, and he was most certainly sleeping, but he had always answered when I called out with my mind.

'Cor! Something strange is happening here. Someone's calling me. They're calling me by name! Cor, can you hear me?'

Again, there was no response, so I had no choice but to figure the situation out on my own. Shoving my blankets away, I slipped my boots on (Had I taken them off before going to sleep?) before making it to my feet. I considered waking Deacon, but he looked so peaceful, breathing deeply and quietly, I couldn't bring myself to disturb him. Instead, I picked up my cloak and drew it around my shoulders, securing it at the throat. The horses stirred slightly as I moved by them. Silently, I stepped out into the night.

Shimmering moonlight lent the glade an ethereal look, and for a moment I was enchanted. How long I stood staring at the impossibly clear, star-filled sky I didn't know, but I startled when the voice called my name once more.

I peered around the glade but saw no one. Try as I might, I couldn't tell from where the voice came. At last, my gaze fell on the millhouse and I noticed warm lights in the windows. The double doors were slightly open and a shaft of light stretched across the landing as if inviting me to come in. A little voice in my head warned me that something wasn't right with what I was seeing, but my curiosity was stronger than any fear I might have. Suddenly I was hurrying across the glade, excitement spurring me on.

'*Emmeline Caulfield must be home now,*' I reasoned silently. '*We must have just missed her earlier!*'

'*And the state of the place? How do you explain that? The roof was rotten, the fireplace crumbling, and the windows were without glass. No one could live there!*' The voice of reason in my head countered.

'*Oh, she's probably just busy fixing up the place,*' my calm, imminently hopeful side naively suggested. '*Let's go meet her. I'm sure she'll explain!*'

'*And why is Cor not answering? Why is the wizard silent? Don't you understand that something's wrong? We should not be doing this! Let's go back and wake Deacon to come with us at least!*'

I slowed my pace as the logic of my thoughts finally sank in, but by that time I was standing in front of the millhouse, my foot about to touch the lowest step. As I glanced up at the open doors and the warm, welcoming light spilling from within, all my thoughts scattered. Joy quickened my breathing as I fairly bounced up the steps to cross the landing. Not pausing to knock or hesitate, I shoved the doors open and walked into the millhouse.

A fire burned in the large hearth, there were lit candles on a long, food-laden table and on the window sills. The aroma of baked bread and hearty stew wafted around me. A woman stood at the fire, back to me, bending over to tend to a large iron cauldron hanging from a hook in the wall. She wore a black gown, gathered at the waist, with long tapered sleeves and somewhere in my mind I reasoned she was a widow in mourning. As I stood there, feeling so comfortable and at home, I became keenly aware that I'd not been invited in. I'd not been greeted or even spoken to. The woman at the hearth continued to tend to her pot and as she did so she began to sing. At first, I couldn't hear her words, but as her voice grew stronger her song grew louder and the lyrics became clear.

"Welcome fetch, hie thee home, come ye breath of blood and bone. Welcome boggle, hear my song, welcome flesh of earth and stone."

It was certainly an odd song she was singing, and for no reason I could clearly say, it bothered me greatly. The tune was fine, but the words sounded like something from a fairy tale about goblins and such. I had just made up my mind to turn around and tiptoe back outside when she stood to stretch, dropping her ladle back into the iron pot. Dusting her palms together, she turned around to look at me. Her expression was not one of surprise or displeasure. In fact, she beamed at me.

"Well, hello there," she smiled. "Where did you come from?"

"I'm sorry," I stammered, "um, I came from, well, I was sleeping out in the glade. I thought, well, I thought I heard someone calling my name."

"Poor child," she cooed, "do come in and sit down at the table. You must be cold and hungry. Z, please fix a plate for our guest!"

Captivated by the vision of the woman at the hearth, I had not even noticed that she was not alone. A girl, likely a few years younger than me, sat at a spinning wheel near a window in the far wall. When the woman called to her, she stood to brush fleece fibers from her skirts before hurrying across the room. She did not greet me or even acknowledge me, but when she drew near her eyes met mine for a moment. Those eyes, beautiful deep blue and thickly lashed, were full of fear. It seemed there was a silent plea for help in her expression. Breezing past me, she nodded at her mother's directions and drew a plate from the stack on a wall shelf.

"I'm Emmeline Caulfield," the woman offered as she tucked the errant auburn curl brushing her cheek back behind her ear. Her beautiful green eyes sparkled, almost outshining the glint of silver from a chain around her neck, though if she wore a pendant it was tucked beneath her blouse.

"I'm Falcon," I replied, suddenly wishing I was someone else as well as somewhere else. "I'm a friend of Jack Adler's."

She looked at me strangely before her expression went blank. I expected she would immediately recognize the name and understand how it was I had come to the millhouse, but instead her image shifted. Her thick, lustrous, long auburn hair shimmered and though it remained auburn, of a sort, it turned brittle-looking, wan, and course. Her cheekbones became obscenely sharp as the flesh on her face drew back. Those eyes, once bright, inquisitive, and full of intelligence, went dark and dead. The flesh on her nose caved in, leaving huge dark nostrils above her lipless mouth now pulled back in a grimace. Emmeline Caulfield's image was skeletal and devoid of light before it suddenly shifted back. Those merry green eyes once more met mine.

"I'm sorry," she smiled so sweetly it was disconcerting, "who did you say?"

"Um," I shifted uneasily from one foot to the other, trying desperately to make up a reason to excuse myself. "Oh, it doesn't matter. I'm Falcon and I'm just passing through the area. I saw your lights and thought I should introduce myself."

"I see," she nodded as she raised one hand toward the girl setting the table. "This is my daughter Z. Z, this is Falcon. Falcon's just passing through, but she's kind enough to stop in to introduce herself."

The young girl stopped what she was doing to look at me silently. She nodded politely before resuming her work. I noticed that she looked nothing like her mother. Z's hair was golden blond, her skin was creamy white, and those eyes were so bright blue as to be azure. Emmeline's hair was long, curly, and a rich auburn. Her complexion was somewhat bronzed, and her eyes a remarkable green. A flash of insight that Z was not Emmeline's daughter at all popped into my head, only disturbing me further.

"I'm sorry, I probably shouldn't have come," I muttered. "You're obviously busy. I don't want to disturb your work. I must be on my way anyway. I have a long way to go. I'll just, um, I'll leave you to what you were doing. It's been nice meeting you."

"No, no, Falcon," Mrs. Caulfield shook her head, waves of auburn curls shimmering around her shoulders, "you can't go! You must stay and have some food and drink. Warm yourself by the fire."

"Thank you for the offer and for your kindness," I responded, putting one foot behind the other, for I dared not turn my back on the woman. "I appreciate it, but I really have to be going."

"No!" Hands slamming down on the wooden table, the woman's anger erupted. Her features again became those of some otherworldly creature. Once more she appeared a skeletal husk that should not have been upright or moving. The effect lasted only a moment, but it was enough to spur me to action. I broke for the double doors, dashing headlong into the safety of the night beyond.

Heart pounding in my chest, breath catching in my throat, I bounded across the landing to take the wide steps two at a time. Suddenly my feet tangled. I felt myself toppling forward, hands outstretched to catch myself when I inevitably hit the ground.

Gasping, I sat bolt-upright, awake and alert. My blankets were wrapped around my legs. I struggled to be free as I realized I had been dreaming. The memories of meeting Emmeline Caulfield and her daughter in the millhouse were so vivid! I could still smell the bread and stew, feel the warmth from the fire in the hearth, and still see the lovely woman's features shift to those of an angry, wicked corpse. I shuddered as I shook off the memories. The storage building was still dark and full of shadows, though I could hear the horses breathing, moving slightly as they dozed. Deacon still slept, head resting on his saddle, but he had rolled over and turned his back to me. Rain continued to patter softly on the roof. The smell of wet grass was thick in the air. Though I really wanted to get up and walk around, move, and dispel the effects of the dream from which I had just awakened, I resigned myself to just straightening out my blankets and trying to go back to sleep. It was too dark and rainy to be doing anything, I silently admitted to myself as I untangled my blankets to pull them up beneath my chin. I lay back, resting my head against Aeon's saddle, closed my eyes, and took a deep breath.

'*Cor*,' I called out softly with my thoughts, '*please send me good dreams.*'

'*It is done!*' To my surprise the wizard's voice rippled through my mind like a kiss on the wind. In that moment I recalled that I had been unable to reach him in my dream.

'*Thank you!*' I responded more to feel the connection between the two of us than out of need or even politeness. The mental link we shared was powerful and comforting. A breeze ruffled my hair as I relaxed in the comfort of the Elemental Wizard's energy.

Reluctantly opening my eyes, I beheld two leather-booted feet and four hooves walking into the dew glistening grass as Deacon led Aeon out to graze. By the time he returned, I was sitting up, folding my blankets, yawning languidly.

"Good morning, Falcon," he greeted me brightly. "Did you sleep well?"

"I did," stretching my arms above my head I yawned again, "and now I'm hungry."

"I'll take Nex out to graze and we'll have some food before resuming our journey." Without waiting for a response, the druid strode past me, untethered his horse, and led him out of the storage building.

As I straightened up our things and prepared to eat, I considered why I had not mentioned my dream to Deacon. I knew he would find it of interest and that he would certainly not make fun of me or belittle my concerns, but somehow sharing it just felt wrong. Maybe, I wondered, I simply did not want to give Emmeline and her silent daughter any more of my attention or my energy. Maybe if I spoke of them, it would somehow make them more real. Though again, maybe it was just a silly dream brought on by our tiring journey. My mind was probably just playing tricks on me, I assured myself.

'*Good morning, Cor!*' Peering up into the rafters of the storage barn, I imagined the wizard's kindly face looking down at me. I knew he was not there, but it felt good to envision him watching over me from above.

'*Good morning, Falcon. I trust you slept well?*'

'*After you sent good dreams I did! Before that was a different story.*' To be honest, I could not remember dreaming after I had awakened from the nightmare, but I thought I did sleep well.

'*I sense you've something on your mind!*'

'*I do,*' I sighed, rubbing the sleep from my eyes.

'*Anything I can help you with?*'

'*No, I don't think so. Just some things I must figure out and try to make sense of, I guess.*'

'*Very well, Falcon. Let me know if I can be of further service.*' My beloved mentor's voice was deep, resonant, strong, and comforting. '*And in the meantime, travel well and stay safe!*'

With reluctance, I let the connection between us dissolve and set about putting together a morning meal. From my saddlebag I withdrew apples, the cores of which we would share with the horses when we finished them, what was left of Corliss's bread, and the Tomcakes. While I waited for Deacon to return, I picked up the water skins as I made my way across the rain-damp grass to the edge of the river. The bank was steep, so I had to go down on one knee to avoid toppling in to the running stream. I pulled the stopper from my leather water skin and held the neck open slightly below the surface to let the river fill it. Once I had closed it back up and placed it on the bank, I did the same with Deacon's water skin before clambering up the steep incline with a heavy bag in each hand. My companion was just returning to the storage barn when I walked in, propping one water skin against each saddle.

"We've fresh water for the journey," I announced, "and if you want tea or coffee, I can heat it up again for you. Well, at least I can try."

"You did well last night, Falcon," he nodded, lifted his water skin, removed the stopper, and drank deeply. "But this is fine for now. Fresh water's always good first thing in the morning and it's a mild day so I don't need hot tea or hot coffee to warm my bones."

"I've put out food," crossing my ankles, I sat down, picked up an apple and tossed it to him. "We've bread and Tomcakes!"

"That's perfect," he laughed, catching the airborne fruit easily. With a loud crunch he bit into the apple as he lowered himself to the ground. He wiped a trickle of juice off his chin with the back of his hand as he picked up a Tomcake. "The horses are grazing for a bit. When they're done, we'll take them to the river for a drink before moving on."

"And where do we go from here?" Once more taking the top from my water skin, I carefully filled my mug, put it on the ground before me, and resealed the leather pouch. With a deep breath, I cleared my mind to focus my attention on the water, on exciting it, and causing it to vibrate. I could hear Deacon munching his apple and a crisp wafer, but I knew the magic was working so long as I kept my eyes on the mug.

"The next place is the Winterbourne's," he replied between bites. "Robert and Margaret Winterbourne live on a nice farm with their twin boys, George and Geoffrey. It's quite a ride from here and the terrain ahead isn't easy, but we'll reach their place by day's end."

Once the water was hot and I could see steam rising from the mug in the cool morning air, I tucked a mint-filled cloth sachet into it to steep. I bit into my own apple after wiping it on my sleeve. The fruit was crisp, juicy, and delicious, I had to admit, and Aeon would not be getting much beyond the core itself.

"What do you mean the terrain isn't easy?"

"There's a ridge of rocky, steep hills we'll have to make our way across. The trails are easy enough to find and follow, but one can't travel quickly over them. We'll have to take our time and let the horses find their footing."

"And after that?" With my apple in one hand, I lifted my mug with the other, blew across the steaming tea to cool it, and carefully took a hesitant sip. It was still too hot to drink, I realized, so I put the mug back on the ground before me.

"Beyond the Winterbourne's, there's a little valley, and beyond that lie steeper mountains. But we don't have to cross those peaks, we're just skirting them to reach Fox Pass. Once through the pass, we'll be visiting Gordon and Anna Reed, a lovely couple with three children, a daughter and two boys. The land becomes more open and wilder the farther west we travel. Homes are farther apart, but with some luck tomorrow we'll be visiting the Reeds and maybe even reach Arlo and Catherine Thorpe's place. The Thorpes are an elderly couple who live by themselves, but their grown children live within a day's ride so they're cared for and their needs are met. Sometimes they're not well, so I make a point to check on them whenever I'm in the area."

"I see," I nibbled the last bit of flesh off my apple core and put it beside me before reaching for a Tomcake. "So, we've many leagues to travel. I guess we should hurry up with our food and be on our way." Lifting the mug of tea to my lips, I blew what little steam remained away before taking a careful sip. The brew was still very warm, but no longer likely to burn my mouth, so I drank it as quickly as I could.

"The horses should have had sufficient time to graze by now." Deacon offered, "So once we're done eating, we'll let them drink at the river and bring them back in to gear them for the ride ahead."

"You finish eating," I suggested, swallowing the last of my tea before brushing my hands on my breeches. "I'll go take Aeon and Nex to the river for some water. You should be done eating by the time they're done drinking."

"You don't mind?"

"No, I'm happy to help," Clambering to my feet, I picked up my cloak, drew it around my shoulders, and tied it at the throat. "I'll be back in a bit!"

As I stepped out into the crisp dawn, I smiled up at the rising sun just peeking over the horizon. Everywhere drops of dew and pale mist shimmered and glinted, making the meadow appear fresh and magical. Feeling good and happy, I pulled the hem of my cloak up to keep it from getting wet on the grass as I made my way to where Aeon stood comfortably grazing, her tail swishing softly.

"Come on, girl," I patted her neck as I collected her reins, "let's get you some water and I've saved you an apple core." Gently, I tugged on her reins as I walked her to the river's edge. She splashed her front hooves into the water, lowered her nose, and began to drink.

While Aeon was drinking her fill, I crossed the glade to gather Nex's reins and happened to glance north to find the dark, brooding presence of the millhouse glowering at me. The breeze was cool, but it was not the air that caused the chill that rode up my spine. The memory of the dream and the appearance of the forlorn and forgotten mill made the hairs on the back of my neck stand up and sent a shiver over me.

"Come on, Nex," I murmured softly to the great white stallion, "let's get you a drink and get out of this place. I don't like it here anymore."

Nex shook his massive head, snorting as I pulled on his reins, and followed as I drew him to the river. He waded into the water beside Aeon and began to drink. I moved back from the horses and rubbed my arms as I looked at the millhouse. The glade had once been beautiful to me, and it still was to some degree, but the influence of the building tainted the place and I was ready to be gone.

"We're all ready to ride," I announced as I led the horses into the storage barn. "They've grazed, had a drink, and I've promised them the apple cores."

"Great!" Deacon smiled, pausing in his work, "I've tidied up here, put your things in your saddlebags and folded your blankets into your bedroll, so give Aeon your apple core and I'll give Nex mine."

He handed me what little was left of the apple I had eaten so I held it on my palm beneath Aeon's mouth. She slobbered a bit as she took the fruit core into her mouth. Munching it contentedly, she looked at me with hopeful eyes.

"Sorry," I shrugged, wiping my sticky palm on my pantleg, "that's all I've got right now. You can have a Tomcake tonight."

Deacon gave Nex his apple core as we both set about saddling the horses. Before the sun had fully cleared the horizon, we were leading our mounts out of the storage building into the misty, warming autumn morning.

Chapter 9

The day moved on as we rode along the smooth, earthen road. The rising sun on our backs grew warmer as it burned off the morning fog. We chatted sporadically, but mostly we just rode in companionable silence, listening to the birds sing, the leaves stir in the breeze, and the leather of the saddles straining and stretching. The road, once heading straight west, began to meander as it followed the lay of the land. Around rising hillocks and down gentle slopes, we began to move in a northerly direction. The trees fell away on either side of us as the terrain opened to harvested fields and rock-strewn clearings. From the change in our surroundings, I could tell we were nearing the foothills Deacon had warned me about.

"At least we'll be traveling south of the uplands, Falcon," my companion offered, noticing my concern. "The foothills are an easy trek compared to those!"

"It's all right," I smiled weakly. "I'm just hoping that Aeon's shoes hold out on the hard and rocky ground. I've been planning on having her re-shod, but the farrier hasn't been by Corhaven when I've been there."

"I'm sure Aeon will be fine," he nodded. "We'll just take our time and go carefully. The path over the foothills is sometimes narrow and it does wind a bit, so I'll take the lead and you can follow."

"What's that over there?" I pointed to my right where some oddly shaped stones stood as if intentionally arranged.

"I don't know," he admitted with an odd expression on his face. "I've never noticed that before and I've certainly come this way often enough. Perhaps we should go have a look?"

"Listen!" Holding up one hand, I strained to hear again what I thought I had heard.

"I don't," Deacon started, but fell silent when the sound came once more. A piteous whimper rose before falling off into sharp yips.

"You hear that?"

"I do!"

"Whatever it is," I turned my mount in the direction of the sound, "it's definitely in trouble."

Without further comment or waiting for him to agree with me, I snapped Aeon's reins smartly and rode as quickly as I dared on the rock-strewn, uneven ground. The sound, I realized, was coming from where the strange stones stood. From a distance the standing stones looked like hunched or cloaked giants and as we neared, I could see there were five grouped in something of a circle.

"Ancient boundary stones?" I queried as I drew Aeon to a halt. "No, that can't be right!"

The whimpering call of distress rose again.

Swinging myself from the saddle, I leapt easily to the ground as I waited for the cry to come once more. As soon as it sounded again, I could sense where it was coming from, so I started in that direction.

"Falcon, wait!" Deacon caught up and swung himself from Nex's saddle, panting as he landed on the ground. "Falcon, wait! It's a nemeton. I've never noticed it here before, but that's what it is!"

"I don't care," shaking my head, I continued toward the circle, "whatever is in there is in trouble and I'm not ignoring it just because there's a nemeton in the way!"

"But, Falcon," my companion insisted, hurrying behind me. I could hear his footsteps as he drew near.

The instant I crossed into the sacred space of the nemeton everything changed. Silence settled over me. A golden white light rose from the ground in the center of the circle, growing brighter and bigger as it moved. I nearly jumped out of my skin when Deacon's hand touched my shoulder as he moved up behind me. We stood together transfixed.

'Should have reached out to Cor first,' I thought as I beheld the energy before me growing and expanding. Suddenly I became aware of the sensation that we were being watched. Though it was difficult, I managed to tear my gaze away from the center of the circle and look behind us only to find that we were not alone. Before each of the stones stood a massive being, though what they were I could only guess. Each entity was slightly different, but they were of the same species. As if carved from the stones themselves, they were pale with powerful-looking arms, broad chests, and grim expressions.

"Deacon," I whispered, "look! Who are they?"

"Guardians," he responded. "They're guardians of the nemeton."

"How did they come to be here? I've never seen such things before!"

"The creator of the nemeton must have made them as well."

"What do they want? They don't look happy or particularly pleased to see us."

"They're just reading us, sensing our intentions. We're of no threat so they won't bother us, I hope."

Suddenly, the yelping cry of the animal in distress resumed, shaking me from my wonder. Ignoring the guardians around us and moving around the swirling energy in the center of the circle, I followed the strident cries until I came to a deep crevice in the ground, peered down and saw a puppy staring up at me. When the beast laid eyes on me it leapt up, only to fall back in defeat. It was clear the little guy had fallen into the gaping hole in the ground and could not get back out.

"Deacon," I called back over my shoulder, "it's a puppy! It can't get out of this hole. We need to help it."

"Are you sure that's a puppy?" He asked as he moved beside me, "Looks like it could be a wolf to me. And are you sure you want to do this?" Casting his gaze around the nemeton, the druid suddenly looked uneasy.

"It looks just like Samson," I reasoned aloud, "though it's a bit more gray than black. It's a puppy. Anyway, it needs help so we must get it out, and yes, I'm sure I want to do this."

"I have a rope in my saddlebag," my companion offered, "so I can tie it to Nex's saddlehorn and lower myself into the hole."

"No," shaking my head adamantly, I responded, "I'll go. I'm lighter than you and we shouldn't bring the horses into the nemeton. You can lower me into the hole and pull me back up yourself."

"What if the beast gets scared and bites you? What if it panics and fights you trying to rescue it?"

"What if he bites you? What if he fights you? The risk is the same for either of us," I retorted. "But I want to do this. Trust me?"

"Very well," he nodded as he turned to exit the nemeton, "I'll be right back!"

While Deacon was retrieving the rope, I released the buckle on ThornSting's scabbard belt to lay the weapon down before getting down on my knees. I spoke gently to the whimpering puppy. He was obviously relieved and happy to see us. His eyes were bright, his muzzle long and sharply pointed, and his ears stood up high on his head. He did look very much like Samson, the Fulton's dog, but where Samson was black this puppy was gray.

"Don't worry, sweetie," I murmured, "we'll get you out in just a minute." Rocking back on my heels I looked all around us. "Wonder where your mommy is, baby. Or maybe you're already on your own?"

The animal yipped excitedly in response as it sat on its haunches. Cocking its head at me, it seemed to be trying to figure out what I was saying and what I was doing.

"Here you go," Deacon returned, a coil of rope in one hand. He offered me one end. "Tie this around your waist and I'll lower you. Be sure and tie it firmly."

"I will," I accepted the rope as I stood and brushed my hands off on my breeches. Slipping the length around my back, I tied a secure knot, added a second, and pulled to test it. It felt secure to me. "All right, I'm ready."

Deacon held the rope firmly as he lowered me into the crevice. Even before my feet touched the bottom of the hole, the dog was leaping up and bouncing off my legs. He was excited to see me and showed no signs of being scared or wanting to bite me.

"All right, now you're going to have to trust me," I spoke in what I hoped was a reassuring voice, "and I'm going to pick you up and Deacon's going to pull us both up, understand?"

Though he did not answer me, the beast seemed willing to cooperate so I scooped him up against my chest and called out to the druid to pull us out. Instantly, my feet left the ground as I began to rise. The dog did not even squirm as we were lifted up the side of the pit. When I was close enough, I lifted the little pup and released it onto the ground. He promptly turned around to yip at me, his bushy tail wagging furiously. Once safely on the ground beside the hole, I untied the rope and Deacon coiled it back up.

"There you go, you're free," I announced to the excited dog, "you can find your way home now." Pausing briefly to buckle my scabbard belt around my waist once more, I adjusted the weight of the sword as I straightened the hem of my tunic.

"I guess it's back on the road for us," Deacon smiled, smacking his thigh with the coil of rope as he started back to where the horses stood.

As I followed my companion, the puppy trotted beside me, joyfully bouncing along.

"You're supposed to go home," I shook my head at him, hands on my hips. "You're free. Go home!"

At that, the beast wandered away to sniff at the base of one of the standing stones, seeming to lose interest in me, so I walked to where Deacon stood packing the rope back into his saddlebag. Gathering Aeon's reins, I put one foot in the stirrup and swung myself into the saddle. Deacon mounted Nex, turned him back to where we'd left the road, and regained the trail at the base of the foothills. I turned my mount to follow, glancing back at the nemeton where the puppy stood on three legs relieving himself against one of the standing stones.

"Not sure that's properly respectful," I shrugged, "but I guess that's what puppies do. The guardians haven't raised the alarm so they must be all right with it."

Leaving the now-free dog to find his way home, we headed for the trail which rose gently up a ridge, winding between boulders and smaller strewn rocks. By the time we reached the crest of the foothills I realized that our four-legged friend was following us, running here and there to investigate the various smells, and marking his territory at will.

"I see you," I smiled at the puppy as he raced to catch up with us. "You were supposed to find your way home."

Yipping in response, his long pink tongue lolling out the side of his mouth in a silly panting grin, the young dog looked at me pointedly. When he sat down and cocked his head to one side, I realized he was tired.

"Fine," I sighed, dismounted, and picked him up. He licked my face a few times before I managed to hoist him across Aeon's back. Quickly, I got back into the saddle, rearranged the young dog between myself and the saddlehorn, and clucked to my mount.

"Seems we're new friends, huh?" I spoke to the puppy, already yawning as it settled to get comfortable. "Don't know what I'm going to do with you, but as you seem determined to come with us, at least for a while, I guess we'll figure it out."

Yawning once more, the puppy peered up at me with adoration in his eyes. That face, those eyes, just melted me inside.

"Oh sure, just give me those big puppy eyes," I chuckled. "Lothar! That's it, your name is Lothar. What do you think? Does it feel right to you?"

Though his eyebrows rose as he looked up at me, he did not respond or react, leaving me to wonder if he would take to the name I had just given him. It seemed only time would tell that tale.

"You realize that still may be a wolf," Deacon called back over his shoulder, glancing with a grin at the sleeping puppy before me.

"Could be," I shrugged, "but it's not. It's a dog, trust me."

The druid had been right when he told me the terrain was not easy and that the trail was tricky. The ground rose then dipped, the path narrowed and widened as it wandered over the ridge. It felt like we were traveling very slowly by letting the horses pick their way along the pebble-strewn ground. When we finally started going down and the level land stretched out before us, I heaved a sigh of relief. Beyond the open valley before us rose a dense forest of dark pines and sun-kissed oaks.

"The Winterbourne's place is just off to the south there," Deacon pointed to our left. "You can just barely make out the roof of their house from here."

"I see it," I nodded. "And you said there are two boys there? Twins?"

"Aye," he replied, "George and Geoffrey. I reckon they're probably six years old by now. Dark hair and dark eyes; it's almost impossible to tell them apart, but unless George has had a spurt of growth, Geoffrey's the taller of the two."

"Anything else I should know about them or their parents?"

"Margaret, that is Mrs. Winterbourne, is reserved. She's a lovely person, but a bit stern. Robert's the outgoing one. Don't think he's ever met a stranger."

We rode on without further conversation. The day had turned warm and the blue sky overhead was free of clouds. A slight breeze blew whisps of hair into my face from time to time, which was annoying, but it also kept the insects from us so I was not about to complain. As we neared our destination, I considered what to do with Lothar. I was not sure how the Winterbournes would take to having a puppy bouncing around their children or their house, but I was not keen on leaving him alone outside either. Looking down at the sleeping canine, I reasoned that he was not yet very big, and he seemed to have attached himself to me. I could only hope that he would behave nicely and that there would be no incidences between him and the family.

The Winterbourne's place was a tall, narrow house of wattle and daub. Obviously two-stories, there were narrow windows below the eaves and slate tiles on the roof. Most of the homes I was used to seeing were thatch-roofed cottages, one story and cozy, but this place appeared more solid and impressive. A garden stood to the south of the home, mostly harvested, though a few vegetables remained awaiting ripeness.

"Hold on a minute, please," I called to my companion as I drew Aeon to a halt. Tucking the sleepy puppy under one arm, I jumped down from the saddle and began digging through one of my saddlebags. When my hand touched the item I sought, I pulled it out, placed Lothar gently between my feet, and offered him half a Tomcake. He munched the crispy biscuit quickly and with obvious delight, before looking up at me, begging.

"You be good," I assured him, "and you can have the other half of the Tomcake later." Satisfied that the puppy had gotten my message, I picked up Aeon's reins and began to lead her behind Deacon on Nex, with Lothar dodging here and there around us.

"I'm hoping Cor's Tomcakes work their magic," I laughed as the druid looked curiously back at me. "And maybe Lothar will behave himself and not cause any trouble."

"Ah," Deacon nodded sagely, "twin boys and a puppy. No, I see no trouble there!" He laughed deeply as he drew Nex to a halt and dismounted. Side by side we led our horses to the Winterbourne's place.

Two muss-haired, giggling little boys ran around the corner of the house, chasing one another in play. Both came to a sudden halt when they noticed us, but the shorter of the two broke away from his companion to leap onto the stoop and bang loudly on the closed door.

"Momma! Momma! We have company," he yelled as he continued to pound. "Momma, Deacon's here!"

The second boy, taller and a bit darker complected, had slowed to a walk, his eyes glued on Lothar as he approached. The dog was busy chewing on a clump of tall grass, snapping the willowy blades, tugging and releasing them.

"Who are you?" Raising one hand to shade his eyes from the sun, he peered up at me, before glancing at the dog. "And what's that?"

"I'm Falcon Rose," I replied with a nod, "and this is my friend, Lothar."

"Greetings Master Geoffrey," Deacon approached the child, hand extended. The boy shook hands with the druid before turning back to me.

"Why are you with Deacon?"

"Falcon is a member of the Order of Healers," my companion answered for me. "And I'm showing her around, introducing her to folks that might need her help one day."

"Why?" The youngster challenged. "You goin' somewhere?"

"No," Deacon shook his head with a wry grin, "I'm not planning on going anywhere, but it's good to have help and it will be easier for the two of us to tend to folks, a little less work for me."

"Hi," the boy's brother joined us, his eyes too locking on the puppy who was still busy with the blades of grass, "I'm George!"

"Greetings, George," I smiled, "you too, Geoffrey. I'm happy to meet you both."

At that moment, a woman stepped out of the house, wiping her hands on the apron tied around her waist. Her hair, as dark as that of her sons, was partially gathered at the nape of her neck while wispy tendrils edged her face. Though I was never particularly gifted at guessing a person's age, it was clear to me that Mrs. Winterbourne was older as the hair at her temples was streaked gray. Wearing a long dark blue skirt and white blouse beneath her apron, she had flour on her chin, and she looked hot and tired.

"Margaret," Deacon greeted the woman warmly, "it's good to see you. You look well!"

"Deacon," she smiled in return, "it's always good to see you. I'm well, thank you, tired, but well. Today is breadmaking day and I'm a bit of a mess. How are you?"

"Excellent, thank you," he replied, extending an arm toward me, "and Margaret, I'd like to have you meet my friend and fellow healer, Falcon Rose. Falcon, this is Margaret Winterbourne."

"How do you do?" I bowed politely, noticing even as I did so that, like those of her children, the woman's eyes were locked on the puppy. "I'm pleased to meet you." Lothar, who had just lost interest in the grass, spun around to notice the boys. Hesitantly, he trotted over to stand beside me before sitting down on his haunches.

"I, uh," Margaret Winterbourne stammered, a confused expression on her face, "I'm happy to meet you too." She managed to return her attention to my companion. "Please, Deacon, do come in. You're welcome to tea or coffee."

Clearly, the woman did not include me and Lothar in the invitation to enter her house. I understood her reluctance to let a strange, possibly wild beast inside, but I was not as interested in her as I was her boys anyway.

"Well, I," Deacon paused, casting a glance at me.

"You go on, please," I beamed. "If it's all right, I'd like to talk to the boys."

"That's up to them," Margaret shrugged dismissively, "but I've no issues with you talking to them if they're willing to talk with you."

With that, she took Deacon by the arm and the two headed for the house. The two boys, meanwhile, stood transfixed before me, both intently focused on Lothar. I could see the desire to touch the puppy in their eyes. Gently, I gathered him up to my chest, petting him carefully.

"Geoffrey, George," I spoke quietly as I knelt to put Lothar back on the ground, "this is Lothar and you're welcome to play together so long as you're gentle and careful with him."

"Yes, Ma'am!" Both boys proclaimed, barely able to contain their excitement.

"And we can talk while you play, yes?"

"Yes, Ma'am," both murmured. I realized in that instant that I could have asked each for an organ or an appendage and they'd have readily agreed, so rapt were they.

"Very well," I released the puppy, who joyfully bounced upon the legs of the nearest boy, wagging his tail and whimpering. "Let's talk."

Chapter 10

George and Geoffrey Winterbourne ran around the garden and the yard surrounding their house, giggling, and calling Lothar's name, encouraging the puppy to race after them. He did so until all three were winded and panting. Finally, the boys went to the well, dropped the rope-tied bucket in, and drew up a pail full of fresh cool water. They used a long-handled ladle that was hanging on the side of the well to get a drink before looking at me.

"Can we give him a drink of water?" George asked, nodding at the puppy, now panting with his tongue hanging out of his mouth.

"Sure," I smiled, "but don't use the ladle. Cup your hands, George, and Geoffrey, you pour a ladleful into your brother's hands so Lothar can drink from that."

"There's a water trough for the horses in the paddock near the barn, but I don't think Lothar's big enough to reach it," Geoffrey suggested as he dipped the ladle into the pail, withdrew the water, and poured it into his brother's cupped hands.

"I'm sure you're right," I agreed, noticing for the first time that the two looked tired. Though both boys had deeply tanned skin, the dark circles beneath their eyes spoke clearly of their health. "So, are you two feeling all right? You look a little tired. Have you been ill?"

George glanced up at his brother who looked pointedly back at him. As twins often do, I had been taught, the two silently exchanged information before both looking at me. For a moment I did not think they would say anything, but finally Geoffrey sighed.

"We've been having bad dreams, Ma'am," he admitted. "Both me and George have been dreamin' about a scary woman. We don't know who she is or what she wants, but she's scary. It's hard to go to sleep when we know she might be in our dreams."

"I imagine so," I nodded. "Have you told your mother?"

"Yes," George replied, nodding at his brother to refill his cupped hands for Lothar, "Momma says it's just a dream and that we should go back to sleep. She says if we're good no scary woman in a dream can hurt us."

"And do you believe her?"

"I don't know," the boy admitted. "We try to be good, but if she's in our dreams that must mean we're not. And if we're not good we don't know how to be good."

"We're good," Geoffrey asserted. "Momma just don't understand and we can't make her understand. So, I stay awake and watch while George sleeps and when he starts actin' uneasy I wake him up. He does the same for me."

"And this scary woman in your dreams," I probed gently, "can you tell me what she looks like? Does she do or say anything?"

The boys exchanged another look before turning to me, their expressions stony.

"No," Geoffrey shook his head slowly, "we can't tell you that. It's like, almost as soon as we wake up, she is gone. We can remember that she scares us, and she really does, but we can't tell who she is, where she comes from, what she looks like or if she says anything. We just remember her, sort of, but not really."

"She's just scary," George whispered as Lothar finished slurping up the water from his hands and proceeded to lick the boy's face in appreciation. George giggled, trying to pull away from the exuberant puppy, but he could only escape by standing up. At that, Lothar took off as fast as his little paws would take him, racing around the garden to disappear behind the house. The boys gave chase, all thoughts of nightmares and the scary woman apparently vanishing as they ran after the pup.

"Is it possible their nightmare woman is the same one Brice dreams of?" I murmured softly to myself. "Could it be a coincidence? Surely not. That's just too fantastic!"

All hopes of gaining further information were dashed when the door opened and the boys' mother and Deacon stepped outside. To me, it seemed they had not been in there very long, but they appeared to be in good spirits, smiling and chatting amicably, so it must have been a successful visit.

"Geoffrey, George," Mrs. Winterbourne put her hands on her hips and called out loudly, "you boys come tend to your chores. You've played long enough, now it's time to get to work!"

Lothar appeared first from around the far corner of the house. He was bouncing excitedly as the boys gave chase, but when he saw Deacon and Mrs. Winterbourne standing there together, he dug his front paws into the dirt, slewing to a sudden halt. He glanced at them, quickly recovered, and bolted to where I stood. His pursuers appeared to obediently give up their chase, pausing before their mother for a quick "Yes, Ma'am."

Deacon said his farewells to the Winterbournes before turning to me, "Falcon, are you ready to move on?"

"Yes," I smiled, "just let me get Lothar a bit more water from the well. The boys gave him quite a workout and he's very thirsty."

"I'll help," he offered, leading the way to the stone well. "I see there's already some water in the bucket, did the boys haul this up for you?"

"They did. If you'll ladle some into my hands, I'll give our furry friend here a quick drink and we can get back on the road."

"Of course," the druid nodded as he poured cool water into my outstretched, cupped hands.

I knelt to let Lothar lap up the water, though he spilled as much as he got into his mouth, I was sure. Glancing up at my companion, I gave him a smile so he refilled my hands once more. Again, the puppy drank, but he had lost interest before my hands were empty, making it clear he'd had enough.

"All right," addressing Lothar as I scooped him up, "you've had your fill, it seems. Let's go!"

Deacon returned the ladle to the pail, wiped his hands on his tunic, and joined me as we crossed the yard to where the horses stood. It dawned on me that I might have asked Mrs. Winterbourne for permission to water our mounts, but it was clearly too late for that now as she and the boys were already going inside. I knew we were not that far from running water so the horses would have ample opportunity to drink further on down the road.

Tucking Lothar into the crook of my arm, I gathered Aeon's reins, put my foot in the stirrup, and hoisted myself into the saddle. Deacon mounted Nex, turned him north toward the open valley we'd skirted, and firmly heeled him in the flanks. We resumed our journey at a comfortable pace as the ground was smooth and grass covered. The land to our left rose higher and higher as we traveled north, and soon we were riding in the afternoon shadow of an ever-growing ridge of mountains.

"So, how did your visit with Mrs. Winterbourne go?" I dared to ask as we rode side by side.

"It went fine," he shrugged, "though I got the feeling she wasn't being completely open and honest with me about what's going on."

"What do you mean?"

"Well, she mentioned the boys are having bad dreams, making up stories, scaring one another as children often do. Though she made light of it, I could tell that she was concerned. I did offer to have you make them some of the sleeping elixir you gave the Fultons, but she insisted they don't need anything. Apparently, they have no difficulty sleeping, they just have bad dreams."

"Yes, they told me about that," I nodded, "and they also told me that while one sleeps the other stands watch. When the sleeper starts fussing or fighting, the one standing guard wakes him. They switch and take turns. It can't be very comfortable trying to get rest that way."

"No," he shook his head slowly, "no indeed. I do wish she'd have let us leave some elixir there just in case, but she's a strong-willed woman and I knew there was no sense trying to change her mind."

"Deacon," hesitantly, I approached the subject, "do you think it's possible that the Winterbourne boys are dreaming of the same scary woman as Brice Fulton?"

"It does seem to be a bit more than a coincidence, doesn't it?"

"But how is that possible and what could it mean?" I wondered aloud, patting Lothar's head as he yawned tiredly.

"You're the witch," my companion shot me a grin. "You tell me!"

"The witch in me doesn't know," I laughed, "but the practical woman in me knows that we don't know enough to even hazard a guess. Maybe it is just a coincidence, maybe the scary woman the children are dreaming about is entirely different for each child. Maybe it's something in the water or something in the air that's giving the little ones bad dreams. We simply don't know, at least not yet."

"I agree," he nodded approval, "so let's go. Fox Pass is a bit further on, and we'll make our way through there to the other side of Serpent Ridge. Beyond, the traveling's a bit easier."

"Serpent Ridge, huh? That's what this line of mountains is called?"

"It is. It continues to get higher and more treacherous the farther north you go. Down here on the southern end the hills are not too bad to cross, but further on? Very dangerous."

"So, we stay south of most of Serpent Ridge, and where do we go after that?"

"We'll move on west, go through Lindenwood forest, cross the Marmeny, and then turn south and back east. Eventually, we'll come full circle."

"I see," I replied as my attention was drawn back to the furry, now wriggling, pup moving against me. Apparently, Lothar's nap was over and he wanted to be free. "I'm going to let Lothar down so he can run and do what he needs to do."

"I...," Deacon's words died on his lips as a look of confusion washed over his face. "What the devil?" He'd drawn his horse to a halt and now sat staring at a pile of tumbled rocks just ahead and to our left.

"What is it?" I queried, "What's wrong, Deacon?"

"This is Fox Pass! It's full of fallen stones. Looks like one of the cliffs has collapsed."

"Is there another way through," I gaped, "or a way around this?"

"Wait here," Deacon swung himself down from the saddle to walk to the mouth of the pass, Nex's reins still in one hand. "The rubble's mostly up against the south wall here. If we lead the horses and walk carefully, I think we can still get through, but we want to be quiet and step lively. Who knows how unstable this part of the mountain is or when it might collapse again? We don't want to be here if that happens."

"Oh, um," I murmured as the image of the towering earthen walls collapsing on us, the horses, and Lothar, came horrifically and vividly into my mind. For a moment I could not move or even think straight. "Are you sure this is safe enough for us to go through? Should we try to find another way?"

"If we go back south and cross the ridge at the tip of the tail, we'll have to go through a very dangerous swamp that lies at the base of the western side. The land is so alive there that it surfaces and sinks at will. Men who have traversed it successfully for years have been known to disappear into the depths when solid ground suddenly sinks taking them with it."

"We can't go past the swamp," I paused in confusion. "Didn't you say we're going through the pass before going south? Can't we just turn back to go south now, then head west?"

"Not if we intend to check in on everyone. The land just isn't passable in some places," he explained with a shrug. "No, this is still the best way."

"I'm not sure about this, Deacon," I admitted, jumping down from Aeon's saddle, one hand supporting Lothar's weight against my middle. Releasing the pup, I drew my cape from my gear, shook out its length, and put it on. The air had taken on a chill in the shadow of the pass and the weight of the woolen cloak felt wonderful on my shoulders. Lothar immediately went sniffing up to the nearest good-sized rock, lifted his hind leg, and relieved himself. Turning my attention back to the matter at hand, I stepped up beside the druid to peer into the rubble-strewn pass. As much as I hated to admit it, Deacon was right. It appeared that if we took our time and walked, carefully leading the horses, we could go through Fox Pass. Still, those sheer ragged walls on either side felt precariously menacing.

"Trust me?" Deacon raised his eyebrows, offering me a grin.

"I do," I sighed in resignation. "Very well, let's do this."

"Now remember," he warned, "we need to be as quiet as we can. We don't know what caused this wall to collapse or how secure it is. Any loud noise might set it off again and we don't want that."

"Right," with a nod I shuddered, "quiet it is."

"Follow me," he directed. Without further comment, he gently pulled Nex's reins and started around the rubble on the floor of the pass.

"Lothar," I called to the puppy who was busy sniffing anything and everything, tail wagging happily. He looked up, cocked his head, and bounded at me. "Come on. I'm going to try to carry you. Maybe that will be safer than letting you scamper around on your own."

Scooping up the panting bundle of fur, I positioned him in the crook of my left elbow as I gave a gentle tug on Aeon's reins. Watching my step as I made my way slowly, I followed Deacon behind Nex, noting how delicately the white stallion moved among the loose stones and pebbles. It became evident, as we made our way deeper into Fox Pass, that the cliff collapse had mostly affected the mouth of the cut. Our path soon became wider and easier to traverse. Lothar, having apparently exhausted his patience with being carried, squirmed his displeasure, so I released him to the ground as I guided my mare. The puppy bounded away to investigate his surroundings, so I clucked at my mount and snapped her reins softly. As we rounded a bend, the end of the pass came into sight, though a fellow traveler heading toward us obstructed the view. A weary-looking man sat hunched aboard a wagon loaded with wares, his bay bobbing its head as it pulled the cart along. The driver was looking down, but when Deacon called out a greeting the man's head popped up as he suddenly halted his wagon.

"Will Perry!" My companion called cheerily as he drew Nex to a halt.

"Eh?" The man shook himself as if waking from a stupor, "Who are you?"

"It's me, Will, it's Deacon. I know it's been a while since we've seen each other, but surely you remember me. I treated your wife's cough last winter."

"Deacon? Oh, yes! Yes," pulling the woolen cap from his head, he smacked it on his knee with a smile, "I remember. Good to see you, man. How are you?"

"I'm well, thanks. You don't seem quite yourself. Is there something wrong? Is your wife well? She normally travels with you, doesn't she? I hope she's well."

"Aye, May's fine. She's back home putting up preserves from the last of this year's harvest."

"That's good to hear," Deacon nodded. "So, something else is bothering you?"

"I've had the strangest journey, Deacon. I make this trip every fortnight, rain, or shine, almost every month, depending on what supplies reach me up the river. Normally, the people I see are nice, friendly, easy-going, and helpful. I've known some of them all my life, in fact, and they've always been, well, I don't even know what I'm sayin'."

"That's all right, Will," Deacon prodded gently, "go ahead."

"Well, this trip folks have been downright mean! People who are usually smiling, laughing, quick with a helping hand or to offer a pint or cup of coffee are suddenly bitter, angry, and are as likely to turn and stomp away as to even return a 'hello.' It's just been strange. I can understand folks having a bad day, one or two being in a foul mood or not feeling well, but it's been everyone I've encountered this time. In fact, you're the first person I've run into who didn't snap at me before I could stop my wagon!"

"That is strange," the druid agreed, turning to me. "Falcon, this is Will Perry. He transports goods from the river across the countryside from village to village. He and his wife May live near the Marmeny river. I've known them both for years."

"How do you do?" I nodded greeting at the man aboard the wagon as Aeon bumped my shoulder with her warm, soft nose. Turning to attend the mare, I patted her muzzle as she shook her head.

"Will, this is Falcon Rose. She's a friend and fellow member of the Order," Deacon completed his introduction. "We're making our journey to check on folks before the winter moves in."

"Nice to meet you, Falcon," Will nodded, idly fingering the leather reins in his hands.

"Mr. Perry," I interjected before the conversation could turn back to his experiences with the people he'd met, "the wall of the pass behind us has crumbled and fallen. I don't think you'll get through it with your wagon."

"Oh no," he sighed, "if I have to go around it will add days to my journey. I don't know what to do!"

"Well," I offered, "Deacon and I can go back and roll the bigger stones out of the way. Maybe we can clear the path enough for you. At least we can try."

"Excellent idea, Falcon," Deacon agreed. "I think we can manage that."

Suddenly, Lothar came running from behind us. He leapt up on my legs. In a blur, I saw Will Perry dive under his wagon seat and pop upright, bow in his left hand, arrow in his right. Even as the horror of what I was seeing coalesced in my mind, I shoved my right hand forward, palm out and screamed, "Nooo…!" In a flash, I snatched the puppy up, turned, and put myself between him and the diminutive driver's weapon. Though time seemed to stand still, everything sped by in inexorable motion. Deacon called out, "Will, no!" just as the driver nocked the arrow. I glanced back over my shoulder, turned, and shot my hand out as if to deflect the projectile. Though the sharp tip was headed directly at my palm, the impact never came, nor did the sensation of metal penetrating my flesh. Instead, the next thing I became aware of was the sound of the arrow clanking off stone and clattering to the ground. My heart pounded in my chest. My ears suddenly roared as I hugged Lothar as tightly as I dared. Tears welled in my eyes, threatening to run down my cheeks as relief washed over me.

"What the deuce?" Mr. Perry gasped, "I never miss, and here I couldn't even get off a shot!"

I heard the wagon groan as he jumped down from the driver's seat before he and Deacon both rushed toward me. Turning to face them, I smiled weakly as I rubbed the puppy's ear between my thumb and fingers.

"It's all right," swallowing back a sob, I sighed. "There's no need to shoot. This is Lothar, my friend."

"A thousand apologies, Falcon. I saw the wee wolf running at you and I thought it was about to attack! When it leapt up on your leg, I was sure it was about to kill you right before my eyes. I'm sorry. I didn't realize it was your," the wagoner paused, clearly unsure how to continue.

"It's all right, Mr. Perry," smiling, I offered quick clarification. "Lothar might look like a wolf, but he's a dog, a shepherd, actually. Deacon and I rescued him and he's taken a shine to me, so I guess you could say he is my companion."

"Dog," the man murmured as he rubbed his chin and looked pointedly at Lothar. Raising his eyes, he looked at me before glancing at Deacon. The druid offered a smile of reassurance with a shrug. "Dog, yes, of course. Lothar. Ah, well hallo Lothar!"

When I released the excited puppy to the ground, he shot toward Mr. Perry and Deacon, bouncing with joy. After leaping on first one man then the other, Lothar trotted off to investigate the horse rigged to the wagon as well as the big wooden wheels, one of which he unashamedly relieved himself on. Clearly the dog held no grudge.

"Well," I clapped my hands together, "I guess we should start clearing the pass so you and your wagon can get through."

"Hold on there, Miss Rose," Will Perry held up one index finger as he returned to his wagon. With one hand, he fished beneath the wide, wooden seat, before proudly displaying the object of his search, "You wear these gloves. I can't have a member of the Order of Healers damaging her hands helping the likes of me. Please, take these."

"If you insist," I chuckled at the thought of my hands being anything worthy of protection. Still, I realized, it was nice of the man to be so thoughtful. Happily, I accepted the proffered soft leather gloves and slid my hands into them. They were much too large for me, but they would offer some protection from the rough stones so I clapped the gloves together and started back the way Deacon and I had just come.

The afternoon wore on as the three of us shoved and rolled stones out of the path of the wagon. By the time we reached the mouth of Fox Pass, I had resorted to cursing the rocks beneath my breath and found, to my delight, that many of them moved of their own volition. That I might be able to use magic for such a mundane feat had not occurred to me, so when the first stone rolled at a mere glance it was all I could do to keep from giggling and jumping up and down in delight. Shooting a glance back at my companions who were still busy bending over and using all their might and weight to roll the bigger stones away, I released a sigh of relief that neither seemed to have noticed me. Deacon, I was sure, would have been happy and perhaps even impressed at me wielding such power, but I was not sure how Will Perry might react. He might be one of those folks who thought such abilities evil or signs of worshipping demons so I had to be careful and not let him see what I was doing. Still, I could not help but give a little assistance to Deacon when I saw him struggling with a particularly large boulder. He had shoved his hands beneath the edge of the stone, pushed his shoulder against it, and was throwing all his weight at the thing, but it refused to budge. Concentrating all his effort on the boulder, he turned to catch sight of me just as I reached out my right hand, index and middle finger extended. Suddenly the boulder heaved and rolled, releasing resistance so quickly that Deacon fell against it as it tumbled away. Dropping to his hands and knees, my companion laughed as he offered me a knowing smile.

"Didn't think you were going to budge that one," I grinned, walking back to where he had been working. I extended my hand to help him up. "Good thing you're persistent!"

"Aye," he winked at me, "I'm persistent and you're Falcon Rose."

"I can be no one else!"

"Looks like that's the last of them," Will Perry observed as he joined us. "Won't have any trouble getting' the wagon through now, thanks to you both."

"You're very welcome, Will," Deacon offered as he stood and brushed his hands on his trousers. "We're happy to help."

"You can have these back," I held up the leather gloves, "and thanks for letting me use them."

"You're welcome, Falcon Rose," Mr. Perry accepted the proffered items, "and I'm grateful to you. Let me give you something for your journey. I have a few extra items on board and the two of you have certainly earned something."

"That's not necessary!" With a shrug I turned and called for Lothar.

"Necessary or not, I insist. Come, let me show you what I have for you both."

Will Perry insisted we accept some of his goods in thanks for our help clearing the pass. He added greatly to the provisions we already carried, foisting preserved meat, fresh fruit, and even the delicacy of dried figs on us. He refused to take no for an answer when he asked if we needed another blanket or cape, as his wagon carried folded stacks of both. So, Deacon received a new blanket and I accepted a lovely blue-gray woolen cape. As he unloaded the wares from his wagon, he warned us that there were robbers about.

"Word is so far they're just targeting folks on the road," he shook his head slowly, "and I've not heard of anyone gettin' hurt, but these are strange days so you both need to be careful in your travels."

"You think King Rowan knows about the robbers?" I interjected. "Would he have any of his men out trying to stop them?"

"That I don't know, Miss. And I don't know if it's one band of robbers or if there's many plaguing Esling. Doesn't seem likely His Highness would have anyone out looking for them, though, as his troops are spread thin, at the moment."

"What do you mean? Esling's not at war, is it?"

"No, Miss," Will grinned, "not at war, but the king's sent several regiments to Gadson. That country's been under attack on more than one front and Queen Lorene's army has been unable to do more than hold the invaders off. So Esling's troops are a bit sparse now."

"We don't know if His Highness is aware of the robbers?"

"Can't say," he shrugged, "and I'm not heading in the direction of Castle deBirch."

"Perhaps you and I should go speak with the king," Deacon suggested to me, "or at least somehow make sure he knows what's happening."

"Will we be travelling that way?"

"Soon, yes. We have one more family to check on beyond Lindenwood," he explained, "so it will be a day or more before we can get there. We'll be crossing the Marmeny too, so we can stop and check in on your missus if you like, Will. Someone should let His Highness know that the roads are dangerous, and it looks like that falls to us."

"You might let him know that his people have turned mean and nasty as well," Mr. Perry guffawed as he climbed aboard the wagon to sit heavily on the wooden driver's bench. Pulling his knit cap back onto his head, he added, "Not that he can do anything about that, mind you. I just find it most strange! And I'd be grateful if you'd check in on May. I'm sure she's fine, but I'll not be back home for a bit, so she might appreciate the company."

"Consider it done," Deacon nodded as he gathered Nex's reins.

"Farewell, Deacon," the wagoner offered a salute, "and you too, Miss Rose. Thank you both for your help. Take care and travel safe!"

"Farewell, Mr. Perry," I waved as he snapped the reins across his horse's rump. The wooden wheels of the wagon groaned complaint as they rolled forward. Lothar appeared as if from nowhere running alongside the slowly moving vehicle. The shepherd jumped and yipped as he raced around the wagon.

Chapter 11

Deacon mounted Nex as I wrapped my new cape around my shoulders and hoisted myself onto Aeon's back. As we headed toward the western mouth of Fox Pass, I could hear Will Perry talking to Lothar, urging him to go away, to get back to his friends and stop following him. At length, I drew Aeon to a halt, turned in the saddle, and called the dog. With a yip, the animal acknowledged the command, bolting back down the pass toward us. From a distance I could hear the wagoner call out thanks, obviously relieved that he would no longer be followed.

"Come on, Lothar," I urged the dog, "let's go. We're already behind schedule and the sun will be setting soon."

"Yes, I'm afraid we'll have to stop and set up camp sooner than we'd planned. Today hasn't gone as I expected and we're still far from where we need to be," Deacon admitted.

"Are we safe?"

"What do you mean, Falcon?" my companion looked at me curiously.

"I mean, the robbers! Are we safe from them?"

"We have nothing a robber would want," laughing loudly, he slapped his knee with one hand, "and no one assaults a druid."

"Why not?" Taken aback by his words, I suddenly realized that in all the time I had known the man I had never seen him armed. He did not carry a sword, a staff, or even a bow, and the realization caught me off guard. "You don't carry a weapon, do you?"

"Not that anyone knows," he smiled slyly. "I do have a dagger in the shaft of my boot, but I've never had cause to draw it. I choose to use my words rather than a weapon. I am, after all, a Healer."

"Doesn't a blade in your boot rub against your leg? Isn't it uncomfortable?"

"Probably would be, were it not for the specially designed shaft. Malamara gave me the boots, and in the outside of the right shaft there's a leather sheath built just for the specific dagger I have. I don't feel it at all."

"That's," I stammered, lost between amazed and confused, "that's wonderful, I guess."

"And besides," he added, "you have ThornSting, all the wisdom the Elemental Wizards have given you, and your own powers. We will be fine in our travels, Falcon."

"All right," I nodded, still considering everything I'd just noticed, "I'm sure you're right. So, where do we make camp?"

"A few miles ahead we'll be coming to Lindenwood Forest," he replied, "so let's make for the edge of the woods and we can have a fire to warm our food and our spirits."

"Sounds great to me!"

The sun had slipped behind the trees well before we reached the edge of the forest. A long, dark, and surprisingly cool shadow stretched out to greet us as we neared Lindenwood. Lothar trotted along with us as we rode at a comfortable pace.

"North or south side of the road?" I asked as I drew Aeon to a halt.

"Not much wind, but what's blowing is out of the north, so let's camp on the south side so the road will be clear of the smoke from our fire," Deacon responded as he halted Nex before swinging easily down from the saddle. "I don't expect there will be a lot of traffic on the road tonight, but at least we'll have the forest to our backs and the open road before us."

"I'll gather some wood for a fire if you'll tend to the horses," I offered as I dismounted, brushing the road grit from my hands on my tunic.

"Fair enough," he smiled, taking Aeon's reins from me. "I'll unload our gear and give the beasts a good brushing, then we'll light the fire and see to supper. Where did your four-legged friend go?"

"Oh, he dashed into the woods over that way," I pointed to the trees south of where we stood. "He's probably chasing a squirrel or a chipmunk or something. Just hope he comes back!"

"I'll warrant he will," Deacon smiled. "That one's taken quite a shine to you, Falcon. I don't expect you could get rid of him if you tried!"

Smiling at the reassurance, I made my way along the edge of the woods, stooping to pick up twigs and branches. I was gathering the smaller pieces first, as I knew we would need kindling, while keeping an eye out for bigger branches and logs for the next trip. Given the hour and the quickly cooling air, I figured I would need to make at least three trips to have enough wood to keep a fire going through the night. And I knew Deacon would need some time to deal with the horses and our gear, so I decided to make the most of it. From within the darkening woods, I could hear Lothar running, panting, and releasing the occasional growl. He was certainly after something, I realized.

Deacon had removed the saddles, blankets, and saddlebags from the horses by the time I returned with an armload of firewood. My gear lay on one side of an open space and his lay on the other. I dumped the twigs and brush on the ground and set to arranging it with the lighter stuff on the bottom so the fire would catch more easily. My companion was busy brushing down his mount, murmuring words of encouragement to the beast, so I silently set about working a little magic. I had a flint in my bag, of course, but Eban Kendall, the Elemental Wizard of Fire, had taught me a few things to make my life easier and I had not had that many opportunities to practice or use them. Sitting cross-legged on the ground, I took a deep clearing breath, closed my eyes, and visualized a spark catching flame. At length, I opened them to project the image onto the kindling. The world around me disappeared. I disappeared. There was only the spark and the flame. Silence fell over me. I did not breathe, did not think, did not move. I focused only on the fire. A tiny tendril of dirty gray smoke rose from the edge of a dry leaf. Stalks of dry grass curled, turning first red then black. Finally, a tiny ember appeared, grew, and snapped as the spark caught and the fire began to burn. I looked up to find myself completely unobserved, smiling that I had accomplished what I intended without need of explanation. As the flames grew, I continued to feed the fire with bigger pieces of wood, fanning away what smoke was building around me. Kneeling in the clearing, I bent over to blow gently on the increasing flames, feeding the fire and causing the smoke to dissipate. Satisfied that the flames would not sputter out, I stood, brushed the knees of my breeches off, and stared into the darkness of the forest.

"Lothar!" I called out as loudly as I dared. It felt strange to disturb the quiet of the place. "Lothar, come back!"

Though I did not expect such a quick response, it was no time before the puppy came bounding out of the forest with something in his mouth. He came near me, but not near enough that I could take whatever it was he had away from him.

"What's he got?" Deacon joined me, having finished up with the horses.

"I'm not sure," I glanced at the oddly shaped mass of what appeared to be flesh with some tufts of fur here and there. "I think maybe it's a rabbit, or rather it was!"

"At least you know he's old enough and fast enough to fend for himself," my companion offered brightly, patting me on the back as he moved past me.

"Ick," I grimaced, "um, little man, a new rule. You can hunt, catch, and eat anything and everything you like. Just don't bring it back for me to see, please? I think you've just killed my appetite."

"Come Falcon," Deacon insisted, drawing my attention away from the shepherd and his carnage, "let us have something warm to drink while we decide what to eat. It's been an eventful day and I'm sure we can both use a good night's rest."

"Yes," I agreed, glancing back once more at the dog who was now lying on the ground, front paws crossed comfortably, munching happily on his catch, "yes, something warm to drink would be good."

We both rummaged through our saddlebags for the appropriate vessels and as I withdrew my stone mug my hand brushed an unfamiliar-feeling item. I shifted the mug to my left hand and stuck my right hand back into the bag, carefully withdrawing the newly discovered object. I gasped as I looked at the details of the shallow bowl and I suddenly realized that it was a water dish for Lothar. Mara and Cor had packed my saddlebags. Had they known that I would be gaining an animal friend on this journey, one that would need something to drink from when we were away from rivers, streams, or ponds? My thoughts went a little further. Was finding Lothar an accident after all? Had the puppy really fallen into that hole or had he been placed there just so we could find and rescue him? Who would have done such a thing and to what ends? Were greater forces having their way with us?

"Come on, Falcon," I muttered beneath my breath, "it's just a bowl and you've no idea if Cor and Mara meant it to be for Lothar. And what if it is his and what if they did mean it for him and even know about us finding him? They're both powerful beings and certainly capable of such feats."

"Falcon?" Deacon paused in his preparations, glancing up at me from where he crouched beside the fire. "Are you well?"

"Oh," I waved a hand dismissively, "I'm fine. Just thinking out loud. Never mind me. Let's have a drink."

"Here," he handed me a water skin, "pour yourself a drink. I found a few nice-sized stones to put in the fire so we can cook on them."

"Thank you! Can I pour Lothar some water?"

"Of course," he smiled kindly, nodding at the vessel in my hand. "I see you've the perfect bowl for it. Cornelius?"

"Cornelius," I beamed, "and Mara, of course." Carefully filling the supple bowl with water, I marveled at its construction, as it seemed to be made of tanned leather leaves laid one upon another. It had been sealed with something clear, but I had no idea what substance had been used. Whatever the technique, the bowl was wide enough and deep enough to hold sufficient water for Lothar, and it was soft enough that I could fold it up and tuck it back in my saddlebag with ease. I lifted the filled dish, carefully carrying it to where the puppy lay happily munching on whatever it was he had caught. As busy as he was, he did not even pause in his eating to acknowledge my gift and in fact, turned away from where I stood as if he was fearful that I might help myself to some of his grub.

Returning to the fire, I brushed my hands on my pants, retrieved the water skin once more and filled my mug.

"We've plenty of bread, meat, cheese, and those lovely fruits that Will gave us. Come, sit down, and rest a bit, Falcon," the druid offered.

"Can I ask you something, Deacon?" I dared ask before I could think twice about it.

"Of course," he nodded, taking my water-filled mug to place it on the stones in the fire. "Ask what you will!"

"How is it that I didn't know you don't travel armed as most folks do? I've known you for years now and I never noticed this? How's that possible?"

"First off, we see one another mostly at my place. Even if I was armed while traveling, I'm not likely to walk about my own home wearing weapons. You don't walk around Corhaven sporting ThornSting do you?"

"No," I grinned, feeling slightly relieved already.

"And you and I have only seen one another briefly over the past year or more. You've been away studying with one wizard or another, so we're just now getting reacquainted."

"True!"

"We've never journeyed together, so there's no way you'd know whether I travel armed or not," he explained with a nod.

"You're right," I shrugged, the relief I'd felt briefly giving way to foolishness. "I'm sorry. I wasn't thinking."

"That was a nice bit of magic you did back there in the pass, by the way, Falcon."

"Oh, that was nothing," I brushed off the compliment.

"Wasn't nothing, lass'," he beamed. "I'd have never been able to budge that boulder if you'd not helped. That was powerful magic."

"Not really," with a grin I added, "well, I mean I guess it sort of is, but Declan taught me that the Earth is alive, not always aware, but alive. He says stones and rocks are often aware and they can move, but they're solid and their weight makes them comfortable not moving. I knew that the boulder you were trying to move had only recently fallen into the pass so it would remember what the freedom of movement was like. I merely reminded it so it wouldn't resist you."

"You spoke to the boulder?"

"Something like that, yes. Now that I think about it, I used to hear boulders sing even before I became aware of what I am."

"I'm delighted that you are what you are, Falcon," Deacon grinned, slipping his index finger carefully through the loop on the side of my mug and withdrawing it from the fire. He placed the steaming cup on the ground to cool for a few minutes.

"Um," I hesitated, not wanting to test his patience, "one more question?"

"Of course," he replied, handing me the now cooling mug.

"You said that no one assaults a druid," pausing to drop a cloth sachet of herbs into my mug, I continued, "but how does anyone know that you are a druid? Is there a secret energy you give off or does everyone in Esling and the surrounding countries just know about you?"

"Look Falcon," was his only reply. I started to protest, thinking it a pause for effect, but realized he was directing my attention to himself. Across the merrily burning fire, he now sat cross-legged, holding his own mug in his right hand. "Look!"

His left hand was extended, fingers together, palm facing me. Though I could not imagine what he was expecting me to see, lines rose in the center of his palm. The skin within the raised lines turned pale pink and shiny, like fresh scar tissue. As I watched, the mark turned a deep, angry-looking red and I realized that had the instrument that made the mark been a blade applied with enough force, he would have lost his index, middle, and ring finger. The scar, which looked remarkably like a shaft of lightning, effectively intersected his palm from the skin above the base of his thumb to just beside his little finger. It was both ugly and beautiful at the same time. I could not look away!

"That's," I gasped, "oh, oh! That's a druid's mark! I didn't know those were real. I've heard tell of them, of course, but I…"

"You figured, since you'd never seen me with one, either druids' marks were just myth or superstition, or I wasn't a real druid," he interjected.

"I, well," pausing to consider my response, I realized it was safe to be honest, "yes. I guess that's it. Why have I never seen this before?"

"Why would you? You've never challenged me. You and I were introduced by friends years ago. There was never any reason for me to show you my druid's mark."

"You mean, it's not visible unless you want it to be? I remember when we first met and I had those swirling, wormy things beneath my skin. You and Cor treated me and I never spied anything unusual in your palm," I insisted.

"That's right, Falcon," he nodded with a soft smile, "that's right indeed. My mark is only visible when I wish it to be so." As he lowered his arm, he shook his hand and, to my amazement, the scar disappeared.

"So that's part of your druid magic. And you claim you're not a witch!"

"I'm not a witch," he laughed, "but we druids do have a few abilities."

"Like what?"

"Every druid is different, but all share a knowledge of the world. Some speak to animals, some heal sickness, some speak and teach languages, and some…,"

"Some what? You really have me curious now!"

"Some read the dead," Deacon replied soberly.

His words took me aback, but I tried to understand.

"You mean, you can see and hear the dead like I do?"

"No, lass," he shook his head slowly, "I'd much prefer that, I think. You see spirits. I read bodies. I must touch a corpse to access its story."

"Oh," grimacing, I admitted, "I don't think I'd like that!"

"Never mind that now. Let us partake of this bounty and get some much-needed rest."

We both sat comfortably on either side of the brightly burning fire, me with my mug of peppermint tea and Deacon with his brew of dark, bitter herbs. The bread we had been given was beginning to dry out and become stale, so we ate it with our cheese and meat, dipping what was left into a small crock of honey Cor had packed for us. Though I tried the dates Will Perry had generously gifted us with, I found they were not really to my liking and gave my portion to my companion. In return, he peeled an orange and gave me most of the juicy, sweet sections. It was a surprisingly delicious meal and, after cleaning up, I was happy to prepare for sleep.

Releasing the buckle on my scabbard belt, I placed ThornSting on the right edge of my blanket and arranged Aeon's saddle for use as a pillow. Careful not to waste precious water, I poured a bit from my pouch onto a piece of cloth to wash my face and hands. Though I was not aware of it, I hummed a little song as I removed the plaiting from my tresses and brushed out my hair.

"That's a lovely tune," Deacon smiled, stretching out on his blanket to rest his head on his saddle.

"I'm sorry," I blushed. "I didn't realize I was humming. I'll be quiet now."

"No, no," he insisted, "I was enjoying it very much. Please don't stop!"

"Maybe someday I'll add some words to it," with a shrug I offered, "but it's just this little tune that keeps running through my mind. I've no idea where it came from or if I've ever heard it before."

"Please, lass, continue," murmuring with a smile, Deacon took a deep breath as he closed his eyes.

Unsure what else to do, I continued to hum as I brushed the tangles from my hair. When I was done, I cleaned the strands from the brush, wadded them up, and tossed them away for the wildlife to use for their nests. As I tucked the brush back into my saddlebag, I glanced away from our camp to where Lothar now lay sleeping. Grateful that he was finally done munching, chomping, and loudly enjoying his kill, I shoved my bag away and curled one hand around ThornSting's hilt, resting my head on Aeon's saddle. I drew my cape more tightly around my shoulders against the chill air. The night was quiet with only a few crickets serenading us. A distant owl hooted in the woods while a gentle breeze rose to fan the flames of our fire. When Deacon's breathing became deeply relaxed, I realized I was the only one awake. I rolled onto my side. Tucking my free hand beneath my chin, I looked out over the land we had crossed. A light mist was rising from the dew-damp grass. Fireflies danced and flickered in the light of the waning moon. With a deep breath, I let my eyes close, realizing how heavy they were, how relaxed I was, and how wonderful it felt. In the distance, I heard leaves stirring but was too tired and sleepy to investigate. I drifted easily off to sleep.

Chapter 12

Running as fast as I could, arms and legs pumping, chest heaving, I raced across the open field. I did not dare risk looking at the ground, as whatever was chasing me was gaining with every step. Something powerful, dangerous, and fast was on my heels. I knew it had every intention of destroying me. I had no idea what it was, nor could I glance back over my shoulder to see it. All I could do was redouble my efforts for speed, keep my head down and my body moving. I could only hope to outdistance the terror. Sliding down a dusty, pebble-strewn hill, I nearly lost my footing before righting myself to leap over a fast-running stream. My pursuer was getting closer as I could hear it breathing, not panting as if it was exerting itself, just taking in deep ragged breaths and exhaling with a rattle. The sound made my skin crawl and I shuddered at the notion of what creature might be capable of making it.

My eyes snapped open. It was still dark, but I could make out a lump curled up in the distance that had to be the sleeping Lothar. I could feel the heat of the fire on my back, the solid and not-so-comfortable ground beneath my hip and shoulder, the cool air on my face. Curious as to why I was awake, I tried to move my head, but was startled to discover I could not. I could blink my eyes, could feel the breath moving in and out of my chest, could feel my heart beating, but otherwise I was frozen. Fighting a rising panic, I became aware of a sound, so soft and smooth as to be almost imperceptible. As it grew louder, I recognized it as that of a snake slithering across the ground. I struggled once more to look around for the source. Still, I could not move, so I closed my eyes tightly. Silently, I begged to be released so I could move, could get up and run away, but I remained trapped. When I opened my eyes once more, I found myself staring directly into the snout of an asp. The creature's head was impossibly big, nearly the size of a human being's, and its tongue flickered in and out rapidly.

'Helloooo, Falcon Roosse,' it hissed, turning its head first one way then another, as if sizing me up. *'So nice to sssee you!'* Its eyes, golden with black elliptical pupils, were widely set. I realized that it was so close to me it could only see me through one eye at a time.

Still frozen, unable to respond, I could only mentally cringe, though I wished fervently to be able to scoot away.

'I'm hungry!' The asp announced in a silky, smoky, deeply feminine voice. It lifted its head as if to investigate what food sources might be nearby and to its liking.

When the sleeping Lothar came to mind, I panicked that the snake might try to attack and eat my four-legged friend before common sense kicked in. Reason assured me the puppy could escape the reptile long before she could strike.

'You're quite the tasssty-looking little morsssel,' the serpent hissed at me, slinking away to the left.

Though I was still unable to move, I could see the snake gliding toward my feet, its bottom jaw lowering, the mouth widening impossibly. Curling its length back upon itself, the creature began to widen its mouth as it swallowed the tips of my boots. Forcing itself further, my feet disappeared as the awful maw made its way to my ankles. The realization that I might soon be swallowed up completely, having to endure being suffocated and digested by this impossibly large asp, made me shudder to my core. All I could do was close my eyes tightly and pray the creature would go away. Sudden hope rose in my heart when I heard the sleeping druid snort. I thought he might be waking to come to my rescue, but when I heard the gentle snoring resume, I realized he was just changing positions in his slumber and was not likely to wake in time to save me. Pressure and the weight of the snake's body continued up my legs as I struggled to move.

The sun was shining on the thatch-covered roof of Corhaven as I walked up the path to the front door. Cor, wearing a pale blue tunic, straw colored vest, and brown pants, sat cross-legged on the stoop. His long white hair and beard were shining and neatly smoothed. Beside him, Lothar was curled comfortably sleeping with his muzzle on his front paws. Cor stroked the dog's thick fur with his left hand as he raised his right hand to me in greeting.

'Welcome home, Falcon,' he called in that familiar voice I knew so well. *'We've missed you!'*

'Missed me?' I waved in return, *'Where have I been?'*

'Where indeed, lass? Where indeed?'

Somewhere, deep in my mind, I wondered what Lothar was doing with Cor and how it was they seemed so comfortable together. Just as that thought materialized another, how it was the puppy appeared to now be a full grown, very large dog, came rapidly behind it. Questioning where I had been as well as how I had gotten back to Corhaven when Aeon seemed nowhere to be found, I drew to a halt when something solid touched my body.

My fingers twitched as my hand jerked. A warm softness rested beneath my fingertips as I became aware of a weight resting against my middle. Inhaling deeply, I was delighted to open my eyes, find myself fully awake, and marvel that I was no longer frozen. Glancing down, I found Lothar curled up sleeping, his back against my stomach and his nose beneath one paw. The sun had not risen above the horizon yet but the sky was growing lighter in the east. Gently scooting away from the sleeping shepherd, I pushed myself upright to glance around the camp. Memories of the strange dreams I'd had surfaced as I observed my companion still sleeping and recalled hearing him snore, hoping he would rescue me. Beside me, Lothar snoozed comfortably, still a puppy and not at all the size he had been with Cor in my dream. Though I was tempted to try to make sense of what I had seen in my sleep, I was more relieved and happier to be awake and free of them all, so I set about stoking the fire. As I piled dry grasses and twigs into the softly glowing embers, they sprang to life, snapping and hissing, erupting to flame.

"Good morning, Falcon," Deacon yawned and stretched with a smile.

"Sorry to wake you," I grinned, "but I was trying to get the fire going again so we could have something warm to drink."

"That's quite alright," he replied. "High time we were up and moving, I expect. The sun is rising and the day will be passing us by if we don't hurry!'

At that, Lothar raised his head, pricked up his ears, and yawned. He got up, wagging his tail as well as the rest of his body, and pushed his length along my side in an attempt to scratch himself. With a laugh, I tossed the dry twigs I had in my hands onto the fire and began scratching behind his ears. Rewarded with a tongue lapping my chin, I swatted the puppy and told him to go play.

Deacon and I had hot tea and bread, sharing an apple before we set about repacking our gear. After brushing my hair, I thirded my tresses, wove them into a long braid, and tied off the end with a strip of leather. Removing my new blue-gray cape from my bedding, silently thanking Will Perry, I shook out its length, making sure any leaves, twigs, and pieces of grass were gone. I smoothed the length of my tunic, happy to find it neither too dusty nor too wrinkled and straightened my sapphire sash. Buckling the leather scabbard belt around my waist, I slid my blade into the sheath along my left leg. Placing the cape on my shoulders, I tied it securely as I swung my braid to my back. Deacon and I tied up our bedrolls, rearranged the contents of our saddle bags, and began saddling the horses. By the time we had quenched the fire and made sure there were no lingering embers, Lothar had explored the area around the camp as well as the nearby woods, returning panting and tired. I gave him a small bowl of water, which he lapped up sloppily, and wiped the vessel free of moisture before returning it to the saddlebag.

"Come on," I nodded at the puppy as I lifted him up into the crook of my right arm, "let's get moving." Grasping the saddle horn, inserting my foot into the stirrup, I started to hoist myself up when Lothar began to squirm in protest. Clearly, he had no intention of letting me carry him. Reluctantly, I released the puppy to the ground before mounting Aeon's wide back. I made sure ThornSting was hanging properly from my left hip, gathered the reins, and nudged the mare forward. Deacon had mounted Nex and was taking the lead heading toward the well-worn, hard-packed dirt road. Lothar darted to the road ahead before disappearing into the woods.

"First we go through Lindenwood Forest," my companion announced. "We'll check on Gordon and Anna Reed and their brood. After that, we'll cross the Marmeny and stop in to see May Perry before we turn south."

"How deep is the forest?" I amended my question, "How long until we reach the other end?"

"We're just crossing a thin stretch of the woods, so it will only take a few hours. The forest itself is quite large and can take several days to traverse if you're going across the widest points."

"So, we should be at or near the Reeds' place by midafternoon?"

"Barring any unforeseen circumstances," he nodded.

"Like having to clear stones from a collapsed pass?" I laughed.

"Just so," glancing over his shoulder, he favored me with a broad smile before nudging Nex to leap up a small rise onto the road.

When I bumped Aeon in the flanks with my heels, she responded with a start and easily jumped onto the road beside Nex. As the trail was wide and smooth, we rode abreast into the mouth of the forest. Overhead, birds were singing their morning song and swooping about from tree to tree. In the distance squirrels chipped and chittered, and a slight breeze caused the drying leaves in the trees to whisper and dance. Lothar ran back and forth across the road ahead, investigating the woods on either side, but he remained close as we traveled.

Deacon and I chatted as we made our way deeper into the forest, but as we both seemed to ease into an appreciation of our surroundings, silence became comfortable. The trees grew closer and closer together, the canopy of leaves overhead became thicker while the woods became darker. The air was cool, but not uncomfortable. Idly fingering Aeon's reins, I became aware of the feeling that we were not alone. I could see no one on the road before us or behind us, and the woods surrounding us were quiet, but I could not shake the sensation. I could feel Deacon's eyes on me from time to time, so I would turn and offer him a silent nod in response to his unspoken questions. It was clear that he too was experiencing what I felt. As we rounded a gentle bend in the road, I noticed a band of soldiers encamped off to my left. There appeared to be at least six of them, and their horses stood together beyond their camp. I could see no fire, nor could I smell wood smoke, but the men, one resting with his back against a tree, others seated cross-legged on the ground, one stretched out in repose, were clearly visible. It was strange, it occurred to me, for them to still be in camp so late in the day. It must surely be coming up on midday, yet they were still resting. It crossed my mind briefly that they might be one of the band of robbers Will Perry had warned us about, but the garments they wore, alike from what I could see, indicated otherwise. Surely, they were soldiers.

'They must have seen quite a battle, or a very hard journey, to be still resting so late,' I reasoned silently. I had just thought to mention my observation to my companion when my gaze once more swept across the woods which I now found empty. Drawing Aeon to a halt, I looked again at where I had seen the soldiers, but there was nothing there.

'Where did they go?' The voice in my head whispered, *'Were they ghosts?'*

"Are you alright, Falcon?" Deacon stopped Nex a bit ahead of me, glancing back over his shoulder.

"I'm fine," I smiled weakly. "It was nothing. Just thought I saw something, but there's nothing there. Must be my imagination getting the better of me."

"In woods this dark, that's understandable," he returned my smile. "But soon we'll be coming to the western edge of Lindenwood. We'll reach the Reeds' place and maybe they'll invite us in for tea."

"That would be wonderful," I nodded, realizing I was beginning to feel hungry. Nudging my mount, I turned my attention back to the journey as we picked up our pace. Lothar trotted along beside us for a bit, but his attention was drawn to something in the woods, and he disappeared to investigate. It was not long before the forest grew lighter, the trees became sparse and the sunbeams began to stream down between the leaves. The autumn forest appeared ablaze with golden light as we reached the end of Lindenwood.

"That wasn't so bad, was it?" Deacon grinned as we left the woods behind us.

"Not at all," I replied, "but I think I'll stretch my legs and walk a bit. I'm sure Aeon needs a break from me as well."

"Good idea," he nodded as he swung lightly down from the saddle. Nex's reins in one hand, my companion waited for me as I dismounted. I stretched my arms above my head with a yawn as I took Aeon's reins in my hand. Together, Deacon and I walked along the dirt road, leading our horses while watching Lothar running around enjoying himself. "The Reeds' place is just over there, south of the road. It sits in the shade of the forest."

"Do we cross the field here?"

"No, there's a trail a little further along. Gordon Reed keeps livestock in that," Deacon began, but faltered. Scratching his forehead, a perplexed expression on his face, he added, "At least he used to keep animals there. But there's no fence rails there now. The field looks empty!"

"Maybe he's rotated his livestock into another field," I shrugged, "or maybe he sold them at market."

"Yes," he nodded hesitantly, "I guess that's possible, though this field's always been enclosed and it usually has cows and other animals in it. This is just strange. Still, I guess we'd better go check on the family and see if they need anything."

"You seem concerned," I patted my companion on the back gently, "so let's ride. Lothar will keep up with us and we can get your mind put to rest."

"Thank you, Falcon," the druid sighed, "you're right. Let's go."

As I threw my leg across Aeon's back and settled myself into the saddle, I called out to the puppy who paused in his investigating to look up at me curiously.

"You follow along, Lothar," I commanded as I urged my mount forward. The shepherd seemed to understand and happily followed along through the grass beside the road. Deacon and I rode the short distance at a good pace and we were soon leaving the road for a trail that turned south. I could see the cottage from the head of the trail and though it looked occupied, there was laundry flapping gently on a line beside the place, it did not look well-tended. Tall grasses had surrounded the house and they too waved back and forth in the wind. When we reached the front of the place, Deacon drew Nex to a halt. He looked at me, worry clearly etched on his face.

"Gordon Reed!" The druid called out as loudly as he could before swinging down from his horse. "Anna? Gordon? Anyone home?"

For a moment the only response was the wind whispering through the grass. Finally, the front door of the cottage swung open and a gray-haired woman stepped out into the afternoon sun. She wore a dark gray skirt and blouse with a black apron tied behind her neck and around her waist. Her coarse hair, tinged with gray, was drawn away from her face. As she looked up at us, she shaded her eyes beneath one hand.

"Who are you and what do you want?" She demanded curtly.

"I'm sorry to disturb you, Ma'am," Deacon bowed. "We are here to see the Reeds, Gordon, and Anna. This is their place."

"Not anymore, it's not," she shook her head, "not since I moved in."

"What do you mean? Gordon and Anna left this place and moved away with their children? I was just here this summer and they didn't mention any plans to move. Do you know what happened, where they went?"

"Well," she looked Deacon up and down before heaving a sigh, "you might as well come on. Follow me. It will be easier to show you than tell you."

"Thank you," my companion nodded, shooting me a hopeful look before tying Nex's reins around a young tree.

As I dismounted, I searched the area until I spied Lothar. He sat chewing on a tall blade of grass under a honeysuckle vine, apparently resting, so I secured Aeon to a young ash tree before hurrying to catch up with our hostess and Deacon. We walked around the cottage, along the south side of the property, past a stable that seemed to be in excellent condition, and beyond two pens, both devoid of animals.

"Here you go," the woman announced as she stopped, spreading one arm toward the clearing ahead.

Deacon drew up short with a gasp. He stopped so suddenly I nearly ran into his back, but I just did manage to dodge to one side. I was about to ask why in the world he had stopped so suddenly when I caught sight of the cause. The question dried up on my lips as I looked at the scene. Four wooden crosses stood side by side before four mounds of dirt. The grave on the left was obviously that of an adult and as I neared the cross, I could just make out the name "*Anna*" etched across the center. The other three graves, smaller, were clearly those of children. As I walked slowly by the crosses, reading the names, I listened to the woman telling Deacon what she knew of what had happened. As gruesome as the story was, our hostess seemed to take delight in the telling so my dislike of her grew profound.

"Seems the Mister had been gone," the woman offered conspiratorially, "and arrived here to find Mrs. Reed, screaming and quite mad, covered in blood and wielding an axe. She'd butchered her wee ones right there in the back yard, chopped them up as if they were cord wood. Her man said she came to her senses for just a minute, but when she looked around and realized what she'd done, she slammed the blade of the axe into her chest and killed herself right in front of him."

"And what became of Gordon Reed?" Deacon shook his head in disbelief. He too seemed uneasy that the woman was so enjoying telling the tale.

"Returned to the king's service," she smiled broadly. "He's off fighting a war somewhere by now."

"So, what happened? Why did Anna do what she did?" I interjected, trying to guide the conversation back to the matter at hand.

"Possessed of a demon, they say," our hostess looked at me pointedly. "Evil took her over and made her kill her children and herself, poor thing. Reckon she'll spend eternity in the fiery burning pit."

"That's horrible," I gaped, shaking my head to clear the images of the bloodbath that had developed in my mind. "How can you bear to live here?"

"Ach," the woman waved a dismissive hand in my direction, "I've no fear of demons or ghosties. The wee ones keep me company, and now that Missus Reed's stopped screamin' it's not so bad. I get to live here so long as I provide Baron Nichol with the required services, as I'm sure not many would want the place now."

"Services?"

The woman was of a goodly age, though she was broad and certainly built strong. Still, I could not imagine what she might do in exchange for the place.

"I'm a seamstress," she replied in a haughty tone, "if it's any of your concern! I sew garments for the Baron and his family."

"Baron Nichol," Deacon interjected, "is in…"

"Banfort," she huffed, turned, and walked back toward her place. We had clearly been dismissed.

"Come Falcon," Deacon sighed, "let's go. There's nothing we can do here. Let's check on May Perry and go on to Banfort. Maybe we can find an inn, get a room and something hot to eat. I think we can both use it."

"Yes," I murmured, unable to take my eyes from the four graves before me. "You're right. Let's go."

As we made our way back to where the horses were tethered, the notion that what had befallen Anna Reed and her children was somehow connected with the nightmares the other children were experiencing came into my mind with uncanny certainty. I knew it was so, though I had no idea how that was possible.

'You know the truth,' Cor's familiar voice echoed in my head. *'You are not wrong!'*

The woman who now owned and occupied the Reed cottage disappeared through the back door without a word. She did not invite us in for tea or supper, did not offer to let us water our horses, or even say goodbye. Deacon did not mention offering her our assistance with herbs or ointments, and I did not have the heart to bring it up. As I released Aeon's reins from the ash tree, Lothar trotted up and sat down beside my foot. The puppy looked at me expectantly and I could not help but smile as I scooped him up into my arms. Soft, wet, puppy tongue licked my chin and cheeks, making me instantly feel happier and lighter.

Chapter 13

As we continued our journey, I took great comfort in Lothar's presence. While rubbing his ears and petting his head, I tried desperately to clear my mind of the images of Anna Reed murdering her children. I could not seem to wipe the thoughts of the poor youngsters lying, in pieces even, beneath those piles of soil. Though I was aware of Aeon's steady movement, of the wind on my face and the sun on my shoulders, everything else around me seemed to close in, as if the world had suddenly grown too small and too tight for me. I could not breathe. I could not think. I just kept reliving the carnage over and over, though I knew it was my imagination and might not even be close to what happened.

When we reached the landing at the edge of the Marmeny river, Deacon climbed down from Nex's back, but told me to stay put. He hurried away to a small cottage nearby, and knocked briskly on the door. When a broad-shouldered, very muscular young man answered, he and Deacon began a conversation I could not hear. Whatever was said seemed to be congenial as the two soon returned to the landing. Smiling up at me, the young man took Aeon's bridle in his hand and carefully led us aboard the wide, low-sitting craft. Once Deacon guided Nex aboard, the ferryman began to move the boat across the water. A heavy rope was tethered on either side of the fast-moving river, and Deacon pulled us along it as the young man used a long heavy pole shoved into the river bed to propel us forward. I started to dismount and lend a hand, but Deacon noticed and insisted I stay where I was. My view of the river, from where I sat astride my mare, was amazing, but it was also unsettling. The water churned briskly and the ferry pitched and rolled with the force. Aeon seemed to take the motion in stride, but it made me feel dizzy so all I could do was focus on the approaching shore and keep my eyes off the river. I silently promised myself, then and there, that I would dismount and stand on my own two legs were I ever to travel by ferry again. Lothar did not seem interested or even affected by the journey across the water.

At the river's edge, the ferryman secured the barge using heavy ropes before he and Deacon led the horses onto dry land. I watched as my companion gave the young man several coins for his services. The two spoke in hushed tones before Deacon mounted Nex and rode up beside me.

"He says his mother is home," the druid offered, "and will be happy to see us."

"That's Will Perry's son?" I smiled, suddenly realizing there was a great similarity in their appearances, "I guess I should have seen that. Mr. Perry is certainly an enterprising man! Between carting supplies inland from the river and having a son as ferryman, his family must be doing well."

"They're hard workers," Deacon nodded, "that's for certain!"

Atop a gentle rise within shouting distance of the river, the Perry's home stood before sparse woods. Its size and construction clearly indicated it was lived in and loved by those with ample resources. Two stories, with mullioned glass windows and a wide, heavy oak door, the place was larger than any home I had seen. As big as Deacon's sprawling home was, it would be dwarfed beside the Perry's, I mused silently. Autumnal grasses swayed gently in the yard while leaves of burnished gold fell from two apple trees growing in front of the house.

May Perry was a lovely, kind, good-natured woman. We had dismounted and tethered our horses to a rail beside the front door when she startled us by appearing on the stoop before we had even knocked. She invited us inside, even calling Lothar, whom I had released for a run, inside for a bowl of water and a leftover ham hock bone. She offered us tea, though it was clear she was busy. The kitchen area was scattered with stone jars, bags of spices, wooden spoons, some clean, some covered in sticky substances, and bowls. A fire burned brightly in the hearth while a cauldron hanging suspended by a hook bubbled gently above it. The aroma of sweet, tart fruit filled the house so when our hostess offered warm bread with butter and fresh jam, I could not refuse.

Lothar, enjoying his first time inside a house, tentatively checked out the room. Lifting his nose to sniff the delicious fragrances of food, he suddenly turned his attention to the boots sitting just inside the door. I realized I was beginning to understand the dog when he sniffed inside one boot only to step back as if sizing it up. Just as he was about to hike his hind leg to mark the thing, I snapped my fingers to get his attention.

"No, Lothar!" I warned him, "Absolutely not! If you want to stay inside you keep that leg down."

It was at that moment our hostess put down the bowl of water and laid the ham hock bone on the floor beside it. Lothar was more than happy to abandon his previous intentions. He snatched up the bone wagging his tail wildly.

"Thank you, Ma'am," I smiled.

"You're welcome," she nodded, "now, you two, come sit at the table and talk with me. I assume you've seen Will, yes?" She indicated with a wave of one hand that we should remove our capes and give them to her. When we did so, she took them both and hung them on pegs near the door.

"We did," Deacon interjected, "and he asked us to come check on you. Not that there's any reason, he just thought you'd like the company for a spell."

"Yes, that's my Will," with a rueful grin she replied. Returning to the table, she sliced two thick slabs of bread from a fresh loaf cooling on a platter, putting each on a stoneware plate. "Help yourself to some butter and jam, or just jam, whichever you prefer. Peach preserves are in the crock there or there's plum in the other one. I've got apple butter simmering over the fire, but I don't think it's ready yet."

"This is wonderful, thank you," I gaped at the bounty. I had tried my hand at making preserves and jellies with less than tasty results. I opened the peach preserves and used a wooden spoon to ladle a blob onto my bread before handing the spoon to Deacon. "Thank you so much!"

"So, tell me, how has your journey been?" May Perry placed an empty mug before each of us. "And what news of the world have you?"

Mouth full of bread and preserves, I glanced up at my partner, wondering how he would respond to the woman's query.

"Interesting you should ask," Deacon responded, "as your husband told us he'd encountered mostly unpleasant and even angry people on his route."

"You don't say!" She looked taken aback.

"And now we've learned about Anna Reed and her children," he shook his head forlornly, "and we've no idea what to make of that! It's curious that Will didn't warn us about the Reeds, as we met him coming through Fox Pass."

"Oh, he wouldn't," she explained. "The poor man took it awful hard, what happened to those children. You see, the two little boys often ran out to meet him and they'd ride in his wagon back to their house. He delighted in telling them little stories and giving them small treats. He thought the older daughter was quite sweet too, and what became of them all, well, it's been hard for him."

"Yes, I can imagine," Deacon sympathized. "It's shaken us deeply as well."

"And the horrible woman who lives in that house now," I interrupted, immediately regretting my words. What if our hostess knew the new resident of the Reed place and liked her, or was even related to her? Suddenly I was embarrassed at my outburst.

"Woman?" May Perry paused in pouring water from a kettle into the mug before me. "What woman is this? I've not heard of anyone moving into the place. It's been less than a fortnight since Gordon Reed came by, a weeping, sobbing mess, and told us what happened. After he buried his family, he packed what he could and told us to take his livestock, which we did and paid him a fair price for them. With nothing to keep him here, he left to rejoin the king's troops."

"She claims to be a seamstress for Baron Nichol," Deacon replied, "but now that I think about it, she didn't even introduce herself. A bit of a gruff one, I should say. We don't know her name or if she has a husband and family."

"She was not nice," I insisted, chewing another bite of bread with peach preserves. "She seemed to really enjoy telling us the gruesome details of what had happened."

"Seamstress for the Baron or not, either she has her own boat or she's come from Banfort the long way around, north through the mountains, because she's not passed by here or taken the ferry. That I'm sure of. Don't get me wrong, James would take the devil himself across the river if he had the fare to pay, but he always tells me when someone new passes by and the boy hasn't said a word about any woman taking the ferry."

"That is odd," Deacon agreed. "Well, we thought we'd go on to Banfort and see if we could find out anything else. And at the suggestion of your husband, we're off to Castle deBirch to warn the king about the robbers on the road. Have you seen or heard of them?"

"Heard tell of at least two bands of robbers, yes," she nodded, "though we've not seen anything of them here. Could be they're avoiding the Marmeny altogether as there's not many places to cross."

"Yes, that's true."

"If Will mentioned folks being mean and angry to you, it must mean something," our hostess added, "and maybe you should talk to Louisa Drew. She's one of the busiest midwives in Banfort. She knows most everyone in the area and if anyone might have an idea of what's going on it would be her. She's a bit of an herbalist as well so I'm sure you'll have plenty to talk about."

"That's a wonderful idea," Deacon nodded, lifting his mug of tea in a toast, "thank you!"

"Think nothing of it," she beamed. "Now, help yourself to more bread and preserves while I stir the apple butter."

We sat at the table near the fire, munching on the bread with preserves, sipping hot tea and talking merrily. Lothar stretched out on the floor as he washed the meat juice from his paws, looking for all the world as if he was born and bred inside. May Perry tended to her cooking as she moved efficiently around the room. Deacon was in the middle of a story, animatedly sharing an adventure, when suddenly the dog stopped licking, looked up and pricked his ears forward. May stopped stirring and stiffened, obviously listening to something outside. I looked at Deacon, who had fallen silent. He looked back at me with one eyebrow raised.

"Sounds like more travelers passing through," May announced, dropping her wooden spoon back into the bubbling pot, wiping her hands on her apron.

The windows, in the south and west wall, were open to let the heat of the hearth out and the fresh, cool afternoon air in. The pounding of hooves drowned out the voices that rode in on the breeze, but it was clear there were several men on horseback approaching. Deacon and I stood, uncertain whether to make our departure or simply make room for others who might join us. Mrs. Perry crossed the room and flung wide the door just as two men reached the stoop.

"Good afternoon, gentlemen," she greeted them politely. "What can I do for you?"

"We're on our way to Corhaven," the man in front, clearly the leader replied, "and we need to cross the river. The ferry is on the other side. How do we alert the ferryman?"

"There's a bell on that post near the landing," she smiled, "just ring it and my son will come for you."

"Fine," the man nodded smartly before turning away.

From my position near the table, I had a clear view of the two at the door and could see they were both King Rowan's guardsmen. My curiosity got the better of me when I overheard the one mention Corhaven and I could not help but interrupt.

"Excuse me," I boldly moved forward to stand beside May Perry, "I heard you mention Corhaven. You seek the wizard Cornelius Welkin?"

"Pardon me," the soldier turned back suddenly, clearly unaccustomed to being questioned. "We are on the king's business. Where we are going and who we seek is of no concern to you. Just who are you, anyway?" With that he placed both hands on his hips, squared his shoulders and cocked his head, angrily awaiting an answer.

"I'm Falcon Rose," I retorted, "and Corhaven is my home, so if that's where you're going it is my concern, sir!"

"Falcon Rose! It is indeed fortuitous that we stopped here, for it is you we seek. His Highness commands to see you at once!" The man saluted as he took one step back, bumping into his companion. "I am Captain Alexander Durand of King Rowan's guard. This is Lieutenant De Groot. My men and I are here to escort you to Castle deBirch."

"Wait," I stammered, suspicion suddenly overwhelming my curiosity, "what business does King Rowan have with me? Have I done something wrong?"

"His Highness has not informed us as to why we're to deliver you," Captain Durand nodded curtly.

"So, I'm just supposed to drop what I'm doing and come with you? Is this about the robbers on the road?"

"What would the king be wanting with this child?" May Perry interjected, putting one arm protectively around my shoulder.

"I was told that I should remind you, Falcon Rose, that you oathed your sword to serve the royal family," ignoring our hostess, the soldier focused his attention on me. I noticed that his face was long, his jaw strong and well-defined. His dark blue eyes regarded me calmly from beneath a fringe of black lashes. Though I knew no reason for it, I had the distinct impression that Alexander Durand had little regard for me and may have even resented being dispatched by the king to fetch me. His second, Lieutenant De Groot, was shorter and stockier built, with a tousle of blond hair falling over one eye. Both men wore the easily recognized ruby cape of the king's guard, and I caught a glimpse of the captain's brooch peeking from beneath Durand's locks.

"Oathed her sword," Mrs. Perry murmured, her hand fluttering to her lips in surprise, "wait a minute! Falcon Rose. You're the one who rescued Prince Rowan and returned him to Esling! You're THAT Falcon Rose!" Clearly the woman was startled, she dropped her arm and stepped back away from me as if I might be dangerous.

"I guess I am," with a shrug I admitted. "And yes, Sir, I remember well that my sword is oathed to serve. I will accompany you on one condition, that my companion, Deacon, be allowed to come too."

"His Highness demands to see only you," Captain Durand replied.

"I'll not leave Deacon behind!"

"Wait, Falcon," the druid took a step toward us, "I need to continue the journey. I still have Arlo and Catherine Thorpe to see as well as others, and I want to find out what I can in Banfort. You go on to the king. Tell him about the children and the nightmares. Tell him about the robbers. I'll continue and see you again at my place when we're both done."

"Are you sure? I feel bad leaving you like this."

"Go on, the king needs you. I've made this journey many times before and I'll be fine," he assured me.

When voices rose from the yard behind the two soldiers they parted, turning to address a man approaching.

"Sir, I've found the bell to summon the ferryman," the newcomer announced, though I couldn't see him from where I stood, "should I ring it now?"

"Never mind, Beck," Captain Durand shook his head, "we need travel no further. We've found what we came for and can now return to Castle deBirch. Tell the men that we will depart momentarily!"

"Yes, Sir!" Came the snappy retort, and I could imagine the man saluting smartly.

Just as the two soldiers turned their attention back to us, Lothar yawned, stretched, and made his way to me, taking position beside my right leg. The shepherd looked up at me before focusing those beautiful eyes on the two men on the stoop. He did not utter a growl or yip, his hackles did not rise, but I felt a wave of tension roll off him. I put my hand on the top of his head and patted him gently.

"Egad, what is that?" Lieutenant De Groot gasped at the pup. He shrank back, obviously surprised at his own reaction.

"This is Lothar," I proudly announced, "and he is my friend and companion."

"He's not coming with us," Durand's voice dropped menacingly as he replied.

"I assure you that if I'm joining you, he's joining you. He goes where I go," I insisted.

A silent moment ticked by as the challenge grew between us. Though neither man moved, in my mind I saw a wicked grin spread across the second man's lips and his eyes twinkled as he offered, "Sir, I could just gut him here and now and the problem would be solved, plus we'd have a nice fur for when the weather turns."

I did not breathe, nor did I move, yet in my mind's eye I clearly saw myself step forward to confront De Groot.

"You lay one hand on him, touch one hair on his head," I snarled, withdrawing ThornSting from its sheath, "and it will be the last thing in this world you ever do! Do you understand me?" I glared at Lieutenant De Groot, the tip of my blade held precariously beneath his chin. My gaze locked on his, I mentally 'pushed' my power at him, refusing to blink or move, in an entirely instinctual act of magical spell work.

At first the man's eyes widened in surprise. For a moment I thought he was going to smile and laugh, but when my energy touched him, he froze. It was clear he knew I had read his thoughts, even though they were in jest. And though he did not understand what had just happened, he knew enough to remain silent. At length, he drew a breath, lowered his eyes, and nodded.

"I understand," he muttered as he stepped back. "The dog goes where you go."

"What was," Captain Durand shook his head as he shot me a look of confusion and stammered, "what was that?"

"What was what?" With a smile, I cocked my head, feigning innocence, "Now that we all understand each other, Lothar and I are ready to join you. If, that is, you're ready to go!"

"Very well," he nodded uncertainly, stepping back from the doorway. I could tell by his expression that he truly wanted to question me at length, but instead he turned and walked down the steps into the yard. His second followed him without further comment while Lothar and I fell into step behind them both.

Four more soldiers stood at the end of the path leading to the Perry home. Two of them were mounted, ready to ride, and the others were relaxing beside their mounts, awaiting orders.

"We ride," Captain Durand announced, "to Castle deBirch!"

"That's what Beck said," one of the men astride a great dapple-gray horse replied, "but we didn't believe him. We really need journey no further?" The soldier looked pointedly at me before glancing at Lothar walking at my side. He fell silent.

"Mount up!" The captain barked. The two men standing beside their horses quickly followed orders.

"Thank you, Mrs. Perry," I turned to smile at our hostess who had followed us into the yard. "And Deacon, you travel safe. I'll see you back at your place when I can."

"I trust you'll let Cor know what's happening?"

"Oh yes," I nodded, "he'll know soon enough if he doesn't already."

"You take care, Falcon," the druid embraced me warmly.

"She'll be amply protected," Captain Durand interjected curtly, obviously anxious for us to be on our way.

"Yes, but who will protect her from you?" May Perry muttered under her breath before beaming a wicked conspiratorial smile at me. She held my cloak, which she had taken from the peg beside the door, spread open in her hands. When I stepped into the garment, she turned me gently and tied it at the throat. For an instant her kindness reminded me of my own mother, and I felt a twinge of sadness.

"It's all right," I winked at the woman, returning a smile, "I can protect myself."

"I've no doubt," she chuckled. "Farewell Falcon Rose. You're welcome here anytime!"

Picking Lothar up, I hurried down the path to where Aeon stood, grabbed the saddle horn, and hoisted myself into the saddle. As the soldiers turned their mounts, heading for the road, I settled the puppy before me and pulled the mare's reins to the right. Glancing back over my shoulder, I waved at Deacon and May Perry before turning my attention to the road. To my surprise, Captain Durand and his lieutenant rode lead while the other four brought up the rear behind Aeon. I was not sure if the king's guards were afraid that I would try to make an escape or if this was standard escort formation, but it did not make me particularly happy and I planned to let King Rowan know about it as soon as we reached Castle deBirch.

A crushing disappointment settled on me, as I realized I would be unable to meet the midwife, Louisa Drew, in Banfort. I desperately wanted to know what was going on and had hoped she might supply me with information that could help me figure it out. May Perry obviously thought highly of the woman and I had looked forward to meeting her. Now I would have to wait for Deacon to speak with her and tell me what he had learned. For a moment, I regretted having oathed my sword and my service to the king. Just as quickly, I realized what my father would have likely felt about that and immediately wiped such thoughts from my mind. It was, after all, an honor to serve the royal family of Esling and my country, I assured myself. I should be proud and eager to drop whatever I was doing and heed the call of the king.

"Just keep telling yourself that, Falcon," I murmured with a sigh, pretending to be speaking to the puppy. "Just keep telling yourself!"

Chapter 14

As we journeyed in formation, Captain Durand and Lieutenant De Groot ahead of me, the other four behind me, the late afternoon wore on to evening. I caught snippets of conversation from the two soldiers ahead of me, but could not really hear enough to make sense of what was being said. The four men behind me, on the other hand, were quite easy to hear, as they loudly boasted and bragged about their romantic conquests. One crowed about his exploits with a certain red-haired barmaid while another was quick to point out that the lady in question was well known to share her favors with any and all interested so long as they had the proper fare. When the one began going into detail regarding the wench's physical attributes, I felt myself stiffen and I prayed no one would notice me blushing. I was tempted to call out to the captain and ask that we stop and take a break, but I held my tongue. I was determined to not be thought of as a weak female and cause for slowing down our progress. Eventually Lothar would need to relieve himself and burn off some energy, I realized, but I hoped I would not be blamed for that.

The sun was beginning to touch the treetops on the horizon when the road we traveled gently turned toward the south. It was a relief to be out of the heat, I noticed as I wiped tiny beads of perspiration from my forehead, thinking I should have long ago removed my woolen cloak. The puppy squirmed and yawned as he looked up at me.

"Captain," I called out at last, as I clearly had no choice, "are we making camp soon?"

"We are not making camp at all," Captain Durand drew his mount to a halt, turned in the saddle and looked at me. "His Highness commanded me to make all haste, so we'll travel on until we reach the castle."

"Can we take a short break soon? Lothar needs to stretch his legs and frankly so do I."

"A break?"

"Sir, please consider carefully before you answer," I challenged. "Am I a willing servant of the king or am I a prisoner? Because if I'm the former, and I believe I am, surely, I'm entitled to a bit of courtesy."

"Very well," he nodded, "we'll take a break. There's a clearing ahead with a tributary running through it. We'll stop there and water the horses as well before continuing our journey."

"Thank you," I nodded politely, though by the time I responded I was thanking the back of the man's head.

Less than a league further, we reached the clearing the captain had mentioned and all left the road to dismount. The setting sun had just disappeared behind the trees and the grassy span lay shrouded in shadows, deep and cool. I led Aeon to the stream as I released Lothar to the ground. The mare dipped her nose in the cool water to drink while the puppy bounded into the brook splashing and playing. The soldiers also led their mounts to the water before walking around the clearing here and there to stretch their legs. When the men moved into a little group and began to talk, I dropped Aeon's reins and quietly tiptoed downstream. Behind a clump of bushes slightly uphill on the bank of the brook, I turned my back on the clearing, moved aside my cloak, and hastily pulled down my breeches to relieve myself. I hoped I could be quick and that no one would notice my absence. Just as I finished and was pulling my garments back up, Lothar came trotting along the stream, romping, and playing. I walked back toward where the horses were drinking as I adjusted ThornSting's scabbard on my hip, yawning, and stretched my arms up over my head. Watching the puppy wagging his tail, sniffing about, I was startled when a force hit me from behind, landing with a great weight on top of me. A rough hand clamped over my mouth as hot breath touched the side of my neck.

"Don't move," Captain Durand commanded, his gruff voice lowered to just above a whisper. "Do not speak. Be still."

Fearing that Lothar might notice what was happening and start barking or yipping at the man on top of me, I struggled beneath the weight to see where the pup had gone. I half expected the beast to pounce on the soldier, possibly biting him or ripping out his throat to protect me. Instead, the shepherd stood still and alert. Lothar began to move stealthily away from us, eyes fixed on something I could not see, stalking silently.

"Torocs," Durand hissed, pointing toward the road with an extended index finger.

As I peered through the shadows toward where he indicated, I noticed the other soldiers all lying flat on the ground. No one moved. The horses, still either drinking or standing near the stream, seemed indifferent to the situation. In the distance I could hear thundering footfalls, and the sound grew louder as the torocs approached. I had never seen a toroc, I realized, and had, in fact, thought them myth.

My heart hammered in my chest; I swallowed hard as the silencing hand left my mouth. I very much wanted to move, to scream, maybe even run, but such actions were clearly not possible. Still, the weight of the captain of the guards was pressing and it was difficult to draw breath. I squirmed beneath the man's body, trying to move to one side of him so I could at least breathe. To my dismay, he grabbed my wrists in his hands and squeezed a warning. I could not move. I could only hope to draw in enough air to keep from fainting or dying altogether. It was painful to keep my head up to see the road, so I had no choice but to press my ear to the ground and look off to one side. I listened to my heartbeat as the moments crept by.

The clamor continued to grow as the torocs drew nearer. Though part of me wished only to close my eyes and remain secure in the belief that they did not exist, another part of me simply had to know, had to see for myself. Once more I lifted my head as I shook Captain Durand's grasp off my wrist and propped my chin on my fist. I was determined to see the torocs without moving, as I had no desire to attract their attention. To my relief, Lothar still watched silently, but showed no sign of attacking the creatures.

Darkness loomed on the road. The height and breadth of the shadows alone made my blood run cold. When the first toroc appeared, spear in one hand, cloth of some sort in the other, I blinked at the sight. The beast was HUGE! I had seen mountains smaller than the massive thing moving along the road. A pelt of fur lay across its wide shoulders and down its back. Its face, if it could be called that, was oddly proportioned with a wide forehead, down-sloping eyes, and a nose that spread wide and lay flat. Its tangle of hair and matted beard were black or brown, I guessed, as the light was insufficient to tell such detail. Massively muscled arms, and a wide chest, it wore what appeared to be scraps of fabric, though a voice in my head suggested its garments were not as they appeared. Behind the first toroc marched another and another. They were so large that they seemed to crowd the road. As I lay prone and silent, I searched my mind for memories of what I had learned about them, but there was scant to be had, I lamented. They were an ancient race of demons, I seemed to recall, and had no regard for life, theirs, or anyone else's. I was certain they ate meat, sometimes decimating whole herds of wildlife, and preferred to avoid humans, but when pressed to service they were a terrible force.

'Who or what would call them?' I wondered desperately. 'And why?'

Briefly, I considered calling out to Cor, to ask of him what I might, though I thought better of it. For all I knew, torocs could sense or hear magic. Perhaps my reaching out to the wizard might attract their attention and I could not risk that. Instead, I watched silently, barely breathing, as the troop moved along the road. When the last toroc had moved out of sight, Captain Durand rolled off me and leapt to his feet. With only a sideward glance in my direction, he strode away toward the clearing without a word.

"No, no," I muttered under my breath as I rolled over and sat up, "don't help me up. I'm good!" With a huff, I began picking the twigs and leaves from my tunic, cloak, and hair.

Lothar shook himself, releasing the muscular tension in his back and shoulders as he wagged his tail wildly. He gave one last glance at the road before bounding towards me.

"You did excellent, buddy," I patted my knee to draw him closer. "You have got to be the smartest dog in all the land, being so quiet and still just now." Scratching beneath his chin and behind his ears, I praised him for his behavior. "And between me and you? The next time Captain Durand throws himself on top of me, you're welcome to sink your teeth into his ankle until he screams like a girl or until your teeth hit bone." With a laugh, I gave the pup a final pat on the head.

The captain of the guard had reassembled his troops, though he had done so quietly, I noticed. I gathered Aeon's reins from where the mare stood yanking the leaves off the low branches of a tree and drew her toward the center of the clearing. Lothar padded along quietly beside my leg, and did not squirm or make a sound when I scooped him up into my arms. Once we were all mounted, Captain Durand motioned me forward.

"You ride up here with me now," He nodded as Aeon and I drew abreast of him on his horse. When he turned his mount onto the road, Lieutenant De Groot fell into place behind us, assuming my previous position in the phalanx, while the remaining four rode two abreast behind him.

We traveled in silence for a time. My thoughts were awhirl remembering over and over seeing the torocs. I kept recalling little details of what I could see from my position lying on the ground, the creatures' size, mass, their hair, and facial features. When at last I could hold my tongue no more, I softly cleared my throat.

"Captain Durand," speaking only loud enough to be heard and no more, I began, "why did those creatures not notice us? We were hardly well hidden."

"I don't know," he heaved a sigh. "Maybe the breeze was just right so they couldn't catch our scent. Maybe their vision isn't good so they couldn't see us in the shadows of the clearing. Maybe they were more intent on getting where they're going than in finding prey or perhaps, they'd just feasted on a herd of wild boars. We should just be thankful that they didn't notice us."

"Of course," I quailed at his tone. I had not intended to be difficult. I was truly curious as to why we had escaped unnoticed. Properly rebuffed, I nodded silently as I looked away across an open field to the west. A few scattered fodder shocks stood sentinel beneath the crescent moon. Darkness was coming quickly and with it came a chill in the air. Moving Aeon's reins to my left hand, which rested comfortably on Lothar's back, I used my right hand to pull my braid from my back to the front of my shoulder before pulling the hood of my cape up on my head. Immediately I felt warmer and more comfortable.

Behind us, Lieutenant De Groot coughed twice and muttered "Pardon me."

"Lady Falcon," Captain Durand addressed me suddenly, as if in response to the Lieutenant's cue, "my men and I, well, we've heard..." The man fell silent, obviously struggling for the right words.

"Yes?" I replied, carefully considering where the conversation might be heading. Raising one eyebrow at him, I forced myself to keep from smiling at his discomfort. I knew I should not take pleasure in his obvious difficulty, but I could not help it.

"Careful Falcon," Cor's familiar and comforting voice echoed in my mind. *"Take care dealing with these soldiers. Tell them only what they need to know. Do not attempt to make friends with them."*

"That's not a problem, Cor," I replied in my mind, *"as I'm not particularly fond of any of them."*

"Where are you, lass?"

"On the way to Castle deBirch. Deacon went on without me when the king's men found us at the ferry. I've been summoned to appear before King Rowan. And Cor, we just passed a band of torocs!"

"Torocs? Are you sure?"

"Saw them myself, I did! Don't care if I never see the likes of them again."

"Falcon this is bad, very bad."

"What do you mean? They kept going, didn't even notice us."

"Torocs do not just go wandering around for no reason, and they do not move in a group unless directed to do so by a greater force. They've been called into action by someone for a reason."

"Oh, that does sound bad!"

"And Falcon?"

"Yes, Cor."

"The other wizards and I have been hearing tales of children across the land being plagued by nightmares. Their fears are keeping them awake and are growing stronger. Parents everywhere are losing patience, losing hope, growing short-tempered and desperate for answers."

"So, this is something we should be investigating?"

"First, find out why King Rowan wants to see you. We shall continue to gather what information we can and will let you know. Travel well, dear Falcon. Stay safe!"

The entire silent conversation with my beloved Elemental Wizard of Air was over in but a few moments. It transpired while the poor befuddled Captain Durand sorted out his words. Closing my eyes briefly, I shook my head, took a deep breath, and returned my attention to the soldier beside me.

"We have heard," the captain started again, "that you are a witch. Is this true? Are you a witch?"

The question took my breath away. I must have blinked several times in surprise as I gathered my wits to respond.

"I am the daughter of Selene Sylvan and Arne Rose, captain of the king's guards and your predecessor. I am a member of the Order of Healers and my sword is oathed to serve the family deBirch," I replied as calmly and succinctly as I could, praying my voice was not as shaky as I felt. The little voice inside my head angrily sneered '*I've heard that you, Sir, are a braying ass. Is this true? Are you a braying ass?*' and taking delight in the notion.

For a moment Durand seemed to ponder my response, his right hand idly stroking the length of his chin. Suddenly, his eyes opened wide. His expression shifted to one of surprise and even alarm.

"Did you just call me a braying ass?" He demanded in haughty dismay.

"Me?" I gaped, head spinning at the realization that he had heard my thoughts. "I assure you that I said no such thing!" Chuckling inside, I feigned innocence, imagining what fun I might have playing with his mind.

"*Careful, lass!*" Cor's voice came once more, "*You're playing with fire!*"

Silently, I nodded agreement with my mentor and vowed to at least try to refrain from such actions in the future.

"*Thanks, Cor,*" I responded mentally, "*you're right. I'll behave!*"

Captain Durand started to say something just as two riders appeared around a curve on the road ahead. Both were dressed in the military garb of Esling's army, black gambesons beneath hard-tanned leather vests. Unlike the king's guards, they wore no ruby nor did they wear cloaks. The two were traveling quickly, their mounts kicking up considerable dust as they approached. When they saw us, they drew their horses abruptly to a halt, both men offering the captain a brisk salute.

"Sir," the nearest soldier addressed Captain Durand, "we've been sent to catch up with a band of torocs seen traveling this road. His Highness, King

Rowan, has dispatched us to spy on them and find out what they're up to. Have you seen them?"

"We did," Durand nodded, "and you're not far behind them. If you make haste, you should have them in sight long before sunrise, provided they remain on this road."

"Aye, Sir," the second soldier responded. "Thank you, Sir!"

Without further comment, the two guided their horses around us, spurring them on. They were soon pounding down the road only to disappear.

"So, the king is aware of the torocs," I reasoned aloud. "I have to wonder what else he's already aware of."

"Little goes on in the kingdom His Highness doesn't know about, I assure you," Captain Durand replied as he heeled his horse in the flanks. "Let us hurry. Castle deBirch lies ahead."

At the captain's urging, I nudged Aeon smartly, tightened my grip on Lothar, and leaned forward in the saddle. Captain Durand's horse, a powerful white stallion, took the lead, but Aeon, being the competitor she was, quickly caught up to match the charger's pace. The captain glanced at me, quickly turning his attention back to the road ahead. We rode hard until we reached the top of a rise where the road branched away to the east and straight ahead. The captain raised his right hand, calling out to draw us to a halt. Below, the road stretched east through a wide vale. Castle deBirch rose on a craggy hill in the distance, burning torches on the walls casting a veil of soft illumination around it. As it was well past sundown, the gate was closed, but sentinels patrolled the ramparts so I knew we would be able to gain entry easily enough.

"Beck," Captain Durand barked, "signal the gate!"

At his leader's command, Beck raised a horn to his lips and gave a loud blast. Lothar, startled by the sudden sound, shuddered in my arms and squirmed against me. In the distance I heard a guard order the gate lowered and the sound of the heavy wheel turning quickly followed.

"Come," Durand commanded, starting for the castle at a more leisurely pace.

It had been some time since I had laid eyes on the castle. I marveled anew at the grand size of the stone structure. Pastures stretched out across the idyllic vale, while pale, ghostlike sheep grazed in the quiet darkness.

Two guards bearing halberds stood on either side of the lowered drawbridge, moving further apart as we gained the bridge to cross the water-filled moat. They snapped to attention as Captain Durand led us inside the castle walls. The stable master, a powerful looking man wearing a leather apron, approached from the open double doors of the building to our right. Four young men in tunics, leggings, and boots, followed at his command and were reaching for the bridles of our horses even before we could dismount. The young grooms were instructed to see to the comfort of our mounts and the one dark-haired groom that touched Aeon's bridle looked at me questioningly.

"Give her a good brushing down," I nodded encouragement, "and don't touch anything in my gear." Knowing that Scorch, the Earth Star, was in my saddlebags, I had to make sure he wouldn't take any dangerous liberties.

"Rest assured, My Lady," the stable master replied before the young man could answer, "your things will not be touched. I'll see to that! I'm Haggerty, at your service."

"Thank you, Mr. Haggerty," I nodded, lowering Lothar to the ground so he could stretch his legs and do his usual canine business.

"No Mr., My Lady," he quipped, "just Haggerty."

"Haggerty, that little four-legged, furball is my friend Lothar. Would you be so kind as to keep an eye on him for me? I don't know how long I'll be and he needs some time to run around and have some fun."

"I'd be happy to do so, Ma'am. I'll take good care of him," the stable master bowed with a broad smile.

Chapter 15

Our footsteps echoed down the long stone corridor. Ornate woven rugs of burgundy and blue muffled the sound of our bootheels, but the spaces between the runners made the noise even more pronounced. King Rowan's steward had met us on the steps of the castle and he led us not to the Grand Hall, but to the personal residence wing of Castle deBirch. Considering the hour, I should not have been surprised that the king would receive us in his personal chambers, but it took me a minute to figure out where we were going and why. Captain Durand and the king's advisor exchanged hushed words as we made our way through the labyrinthine hallways while I followed silently, admiring the tapestries and displays of weapons on the walls. My arms felt strangely empty without Lothar, though I had left him in the safe keeping of Haggerty and his boys. I would have kept the pup with me, but I knew he needed to run, expend some energy, and relieve himself. I had glanced back over my shoulder as the captain and the steward began moving through the arched doors of the castle, only to see the little pup romping and chasing two of the young stable hands around the courtyard. Smiling despite the pang of regret, I took a deep breath and followed the men into the castle, resolving to trust Lothar to the king's servants.

When we reached the royal chambers at the end of a long corridor, the steward stopped to knock twice on the door, as he directed us to remove our weapons. A young page stood at attention as we arrived, and at the word of the advisor he stepped forward, extending his arms. As Captain Durand placed his sword across the young man's forearms, I unbuckled my scabbard belt, hurrying to place ThornSting there too. Pulling down the hem of my tunic, I nervously brushed any road dirt off the garment and tidied my sapphire sash.

At length, the door was opened and the steward stepped back to let us enter the king's chambers. My eyes were immediately drawn to the splendor that filled the room. I had never been in King Rowan's private rooms, though I was in Princess Laurell's years before while she still lived, but the antechamber into which we stepped almost took my breath away. The walls were covered in rich fabrics, the furniture was dark sculpted wood accented with gold. Torches burned along the walls, while white tapers cast illumination from candelabras on tables, an ornate desk, and various shelves. Thick, beautifully woven rugs were scattered across the stone floor and a large, gilded-frame looking-glass hung above the fireplace. So amazed was I with the beauty of the place, I had to pause and simply take it all in. When, at last, I was able to look away from the splendid décor, the first person I laid eyes on was the warlock, resplendent in robes of crimson and gold. I could not help but gasp when I saw Abra. Surprised and delighted, I favored him with a smile, though I was startled speechless.

"Milady Falcon Rose," Abra beamed, taking my hands in his, "let me look at you. My, you've grown since last I saw you. You look well."

"I, um," I stammered, struggling to gather my wits, "I am well, thank you. Abra, it's, um, it's lovely to see you. It's also quite a surprise. What are you doing here?"

"Just enjoying a game of chess with His Highness." He smiled, leaning near to add conspiratorially, "He's quite a cut-throat player, but he lets me win from time to time just to keep me coming back."

"Here now, you dusty old warlock," King Rowan lifted an index finger in protest as he sat before the chessboard, "I never let you win!"

"As you say, Sire," Abra bowed deeply. "It is as you say. A thousand pardons, Your Highness."

"Enough," the king sighed as he shook his head. "Captain Durand, I see your journey was a successful one."

"Yes, Your Highness," the captain saluted, standing at attention.

"Please, relax. I'd like you to stay, as my reason for having you bring Lady Rose to me involves you as well."

"Yes, Sire!"

"Falcon Rose," King Rowan addressed me from his seat at the chess table, "thank you for coming. It is good to see you again. I trust you and the wizards are well?"

"Yes, Your Highness," I reluctantly stepped past Abra to bow before the king. "How may I be of service?"

When I looked up, it was with a mighty struggle I managed to keep my surprise at the king's appearance from my face. He looked well, healthy at least, but he bore no resemblance to the prince, the young adventurous man Abra and I had rescued from captivity a few short years ago. His hair, still long and lustrous brown, was shot through with fine streaks of silver, his beard, neatly trimmed, also tinged, and there were small creases at the corners of his eyes. Across his brow deep furrows were etched. His eyes were bright, he looked strong and happy, but the responsibility of the throne had clearly aged him quickly. I knew he was not that many years older than me, but he certainly looked it.

"Perhaps you've heard that I'm to wed this year?"

"I had heard that, yes," I admitted, looking nervously at the tops of my boots, "though I understood that it was rumor and did not take it for fact"

"It actually is fact, Falcon," he nodded as he looked up from beneath heavy brows. "May I call you Falcon?"

"Of course, Your Highness," surprised at the question I gasped. "You may call me what you will."

"Very well, Falcon it is." With a gesture of one hand, he offered me the chair across the chess table before adding, "Please do sit down. You need not stand on ceremony, after all, we're old friends."

"Thank you, Sire," with a nod I took the seat offered, my curiosity building. I noticed Captain Durand still standing at attention behind me while Abra silently stepped from the room.

"My intended, Princess Merilda of Ayndor, her father, King Radolph, and sister, Princess Eleanora will be brought here to Esling," King Rowan explained, taking a carved ivory chess piece from the board, turning it over in his hands. "And I would like you to escort her."

The room went silent. The fire that had been merrily crackling and popping in the hearth suddenly fell quiet. A heavy pendulum clock on the ornate fabric covered wall continued its ponderous toll, but all else stood still. King Rowan raised one eyebrow in question as he awaited my response. Captain Durand, still standing at attention behind me, made no sound but I could swear I felt him tense.

"Me?" I gaped at the notion, "Why me? Surely you have men aplenty to escort your fiancé and her family."

"Yes, you," he nodded thoughtfully. "For I remember how you served my sister, Laurell, while I was away. I would like you to do the same for my bride-to-be."

"Um, well," I murmured uncertainly, struggling to imagine how such a journey would go, "I am sworn to serve you, of course, Your Highness. But would it not be better to have your guards escort the princess here to Esling? I'm sure they're much more capable and experienced than I am."

Captain Durand, clearing his throat, stepped forward to stand very near my chair. I glanced uneasily over my shoulder at him.

"If I might be so bold, Sire, my men and I are most capable and we have no need for this, this," obviously unsure how to refer to me, Captain Durand began before faltering. Raising a hand only to drop it to his side, he bowed his head before moving back from my chair.

The hairs on the back of my neck stood in response to the captain's words. A fire burned deep in my gut. Suddenly, it was all I could do to hold my tongue. Though I was sure it was not his intention, he had just inspired me to want to, no, to demand to escort the king's intended back to Esling. With a renewed sense of purpose, I rose from the chair, slapping one hand on the chess table hard enough to rattle the pieces on the board.

"Your Highness," I beamed, "on second thought, I'd be delighted to accept this assignment. I'm sure I'll be of great help to Princess Merilda and her family, and I'll make sure they arrive here in Esling safe and sound."

"It won't be a huge caravan," King Rowan explained, "just the royal family, their servants, and a few personal things Princess Merilda will want in her role of Queen of Esling. Her mother, Queen Gloriana, passed away many years ago and the girls were raised by the king, their nannies, and mentors. I should think three wagons will likely make the journey from Ayndor."

"I know Ayndor lies to the south and the west of Esling," I shrugged, resuming my seat, "but how many days travel is it? How long should this journey take?"

"Barring bad weather or unforeseen issues, it should take roughly a fortnight. My guards and you should make it to Ayndor in five days or so," he nodded. "It will likely take the royal family a few days to get their things packed and loaded into the wagons. The return trip will be a bit slower, of course, as you'll be traveling in caravan."

"Right," with a nod, I muttered, "there's many details to consider. I understand. And when shall we leave, Sire?"

"As soon as possible. I would like the princess and her family safely ensconced in the castle by the next full moon," he replied. "Now, if you'll excuse us, Falcon, I will have a word with Captain Durand. My servant will show you to your quarters,"

"But," I began to protest before changing my mind, "yes. Thank you, Your Highness."

It was clear I had been dismissed, and for the first time in my life. I realized that I did not like the feeling, but I had no recourse. Though I wanted desperately to speak to the king privately, to discuss the plague of nightmares the children of the kingdom were experiencing and what they might mean, it was clear this was not the time. With a bow, I muttered good night as I followed the woman who had entered the room from a side door, apparently at some cue from the king. She was gray haired, though her face was smooth and unwrinkled. Dressed in blue the color of the sky, she exuded an air of calm officiousness, and when she paused before the closed door to make sure I was behind her, she offered me a gentle smile.

"This way, please," she directed as she opened the door to step into the corridor. "Your things will be brought to your room directly."

"What about Lothar?"

"Lothar?" She drew to a halt, looking at me with eyes of silver-blue.

"My dog," I smiled, "well, he's really a puppy. He's playing with the stable boys at the moment, but he's really a good dog and I'm sure he'll be no trouble."

"You may collect your dog whenever you wish," with a nod she resumed walking down the corridor. "I'll show you your room first. His Highness is quite fond of hounds so I'm sure he'll have no qualms with you having yours in your room."

"Thank you," I sighed in relief, "he's young enough that I'd not want to leave him unattended."

"Right this way," the woman encouraged, "and by the way, my name is Madam Anna, I'm His Highness's chambermaid. Should you need anything there are pages stationed on each corridor. Simply give a message to a page and he will see that it gets where it needs to go. Your room is right here. A fire's been laid in the hearth, there's fresh water for washing, clean garments in the wardrobe and the bed is newly made. I'll have tea and biscuits sent up if you'd like, or there's cold meat and cheese available at this hour if you'd prefer something more substantial."

"Tea and biscuits would be nice, thank you," I replied absently as I looked around the room. Bearing little resemblance to the king's quarters, it was still an opulent place, with a carved mantle above the fireplace and mullioned windows framed with green velvet drapes.

At the sound of a gentle rap, Madam Anna crossed the room to open the heavy oak door and allow a page to enter. He carried ThornSting carefully, almost reverently, across his extended forearms.

"Ma'am," he bowed slightly, "your sword!"

"Thank you, um," I paused, not quite sure what to call the lad.

"Luc, My Lady," he blushed. "My name is Luc."

"Very well," I nodded, "thank you Luc."

"Ma'am." With another bow he turned and silently left the room.

"I'll see to your tea and biscuits," Madam Anna offered as she breezed through the door following the young page into the hallway.

Suddenly alone in the room, I took a deep breath as I inspected my surroundings. Heavy column candles burned on either end of the mantle, so I carefully lifted one from its holder to pour the pooled melted wax from around its wick onto the wood laid in the hearth. Replacing it without spilling a drop, I pulled a twig from the faggots, lit one end in the candle's flame and tossed it into the wax. Flames burst brightly as the wax caught fire, twigs quickly flashed and curled before the larger pieces began to burn. I knew the air outside was not cool enough to warrant a fire in the fireplace, but inside the stone walls of the castle held no heat so a fire was needed to ward off the chill. The heavy drapes on the mullioned windows and beautifully woven tapestries on the wall did little to dispel the cold, harsh feeling of the room. Rubbing my hands together as if chilled, when I really was not, I jumped onto the large bed, reveling in the feel of the counterpane. I had no experience with silk, but as smooth, tightly woven, and delicate as the fabric of the bedspread was, I guessed this was the stuff. Deep rose with tied tassels along the hem, the coverlet was quilted and tucked, and it felt soft and glorious. I looked forward to sleeping beneath its beautiful warmth. Stretching my arms over my head, I stared at the arched ceiling, noticing the details of its construction, when the raucous sound of raised voices and heavy footsteps approaching in the corridor tore my attention away. I sat upright, smoothing the spread as I climbed off the bed, feeling guilty for what I had just done. A sharp knock on the heavy door shook me from my silliness.

"Abra," I smiled as I opened the door. The warlock was accompanied by one of the stable master's pages who was struggling to hold onto the squirming Lothar. "Please, do come in, both of you."

"Milady Falcon," Abra nodded as he strode in, my saddle bags hanging on his forearm, "this is Edward. He's been taking care of this beast whom I'm told is yours?"

"Lothar!" With a mixture of delight and relief, I took the wiggling puppy from the young page's hands, scratched beneath his chin, and hugged him quickly. His excitement and anticipation of investigating the room was almost more than he could bear, so I released him onto the floor with a word of warning. "And you remember, young man, you're inside now so you behave yourself accordingly! No relieving yourself and no marking your territory. We're guests here."

"The animal's name is Lothar?" My warlock friend interjected with a grin. "Where ever did you get that name?"

"I don't know," I shrugged. "It just came to me. Why do you ask?"

"No reason," he quipped. "That will be all, Master Edward. You may go now."

"Well, I," hesitantly I stepped forward to thank the young boy, but Abra stopped me with a simple gesture. His index finger before pursed lips, he made it clear that I should say no more until the page had left the room. Once the lad had departed and the door was closed, my quixotic mentor turned to me.

"Edward's in training, Falcon," he explained, "and I take great care to let no one believe me kindly or, even worse, pleasant."

"Your secret's safe with me," I shook my head, "though I can't imagine why you would care what anyone thinks of you."

"Let's just say I have a certain reputation to uphold. I come and go from Castle deBirch, when and how I please. I explain myself to no one and I have no desire to grow close to anyone here. I play chess with His Highness in order to keep an eye on things in this realm."

"Does what's happening now have something to do with the talisman?"

"Indeed, that is most likely." With a heavy sigh, he gathered his robes around his middle as he crossed the room to sit down in one of the arm chairs flanking the fireplace. "I'm not sure exactly what is happening yet, my dear, but something is stirring. I've felt the vibrations in the air and heard rumors of strange comings and goings in this land and others."

"Yes, I've noticed that."

"So, tell me, how is it you came to be traveling with this…Lothar?" He nodded at the puppy who was busy sniffing along the floor near the wall.

"I rescued him from a pit he fell into in the middle of a nemeton," with a shrug, I explained. "Well, Deacon and I rescued him and he sort of grew attached to me. He believes I am his, I think."

The broad smile that spread across the warlock's face and the twinkle in his eyes began just seconds before he broke out in gales of laughter. In confusion, I could only sit and watch as over and over again he roared in delight.

"What in the world could possibly be so funny?" I demanded at length, having exhausted my patience with the Aerienesse.

"Oh, Falcon, my dear," he wiped tears of joy from the edges of his eyes as he shook his head slowly, "only you could snatch a sacrifice from the altar of the Gods and Goddesses and not think twice about it!"

"Sacrifice? What in the world are you talking about? Lothar had just fallen into a hole in the ground in the nemeton. That's all. There was no altar!"

"Lass, do stop and think about this for a moment. What are the odds of there being a naturally occurring hole in the ground within the sacred space of a nemeton? That hole, as you call it, is an altar. Live sacrifices are left there for the Gods and Goddesses."

"What would possess anyone to put a live anything into a hole so it would die of starvation or thirst? How would that please the Gods and Goddesses? That's barbaric! It's obscene!"

"Barbaric or not," the warlock sighed, his laughter finally dying out, "I assure you this is what happened. Your beast there was meant as sacrifice and you snatched him away from deity!"

"He was not!" I insisted, calling the puppy to me. "Lothar, come. Come see me."

At my command, the shepherd ceased his snuffling inspection of the room and came padding over to me. He laid his head on my knee to stare up at me with eyes full of adoration. How could anyone treat such a beautiful animal with so little disregard? How could anyone be so cruel? And how could any God or Goddess demand or accept such a precious sacrifice? Deity and I had not gotten along since my parents' murder; I had yet to forgive them for allowing it to happen, and learning of this obscenity just added fuel to the flame of distrust I held for them in my heart.

"Milady," Abra said softly, leaning forward to place one hand on my knee, "I am sorry to have laughed at you. And I apologize for the way I explained the situation with Lothar. I did not mean to hurt you."

"It's all right," I sighed, still staring into the puppy's eyes, stroking his thick, soft fur. "Whether I stole a sacrifice meant for deity or not, he's my friend now and I'll not let anything hurt him."

"I understand. He looks like he'll be a fine friend at that!"

Suddenly, a sharp rap on the door made Lothar sit up at alert. For a moment I could not think who would be knocking on my bedroom door.

"Ah, tea and biscuits!" I smiled as I rose to answer, "I trust you'll stay and join me?"

"Of course," Abra replied, gently calling Lothar to his side. To my surprise, the shepherd heeded the warlock and was soon enjoying more scratching and petting attention.

Chapter 16

Abra and I talked into the wee hours. I had not seen the warlock since he had guided me through a portal to recover the talisman some years ago. I shared with him how I had been training with each wizard and how I had recently been initiated into the Order of Healers. He seemed to be pleased with my story, but I could feel that something was bothering him. At last, he stood, stretched, and announced his departure.

"It's been lovely spending this time with you, Milady Falcon," he bowed slightly, "but I must be away now. As you remember, I cannot stay long in this world of yours. I shall continue to watch over the situation here and should anything of importance arise, I will let you know, of course."

"That's it?" I gaped as I stood to escort him to the door. "That's all? After all this time you're just going to leave me here alone? You're not coming with me to bring the king's intended back to Esling?"

"Alas, no," he smiled kindly, "but I will do what I can. Be assured that I am not leaving you alone here. And you do have Lothar, of course!"

"Sure," unable to hide my disappointment, I turned my eyes away as the tears began to well, "yes, you're right, I do. Thanks, Abra. Thanks for a lovely visit."

"I will see you anon," gently kissing the back of my hand, he looked up at me from beneath a heavy brow. "You are well?"

"Yes," I nodded, feigning a yawn, "I'm fine. I'm just tired. Best get some sleep. Good night Abra."

Without another word, the warlock slipped silently into the hallway. I closed the door, leaning my forehead against the wood, wondering why in the world I was experiencing the feelings stirring down deep. Heaving a heavy sigh, I crossed the room to draw back the covers from beneath the pillows on the massive bed. Part of me was looking forward to sleeping beneath the beautifully woven, soft blankets, while another part was quite intimidated. I had never slept on such an elaborately designed and created piece of furniture. The bed I slept on growing up had been small and comfortable, the coarse fabric covering a mixture of straw and goose feathers, but nothing at all like the massive four-poster before me. The fire still burned in the hearth, so I decided to leave the heavy velvet drapes surrounding the bed open to the warm air. Crossing the room, I opened the chifforobe and withdrew a simple linen shift. After pulling off my boots and stockings, I yanked my tunic over my head, stripped my breeches off, and slipped on the clean, soft gown. Tiptoeing across the cool stone floor, I grabbed the remains of the last biscuit from the plate on the table, tossed it to Lothar, who had assumed a comfy position near the fireplace, and climbed into bed.

As I lay there beneath the lovely blankets, I kept thinking of what Abra had said about the puppy and how he had likely been put into that pit as a live sacrifice. It made my stomach turn to think anyone could be so cruel, so uncaring, and so superstitious. The mere idea made me dislike the gods and goddesses even more, for who else could possibly think of such horrible things? Surely, that was nothing humans could devise, I assured myself as I rolled over and drew my knees up to my chest. A heavy thump on the mattress beside me announced the arrival of my four-legged companion, so I reached out in the darkness to find his furry head. He walked a tight circle on the blankets a few times before lying down behind my knees. It was nice, I realized, to have his warmth and weight beside me. It was reassuring to have a friend with me, I admitted to myself as I closed my eyes.

'Good night, Cor,' I sighed as I drifted off to sleep.

The sudden snap of a crackling ember startled me awake. Rolling over, I watched the tiny speck of burning wood turn black on the floor in front of the hearth. Beside me, Lothar lay awake, his head raised, ears perked up to listen. I too listened, but heard nothing beyond the fire burning. I had no idea if the sun had risen beyond the castle walls yet, or if the world stirred outside my closed windows, but I was fully awake, rested, and could find no reason to remain in bed. Finally, I sat up, stretched my arms over my head, and with a yawn, threw back the covers. The stone floor was chilly to my bare feet, but my clothes lay neatly draped across a chair near the chifforobe, so I hurriedly made my way to retrieve my stockings. Dressing as quickly as I could, I donned clean breeches and a fresh tunic before securing the sapphire blue sash of the Order of Healers around my waist. I buckled on the leather sheath and slid ThornSting into the scabbard on my hip. As I drew my brush through my unruly tresses, I poured fresh water from a stone pitcher into a bowl meant for washing before placing it on the floor so Lothar could have a drink. Once I pulled on my stockings and boots, I neatly re-packed my things into my saddlebags before donning the blue-gray cape Will Perry had given me. I tied a bow in the cape's cords as I opened the heavy wooden bedroom door. Not sure of the day's itinerary, I left my belongings beside the door, just inside, and followed Lothar down the corridor.

The young page, Edward, stood leaning against a stone column beside the wall, asleep. I would have let him remain so, but the puppy had other ideas. He nudged the boy's hand with his nose and instantly the page was awake, apologizing profusely for having been sleeping.

"At your service, My Lady," he straightened himself, nodding smartly. "Good morning, Ma'am."

"Good morning, Edward," I smiled, "I'm sorry to have awakened you. Lothar and I are on our way out for some fresh air. Could you show us the way?"

"Of course, Ma'am, just this way. And," he hesitated, chewing on the inside of his lip, "might I be so bold as to ask a favor of you, My Lady?"

"Ask away!"

"Would you please not tell anyone that I was sleeping? We're not supposed to fall asleep."

"Your secret's safe with me, Edward. So, are you allowed to sleep at all while on duty?"

"When our services are no longer needed and we're dismissed," he replied as he started down the long corridor, "or when another page takes the duty."

Torches still burned in sconces on the walls of the hallway, but for all I knew they burned all the time, as there were no windows for illumination. I could have asked the young page if it was daylight outside, but he seemed reluctant to carry on a conversation as he led me through the labyrinthine castle. Around myriad corners we went, down two wide staircases, and through a low-arched doorway into what could only be the kitchen. There were three large hearths along one wall, wrought iron hooks and grates of various sizes and shapes hanging along their stone facades. Three large tables stood in the center of the room upon which were stacked different sized bowls and serving platters. In a niche between two of the fireplaces a young girl sat leaning against the wall, her knees drawn up to her chest, her head drooped forward. A tangle of blond hair obscured her face. I realized, as we made our way to the door on the far side of the room, that the child was the keeper of the fires. It was her lot in life, at least at her age, to keep the fires in the hearths from going out completely. I knew she would doze during the night, only to wake and feed the fires until the cooks, maids, and other servants arrived to start the morning meal. The heavy oak door squealed softly as I opened it, stepped into the courtyard, and watched Lothar race past me. Edward gave me a questioning expression, looking relieved when I told him he could return to his post.

"Don't worry," I assured the page, "Lothar and I can find our way from here. Thank you!"

With a silent bow, he turned and disappeared back into the dark kitchen.

Taking a deep breath, I shrugged the cape back off my shoulders to stretch my arms over my head as I looked at the pale pink sky above. It was morning, albeit very early in the morning, I realized. Lothar ran around the courtyard, chasing the chickens that provided the denizens of the place with fresh eggs. He seemed to be just teasing them, showing no interest in doing them harm, so I let him be as I investigated my surroundings. Across the wide stone-covered yard, the doors to the stable were already open and I could hear voices as well as horses snorting within. It was such a lovely morning, and a beautiful place, I mused, yet I was filled with dread over what I would soon face. I truly hated the idea of riding for days with Captain Durand and his men, though I was oathed to serve the king as he willed it. With a sigh, I pulled a blade of grass from beside the stone stoop near the door. Wrapping my voluminous cloak around me, I sat down heavily, considering how I might avoid what lay ahead.

'*You're sworn to escort the princess and her family from their home to Castle deBirch, yes?*' Cor's calm, familiar voice filled my head and made my heart sigh in relief. '*But you've no need to travel with the king's guard to get to Ayndor. You need only be there when they arrive to see the king's intended back to Esling.*'

The truth of the wizard's words felt like a weight being lifted from my shoulders. He was quite right! I had no obligation to travel with the king's guard to get to Ayndor. I could make my own way there. All I had to do was see Princess Merilda, and her father and sister, back here safely.

'*Thank you, Cor! You're so right. I can make it there without Durand and his men. Lothar and I can get there somehow.*'

'*Vesta is on her way to you, lass. She'll guide you to Ayndor.*'

'*I don't know how to thank you, Cor, you and the other wizards. You've made my day. Thank you so much!*'

'*We're with you always, Falcon. Take care and travel safe!*'

'*Thank you!*' With renewed joy and fresh hope, I stood, shook out my cloak, tossed the blade of grass to the ground, and rubbed my hands on my breeches. Humming a jaunty tune, I crossed the courtyard to peer into the shadows of the stable. The scent of straw, dust, and horses wafted around me as I entered.

"Hello! Haggerty? Anyone here?"

"Aye, My Lady," the stable master responded as he stepped out of a stall, wiping his hands on a cloth. "How may I help you, Miss?"

"Please have my horse saddled and ready to go as soon as possible."

"You'll not be leavin' with those you came in with?" He cocked his head, offering me a sly smile. "Not that it's any of my business, mind you."

"I'll not be leaving with them, no," I shook my head while repressing a shudder. "In fact, I'll be leaving by myself as soon as I can."

When he hesitated, casting me a sideward glance, I could see he wanted to say something. I was about to ask what he had on his mind when I clearly heard his thoughts as if he were speaking.

'*You watch out for Captain Durand, My Lady. You just watch out for that one.*'

Disappearing into a stall, he reappeared leading Aeon by the bridle.

"This is your mare, yes?" He smiled politely as he patted the horse's nose.

"Yes, sir," with a nod, I replied, still puzzled over his thoughts and his warning, "that's Aeon. Please ready her to travel."

"Yes, Miss," he responded. Without further comment, he pushed the horse back into the stall and disappeared behind her.

As I strode across the courtyard, I whistled to get Lothar's attention. He stopped sniffing the edge of the herb garden to look up before bolting toward me, his excited tail wagging the rest of his small body. I bent over and caught him as he leapt toward my knees, snuggling him to my chest to enjoy puppy kisses. As he licked my chin, I crossed the stoop, opened the door, and stepped into the now bustling kitchen. Fires burned brightly in each of the hearths and the fragrance of meats and breads filled the room. Ignoring the grumbling in my stomach, I lowered my eyes and tiptoed as inconspicuously as possible toward the far door. I had almost made it to the hallway when one of the cooks turned from where she stood kneading dough at the table and called to me.

"My Lady," she raised her voice to be heard over the clattering of dishes and utensils, "may I help you with something?"

"No, thank you," I blushed, feeling guilty about carrying Lothar through the kitchen, "I just had my puppy out for some exercise."

"Madam Anna's been in already," the woman in the white apron offered kindly. "She ordered a tray of food be taken to your room. There's a bowl of scraps for your animal there too. It's all waiting for you upstairs, Ma'am."

"Thank you," I bowed slightly, desperate to make my escape, "I'm sorry to have bothered you. Thank you."

"You're welcome, My Lady," she nodded succinctly as she turned her attention back to the dough on the table before her. "Mind how you go now!"

"I will, thank you," murmuring softly, I could not be sure she heard my reply, but I was just happy to be out of the busy kitchen. I made my way quickly down the corridor. "Did you hear that, Lothar? Madam Anna's had a bowl of food for you taken to our room, so we'll go eat. I hope to have a brief audience with the king, as he needs to know about the nightmares the children of his realm are having and I'm going to do my best to talk him into letting me travel by myself to Ayndor. I so want to leave right away."

Rubbing the puppy's ears, I retraced my way around the various corners and up the two wide staircases to my room.

The fragrance of fresh bread and sausages greeted me when I opened the bedroom door. Lothar leapt from my arms to race across the room to the bowl on the floor beside the hearth. Wagging tail and wobbling body, he excitedly started eating. I removed the white cloth covering the tray on the table between the two armchairs and picked up a link of sausage with my fingers. As I munched one end of the meat, I pulled a hunk of bread from a warm loaf on the plate. A crock of butter sat beside a dish of fresh honey, and both or either would have been good on the bread, I realized, but I shoved a bite of it into my mouth to find it was excellent without either. I poured a mug of fresh milk from a stone crock beside the tray and thirstily drank it down. Realizing there was little point in eating quickly and denying myself the pleasure of the repast, I pulled my cape aside to relax in a chair beside the table, nudging the tip of ThornSting so it rested beside my outstretched leg. Finishing up what was left of the loaf of bread, I tossed the end piece to Lothar and was about to pour myself some more milk when a knock on the door startled me. Wondering who in the world it could be in the corridor, I rose from my chair to cross the room.

"Luc!" The surprised greeting escaped my lips when I opened the door, "Good morning, Luc. What can I do for you?"

"His Highness wishes to see you, My Lady," the young page bowed deeply, "at your earliest convenience."

"That's," I stammered, not sure how to respond, "I mean, of course. Anything His Highness wants. I'll come now. Just let me pour Lothar a bit more water." Quickly, I returned to the table near the window where the pitcher of fresh water sat beside a washing basin. As I poured part of the water into the bowl, I decided it only proper to use the remainder to wash my face and hands before seeing the king. Last night's audience had been hurried and I had not had the time to freshen up before being ushered into the royal chambers. This morning would be different, I silently assured myself. "Just one moment," I nodded to Luc who stood waiting patiently in the doorway. Soaking a cloth in the cool water, I wrang out the excess, washed my forehead, cheeks, chin, and neck, before wiping my hands and fingers clean of my breakfast crumbs. I patted my hair down as best I could, straightened my tunic and cloak, and righted ThornSting on my hip.

"All right, I'm ready," I announced as I made my way to the door, "and Lothar, you stay here and behave yourself. I'm sure I won't be long."

"This way, My Lady," the page offered with a sweep of his hand, "if you'll follow me?"

"Of course."

As we walked briskly along the wide stone corridors, I wondered why the king would be summoning me. I had intended to seek an audience with him, of course, but could fathom no reason he would request my presence. Madam Anna was just coming out of the double doors to the king's chambers when Luc and I rounded the corner. She greeted me politely and succinctly, excusing herself to bustle by me in haste. Before my young escort could put his hand on one of the doors to knock, the other door swung open and the king's steward nodded a silent greeting. He stepped back to usher me in while Luc backed away to discreetly disappear.

"Lady Falcon," King Rowan's voice reverberated around the room, though I could not tell from where it issued. "Do come in, Falcon. Please, make yourself comfortable. I won't be but a minute."

Unsure of protocol in such a situation, I moved further into the room, but remained standing. The heavy pendulum of the clock on the wall swung slowly back and forth as a singing bird drew my attention to the open window nearby. Fresh air wafted into the room as the sparrow chirped brightly, sunbeams glinted off crystal, silver, and brass fixtures and decorations, and the fragrance of freshly brewed coffee filled the air. On a tray atop a low table before a long, upholstered lounge, an ornately decorated silver urn sat between delicate porcelain cups and I couldn't help but crave a cup of the warm brew.

"There now," the king announced as he stepped into the room from between heavy, velvet drapes, "I'm sorry to have kept you, Falcon. As you can see, I am preparing to go hunting with my birds of prey."

King Rowan did indeed look ready to go hunting. He wore a beautifully tanned leather vest over a natural linen tunic and matching vambraces covered each forearm. His dark brown trousers were tucked into soft-looking leather boots, and an ornately woven leather belt hung at his waist. Dark hair pulled back from his brow, Rowan looked younger than he had the night before, I realized, or perhaps his anticipation of the hunt lifted years from his appearance.

"You wanted to see me, Your Highness?" I bowed, one hand on ThornSting's pommel.

"I did, yes," he nodded as he moved to the table near the lounge. "Would you like coffee?"

"Please, let me," I gaped, suddenly aware that we were alone and there was no servant to pour the king's coffee.

"No, no," he dismissed me with a wave of his hand, "I'll do it. I rather enjoy doing some things for myself. Please, sit down, make yourself comfortable."

"As you wish, Sire."

"The reason I wanted to see you, Falcon," he began, pausing as he concentrated on pouring the hot liquid into the porcelain cups, "is because frankly, I had the sense last night that you had something on your mind. I had business to attend with Captain Durand and I dismissed you rather abruptly."

"My Lord?"

"Was I mistaken? Did you not have something else on your mind, something you wished to discuss with me?"

Taken aback by the king's insightfulness, I accepted the offered cup of coffee with slightly trembling hands, praying fervently that I would not spill any or drop the cup and saucer entirely. King Rowan moved across the room, pulled a heavy, carved wooden chair from beneath the chess table, and sat down. Placing his coffee beside the chessboard, he indicated I should take the chair across from him so I hurried to do so.

"You were not mistaken, Your Highness," I admitted as I carefully placed my cup and saucer on the table as he had done. "Indeed, you were not mistaken at all."

As I took a seat across from the king, I explained all I had learned as Deacon and I had journeyed across Esling and how many children had been experiencing nightmares. When I told him exactly what Cor had told me, I realized what a relief it was to get the information off my chest, and to put the matter into more powerful and capable hands than my own. We sat sipping coffee, exchanging information, and thinking deep thoughts. At length King Rowan heaved a sigh.

"Very well, I shall have my advisor Ubrus look into the matter," he nodded, tapping one index finger on the edge of his coffee cup. "Was there anything else?"

"I am happy to escort your bride-to-be and her family from Ayndor," I began my argument as convincingly as possible, "but as you know I've recently been initiated into the Order of Healers and Deacon and I were on our journey to tend to folks before winter sets in when your guards...."

"Took you away?" He raised one eyebrow as he took a sip of coffee.

"Well, something like that. It occurred to me that if I were to leave today, right now even, I could continue to look in on folks as I travel to the border of Esling. I could check in on your subjects as I go and still be in Ayndor either before or at the same time Durand and your men arrive." Placing my now empty cup on its saucer, I moved my hands to my lap where my fingers nervously braided and unbraided themselves.

"You wish to travel alone?"

"I do, Your Highness," I nodded excitedly, sensing that he might be grasping my intentions. "That way I could still serve you in my capacity of healer while making my way to Ayndor. I assure you that I'll not delay your intended and her family's arrival back here in Esling. I will be there when your guards arrive, I promise."

"Is there another reason you don't want to travel with my guards, Falcon? You know you can tell me," He pried gently but firmly. "You and I have been through much together and though I am your king I also consider myself your friend. Is it truly your desire to continue doing your work as a healer that has you anxious to depart alone?"

As tempted as I was to blurt out the truth, that I did not care for the captain of his guards and that I felt uncomfortably outnumbered by his men, something made me hold my tongue. This was the king of Esling after all, and he had more important things to deal with than my foolish sensibilities. He obviously trusted Durand, I reasoned, so there must be some good qualities hidden behind that sour countenance. I would remain silent and deal with my own issues in good time.

"I assure you, Sire," smiling as sweetly as possible, I feigned sincerity, "I only wish to continue my journey as healer. I seek only to serve you and the kingdom."

"Very well," King Rowan emptied his coffee cup, returning it to its saucer as he shoved his chair back to stand, "you may travel alone, Lady Falcon, and you may leave at once if you so desire. There's a ruby cloak in your chifforobe. Please, take it to wear when you enter Ayndor."

"But Your Highness," I stood as he did, following what protocol I knew, "I am not a member of your royal guard. Surely, I'm not worthy of such an honor."

"You will be acting under my orders and will be, temporarily, an emissary of mine, so you will take and wear the cloak," he commanded succinctly.

As it was clear there was no further point in protesting, I nodded silently. I knew full well there was a similar cloak in my chifforobe at Corhaven, for Rowan, Prince Rowan at that time, had gifted me one when I had left Castle deBirch after returning him from captivity. Though I had both King Rowan's brooch and one of his guards' ruby cloaks, I was not actually in active service to the king so I would not be so bold as to wear them.

"Your Highness," I bowed, "I thank you for your time and for the coffee. I shall depart now and meet your guard in Ayndor."

"Farewell, Falcon Rose," King Rowan turned his attention to his steward who had just entered the room from between the closed velvet curtains. "Travel safe."

Feeling both relieved and annoyed, I left the king's chambers to make my way back to my room. Luc had offered to escort me to my quarters, but I assured him I knew the way and that his services would not be necessary. A twinge of guilt stirred in my heart over not being completely honest with King Rowan, but I knew to trust my instincts so I brushed it aside, eager to gather my things, Lothar, and be on my way.

I was greeted by a guilty-faced puppy curled atop the opulently covered bed when I opened the door to my room. Lothar lifted his head slightly and thumped his heavily furred tail, awaiting my response to his napping without me, apparently. Though part of me cringed at the dog's audacity, another part was proud and delighted that he was clever enough to know how best to be comfortable.

"Come, Lothar," I patted my thigh, "you and I have to be going now."

Opening the chifforobe with something akin to dread, I withdrew the ruby cloak hanging among the other garments to drape it over my arm, making mental note that I now had several cloaks. I picked up my saddle bags from beside the door, tossed them across my shoulder, and scooped Lothar up with my right hand.

"We've spent enough time here," I reasoned with my four-legged friend, "and now it's time to get back on the road. We have people to see. I just hope Vesta arrives before I'm out of the territory I know."

Lothar squirmed against me, trying to reach my chin for a wet-tongued kiss, so I shifted him deeper into the crook of my elbow as I stepped into the corridor. No one was about as I made my way out of Castle deBirch, and though I was disappointed that Abra had not appeared to at least wish me farewell, I was relieved to not be delayed by the obligatory pleasantries of court.

Chapter 17

The morning was cool when I stepped into the courtyard and I only realized how warm my furry companion was when I released him to the ground. Drawing the length of my cloak around me, I shivered, realizing the ride ahead would be chilly until the sun rose higher to warm the day. Lothar followed me from the castle to the open doors of the stable, sitting patiently by my right leg when I stopped to look into the shadow-filled structure.

"Hello," I called out.

"Here's your mount, My Lady," Haggerty announced as he led Aeon out of the darkness into the weak sunlight just beginning to stream between the shuttered windows of the stable. "She's all ready to go."

"Thank you, Haggerty," I nodded as I handed the stable master my saddle bags. "Would you please put these on her?"

"Yes, Miss," he replied, easily taking the leather pouches from me to secure them behind the mare's saddle. As he turned to his task, I noticed that his arms were thick and well-muscled, his shoulders broad and strong. Though his long coarse hair was tinged with gray, he was obviously still able-bodied, well fitted to his position as stable master.

"My Lady Falcon," a young voice called out from nowhere. I stepped back from Aeon to look around the courtyard only to see the young page Edward hurrying toward me. Almost out of breath, he paused to collect himself for a moment before presenting me with a large cloth bag. "His Highness bade me bring you this. It's for your journey."

"Thank you, Edward," taking the bag from the young man with a nod, I noticed there was a loop of twine tied at the neck and realized it was meant to hang from the saddle horn. "Please tell His Highness that I said thank you and that I'm most grateful for his thoughtfulness."

"Yes, Ma'am," Master Edward bowed deeply, backed away, and sprinted across the courtyard to disappear back into the castle.

"Well," I chuckled as I slipped the loop of twine over the saddle horn, "I guess I'll not starve on the road." Checking to make sure my gear was secure, I scooped Lothar into my right arm. Left hand on the saddle horn, left foot in the stirrup, I hoisted myself up to swing my right leg over the saddle. Once both feet were securely in the stirrups, I moved the puppy into his riding position as I accepted the reins Haggerty handed me.

"You take care traveling, Miss," he offered me a look of genuine concern, his blue eyes darker than my beloved wizard Cor's but just as kindly. "I've heard tell there's trouble about."

"I've heard that as well," with a shrug I replied, "and I'll certainly be careful. Thank you and farewell Haggerty!"

"Farewell Lady Falcon," the stable master lifted a hand to wave. "Lovely to meet you, it was."

Nudging Aeon in the flanks with my heels, I pulled the reins to the right to head the mare toward the castle wall ahead. Two guards stood on either side of the arched entry and as I approached, they pulled the gates open wide. I realized that I must be the first person to come or go as the heavy iron portcullis just past the gates lumbered slowly and noisily up into the wall above the entryway. The guards resumed their positions, nodding smartly as I passed by. At last, I was beyond the castle walls, crossing the solid wooden bridge, and once more on the road.

Though the sky had changed from its dawn-pink to a crisp, pale blue, the sun had not cleared the tree-tops behind me. A frosty mist still hung just above the ground making the wooly sheep grazing in the fields appear phantom-like. Aeon's warm breath swirled around her nostrils as she moved easily down the road, head bobbing with each exertion. Still slightly disappointed that Abra had not made an appearance to bid me farewell, I kept glancing back over my shoulder expecting to see him racing up astride some great steed behind me, beard and long hair streaming in the wind. But the road behind me remained empty and by the time I had ridden to the upper edge of the vale where the road turned in either direction, I had given up hope of seeing the warlock. With a sigh, I turned my mount to the left, heading toward the south, though I intended to make my way west at some point. Casting my eyes skyward, I searched the blue for any sign of Vesta, Cor's raven, but saw nothing but a flock of geese circling smoothly, likely looking for a place to land and feed.

"Let's get some exercise, Lothar," I suggested to my furry companion as I drew Aeon to a halt. "I'll walk the mare and you can run around and explore for a bit. It's a lovely morning and the sun's going to be cresting that line of trees beside us any minute. We might as well enjoy ourselves."

Swinging easily from the saddle, I leapt softly to the ground, bending to release the puppy from my arm. Gathering Aeon's reins, I led her along as I watched Lothar race from one spot to another, sniffing, rooting, and marking things here and there. Though the puppy would run ahead, I noticed that he never ventured beyond where I could see him, or perhaps it was that he never ventured beyond where he could see me. Whatever the case, I reasoned, it was further evidence of how clever the shepherd was, and I realized it was a perfect time for a little training, though I had no clear knowledge on how to do so.

"Lothar," I called, snapping my fingers to get his attention, "come here!"

At the sound of my voice and the noise I made, the puppy did come to a halt. He looked at me curiously, cocking his head, before bouncing back to where I stood beside my horse. Though the speed at which he approached suggested I was about to be jumped upon, I held out my hand and told him to halt in what I hoped was a stern and commanding voice. The puppy did slow down and though he might not have understood my words, my tone must have at least confused or concerned him enough that he did not launch himself at me in excitement.

"Sit, Lothar!" I stood up straight and held my hand up to gain his attention.

Whether it was the dog's intelligence and willingness to please me or my own instinctual way to teach him, he did sit down and look up at my hand. I praised him, patting his head, telling him what a good boy he was before snapping my fingers and releasing him to go play. Obviously proud of himself, he took off at a run, head down, tail out straight. I could not see what he was after, but trusted that he would not go far. When the sun rose above the treetops beside us, its beams washed over the road, surrounding me in heat and light. I realized that it would not be long before I would have to remove my cloak and possibly even roll up the sleeves of my tunic to be comfortable.

Out of nowhere, a screech broke the stillness of the morning as the dark shape of an approaching bird grew larger. Vesta had found us, I smiled in relief.

"Vesta!" Shading my eyes with my hand, I watched the black raven flapping her wings gracefully as she flew toward me.

She shrieked once more in acknowledgement as she circled overhead. Realizing her intentions, I lifted my right arm and after circling me once more, she landed expertly on my forearm. As focused as I was on the beautiful raven on my arm, I failed to hear the over-excited yip of the puppy, nor did I notice his rapid approach until it was too late. The moment I touched Vesta's feathers, Lothar's projectile form appeared headed right for her. I screamed, the bird screeched, Aeon whinnied in alarm and rose on her hind hooves. The impending disaster seemed to rush at me, though I felt frozen. With tremendous effort to move and in desperation, I hoisted the raven skyward, protecting her departure with my own body. I managed to block Lothar's attack.

"Arrêt!" I screamed to the Universe as the possible catastrophe rushed through my thoughts. "Arrêt!"

Everything stopped! Vesta ceased her rise into the sky, impossibly frozen above my outstretched hand. Lothar hung in the air near my left shoulder, eyes bright, sharply-toothed jaws open for the kill. Aeon ceased her excited movement with her front hooves just above the ground, one knee bent and slightly higher than the other. The horse's eyes were wide in alarm, her nostrils flared, and her lips stretched back over her teeth in a now-silent cry of distress. My heart thudded in my chest, my breathing was shallow and rapid. I could not grasp what I was seeing. Suddenly, I understood that I had cast a spell of protection. First, I pulled the mare's reins down and her body followed, both front hooves landing solidly on the ground. I wrapped my arms around Lothar's chest, pushed his front feet down and placed him on the road before straightening his hindlegs and releasing him. Lastly, I stretched up on tiptoes to pluck Vesta from the sky, gently settling her back on my forearm and smoothing her wings down. It was clear that we were no longer in peril, though I wasn't sure what to do next. I had cast the spell, if that was indeed what it was, instinctively and without consideration. I had simply acted and now I was unsure how to proceed. Though I was sure Cor would be able to offer sage advice were I to reach out to the wizard, I was determined to figure things out on my own.

"All right, Falcon," my voice quivered slightly as I addressed myself, "you did this, you can undo it. Just take a breath and clear your mind. You can do this. You can do this, probably."

As I calmed myself down to recall what had just happened, I realized I had used my powers and my words to stop everything. Surely, I reasoned silently, that meant I would need to use the same to undo the situation. Closing my eyes, I drew in a deep breath. Rather than scream, as I had in my alarm, I whispered with all the passion and intent I could muster, "Commencer!"

The sound of feathers brushing together startled me into opening my eyes. Vesta looked at me curiously, her black eyes bright and alert. She pecked the back of my hand with her sharp beak, and regarded me once more. Beside my left leg, Lothar paused to scratch beneath his ear with his hind foot, a silly grin of pleasure spreading across his face. Aeon shifted her weight restlessly from one hoof to another, tossing her head back and shaking her mane. Barely daring to look around me, I sighed in relief that everything seemed to have returned to normal, and I had done it all on my own. I had not reached out to any of the wizards, nor had I tried to access the warlock Abra.

"I did it!" I murmured in awe. "Maybe not spectacularly or smoothly, but I did it!"

Reaching down to settle the puppy by putting one hand on his head, I drew Vesta near so I could look into her eyes.

"Now, Vesta," I instructed, "you fly. Show me which way to go to get to Ayndor, but remember that I can't travel as fast as you do so be gentle with me." At that I lifted the raven who took off into the sky, wings stretching wide, flapping powerfully.

"And you," I turned my attention to the puppy who now sat near my foot with a slightly confused expression on his face, "you and I need a moment." Kneeling so I could look him directly in the eye, I searched his mind until I found a clear light more vivid than anything around it. With a mental '*push*' I connected with that light in his canine mind and hoped it would be enough to forge a clearer and stronger bond in the future. Aeon, my father's great black mare, and I had developed a very close understanding over the years so I was comfortable with her actions and reactions, feeling no need for further bonding.

"Come on," I murmured at last, lifting Lothar into my arms before straightening, "we'd best be moving. We have a bird to follow!"

Swinging myself back into the saddle, I took up Aeon's reins, settled the puppy before me, and heeled the mare in the flanks. What started as a gentle trot soon grew into a gallop and I realized the horse needed to burn off some energy to settle herself. Part of me envied the beast as my nerves were still jangled and only time would settle them.

As the road climbed a steep hill, Aeon's pace slowed as she dug into the ground to gain purchase. By the time the mare reached the crest of the rise, she had drawn naturally to a comfortable pace so I halted her, taking a moment to gather my thoughts. Lothar yawned as he carefully rearranged himself on the saddle before closing his eyes to sleep. Vesta had flown ahead and now sat perched on a tree branch near the side of the road. Apparently, she was waiting for us to catch up with her and I had intended to do so until I glanced off to the left where I noticed a small cottage tucked between the trees at the edge of the forest. As I could see no path to the place, I tugged Aeon's reins to the left and let her find her way through the woods. The scent of wood smoke soon surrounded me, indicating a fire burned in the hearth so someone was likely home.

"My first home to visit alone," I announced to no one. "Let's hope this goes well."

A rhythmic thrumming sound caught my attention just before I reached the cottage. I realized it was a swing moving back and forth, suspended from the branch of a white oak tree. The little girl swinging there wore a pale green dress with a tattered brown shawl tied around her shoulders.

She wore stockings but there were no shoes on her feet. Her pale blond hair streamed behind as she swung forward then covered her face as she went back. Cheeks flushed and the tip of her nose red, she was lovely, but I could not tell if her coloring was from the cold or if she had been crying. I urged Aeon forward to a small wooden gate which hung crookedly closed in the stacked stone fence surrounding the place. Drawing her to a halt, I dismounted and released Lothar to the ground. I stood and stretched, taking in the details of the cottage. The instant I put my hand on the latch holding the gate closed, the sound of the swing stopped. A soft breeze soughed through the trees behind me, but otherwise all was quiet. To my dismay, when I looked at where the little girl had been swinging, she was not there, nor was the swing. The white oak stood as it had, low, long branches reaching in all directions, but there was neither rope swing nor child there at all. Startled, I froze where I stood, simply staring at the tree. The sing-song moaning of the ropes straining around the tree branch still echoed in my mind, but all signs of the swing and the child were gone. Shaking myself from my stupor, I pulled the latch up to swing the gate open. As I approached the ancient-looking wooden front door, it opened, and an elderly man, with hair as white as snow, stepped onto the stoop. A wreath of smoke surrounded him from the pipe he held tightly in his mouth. Eyes pale green and rheumy, he shuffled forward, taking the pipe from his mouth with a shaky hand.

"Can I help you?"

"Hello," I began, not sure how to proceed. "I'm Falcon Rose. I'm a member of the Order of Healers and I'm making my way around the countryside before winter sets in to see if anyone needs anything. I have elixirs, potions, ointments, and healing supplies if you're in need of anything."

"Got no money," he shook his head as he spat out of the corner of his mouth.

"You don't need any money," I explained quickly. "We members of the Order do this work for the benefit of all and it will cost you nothing. We just want to help!"

"Alright," the gentleman nodded his head succinctly as he placed the pipe back in his mouth, "the wife hasn't been feeling well for the last few days. Maybe you can look at her and see if there's anything you can do. The name's Abraham Montague, but you can call me Abe."

"Nice to meet you Abe," nodding, I replied, "please, call me Falcon."

Stooping to clear the low front door frame, I followed Abe into the cottage hoping that Lothar would behave outside on his own. I would go out and round him up, I resolved, if the visit began to take more time than I expected.

The house was cozy and clean, though the furnishings were spare. The ceilings were low, and the windows were clouded over with age. A fire burned in the hearth while a single candle barely touched the darkness across the room where a still figure lay buried beneath heavy blankets.

"That's my wife, Rachel," he gestured toward the bed with one outstretched finger. "She's been like this for a few days now. Sleeps a lot, she does. I can't get her to eat much and she barely drinks. I don't know what to do for her."

"How did this all start?" I asked as I moved cautiously toward the bed, "Did she have a cough, cut herself, get bitten?"

"She woke up one morning last week all hot and sweatin'," he explained. "She did cough and said her throat hurt, had a hard time swallowin',' and felt achy. She took some stuff she makes for fevers, but it didn't seem to help."

Abe picked up an ancient-looking wooden rocking chair and carried it across the room to put it beside his wife's bed.

"Here," he offered, "you can have a seat here. Maybe she'll answer if you talk to her, sometimes she does."

A pale figure stood in the dark corner farthest from Rachel's bed. The woman there appeared emaciated and wan; her skin as white as the hair on her head. She neither moved nor spoke, merely stared at me with unblinking eyes.

"Is it just you and your wife living here, Abe?"

"Aye," he scratched his bearded chin as he shuffled toward the fireplace, "just me and my Rachel. We had children, four in fact. The oldest, we called her Mim, died when she was but a child, and the other three have grown and moved away. Rachel did some healing in her day, nothing as fancy as being a member of the Order, mind you, but she could mix herbs to help when someone had a fever. And she helped bring more than just her own babes into the world. But just me and her now, and I guess our days are dwindling."

"I don't know about that," I smiled, trying to be encouraging. "You look well. Now, if you'll excuse me, I'll see what I can do for your wife."

"You do that," he responded, carefully placing his pipe in a dish on the table in the center of the room. "I'll go bring in some more firewood and put on some water for tea, if you'd like some."

"That would be nice. Oh, and my puppy is running around your yard somewhere. I hope he's not getting into trouble or hurting anything."

"Nothin' out there for him to hurt, Miss," Abe shook his head sadly. "The garden, such as it was this year, has already been harvested and there's nothing else for a puppy to get into. He's fine, I'm sure."

Without further comment, Mr. Montague stepped outside, closing the door behind him, leaving me alone with his wife. As soon as he was gone, a strange quiet fell over the room sending a chill up my spine. I scooted my chair closer to the bed and leaned over the sleeping woman's form. Heavy woolen blankets were pulled up to her chin, but by the meager light of the single candle flame I could see her eyes were closed. Rachel's skin was pale and papery. Her cheekbones were pronounced above her sunken, angular jaw, and her lips were thin and dry-looking. White curls framed her once-lovely face, adding no color to her countenance.

"I'm Falcon Rose, Mrs. Montague," I murmured, searching her face for any indication that she heard me. "I'm here to help you if I can."

"You've seen Mim," came a wispy voice from across the room. "You've seen her, haven't you?"

Gasping, I turned to see the wavering image of the woman who now slept before me standing in the corner. Her lips did not move, yet she spoke.

"You've seen Mim. She's come for me, but I'm not ready to go."

"I, um," pausing to gather my wits, I realized she must be referring to the child I had seen in the swing outside, "I guess I have seen her, yes. She was swinging in the yard."

"Yes, she keeps coming around, but I'm not ready," the pale image flickered like the flame of a candle.

"Can I help?"

"There," the ghostly-woman pointed to the mantle above the fireplace where an array of stone jars and wooden boxes stood perfectly in line. "I need that elixir, the one in the second jar."

"Abe told me you were a healer," I replied, feeling anxious that the gentlemen might return to the cottage at any moment to find me talking to myself. I stood quietly and tiptoed to the mantle where I picked up the jar second in line from the left. "This one?"

"Yes," came the response, though the image had vanished. The cottage was empty but for me and Rachel Montague.

Chapter 18

The scent of bitter herbs and decay wafted from the stone bottle the moment I removed the cork. I could not identify all the herbs, though I was sure I smelled nettle and possibly burdock. As I stood there breathing in the fragrance, I became aware of a presence near my back. Cold air coiled around me as the flickering image reappeared.

"For heaven's sake, child," it admonished, "don't just stand there!"

"But," I hesitated, not sure how to begin, "I don't know…"

"Just put six drops of the tincture in a cup of water," the entity directed, clearly short on patience. "Put your hand beneath my neck, tip my head back, and slowly pour the fluid into my mouth. Don't pour too fast or I might choke."

"Six drops?" I blinked at the stone jar in my hand wondering hopelessly how I could get exactly that amount into a cup of water.

"On the mantle," came the sigh. "There's a jar of hollow reeds. Put one in the tincture and put your fingertip over the open end as you withdraw it from the fluid. Gently move your fingertip to release exactly six drops into a cup of water."

"Oh," I exclaimed, suddenly recalling the technique I had learned from Cor and Deacon as well, "of course! Yes, of course."

"Now be quick, girl. My time is short!"

A stone crock stood at the end of the table in the center of the room, and from it I ladled water into one of the cups stacked beside it. Taking a hollow reed from the jar on the mantle, I withdrew tincture from the stone bottle and carefully dispensed six drops into the cup. As quickly as I could, I slipped my right hand beneath the sleeping woman's neck, tilted her head back gently, and slowly poured the contents of the cup into her slightly open mouth. She did not cough, nor did I see her swallow, so I laid her head back onto the pillow and withdrew my hand. I sat down in the rocker, watching and waiting.

Rachel Montague's eyes fluttered open as she turned her head slightly to look at me.

"Please," she whispered in a raspy voice, "get Abe for me."

"Oh," I leapt to my feet, "of course. I'll get him!"

Rushing to the door, I flung it open and called Mr. Montague's name as I stepped out into the sunlight.

"Abe! Mr. Montague! She's awake! Your wife is awake and she's asking for you!"

I did not dare wait to watch the man respond, though I did see him drop an armload of firewood as he looked up at me. Rushing back inside, I leaned over the pale woman beneath the covers.

"Can I do anything else for you, Ma'am?"

"Go," she shook her head, though it looked like it took tremendous effort, "just go. I need to speak to Abe. I waited for you and now you can go. My time is short. Hear that?"

At first, I was not sure what sound she was referring to, but I quickly realized I could once more hear the singsong moaning of the swing going back and forth in the yard.

"Mim's coming for me," the woman's pale gray eyes shimmered with tears, "and I'll soon go. You go now. Thank you."

"Rachel!" Abe's voice held a touch of relief as he hurried into the cottage. "Thank goodness, you're awake."

"I'll leave you two alone," I stammered as I backed away from the bed. "I have others to see, so I'd better be going. Farewell to you both."

Neither Abe nor Rachel responded to my comment, so rapt were they at being with one another again, so I made my way out of the cottage and headed for my mount.

"Lothar," I snapped my fingers, calling to the shepherd who lay panting in the yard beneath the white oak tree, "come on, boy! Time to go!"

At the sound of my voice, the puppy leapt to his paws to bound across the autumn-dry grass toward me, but as he neared his excitement disappeared and he halted. Cocking his head, he sniffed at me before settling back on his haunches. My hand, resting on the leather saddle, slipped to touch Aeon's shoulder and I could feel the mare tremble beneath my palm. She shook her head up and down, tossing her mane as she stamped the ground with her front hooves.

"What's going on?" I looked around, as if I was missing something my four-legged companions noticed, but I saw nothing. "Come on, Lothar, we need to go."

Reluctantly, the puppy rose to move toward me, though his hackles were raised.

"Come on," I repeated, as I scooped him up in my arms and placed him carefully on the saddle before swinging myself up behind him. Gathering Aeon's reins in my right hand, I turned my mount from the Montague's cottage and nudged her forward. Instinct insisted I keep my left hand on Lothar's back, as it was clear he was still uneasy.

The sun was near the midpoint in a crisp blue sky, I noticed, as we reached the road. Vesta perched in a tree nearby and when she saw us, she spread her wings to launch herself into the air, screeching as if impatient. I turned my horse to follow the raven's flight, enjoying the warmth of the sun on the top of my head. Suddenly, I felt a cold weight relax and slip from me, though I had been unaware of its presence before. A chill ran up and down my spine. I shuddered as the strange sensations left me. Lothar stilled beneath my hand, looking up at me with bright eyes, an expression of joy on his face.

'There you are at last! I thought I'd lost you.' Cor's familiar voice wrapped around me like a warm, comforting blanket.

'Lost me? Were you looking for me?'

'Indeed! I have news, but I see you've returned to the land of the living. I'm glad.'

'What do you mean, the land of the living? I didn't go anywhere, did I?'

'The chill you just shook off, that was the effect of dealing with the undead, Falcon. Distance and the sun have displaced the chill of the otherworld.'

'Rachel Montague's spirit was out of her body, so she was undead,' I reasoned in the silent language my beloved wizard and I shared, *'and with her help and her tincture, I helped her back into it?'*

'For a time, yes.'

'But she will soon leave her body for good?'

'That is up to her, lass. You did what you could, and what she asked of you.'

'She did say she'd been waiting for me. Is that possible?'

'It is indeed, Falcon. If she is blessed with far-seeing, she may have envisioned your arrival. She could have seen everything that just transpired long before it happened.'

'I don't think I like that, Cor!'

'What do you mean?'

'It makes me feel small, like I have no control, no say in anything.'

'I see Vesta found you,' He subtly changed the subject, I noticed without comment.

'She did, yes. And we're on our way, heading to Ayndor. So, what news do you have for me?'

'Declan has discovered torocs aren't the only magical beings moving about the land. There are several others being called to service, though we've yet to determine who or what power is directing them or why. The Undines are quite disturbed as are the Sylphs.'

'And Eban? Any insights from his Salamanders?'

'Only that they're hungry and excited. They sense some sort of destruction lies ahead and they're looking forward to the feast. All I can tell you right now is there does seem to be magic afoot, though we cannot say why or from whom it's coming. We are working on the matter.'

'That sounds ominous. What can I do?'

'Travel safe, lass. Do what you can as healer for the people of Esling and keep moving toward the completion of your task. Remember, I'm but a word away if you need me.'

'Thanks Cor,' I replied in my mind, adding, 'and thank the others for me too.'

'Stay safe, Falcon!' The wizard's voice faded as he withdrew from me. I felt strangely alone as I made my way down the hard-packed dirt road, despite the puppy beneath my hand, the mare I was riding, and the guiding raven wheeling in the sky overhead.

I had learned about the Elementals long ago when I was first rescued by Cornelius Welkin. Oh, my mother, Selene, had taught me some about them, but our time together had been cut short and there had been so many other things she felt I needed to learn, that my understanding of them was slight, at best. Cor and the other wizards had taught me the details of the Undines, Elementals of Water; Salamanders, Elementals of Fire; Sylphs, Elementals of Air; and Gnomes, Elementals of Earth. I knew that the torocs were related, albeit slightly, to the Gnomes and that their power came from the earth itself. I learned early on that the Salamanders were always hungry, always ready to devour what they could to release energy and transform it into something else. I had witnessed them consuming the thatch-roofed cottage I had been raised in when my father set fire to it as he lay dying. An Undine, shimmering in the shape of a liquid girl, had entered the camp Cor and I shared one night in our journey and she had taken a hair ribbon of mine, only to leave it for me to find the next morning. And I had watched the Sylphs dance and spin across the fields and down the roads as they kicked up dust and leaves in their wake. That they all were aware of something going on, some strangeness about to happen, gave me great concern, for Cor had explained that they are seldom interested in the goings-on of people, most of whom do not believe in their existence anyway.

"If someone, or something, is gathering forces," I reasoned aloud to myself, feeling not at all concerned that I might be overheard and taken for daft at doing so, "that must mean there's a battle of some sort ahead. Someone's raising and rallying torocs, and who knows what else? Time to focus on the road and get King Rowan's intended to him. There's work to be done!"

I traveled quickly, that first day away from Castle deBirch. My encounter with the Montagues weighed heavily on my mind, and the physical effects of being so near the undead left me troubled indeed. I'd had experiences with such things before, but mostly from a distance, and though I had been uneasy seeing them, I had been unaffected otherwise. The memory of the chill that had settled on and around me in Rachel Montague's cottage remained vivid and my thoughts went back there often. Though the road Vesta led me along went mostly south, I noticed that by the time the sun began to set that day, it was gently veering west as well. The sunset now warmed my face as I entered a sparse forest of evergreens to look for a place to camp. Not far into the woods, the pines on the right side of the road seemed to step back, creating a small natural clearing, a place perfect for my camp. I dismounted, released Lothar to the ground, and led Aeon to the far side of the clearing. So the mare could graze on what fall grasses and tender leaves she could find, I tethered her loosely. The ground was covered with pine needles and I would have to scrape a good-sized clear spot with the edge of my boot before gathering kindling for a fire. I had just started nudging the dried needles when an excited Lothar bounded at me, water spraying from his muzzle. He bounced off my thighs with wet paws. Clearly, the puppy had discovered water and was letting me know in the only way he knew how.

"Alright, alright," I laughed, giving up clearing the ground for a fire, "you lead the way. Aeon and I will follow."

Apparently, delighted that he had been given a task, Lothar ran two tight circles around the clearing before trotting off between the trees, moving north and away from the road. I gathered my mount's reins, pulled her away from a clump of grass she was eating, and led her behind me. Vesta screeched from somewhere overhead to let me know she was still with us. Ahead, the puppy ran sniffing the ground as he disappeared over the crest of a hill. I followed as quickly as I could pull Aeon, and when I reached the top of the hill, I saw what Lothar was so excited about. Below, a small pond lay still, shimmering darkness in the gathering gloom. Grasses and weeds grew along the banks of the water, while a few short olive trees stood just beyond its far edge.

"Good boy, Lothar," I called as I started down the hill, "good boy! That water looks great."

Once more excited, the shepherd bounced to the pond's edge and hurriedly lapped up a drink. He lifted his head to shake the water from his muzzle before dashing off to explore the area. Aeon, nostrils flaring at the scent of fresh water, pushed past me as she made her way to the pond. I knew my water skin was still filled so rather than join the horse at the water's edge, I moved up beside her to unfasten her saddle. Up the hill a short way, the ground leveled nicely, offering the perfect spot for me to make camp. The water was close, the rise of ground behind me offered protection from view, and I realized the spot Lothar had discovered was far superior to the meager clearing beside the road. Pine trees had given way to younger, wispier species, so the ground was free of needles, making my work of starting a fire much easier. Placing Aeon's saddle on the ground, I tossed the saddlebags down before unfurling my blankets to spread them out. I unfastened my cloak and dropped it on the blankets. Unbuckling the leather scabbard from around my waist, I laid it and ThornSting beside my makeshift bed as I stretched and yawned.

"Night's coming on quickly," I said to myself, "so I'd best get to it and get my fire started."

An abundance of sticks, dry grass, and small tree branches lay scattered on the ground and in no time, I had gathered the makings of a fire that would last through the night. As I worked, I could hear Lothar running and jumping in the woods surrounding the place. When Aeon, apparently having drank her fill of water, ambled up the hill to where I stood building a pile of kindling, I dropped what I had in my hands, brushed my palms off on my breeches, and gathered her reins. I tied the mare loosely to a small tree that I suspected was an ash before returning to light the campfire. Striking two flint stones together, I shot a spark into the tinder and began feeding the growing flames bigger pieces of wood.

Sitting cross-legged on the ground, I drew the Earth Star, Scorch, from my pack, unwrapped it, and placed it near the fire. I removed the wrapped bundles of food from the cloth bag I had received from King Rowan. There was, I discovered, ham, beef, and something I could only guess was some type of fish, because whatever it was, I had not seen or smelled it before. Soft bread and sweet wafers were wrapped in separate cloths, and beneath them were apples, oranges, and berries. There was a tremendous amount of food in the bag, I realized, and if I rationed it and what I had brought with me, it would be more than enough to get me to Ayndor, even sharing with Lothar.

By the time I had eaten, drank some peppermint tea, and washed my hands and face at the pond's edge, my four-legged furball friend had returned from his exploring. He helped himself to a drink before making his way up the slope to where I was sitting on my blankets. Settling beside me politely, he happily accepted scraps of meat and crusts of bread. He even enjoyed a piece of apple before yawning hugely, circling a spot on the ground beside me, and curling up to go to sleep. Aeon stood quietly in the distance, saddle blanket still draped across her back, shifting her weight from one hoof to another in an attempt to get comfortable. Overhead, clouds began moving in, the stars disappearing from the night sky. After wrapping the freshly charged Earth Star and returning it to my saddle bag, I moved ThornSting aside to lie down, pulled the covers up, and rolled onto one hip. Resting my head on my left hand atop the broad saddle seat, I drew up my knees and watched the fire merrily burning. Right hand resting reassuringly on Lothar's warm back, I released a heavy sigh as my eyes gently closed. Weary from the road and comfortable beneath the blankets, heat from the fire caressing my face, I slipped easily off to sleep.

A portal hovered above the pond. Night still claimed the sky, but the shimmering doorway emitted its own light. Walking around the pond, mesmerized by the image above the water, I realized I had no recollection of getting up, but I could not look away. From every spot at the water's edge, the portal faced me. There was no front or back, no sides, only the shimmering circle no matter where I stood.

A voice rang out around me, *'Come Falcon, join me. There is much you must know!'*

My warlock mentor had instructed me on the use of portals, and I had even done so a few times with moderate success. Mala and Mara, separate and in human form, had stood beside me before a portal opening onto the circumstances of my birth, holding me as I wept when the Goddess denied my mother's plea to save my life. They had explained all that had transpired as I entered this world, how the God had saved me, and how I came to be a solar witch. Absently, I touched the amber stone hanging from a leather cord around my neck as I stared at the beckoning portal.

'Come Falcon, now!' Insisted the voice from within the shimmering, floating circle.

The voice of reason, somewhere deep in my mind, piped up with some urgency, *'Is that the warlock's voice? Would he say that?'* But I had no time to stop for such considerations.

Glancing back at my camp, I noticed Lothar sleeping, curled up in a ball, near the still brightly burning fire, my blankets piled at his back. It crossed my mind that it was odd he had not stirred when I rose to investigate what I was seeing, but the thought quickly fled as I turned my attention back to the portal. I straightened my shoulders, took a deep breath, and stepped out over the water's edge. Instantly the energy of the portal drew me in. I was sliding along a smooth cylinder of silver, the light around me emitting a soughing vibration as I moved. My past experiences with portals had taught me that each was unique, each had its own properties, and their energies could be experienced differently each time they were used, if one were obliged to use the same one more than once. I had traveled through a portal that appeared as fragile as wasp nest paper while another was nothing but a swirling vortex of wind. Abra had tried to explain how it was they appeared and how they could have their own will and purpose, though I had a hard time accepting that as truth. This portal shone as solid as steel, was smooth and bright, and I moved through it quickly and without incident.

"There you are," wavered a voice as a hand appeared before me.

Grasping the offered hand firmly, I was able to stop my forward motion with its help, though I could not see Abra, only his hand. There was movement all around me, I found, but it was not the wind. I was surrounded by water, but I was not in water, nor was I wet. Ripples and rivulets swirled by, yet I was not touched. Finias Marin appeared beside me, but when I reached out to touch him, his image shimmered and shattered before coalescing again. The Wizard of the Element of Water smiled crookedly at me.

"Where am I?" I gasped, "And why am I here?"

"You must see this," my invisible companion replied. "The Elementals insisted. In fact, it's at their request you were drawn here. Look, Falcon." With that, my hand was tugged, directing my attention to what appeared to be a whirlpool, though as I watched the circling fluid seemed to clear.

"Another portal," I gaped, having never even considered the possibility that one might appear under water.

"Yes," the voice murmured.

Within the newly formed portal, a body plunged into water. Pale night gown clinging to its torso, twining between small legs, the child's body rolled in the deep. Dark hair streamed out as the little boy's head sank beneath the surface. His eyes were wide in shock and terror. Lips stretched back in a silent scream, he panicked, taking in huge gulps of water as he drowned.

Struggles subsiding, the young boy succumbed to the water, his lifeless form rolling gently in the waves.

"What am I…" whispering to Abra, I squeezed the hand I held as the horror of what I had just witnessed sank in.

"Shhh…" came the response. "Watch!"

Shaking off the horror and sadness, I turned my attention once more to the portal, where again, a small body broke the surface of the water. Cream colored shift turning dark as it absorbed moisture, the fabric swirled around a little girl's middle. Her stockings, peachy pink, were gathered at her ankles above the black leather slippers on her small feet. Long blond hair turned dead brown in the dark water, swirling around her head and obscuring her face. Whether she had been asleep or already dead when she hit the water, I could not tell, but she gave no resistance to the deep. Her body stilled as it floated away. The spectral being beside me squeezed my hand as if imparting some reassurance.

"Wait," I growled, "I can't see any more of this! This is madness! It's obscene! Why am I being shown this?"

"Come, there's more," came the response. I was suddenly propelled forward by a force more powerful than I had ever felt before.

Chapter 19

To my relief, I was drawn away from the watery depths to the edge of a sheer cliff. Sylphs flowed around me, invisible yet noticeable. Their soft singing and gentle touch as they moved by assured me of their presence. I felt reassuring hands on my shoulders, but when I turned to address my companion there was no one there. The sky was bright blue, devoid of clouds, and the sun beat down on the arid land below. I was just beginning to enjoy the scenery when my hand was squeezed sharply as my unseen guide demanded my attention. As I watched, a pair of little boys, dressed in dark breeches, light shirts, and dark vests, chased one another, screaming and crying. Tears streaked down both little faces, their mouths were wet with slobber. The growing sense of dread hit me just as the first boy leapt off the edge of the cliff, the second screamed as he followed. The ground trembled beneath my feet as the song of the Sylphs changed to one of sorrow and despair. Once more, hands squeezed my shoulders before the sensation disappeared. I could only hope it had been my beloved Cor behind me.

"Um," I shook my head, trying to clear my mind of what I had just witnessed, "I don't like this. I'm done with this. I can't take any more. Please, take me back."

"Soon, Falcon," is all that was said.

Suddenly I was surrounded by a wall of guttering flames. Heat from the fire buffeted me from all sides. Though I could smell the smoke from the wood feeding the flames, I did not burn. Eban Kendall, his red hair and beard crackling like flames, appeared in the flickering light, his image wavering in the heat. I stood there, holding hands with Abra, my invisible escort, witnessing the immolation as children walked into the fire. Some screamed and writhed in their torment as the flames licked and cracked their flesh. Others simply lay sobbing and moaning until the smoke choked the life from their bodies. Eban turned to look at me as his image was consumed by the fire.

"No more," my voice cracked as the tears welled in my eyes. "Please, no more."

"One more," the voice rasped. In an instant I was standing at the edge of an open maw in the earth. Piles of fresh dirt lay on either side of the chasm and already there were bodies piled at the bottom. Declan Terrene stood surrounded by gnomes, their shovels and picks at the ready. Clearly, those about to be buried in the earth were children, and some still stirred weakly. The earth began to vibrate and the piles of loose soil began to slip and slide down the edge of the makeshift grave as the gnomes began their work. Declan laughed as the earth swallowed the innocents, then he faded away.

"NO!" I screamed, yanking my hand away from the unseen grasp. I turned from the horror of all I had seen to run blindly back through the portal. I could hear the heavy tread as Abra raced after me, but I could not stop. Terror had clutched at my very soul and all I could do was flee.

"Falcon!" A strong arm shot out before me, catching me just beneath the ribs. The breath pushed out of me; I gasped as I was caught. My flight stopped.

Cold trickled into the corner of my eye as I sputtered awake. Gasping, I sat up quickly, heart racing and pulse pounding. I threw the snow-covered blankets off me, still trembling from the effects of the dream.

"It was a nightmare," I marveled at the revelation. "I've never been through a portal in a dream! The wizards would never, ever, take delight in children dying such horrible deaths. And was that Abra? I never saw him. The voice might have been his, but it might not. It was all a dream! It was all a nightmare!"

Lothar jumped up, shaking the light dusting of snow from his fur, and turned to me with a silly grin, tongue lolling out one side of his mouth. I could not help but return his smile and with his loving energy the memories of the night's horrors began to release their hold.

The snow had almost killed my fire, though what had come down was certainly light and was no longer falling. I decided it was worth the time and effort to stoke the flames. A cup of hot tea and a few minutes to melt the snow and warm my blankets before rolling them up to travel would be a wonderful way to begin the day, I decided as I gathered more branches and twigs. Shaking the snow from the tinder, I added a pile to the remaining embers as I knelt beside it to watch as the flames crackled and grew. Warming my hands before the fire, I took a deep breath and observed my surroundings. A soft mantle of white covered the grass, the weeds surrounding the pond, and some of the branches in the olive trees, but the rising sun would soon melt it all away. Birds sang in the distance while some creature deeper in the woods scampered in the dry leaves and snapped fallen twigs. Day was dawning.

"Time for a fresh start," I smiled at the sky, drawing strength and encouragement from my surroundings.

As I withdrew rations from my saddlebags, as well as my mug and loose tea, I considered contacting Cor about the nightmare I'd had. Part of me wanted very much to tell him everything I had seen and felt, to release the horrors to him, and to have him explain it all away to make me feel better, but I simply could not.

"Maybe later," I mused as I poured water into my mug and set it as close to the fire as I dared. "I think I need to think about this for a while. Maybe I can make sense of it all on my own."

Lothar, having paused in his sniffing the ground near the base of the nearest tree, looked at me curiously. It was clear from his expression that he did not know how to react, or if he should react at all.

"It's all right," I laughed, "I wasn't talking to you. You're a good boy. I was just talking to myself, because, well, I guess it's because it's better than not talking to anyone. My way of dealing with traveling alone, probably."

The puppy, relieved at the tone of my voice, bounced across my lap, dashed a tight circle, and came back panting. I tossed him a crust of bread, some dried meat, and a rind of cheese, which he happily consumed quickly. When he realized he had gotten all he was likely to get from me, he loped off into the surrounding woods for more, or simply to explore.

As my water warmed, I walked through the quickly melting snow to where Aeon stood grazing on clumps of grass. Raising her head, she nickered a greeting as I drew near.

"Let me shake the snow off," I spoke to the mare as I pulled the saddle blanket from her back and shook it briskly. "In fact, we have a few minutes yet, so I'll take this to the fire and let it dry for you. Shouldn't take long at all."

Soon it was time to pack up my gear and return to the road. I had my peppermint tea with a piece of cheese on bread, and munched on an apple as I gathered up my things. Brushing my tunic free of any dust, grass, or leaves, I buckled my scabbard around my waist and resheathed ThornSting. As I bent over to pick my cloak up from the ground, my amber pendant slipped from inside my shirt and smacked me sharply on the chin. As much as it smarted, I was happy to feel it still there around my neck as I donned my cloak against the morning chill. I saddled Aeon, after replacing her newly warmed saddle blanket, and slung my saddlebags over her rump. Finally, I lashed my bedroll to the back of the saddle, whistling for Lothar. As I waited for the puppy's return, I scattered what was left of the fire, pouring a bit of water on the ashes before stirring them with a stick. I had just gathered Aeon's reins to turn her around when my four-legged, furry companion appeared, panting, and wagging his tail.

"You'd better get yourself a drink at the pond," I nodded, "because we must go now. Hurry up!"

Without waiting for Lothar, I led the mare back up over the hill, through the pine forest, and to the road. Vesta flew by overhead, giving her raven call, before disappearing into the trees ahead.

"Let's go," I picked the puppy up the moment he reached me. "You can ride with me for a while and take a little rest. Not sure what you've been up to, but you do look tired."

One hand on the saddlehorn, one foot in the stirrup, I hoisted myself onto Aeon's back and settled Lothar before me. Bumping the mare's flanks with my heels, I clucked to her smartly as she responded with a lively step.

The day was warming nicely as I traveled southwest along the well-worn road, and by the time I reached the end of the forest I was releasing the cloak from around my shoulders. Vesta cleared the trees before Aeon and I did, so she wheeled in the blue morning sky, waiting for us to catch up. I met no other travelers on the road, though there were muddy places in the earthen tracts which showed both horses and wagons had passed recently. Before the sun had made it to the midpoint in the sky, I noticed a house sitting back off the road a bit, but as I drew nearer, I could see it was empty and had apparently been that way for some time. Weeds choked the land surrounding the structure, there were scrub trees poking through a hole in the roof, and the front door hung askew in its frame.

"No need to check there," I assured myself aloud. "Looks like we must move on to Stillmoor."

Deacon had explained to me, while I was still under his tutelage as well as training with the wizards, that most folks built their homes close together. Small settlements were scattered here and there across the land, with only a few hardy souls brave enough to live alone in the wilderness. From time to time a king's guard was awarded a large parcel of land, and this often attracted others willing to work for the privilege of enjoying that guard's protection. This, I knew, was the case with Stillmoor. Drake Stillmoor, a guard of some repute, had served King Stephen's father, and when Stephen claimed the throne upon his father's death, he had given Drake many hectares of land upon which to retire. The village of Stillmoor had grown up around its owner's modest castle and though Drake had long since departed this world, the place was still thriving. Castle deBirch, an actual castle built long ago by the current king's predecessors, had started out as just a home for the royal family, but overtime a mighty wall, tall, thick, and topped with parapets, had been built to surround and protect not only the deBirch family but many of their servants and other subjects. Like the village of Duhne, where my aunt and uncle had once lived, Castle deBirch was now fully enclosed, allowing entrance and exit only through a guarded main gate. I knew there were smaller passageways in and out through the wall for those residents whose work required such movement, but even those were closely watched and not easily accessible. Stillmoor, on the other hand, had no such protection; there was no wall surrounding its inhabitants' homes, no gate, and no guards. From what education I had received from my mentors, I knew the settlement lay ahead to the south and I hoped to reach the place before sundown.

Hills rose on the horizon as the day wore on. The road apparently led off to the north, but Vesta, my fine feathered leader, flew away to the left of the road, banking for a turn before coming back toward me. She shrieked her raven call, again soaring away to the south. Clearly, she was letting me know it was time to leave the road, so I drew Aeon's reins to the left and let her jump across a narrow ditch to the open field beyond. I dismounted briefly to release Lothar to the ground, stretched, and climbed back up in the saddle. With the land ahead wide open and devoid of trees or brush, it was easy to keep my eye on Cor's raven while watching Lothar run around investigating one smell after another. Aeon made her way across the grass-choked ground, coming to a halt atop a slight ridge. Lothar had already raced down the incline and was headed toward the people working the field beyond. When I called to him, he slowed to look back at me, but continued toward the strangers. I nudged the mare to quicken her pace, lest I need to apologize if Lothar leapt or startled anyone, and called out a greeting when I deemed it likely they'd hear me. No one in the field ahead stopped or acknowledged my call. A man in baggy trousers and a tattered tunic worked the dusty ground with a long-handled hoe. His hair, brown streaked with gray, was a matted tangle and his shoulders were stooped. He didn't slow in his work, nor did he look up at me. A woman, presumably his wife, wearing an equally tattered dress of what once might have been blue, carried a basket on one hip, and she bent over to pick up something from the ground as she shuffled slowly forward. Her hair, long, brown, and wild, hung in twisted locks and had surely not seen a brush in a very long time. She shambled ahead, stopped to stoop, and straightened to shamble on. Three children, two boys and a girl, also worked the field, all of them dressed as pathetically as their parents. One of the boys, the older, I guessed, looked up at me briefly with something like hope in his eyes. Suddenly, he shot a frightened look toward his father before once more looking down at the ground.

"Hello!" I called out again as I drew near the workers. "I'm Falcon Rose. I'm a member of the Order of Healers." Straightening the sapphire sash at my waist so they could see the truth of my words, I waited for a response.

The family kept at their laboring as if they had not heard me at all. They continued to work the field, though there was obviously little left to be done with the overworked ground.

"I'm happy to help if there's anything you need," I carried on speaking as if someone was interested. "I have salves and ointments for wounds and burns. If you require elixirs or tinctures for anything I can make them for you. I have bandages and such if you have need of them or if you'd just like to have them on hand."

Finally, the man stopped scraping his hoe in the dirt, raised the handle to rest one hand on the top, and looked at me. His face, haggard and streaked with dirt and sweat, was devoid of emotion, his eyes were flat with disinterest. He blinked at me, simply saying, "No," before returning his attention to the hoe.

"Do you live somewhere around here?" I tried to engage any member of the family in conversation. "I don't see a house nearby, but surely you can't be too far from home."

No one responded. None of the family stopped what they were doing.

Lothar, who had initially trotted up to the children in hopes of getting a little attention, maybe having some play, had apparently sensed something wrong, and he had returned to where Aeon stood. Sitting back on his haunches, the puppy cocked his head curiously, as if trying to understand why no one wanted to play. I was beginning to feel the same way, I realized.

"There's no charge for my goods or services," I continued my plea, "as I'm just here to help in any way I can."

"No," once more the man stopped briefly, uttered the single-word response, and resumed his work.

"Um, all right," shaking my head, I sighed, "well, if you don't need anything, I guess that's fine. I have food and water, if you'd like something to eat and drink. You must be tired and thirsty doing such hard work."

Heaving a deep sigh, the man once more paused, hoe in mid-strike, and merely glared at me. He said nothing, but the expression on his face was clear. He wanted nothing from me, would not accept anything, nor would he allow me to give anything to his family.

"Can you tell me if I'm going in the right direction? I'm heading for Stillmoor."

The sound of the hoe biting into hard, dry ground, and the snap of clumps of plants being yanked from the soil was the only response I got. Aeon shifted her weight uneasily from one hoof to another, anxious to be moving on, so I turned her away from the field and the strange family working it. A pang of regret clutched my heart as I glanced back over my shoulder at the children trudging along the rows, but it was clear my help was not welcome. Lothar made one last attempt to make friends with the little girl, but she kept her head down and continued her work, paying no attention to the tail-wagging puppy.

"Come on, Lothar," I called out as I let Aeon move forward at her own pace, "let's go, boy!"

Ahead, Vesta appeared, arcing up over a rise, her black wings stretched wide as she sailed. When she flew toward me, coming unusually close, I realized she wanted to land on my arm. Shifting Aeon's reins to my left hand, I lifted my right arm at an angle as I called to the raven in the whistling sound Cor had taught me. Responding with a similar cry, the bird landed on my forearm, clutching both sleeve and flesh as she settled her weight. Black eyes shining, she turned her attention to me, looking at me closely as if imparting some wisdom. I looked back at the beautiful creature, noticing the details of her feathers, her beak, and the wisdom in her eyes. As if in acknowledgment, she closed her eyes, bobbing her head before releasing my arm to leap skyward. Puzzled by the incident, I rode on, shaking off my sleeve before relaxing my arm once more.

"That was strange," I murmured as I watched Vesta soar over the top of the rising hill ahead. Making a mental note to ask Cor what my feathered companion meant by the exchange, I clucked to Aeon and set off at a brisk trot. I knew exactly where on the horizon Vesta had disappeared and I didn't want to lose that spot before I got there. Lothar had apparently noticed the increased pace, as he dashed ahead of me excitedly.

The hill Vesta had flown over turned out to be farther away than it looked, but when I finally reached it, letting the mare dig her hooves in to climb the steep rise to reach the top, I understood what she'd been trying to convey to me. My breath caught in my throat at the sight I beheld. The hill upon which I stood was merely the first in a series of such rolling foothills and beyond, rising magnificently to touch the blue sky, rugged, jagged stone mountains dwarfed their smaller brothers. The foothills were covered in green-brown grass, but beyond them snow lay scattered here and there atop the mountains. My heart sank at the thought of crossing those mountains. I prayed fervently that Vesta would reappear and guide me away from their terrifying peaks.

'*Cor,*' I called out in my mind, '*Vesta has led me here to where the foothills give way to mountains. I can't cross those mountains!*"

'*Falcon, my dear,*' My beloved mentor responded, amusement in his tone, '*you'll not be crossing the mountains ahead. Vesta will lead you safely along them once you've cleared the foothills.*'

'*I'm beginning to regret this,*' I sighed, feeling suddenly that I had taken on a task greater than I could handle. '*There's such strangeness going on. Nightmares, dealing with the undead, trying to help a family apparently beyond help, and now this. Even the land's challenging me! Maybe I should have stayed at Castle deBirch and traveled with the king's guard after all.*'

'*Second-guessing yourself, lass? That's not like you.*'

'*Well, yes,*' I admitted with a shrug Cor could not see, '*I'm not feeling very much like me.*'

'*Falcon,*' came the comforting voice, '*take heart. You are not alone.*'

A warm weight touched my back, just between my shoulder blades, and I knew immediately it was the hand of the wizard. The sun was just beginning to go down to my right, and though its rays were warm on my right arm, there was no mistaking the sensation of Cor's strong, reassuring hand. Magic, I had learned by experience, appeared in many forms, some as complicated as a ritual that might take three days and nights to complete. But the purest, most powerful magic happened in an instant, though its effects lasted much longer than that.

'*Thank you, Cor. I guess I just needed to be reminded.*'

'*Ride until the sky grows dark and full of stars before you rest. Travel well, Falcon.*'

With that, the connection with the wizard was broken, though I realized, with a smile, that I was indeed heartened. I felt better than I had all day, since waking from the nightmare that had vexed my sleep. Before me the land opened to a vista of beauty I had never seen before. I sat there astride my father's magnificent black mare and allowed myself a few minutes to simply drink it all in.

Chapter 20

Though when I had first seen the rolling foothills before me, all I could think was how long it would take to travel beyond them, Vesta led me down the first rise into a series of valleys. The way curved around the base of the hills making my journey shorter and faster than I had imagined. Before dark, I had put several foothills behind me and made my camp near a small stream fed by a spring erupting from the side of a hill. I found the night was mild enough that no fire was needed, and the sound of the gurgling water lulled me easily to sleep after a light supper. Lothar curled up beside me, resting his head on my knees, while Aeon grazed on the abundant vegetation covering the valley floor.

To my surprise, I woke to a clear, quiet morning. I had slept well, without nightmares or even dreams. I knew it was Cor's magic that kept me sleeping safely overnight, and I sent him a silent, *'Thank you, Cor'* as I sat up. Dampness on my chin indicated I had either been drooling in my sleep or my furry companion had been trying to wake me with puppy kisses. As Lothar stood nearby, head cocked and tail unmoving, I realized he had been at my chin when a sound had distracted him. Clearly, whatever it was, he was still hearing it, though I heard nothing unusual.

"Hey, Lothar," I tried to get his attention to no avail. "What's wrong? What are you hearing?"

Several moments went by, but still the shepherd did not move. I strained to hear something, but could only catch the murmur of a gentle breeze and the gurgling of the nearby spring. As it was clear I would get no response from Lothar, I drew back my blankets and rose to start the day. I filled my water skin from the nearby spring, gathered Aeon's reins, and led her to the brook being fed by the trickling stream. As the horse drank, I returned to roll up my blankets and have a quick bite before setting off. Lothar finally shook himself, wagged his tail, and came to get a little attention as I ate a crust of bread. He helped himself to my cheese and a good part of a sweet biscuit, before dashing off to investigate some wonderful smell or sound.

Aeon saddled, my saddlebags securely across her rump and my provisions strapped to her saddle, I whistled for the puppy as I donned my cape and secured my blades. While waiting for Lothar's return, I became aware of a strange sensation, which at first, I could not discern clearly. A rumbling rose from somewhere, but I could not tell if I was hearing it or feeling it. So deep, so powerful, the vibration echoed around me, growing louder and nearer, it seemed.

"That sounds," I paused to consider just exactly what it did sound like, "as if giants are rolling boulders around on the ground!"

Looking around, I found there were no boulders in sight, certainly none big enough to cause such a sound. The land was smooth and grass-covered, the hills surrounding me gently sloped.

"Whatever it is, it must be far away," I assured myself. "And frankly, the further away the better. I don't like that sound at all!" Even as I spoke the words, I realized the profound truth in them. The rumbling sound was terrifying, the power it implied almost too much to imagine. Shuddering, I called once more for the puppy, and when he bounded to me, excited and panting, I picked him up in my arms.

"Let's get out of here," casting an uneasy glance around the place, I muttered as I swung myself up into the saddle.

Vesta appeared in the sky, circling, wheeling freely before banking left around a foothill ahead. I clucked to Aeon and hastened her pace as I settled Lothar on the saddle before me. The morning sun began to paint the foothills with a magical light, and the breeze stirred gently through the valley as we meandered around the base of the foothills. The brook, whose origins stirred deep in the earth and burst forth from the crevices of moss-covered stones, followed the same path I traveled, and as we went further west and south it grew wider, swifter, and likely deeper. What had begun as a gentle gurgle grew as the stream became a river, and soon the sound became a roar. The rolling hills on either side of the rushing water began to move back, as the powerful stream cut deeply into the earth. As I rounded the base of one of the few remaining foothills, I found it had been sheared off, the soil eroded and carried away over time. The water curled around the bottom of the cliff, leaving no path to follow. The far side of the river was distant and the swift moving current rendered the channel impassable. I drew Aeon to a halt to consider my options. I could go back far enough to where the river was narrow to cross to the other side, and hope that way would take me to where I needed to be. I could dismount and let the mare swim across the river while I held onto her saddlehorn with one hand and Lothar with the other, or…

Just as I was about to give into despair and consider myself a failure, the raven flew by me, banked left, and rose up the face of the cliff to disappear beyond its summit. As my gaze followed Vesta's flight, I noticed there was a path up the side of the cliff, narrow and a bit steep, but passable.

"Thank you!" I smiled at the sky and the now distant bird. "This doesn't look like an easy trail, I admit. But it's worth a try. Aeon, I'll get down and lead you. Lothar, you can walk with us if you behave yourself and don't go bouncing all over the place."

As I dismounted, I released the puppy before removing the water skin from my gear for a drink.

"I don't know how far away from the river this path will take us," patting the horse's neck, I admitted, "so you might want to get a drink before we start. Go ahead, girl. Get a drink. I'll have a bite and take a short rest before we go." Digging a good-sized apple from my bag of provisions, I bit into its juicy flesh as the mare mosied to the river's edge. Lothar wandered here and there, sniffing, and marking territory, before following the horse to the water. Both creatures stood side by side drinking, the mare pulling water in gently between her pursed lips while the puppy lapped and splattered it excitedly. When they were done, Lothar came trotting back to me while Aeon moved along the river bank munching on grass. I gathered her reins as I offered her my apple core. Lothar caught a bit of dried beef I tossed to him before we started up the trail.

To my surprise, and relief, the path was wider than it had appeared from below. There was room enough for me to walk beside the mare, near her neck and shoulder, and keep an eye on Lothar as he followed along behind us. As the day was growing warmer, I removed my cloak, rolled it up, and tucked it under my bedroll behind Aeon's saddle. We had been steadily moving along the climbing trail when Vesta flew by me at arm's length making me realize just how high up the cliff we were. I forced myself to keep my gaze on the distant vistas, as the mere thought of looking down made my stomach roll and lurch. As the trail narrowed, I moved nearer Aeon's neck and rearranged her reins in my hand. The puppy, I noticed, had grown more pensive and was carefully picking his way along the path in our wake.

As the trail curved left around the face of the cliff its incline grew steeper. When at last I was able to make out where the path reached the plateau ahead, and was breathing a sigh of relief, my right foot came down on the edge of the trail. Suddenly the rocks and dirt gave way. I pitched sideways, arms flailing, but the trail crumbled beneath my feet too suddenly. Aeon's reins slid out of my grasp as my body slammed into the shifting cliff face. Scrabbling for purchase, I tried to dig my fingers into the earth, to catch myself from sliding. I dug the toes of my boots into the loose rocks and dirt, hoping to find a solid ledge to stop myself, but there was nothing and I continued to slide. Panicking, I froze, pressing my body against the sheer cliff. The sliding stopped. I had no ledge to hold onto with my hands, nor was there anything solid beneath my feet, but at least I was no longer moving. Pulse racing, heart throbbing, ears roaring, I could not think. I dared not move. My thoughts were rushing at one another making a rational plan impossible to grasp.

"Calm down, Falcon," I whispered to myself. "Calm down and think. There's got to be a way out of this."

Loose pebbles showered down the cliff along the left side of my body. When I dared to look up to find the cause, I saw Lothar stretching out toward my left hand, his haunches still firmly on the trail.

"Lothar," I continued to whisper, not daring to raise my voice, "I appreciate the thought, buddy, but you're not strong enough to pull me back up to the trail. And if I go down, I don't want to take you with me. Please, get back. I'm all right, please, go!"

Even as I finished my plea, the beast opened his jaws and nabbed the sleeve of my tunic. He did not tug, as I feared he might, but he held the fabric firmly in his mouth. He was determined, it seemed, not to let me go.

"Aeon," I raised my voice just enough that the mare might hear me. "Aeon, can you lower your head and drop me your reins?" I knew even as I said it that my idea was ridiculous. As intelligent as the horse was, she was not going to understand and follow directions.

"Oh well," I sighed bitterly, "I guess this would be an excellent time for a miracle!"

Clinging to the side of the cliff, hot tears stinging my eyes, with the weight of gravity pulling me inevitably down, I sobbed. Had I not been so judgmental, had I not been so prideful and hard-headed, I realized, I would not be in this situation. I could have easily traveled with the king's guards and would not have ended up alone and about to meet such a terrifying demise.

'Falcon,' Declan's voice swam to me through my fear, *'harness the earth's power. Meld it with the air's force and bend it to your will. You can do this. You've learned this well. It's no miracle, dear, it's magic, and it's your power.'*

'Falcon, child,' Cor's voice chimed in, *'hear us. Wield our elemental energy. Hold to the earth and let the air lift you. Lothar will help. You can do this!'*

If anyone else in the whole world would have offered the suggestion the wizards had, I would have thought them daft, but I loved them both and I knew they were right. Declan, the Elemental Wizard of Earth, had taught me the strength, solidity, and movement of the earth's energy. Cor, Elemental Wizard of Air, had instructed me on stirring up the wind and using it to my will. I knew they were right, but clearing my mind, letting go of the fear and panic that clutched at me, would not be easy. Still, I knew I had to try, so I looked up into the bright, intelligent eyes of the shepherd, who still had my sleeve in his mouth.

"You're not going to let me give up, are you?"

Lothar merely looked at me.

"Just," I sighed, "give me a minute here. Let me focus."

Closing my eyes tightly, I drew in a deep, calming, breath. I tried to focus, tried to imagine how to manipulate energy to get myself out of peril, but my mind went blank. Feeling the moments rushing by and the deep gorge beneath my feet pulling at me, I struggled. I wanted nothing more than for it all to be over, for me to be past the pain and terror of the death that awaited me below or for me to be safely and securely back on the trail above, but I felt powerless to accomplish either. I was frozen!

"Earth," I whispered desperately, "if you'll just be solid enough, stop crumbling and falling, if you'll just be strong for me, I think I can maybe crawl back up."

There was, of course, no response from the ground beneath me, but there was no movement either, so I took that as an affirmation.

"Air," I continued, "if you'll just work with me, help me to stay safe against the ground and not let me fall, I think I can make my way to safety."

No answer came from the air, but a gentle, warm breeze touched my exposed cheek and dried a streak of tear there. Hesitantly, I moved the fingers of my right hand, just a little bit higher up the face of the cliff, and found slight purchase there. A force, unknown but strangely comforting, settled over the back of my body causing my panic to disappear. I realized, as I dug the toe of my right boot into the ground and rose ever so slightly, that I was going to survive. Excitement threatened to undo me momentarily when I reached up with my left hand, eager to be closer to the trail, and touched only a mound of loose dirt. I waved my hand a bit, regaining my balance, and stretched again. When my hand touched the edge of an exposed rock, I exerted the last bit of energy I had to stretch up to catch it, but I managed. Lying there, pressed as firmly as I could be against the near-vertical cliff wall, I held onto the handholds I had found as my left foot sought a stable spot. Ever so slowly, I inched my way back up the cliff, Lothar refusing to release my sleeve. When at last my hands touched the newly-broken edge of the trail, I hung briefly, sighing, and sobbing in relief. Lothar growled deep in his throat as he edged backwards.

"I get it, I get it," desperately trying to refrain from giggling, I assured the animal. "I get your message. I'm coming. Just let me get one leg up and I'll be there!"

Finally, I managed to get my right knee up on the edge of the trail, and forced my weight up to roll my body onto the level ground. I lay on my back, straightening ThornSting's scabbard on my hip, laughing and crying at the same time. Lothar, having at last released my sleeve, licked my face, wagging his tail wildly. Though it felt like I had been clutching the side of that cliff for ages, the whole incident probably only took a few moments, but I knew it was something I would never forget. Looking up into the blue sky, watching a fluffy white cloud float by, it was impossible to think that anything in the world could go wrong, but it certainly almost had. I shook my head, feeling the enormity of that realization.

"Cor," I said aloud as well as silently in my mind, "I could have just died!"

'But you did not, Falcon. You are safe.'

"I think I'm going to be sick," I moaned, head spinning and stomach lurching.

'Lie still and take a few deep breaths. The sensation will pass. When you feel up to it, get up and have a drink of water. That will help settle your stomach,' the kindly wizard offered before his voice in my head went silent.

Lothar sat beside me, one paw on my upper arm, until my pulse returned to normal and my breathing calmed. At last, I sat up, petting his fuzzy soft ears before pulling him into my arms for a hug.

"Thank you, sweetie. I couldn't have done it without you. You've earned something extra come time for food."

The puppy squirmed and wriggled in my embrace until I released him. Struggling to my feet, I brushed the dirt and pebble flakes from my clothes as I rearranged my sapphire sash and the leather scabbard belt around my waist. I wiped the tears from my cheeks with my sleeves and touched the amber pendant around my neck to reassure myself it was still there. Aeon flicked her tail and shook her head, snorting impatiently as she stood on the trail just beyond where I had gone down.

"I agree," I patted the black mare's neck as I made my way past her to gather her reins once more, "let's get off this trail, and now!"

Lothar scampered past us to take the lead. I walked beside Aeon, holding onto her bridle until we reached the end of the trail at the summit. Pausing briefly, I followed Cor's instructions and drank a few sips of water before returning the leather water skin to the mare's saddle. I was wiping the excess water from the corner of my mouth when I realized I was no longer alone. With a start, I turned to see Abra, stepping out of a portal.

"Abra!" I gaped, "What are you doing here? And where were you a few minutes ago when I needed your help?"

"You needed me?" Puzzled, he hesitated before taking a few steps closer, "That is odd. My timing is usually impeccable!"

"I slid down the side of the cliff!" Exasperated, I gestured at the trail behind me. It was all I could do to keep from raising my voice, "I nearly died!"

"That explains why I had such a hard time finding you," he nodded. "One doesn't expect to find a warlock clinging to the side of a cliff like a fly on a wall!"

"Why were you looking for me? For that matter, why didn't you come see me off when I left Castle deBirch? I expected to see you before I left."

"Yes, Falcon, I am sorry about that. I had hoped to see you to say farewell, but I got held up elsewhere and could not get away. But it seems you've done well so far."

"I wouldn't say that," I huffed. "I almost died! Did you not hear me? I nearly fell off the cliff into the raging river below! I wouldn't call that doing well."

"Falcon, Falcon," the warlock shook his head with a wry smile, "had you truly been in peril I'd have been there. Though you may have believed yourself in danger, you never were. You were merely being tested!"

Clearly my emotions had not settled because Abra's words made my blood boil. The thought that my terrifying experience was nothing but a test infuriated me. Just as I was about to unleash a torrent of angry words, Lothar appeared from behind a mass of bushes and when he saw Abra he excitedly bounded at him. The warlock, in response, laughed as he bent to pick up the exuberant animal.

"It's good to see you too, Lothar," he smiled as he scratched the shepherd's ears, "but if you'll excuse me. I need to have a word with your mistress here." With that, he released the puppy to the ground, adjusting the hem of his tan tunic as he straightened. His hair, normally wavy and loose, was gathered at the nape of his neck and his long beard was braided and adorned with beads of bone and wood. He wore brown boots and trousers, while the cape on his back was black with fur on the shoulders. Despite my angst, I had to admit, if only to myself, that I was more than happy to see him. Though I did not mind traveling alone, or in the company of animals, the incident on the cliff made me realize there was some safety in traveling with others. I was happy to no longer be alone.

"Why have you come?" Blurting out my question as I realized there was something ominous in his finding me.

"Your assistance is needed, Falcon," he spread his hands and shrugged, "and time is of the essence."

"Is that why you used a portal?"

"It is," he replied soberly. "Please tether your mount. The horse and Lothar will stay here."

"But," I started to protest as I picked up Aeon's reins to lead her away, just as everything suddenly shifted. It was no longer my mare before me, it was a man and he stood very close. His upper body, shirtless and solid, was warm beneath my left hand. I could feel his breath on my cheek and smell his skin and hair. His lips parted as I looked up to find his eyes.

In an instant, the vision was gone. Shaking myself to clear my head of the image, I turned to see Abra standing exactly where he had been when he picked Lothar up for a brief snuggle. He seemed oblivious to what I had just experienced so I struggled to hide my emotions.

"Falcon," he looked at me curiously, "are you well? You've suddenly gone pale as a wraith!"

"I'm," waving his concern away with one hand, "I'm just, I'm fine. Probably just another silly effect of my harrowing ordeal. I mean, my dangerous-not-at-all-dangerous experience. I'm still not real clear about that, by the by."

"Trust me," Abra extended his hand as he approached, "you were in no real danger. But we can discuss that further at another time. We must go. The portal awaits even now."

Tethering Aeon's reins loosely to a few branches of a bush, I patted her neck as I directed Lothar to stay put. Hesitantly I took the warlock's offered hand. A charge of energy sparked as my skin touched his, and I felt myself blush as I looked up into his eyes. I could not speak for fear of falling apart and confessing what I had just seen, so I lowered my eyes and let him lead me to the portal's edge. Realizing that I was assuming the vision I had just had was of Abra, and that I had not actually seen the face of the man in it, I took a steadying breath.

"Come, Falcon," he said firmly as he stepped into the shimmering portal. "Follow me!"

'Let this be a dream,' I silently pleaded as I stepped into the portal behind the warlock. *'Please just let this all be a dream!'*

Chapter 21

I knew well that every portal was unique, and often I was surprised by how varied they seemed, but this portal was simply…short! Rather than the tunnel-like energy manifestations I had previously used, this one was almost non-existent. Abra and I simply stepped from one location to another, though we had clearly moved from day time to the night. Insects buzzed and chirruped around us, a gentle breeze stirred the leaves in the trees nearby, and the clear sky overhead glittered with stars. I was about to ask my companion where we were when a vile scent assaulted my nostrils. Dropping his hand, I clapped both my hands over my nose and mouth, struggling to keep the fetid stench from turning my stomach.

"What is that smell?" I spoke as clearly as possible beneath my hands, "Where are we and why are we here?"

"The question shouldn't just be where are we," Abra replied with smile that shifted into a grimace, "but when are we." Though clearly affected by the putrid smell around us, he was somehow able to keep from covering his nose and mouth.

"Fine," coughing, I moved my hands from my face to bury my nose in the sleeve of my shirt, "when are we?"

"We've stepped back in time but a short way. We are now in what would be to us last night, or the wee hours of this morning."

"And the stench?"

"Torocs," Abra said simply. "And they are why we're here. Come!"

In his usual subtle way, my companion took my hand to pull me along a stand of trees to our left. In the darkness, I could not tell if we were on the edge of a forest or just near a random copse, but since the warlock hunkered down as he ran stealthily, I followed suit. As we neared a deadfall, thick and heavy with downed trees, the awful smell became stronger. The light from a nearby fire threw flickering shadows around us. Abra came to a halt, put one finger before his pursed lips, and drew me in close.

"The torocs have captured King Rowans guards," he whispered. "I only hope we've arrived in time to save them. Torocs seldom hold onto their prey very long."

"Their prey?"

"Yes, of course. The guards. Torocs find humans especially tasty."

I had heard tales of torocs as a child, of course, but I had always believed they were just stories and I never, ever, expected to encounter them in my life, let alone a whole company of them and more than once. That the tales of my youth might be true, that they might eat humans, rip them apart with their powerful fangs and jaws, and devour them, truly startled me.

"What are we going to do?"

"We're going to rescue them, Falcon." Abra looked at me incredulously, "Why else would we be here?"

"But how?"

"These loathsome creatures are notoriously ignorant. They lack the ability to think or reason. Mostly nocturnal, they avoid daylight and especially the direct light of the sun."

"How does that help us?"

"Look, Falcon," he pointed into the woods where a small clearing glowed brightly in the light of a fire. "See how the captives are held? Torocs have only the most rudimentary knowledge of restraints. They don't make rope, though they do steal the stuff and use it if they can find it. Otherwise, and in this case, they use vines to bind their prey. The guards are only barely restrained, but they're beaten enough to know they can't escape on their own. That's where you and I come in."

"I still don't...," I started to complain before the warlock hushed me by clamping his hand suddenly over my mouth. With a start, I realized the captive men I was looking at were those I had seen in the brief vision I'd had in Lindenwood Forest. Though I could not see horses beyond them, as I had before, the soldiers were in the exact positions I had seen in the woods. They had not seen battle or traveled hard, as I had assumed when I had seen them camped so late in the day. They had been captives.

"The Solar Sword, Falcon," the warlock whispered into my ear, a touch of desperation in his voice. "You wield the magic of the sun. That sword will destroy most of them and if any are left, they'll go running as fast as their legs will carry them. Do you understand?"

Abra did not remove his hand from my mouth so I had little choice but to nod my head firmly. Finally, he lowered his hand, put one arm around my shoulders and directed my attention to the torocs' camp.

"See that fellow right there? That one nearest the fire is the leader. He's the biggest and presumably the most powerful," he explained. "That's the one you must deal with first. The others will probably be too startled to react to try to protect him, but if they do, I'll be behind you to handle them."

"Wait, me? You want me to do what? Rush in there with the Solar Sword and just run him through?"

"Don't think of a toroc as a he, Falcon. They're not human. They're made of earth, darkness, mold, vile substances, decay, and slime."

"But, but," I stammered, pointing at the massive, stooped and drooling monsters around the fire, "you want me to…"

"Don't worry," he squeezed my shoulders reassuringly, "we have intelligence and power on our side. They're still building the fire up, but once it's ready, they'll begin to feed. We must act quickly."

"Wait, what…," I started to object.

"You draw your Solar Sword, be ready to rush into the clearing and dispatch the leader. I'll start things off with this," not pausing for me to finish my thought, let alone my question, he explained as he produced an elegantly designed long bow from beneath his cloak. Shifting the weapon to his left hand, he withdrew three wickedly tipped short shafted arrows from a quiver hanging from his belt beneath his cape and as I rushed my thoughts to catch up with what he was saying, he nocked them smoothly. "Ready Falcon?"

Willing the Solar Sword into my left hand, as I had been trained, I held it firmly, watching as the sunburst-shaped hand guard burst into light.

"Whoa!" I gaped, "That's never happened before!"

"You've never used it in actual battle before, Falcon," Abra quipped. "Now!"

With that, he pulled back on the bow string, aimed into the clearing, and released the arrows. They arched and flew silently, their tips bursting into flame as they flew.

I wanted nothing more than to stand there and watch the beautiful projectiles as they soared through the air, lighting up the woods, but I knew I had no time for that. The king's guards were in peril and it was up to Abra and me to save them. As I drew ThornSting from its scabbard on my hip, its magically etched blade immediately began to glow green. One blade in my right hand, the Solar Sword firmly grasped in my left, I rushed past Abra, who even now was nocking more arrows on his bow, screaming what I hoped was a terrifying bellow. As I ran toward the leader, I noticed two of the torocs had already been killed by the warlock's arrows. Most of the remaining torocs were gaping around in wonder, trying to figure out what was going on. The leader of the group, tallest and strongest of the torocs, stood snarling, his red eyes glaring, seeking something or someone to destroy. I rushed at him, Solar Sword pointed directly at his chest, where I assumed his heart would be, but instead of the blade piercing his chest it shot a bolt of blinding light from its tip. The energy went right for the toroc and, with a sickening 'pop,' the monster's head exploded into a cloud of shimmering goo. I had no time to stop to appreciate the victory, as two more torocs stepped away from where the guards were tethered to confront me. The left-most monster went down quickly when the Solar Sword sang her song again, while Abra's arrow struck the creature on the right in the neck, forcing him to double over in pain. Of course, the wounded toroc yanked the arrow's razor-sharp tip from his neck leaving the gaping maw free to gush inky gore down his front. He staggered as he looked down to see himself bleeding, his red eyes rolled back in his head, and he toppled over backwards. Another toroc rushed at me from across the fire, but when the Solar Sword released its energy at him, he crumpled into the flames, screaming, and clawing at the air as he perished. Two other torocs, having witnessed the demise of their counterparts, no longer had the desire to protect their prey, so they turned and fled from the clearing.

When the moaning of the dying monsters ceased, an eerie quiet settled over the area. I looked around in amazement, as the scent of the creatures quickly dissipated. Abra made his way to my side, collecting his arrows as he did so.

"You did well, Falcon," he smiled, patting my back. "Now, let us release the guards and be on our way."

"Bet they'll be happy to see us!" I laughed as I tossed the Solar Sword into the air, watching it disappear before re-sheathing ThornSting.

"They'll not see us," Abra shook his head. "We traveled through the portal back in time. We were not in the clearing last night when this happened. We interrupted the flow of time to change the outcome, but we are not visible in this 'now' because we are not of this time."

"Wait, what? So, we rescue these men and they won't even know we were the ones who saved them? What will they think happened?"

"Heaven only knows, my dear," he offered with a wry smile. "They will struggle to grasp what befell them, probably make up stories they think will be the truth. One or two of them might suspect something extraordinary has happened, but they'll not know."

"So, we risk our lives and don't get so much as a 'Thank You'?"

"That's right," nodding, he tucked his long bow back beneath his cloak as he walked to where the king's guards stood and sat, some beaten and barely breathing, others glassy-eyed and dazed. With a touch of his hand, the warlock caused the bonds restraining the men to crumble and fall. All, including a black-eyed and bloody-jawed Captain Durand and a confused-looking Lieutenant De Groot, were suddenly free, gaping at their surroundings, and too stunned to move.

"Come, Falcon," Abra commanded yet again, "we must be away!"

Clasping my elbow, my companion led me through the trees and back to the forest's edge. It was all I could do to keep up with his long strides while I was trying to process everything that had happened. Part of me was furious at him for being so forceful, so in-control, so demanding, while another part admired him tremendously. Suddenly, my thoughts went back to the vision I'd had before we stepped through the portal and a rush of heat climbed up my throat and cheeks. Had it been Abra who held me close, grasping my arms? I had felt the warmth of his skin, smelled his breath and hair as he drew near. Had the lips I had seen parted in an approaching smile, or had the man been about to say something? Had it been a premonition? Was it just my imagination? Had I wanted it to happen so I had created it in my mind? I had to admit I did not really hate the idea, well, not like I would have expected, anyway. And though he had never shown any indication he might be interested in me romantically, I had entertained the fleeting notion there might be something between us, though romance was not something to which I felt naturally inclined. I did not, as a rule, like anyone getting too close to me, and it had taken quite some time to adjust to the hugs and friendly touches the wizards were wont to give me. I endured the embraces to eventually discover they were much more than that, they were an exchange of energy and what the wizards gave me was always more than they could ever take. Hugs were magical, I had come to realize, as were those pats on the back or head, but the vision simply left me confounded.

As the warlock hurried me along to where the portal awaited us, I vowed to consider the incidences of the day. From morning's first light to the darkness through which we rushed, it had been an adventure, and one that would require time to understand, I realized.

Stepping through the portal, I blinked, shielding my eyes with my hand as I adjusted to the sudden change from darkness to daylight. Abra had led the way back to where Aeon and Lothar waited, and now there was another horse, saddled and bearing full gear, standing beside my mare.

"Whisper!" I gasped at the massive dapple-gray charger, "How did he get here?"

"I summoned him, of course," the warlock replied as he tossed the side of his cloak back over his shoulder. "I do hope you won't mind if I ride along with you?"

"Well," I stammered, taken aback by his proposal, "I guess not. No, I mean, of course I don't mind. I'll be happy to have the company."

"I'll not tax your patience with my presence for long, my dear," he grinned. "I'll be escort until you gather your wits about you. You've certainly had a trying day."

"It looks like sundown isn't far off. Perhaps we could make our way down this mountain and make camp at the base. If Vesta shows that we're to continue following the river below, that is."

"Where is your fine feathered guide?"

"Vesta!" Lifting my gaze to the sky, I searched for the raven as I called again, "Vesta! Where are you?"

A dark spot appeared in the sky, growing bigger as it neared, and soon I could make out the shape of the raven, her wings spread and flapping gently. She screeched in acknowledgment as she soared around us, wheeling south, away from the river below.

"Looks like we are going south, yes?" Abra raised one eyebrow at me as he gathered Whisper's reins in his hands.

"Yes," with a nod I agreed. "Come Lothar, you can ride with me." I snapped my fingers at the puppy, who immediately turned away from sniffing at a hole in the ground and trotted to me. Picking him up, I hefted the dog into the crook of my right arm before hoisting myself up onto Aeon's saddle. Abra swung onto Whisper's back and looked at me.

"Would you like to take the lead, or shall I?"

"You can," I yawned, suddenly exhausted. "I'm happy to follow you."

Abra spurred Whisper in the flanks, moving the dapple-gray stallion ahead so Aeon and I could fall in behind them. Lothar snuggled easily into the gap between my legs and the saddlehorn, yawning as he looked around. My mount's reins rested loosely in my hand as I let the mare follow at her own pace. As we rode, I kept replaying the battle with the torocs in my mind. Abra was apparently correct as the monsters showed little intelligence, and though they were massive, with broad shoulders and well-muscled arms and legs, they really seemed to have posed little threat.

"Abra," I kicked my heels into Aeon's flanks, urging her to catch up with my companion, "I have a question!"

"The way seems a bit narrow for conversation," he replied. "Can your question wait until we make camp?"

"Yes," I sighed, "I suppose so."

"It appears this path winds gently down the mountain. We'll find a nice level spot once we get down."

"Of course," I mumbled, considering I would have that much more time to come up with additional questions. Once more my mind went back to the battle in the clearing and how the king's guards might have possibly been captured. These were well-trained soldiers with speed and intelligence on their side. How could they have fallen prey to the lumbering torocs? A clear vision of Captain Durand, sitting cross-legged on the ground, his hands bound, one eye blackened and his mouth bleeding, came into my mind's eye. Lieutenant De Groot stood leaning against the trunk of a tree, one hand bleeding, his eyes wild, clearly confused. Two other guards lay on the ground nearby, though I had not been able to tell if they were sleeping or dead. Beck and another guard whose name I could not recall sat back-to-back on the ground, knees up and heads down. Now that I had time to consider what I had seen, it did not make sense, and I could only hope that my warlock mentor had some explanation, some answer to the questions building in my mind.

"Whoa!"

Startled from my reverie, I realized that we had made our way down the gently curving trail and had reached the base of the mountain. Though the sky above was still blue, the sun had already slipped behind the hills and their shadows were affording us an early sunset. Abra had drawn his great horse to a halt and swung lithely from the saddle. I drew Aeon up before dismounting too, releasing an excited Lothar to the ground.

"This looks like a good place to make camp," Abra stretched, looking around. "There's a stand of trees just over there where we can likely gather some wood for a fire. Not that it shall be that cold overnight, but a fire makes a cozy camp and a wonderful accompaniment for tales and explanations."

"I agree," nodding, I dropped Aeon's reins to relieve her of her gear. "And I have many questions."

"I'll gather wood while you see to the horses," the warlock quipped as he turned, starting toward the trees.

Grumbling at having been directed, I set about removing Whisper's saddle, blanket, Abra's saddlebags and other gear, before tending to my own horse. The spot the warlock had chosen for our camp was level and mostly devoid of stones, but there were a few pebbles here and there, so I used the toe of my boot to scrape them away. Lothar, I noticed with a twinge of jealousy, had bounded off to follow Abra and I could see the puppy trying to take the sticks the warlock had gathered out of his hands. Apparently, the shepherd was determined to play a game with him, though that was not on Abra's agenda. The ensuing tussle was hilarious to watch.

"Here now," my companion huffed as he hurled a thin branch as far as he could, "go get the stick and let me get this job done, Lothar! Your mistress awaits us both!"

As Lothar raced off to find the projectile, Abra quickly gathered wood for the fire and made his way back to camp. I had placed our respective saddles on the ground, one on either side of the spot I cleared, and spread our blankets on the ground. As my companion stacked the kindling, topping it with bigger sticks, I opened the saddle bags and began removing what provisions we would require to eat.

"I sense you're about to burst if you don't ask your question soon," Abra looked up from his work and raised one eyebrow. "Am I correct?"

"Well, I don't know about bursting, but yes, I am anxious to ask you something."

"Ask, by all means!"

"You said the torocs are not very smart," I began, setting my question up carefully, "and that certainly seemed proven when we dealt with them."

"Yes?"

"Well, if they're that slow," hesitantly, I searched for the right words, "and if they're that mindless, how did they manage to capture the king's guards? Those soldiers are intelligent, they're fast, they're well-trained, and they're well-armed! How could they have been captured?"

"Indeed," the warlock stroked his beard thoughtfully. "That question had occurred to me as well."

"Have you an explanation?"

"The only plausible explanation is that they must have had help. I assume that whatever powerful entity roused them and sent them moving off across the land for whatever purpose must also be aiding them," he explained as he pulled his long robes around himself, crossed his legs, and sat down. Staring intently at the center of the pile of wood, the warlock's eyes flashed briefly before tendrils of smoke began to rise. I had seen him make fire in such a manner before, and though I understood the process and had even managed it myself a few times, I had yet to master the feat. Still, it was always a delight to witness such magic.

"So, how would they have helped the monsters capture the men?"

"If we knew that," he smiled up at me as the embers began to flame and grow, "we would have a clue as to who or what might be behind this, but alas, we do not."

"I see," I sighed as I pulled Scorch from my saddle bag and placed it on the ground beside the growing fire.

"Something else on your mind, Milady?"

"I feel bad," with a grimace, I admitted.

"Bad? How so?"

"After the battle with the torocs, I wanted Captain Durand and the other guards to see me, well, me and you, rescue them. I wanted them to know that we saved them. I wanted to revel in rubbing that in and when I learned they'd never know it was us, I was disappointed."

"Understandable," Abra nodded, "but keep in mind that your emotions are greatly heightened after battle. You think and feel things more intensely when you have emerged victorious. It's a natural reaction."

"Did you feel that way?" I grinned, hopeful.

"Alas, no. I am not human, my dear, so I do not have such human reactions and emotions. I am Aerienesse."

"But you told me that I'm Aerienesse and I have these feelings!"

"I said your spirit is Aerienesse, Falcon," he raised one finger, "but your body is human. You may not have the exact emotions and reactions of a human being but you do have some."

"Oh," murmuring, I considered his words. "So now that some time has passed since the battle, I'm seeing things differently."

"Yes, I would expect that to be the case."

"I don't want to gloat about us saving them anymore," I shrugged as I tossed him an apple. "I don't want them to ever know. Looking back on what happened, I can see how truly broken the men were, especially Captain Durand. He looked completely defeated."

"I'm sure that's how they all felt," Abra replied, catching the fruit handily.

"And I don't ever want to know what that felt like. I feel horrible for wanting to make them feel bad."

"I agree, my dear," he nodded, taking a huge bite from the apple. Wiping juices from his lips and beard with the back of his sleeve, he stared thoughtfully into the fire. "You and I shall speak of this matter with no one else."

Suddenly, an excited and panting Lothar bounded into camp, wagging his tail, sniffing me and my companion. I pulled a strip of jerky from my saddlebag, tossing it to the puppy who snatched it out of the air easily. He stretched out on the ground, put the dried meat between his front paws, and began chewing contentedly.

"How is it you came to know the guards were in trouble?" I asked, turning my attention back to the warlock.

"King Rowan asked me to check on your progress," answering while chewing, he nodded, "and the progress of his men. That's when I discovered they had been captured."

"So, what will you tell the king? Surely, you'll have to tell him the whole truth," I reasoned.

"I shall tell him the truth, of course. And the truth is that his men are traveling on their way as planned."

"You'd lie to the king?" I gaped.

"I would not lie, Falcon!" His expression suggested he had been insulted, but he continued, "But telling the king of his men's capture and subsequent release would serve no purpose. The truth is that they are now free, healing, and traveling as planned. You and I agreed that we'd speak to no one about the matter, did we not?"

"Yes," I nodded, almost grasping the warlock's reasoning, "you're right, we did. I guess I understand. So, you'll not tell the king of my near-brush with death on the face of the cliff either, right?"

"That is correct," he smiled as he tossed his apple core to where Whisper stood munching on a clump of grass. "So, let us finish our meal, enjoy the fire, and get some rest. The road awaits us come sunup!"

Though I wasn't entirely happy with the warlock's explanations or the way he seemed to think, I finished the apple I had been eating and tossed the core to Aeon as he had to Whisper.

Chapter 22

Whether it was due to my physical and emotional exhaustion or the presence of the warlock, I slept deeply through the night. When my eyelids did flutter open, the first thing I saw was the pile of puppy fur before me, as Lothar had curled himself up on the ground near my chest. I lay beneath my blanket, right hand under my head on Aeon's saddle, left hand resting comfortably on the sleeping puppy's back. The fire still burned brightly, with Abra sitting on the other side of it feeding fresh wood into the flames. With a sigh, I rolled over, sat up, and stretched my hands over my head.

"Good morning, Falcon," Abra greeted me brightly. "I've stoked the fire so we can have a nice meal before starting off, if that's agreeable."

"Of course," I yawned, "if you think there's time."

"There is indeed time," he nodded, "and later today we shall reach Stillmoor, where we will get a room at the inn to dine and sleep in comfort."

"We will?" Regarding my companion skeptically, I threw back my blankets as Lothar stood and shook himself from the end of his nose to the tip of his tail.

"We will. You and I shall reach Stillmoor," with a grin he added, "and we shall avail ourselves of the local cuisine and hospitality."

Though I had the sense that he was offering me some clues of which I was supposed to make sense, it was clear that he was withholding information as well. The mischief in his eyes was unmistakable. As I looked at my companion, I recalled the vision I had seen before we stepped through the portal. Once more, I wondered if it was Abra who had stood before me, who grasped my upper arms firmly and drew me close. Part of me hoped for that to be the case, I realized in a moment of abject clarity, while another part felt aghast at the mere notion. The warlock and I cared for one another, of course, and in at least one respect we were the same, as he assured me my spirit was Aerienesse. But the thought that there could be anything more than friendship, respect, and polite mutual affection between us seemed almost obscene. Still, had it been him in the vision, that would certainly change everything, I silently considered. Searching his countenance for some sign, some indication of secret understanding, I felt both relieved and disappointed. There was nothing in his expression, in his manner, to indicate deeper, more intimate feelings.

'Was it him?' The tiny voice in my mind inserted itself, *'You know how to tell! Project your thoughts, imagine what it would be like to be so near him, replay all the details as you do so, and test the results.'*

"The fire is ready, if you'd like to fill your mug with water for tea." Abra offered, pausing with an odd expression on his face, "Are you well, Falcon?"

"What?" Startled from my reverie, I smiled at the warlock as I silently promised myself to heed the wisdom of the tiny voice at another time.

"Still dealing with the effects of yesterday's excitement, are you?" Leaning over, he grabbed his saddlebags and began withdrawing pouches of food from one of them. Once he had laid out his fare, he filled a mug from his water skin, but rather than put the mug near the fire to heat, he placed it carefully on the ground near his knee as he looked up at me. "What say ye? Shall you and I practice our abilities to heat our own water?"

"Um," I nodded with a grin of anticipation, "of course! And yes, I'm probably just still a little overwhelmed from yesterday. But I'll be fine soon." Following the warlock's lead, I filled my mug with water and placed it on the ground before me. Lothar had wandered off and was lifting one hind leg to relieve himself on a nearby bush. "Just a minute," I snapped my fingers. Digging into my saddlebag again, I brought out a cloth-covered bundle, unwrapped several pieces of ham and tossed the one with the most rind on it to the puppy. He snatched it out of the air and immediately began chewing merrily. As I knew Abra and I would need uninterrupted time to focus and direct our power, I gave Lothar the rest of the ham, wiped my fingers on the now-empty cloth wrapping, and wadded it back into the saddlebag.

"Ready?" Abra looked at me.

"I am," I nodded succinctly. Breathing deeply, I began to focus on the water in my mug. I went through each of the steps I had learned from the wizards, visualizing and projecting, always focusing, focusing, focusing. My world narrowed to the size of the mug. Everything around me disappeared. There was no sound, no smell, no taste. I could feel no ground beneath me, nor air around me. There was only water. Time stood still. At length, a tiny bubble rose to the surface of the fluid to pop. A second one was quickly followed by a third. Steam erupted from the mug, curling gently into the air. More bubbles appeared as the water grew hotter and hotter. At last, I held out my hands to feel the heat rising off the vessel. With a smile I glanced up at my companion, who had lifted his mug and was gently blowing steam from the hot liquid within.

"Well done, Falcon," Abra nodded. "You've learned well."

"Thank you," I beamed. "I'm getting better at it with time and practice."

"So, will you have peppermint tea or something stronger?"

"Tea is fine," I replied with a shrug, "and a sweet biscuit, I think."

"Excellent," the warlock offered as he bit into a chunk of dried meat. "We shall enjoy a leisurely repast before loading our gear and traveling on."

Without response, I dropped a pouch of dried herbs into the hot water in my mug before drawing an orange from my pouch. Abra seemed focused on his own meal, so as I tore the rind from the fruit, I was able to observe him. As the tiny voice in my head had suggested, I imagined standing very close to him, his body almost touching mine, his strong, sinewy hands wrapped around my upper arms. With as much detail as I could recall, I replayed the vision in my mind while inserting Abra in place of the man I could not see. At first it felt fine, even seemed reasonable, but I noticed the disparity of height. The man in my vision was certainly taller than the warlock. The energy exuded from the vision man was different than what I felt when I was near Abra. It was a relief to realize, with certainty, that the vision I had experienced did not include my companion, yet it was also somewhat disappointing.

'At least you can look at him now without blushing!' The tiny voice in my head chirped joyfully.

Separating a section of orange, I bit into one end, letting the tart juice explode in my mouth. Chewing thoughtfully, I lifted the remaining fruit in offering to Abra. He looked up, a surprised expression on his face, accepting with a silent nod of thanks.

At last, the leisurely meal ended and we had our gear gathered and loaded onto our mounts. Lothar had run around investigating our surroundings after eating, and upon his return I offered him a quick bowl of water, which he lapped up happily. When we had doused the fire and made sure the embers were no longer in risk of reigniting, Abra swung himself onto Whisper's back. I gathered the puppy up in my arm to mount Aeon, taking her reins loosely in my hand.

"Follow my lead?" The warlock turned to me questioningly.

"Sure," I nodded, glancing up at the sky where the raven was even now gliding effortlessly. "You follow Vesta and I'll follow you!"

The day was mild, the air felt fresh and clean, and the sky was bright blue and cloudless. Lothar snoozed comfortably on the saddle before me, his muzzled tucked beneath the fabric of my cloak. ThornSting bounced gently against my thigh as Aeon walked briskly along the trail. I could feel her straining to catch up with Whisper, likely to overtake him but I firmly reined her in to keep her from doing so. Strangely, I found I was enjoying following the warlock. It was nice to be unconcerned with where I was going, which trail to take, what obstruction to avoid. And by being behind him, I realized, I was free to journey unobserved. I could pick my teeth, scratch my head, make funny faces at the world if I felt so inclined. Best of all, I was free to think without interruption. My mind wandered back to Corhaven as well as Deacon's place, recalling various lessons I had learned from the wizards, some fun, some not so much. I wondered about the felinetrix and if or when I might see either Mala or Mara on my journey. Of course, the dream of Emmeline Caulfield and her daughter Z remained vivid and I could not help but wonder still what it might have meant. Next came to mind the folks that I had met when traveling with the druid; Jack Adler, the Fultons, the Winterbournes, and Will Perry and his wife and son. They all made me realize how vast the world must be and how comfortable I had been seeing very little of it. Despite the battle with the torocs and almost sliding down the face of the cliff, I suddenly realized I was happy to be journeying and I was excited to find out what the future might hold.

The path Abra had been leading us on disappeared as the land before us spread out wide. The settlement of Stillmoor lay ahead, comfortably nestled between two gentle hillocks. There was no protective wall, no massive gates, no guards patrolling, but the land itself obviously offered some protection. A wide river meandered down through the valley, skirting the village along its southern edge, while stony foothills and rough terrain made entrance from the north risky. Nudging my horse, I rode abreast of Abra on Whisper and together we stood for a moment taking in the beauty of the scene.

"That's Stillmoor," I sighed. "It's lovely!"

"It is indeed," my companion agreed. "It's still some leagues ahead and the day is waning. Are you in need of food or a rest?"

"We got such a late start," I shrugged, "and I'm not all that hungry. Let's keep going at least until we reach the river ahead. We can water the horses and let Lothar have a drink while we stretch our legs."

"Excellent idea! I was hoping you would say that! Let us continue."

With a snap of the reins, the warlock eased his horse forward so I followed suit. Whisper quickly set off at a run, while I had to rein Aeon in to a gallop, to avoid losing my hold on Lothar. My mare might have wished the freedom to catch up or even pass the stallion, but I could sense that she was just happy to be burning off some energy so she easily settled into a comfortable rhythm. We reached the river in a short time, where we drew our steeds to a halt and dismounted. I released Lothar and all three of the animals moved to the river for a drink. Abra and I walked upstream where we both filled our water skins, washed our hands and faces, and drank our fill. Rising from my kneeling position on the river's bank, I stood, raised my hands over my head, and stretched my legs walking about. Lothar had lapped up his fill of cold water and was joyously racing around slobbering, first on the warlock then on me. As we had agreed neither of us was particularly hungry, so when Aeon stopped drinking, I gathered her reins and turned her away from the water. Abra picked up Whisper's reins and together we began walking toward the settlement ahead.

As we neared Stillmoor, I glanced up at the sky, judging it to be nearing when most folks would be eating, or at least preparing, their evening meal. The scent of cooking food did reach us as we approached the place, but it was scant at best. The village seemed very quiet, even from a distance, and a sense of unease settled on me. Lothar, apparently oblivious to anything but the scents and tastes of whatever was growing or lying on the ground, scampered about merrily as the warlock and I walked our horses along the road leading into the village proper.

"Should we ride in," I paused to ask my companion, "or walk in?"

"Ordinarily, I'd recommend we ride in, so as to allow us a view of the place and an idea of who is stirring, doing what and where," he replied, stroking his beard between his thumb and forefinger, "but under the circumstances we might as well walk. Stillmoor looks unusually quiet, does it not?"

"It does!" I agreed as I suddenly raised my hand, "Wait! Do you hear that? Someone's doing something. Is that an axe chopping wood I hear?"

Abra paused for a moment as he turned his eyes to me, "I believe that's exactly what it is, Falcon. At least there's someone alive and working in Stillmoor. Let's see if we can find the inn and have some food."

"Yes!" We picked up the pace as we entered the settlement. When I called to the puppy, he instantly stopped what he was doing to race at me. With a few words of encouragement and some scratching beneath his ears, Lothar fell into step between us, wagging his tail and sniffing the air.

We passed several homes, some made of stone, some wood and thatch, heading toward the source of the sound we were hearing. At some point the earthen road became cobblestone and the sound of Aeon's and Whisper's hooves echoed through the quiet streets. A weaver's shop stood off the street slightly, its sign proudly proclaiming itself, but the door was closed and no lights shone from within. I nodded at Abra who had already noticed the closed shop. Further along the street a green opened to our left where the village well stood silently unattended. A few sheep grazed on the grass, but there was no shepherd to be seen. Ahead, a building with large wooden doors flung open stood nestled between two smaller stone structures, the smell of wood smoke reached us just before the ringing of metal against metal assured us it was the blacksmith's place. The smell of warm earth and hay dust wafted from within, so we paused at the open doors to await the notice of the smith. Lothar, more excited to meet strangers and less patient, bounded away from us to run circles around the bare-chested, black aproned man with a hammer in one hand and a rod of metal in the other. Startled, the blacksmith paused in his hammer stroke and looked at the puppy as it circled him.

"Here now," he coughed, "who're you and where did you come from?"

"That's Lothar," I interjected as Abra and I stepped into the shade of the forge. "I'm Falcon and this is Abra."

With Aeon's reins in one hand, I straightened the sapphire sash around my waist with my other hand so he could see it. When the sash was properly visible, I extended my hand in greeting.

"I've no need of a healer," he raised one eyebrow, nodding pointedly at my hand before stepping back, "so you might just as well move along."

Surprised, and a bit crestfallen, I dropped my hand.

"Why is Stillmoor so quiet?" Abra pushed by me to confront the man. "Where is everyone? What's happening here?"

"Don't know," the man muttered, returning his attention to his work. Once again, he struck the metal rod he was working on with the hammer. The sharp retort rang out around us. Lothar startled, running back to stand beside me.

"Don't know," insisted the warlock, "or won't say?"

The blacksmith turned to look at the two of us, his hammer held in the air behind him. Shaking his head emphatically, he refused further comment as he slammed the hammer down.

"Come Falcon," my companion turned to me, "it's clear this man knows nothing. Let us make our way further into town where the more intelligent people must be."

The man at the forge harrumphed, but he did not respond further to Abra's obvious attempt to get a response or an argument. He merely refocused his attention on his work so we turned and walked out of the darkness back into the sun-washed street.

The light in Stillmoor was changed, tinged gray and chilled. The sun still hung in the sky, sidling west in its ever-moving journey, but it no longer offered warmth. Scents of food cooking, once slight but appealing, now seemed bitter, sour, and wholly unappetizing. A couple of dogs, their breed unrecognizable, wandered down the street, sniffing at this and that in a search for food. Though the pair were dusty and a bit scruffy looking, they appeared well-fed indicating their master must be somewhere in the village. As they drew near, they paused to look at us, specifically at Lothar, before continuing in their trek, suddenly disinterested in the strangers before them. Lothar wagged his tail a few times, but he did not stir to approach the dogs. He merely looked up at me with that silly puppy grin of his, and nudged my hand with his nose. In the distance, the axe continued its *whoosh, crack* as it bit into wood.

"Abra," I spoke in a hushed tone, without being entirely clear why, "do you feel that? Do you see what I'm seeing?"

"I do, Falcon," he responded in an equally quiet voice. "Let us move on. Perhaps the wielder of that axe we're hearing will be more helpful."

Without further discussion, we led the horses along the cobblestone streets, the puppy walking with us instead of scampering around as he usually did. I became aware of an uncomfortable sensation as the hairs on the back of my neck prickled to attention. Though Stillmoor appeared empty I knew quite well that we were being watched. Furtive glances from behind shuttered windows followed our progress as we passed small cottages and larger homes, as well as shops and storefronts. The door of the bakery was closed and locked, a sign hung askew from the doorknob announcing the business closed, but a curtain on one window stirred as we walked by so it was clear someone inside was watching. Shaking off the uneasy feeling, I took a deep breath and focused my attention ahead to where a young man in brown trousers and leather boots worked shirtless, swinging his axe. Again and again, he raised the blade, bringing it down with enough force to split the upturned logs with one blow. His chest shown glistening with perspiration, taught muscles rippling with each exertion. Though a pile of logs remained, he had already split and stacked a formidable amount of wood.

"What, ho there!" Abra called out to get the man's attention.

At the sound of the warlock's voice the lumberman raised his head to look at us, paused, and dropped his axe to the ground.

"Hello! What can I do for you?" Wiping his hands on his trousers, he leaned over to pick up his shirt, which he had draped over the end of a nearby sawhorse. As he slipped his arms into the sleeves of his tunic, he nodded at me, "You're a healer, are you? Here to save us all, are ye?"

"I am a healer, yes," I smiled in response. "Are you in need of saving?"

"Probably not your sort, I'm afraid," he quipped as he ducked his head into his shirt and pulled its length down over his chest. "But the place sure could use some healing."

"What's wrong here?" Abra interjected.

"'Tis the damn dreams," the man explained. "Well, they're really nightmares, I reckon."

"Nightmares?" I prodded gently.

"Started out with the children first. Poor little ones would wake screaming and crying, refusing to go back to sleep. It went on and on. Eventually the older children and even adults started being plagued by them, terrible, terrible ugly dreams."

"And now?" Peering around the town, I was once more startled by how quiet and empty it felt.

"Everyone stays inside," he shrugged. "Oh, I'm Robert Allen, by the way." In three long strides he reached the side of the road where we stood to extend his hand in greeting. Abra shook his hand before nodding toward me.

"I'm Abra, this is Falcon," my companion offered, "and we're sorry to hear of the trouble you're having here. You don't look overly tired, I must say. How is it you've avoided the effects of the dreams?"

"Didn't avoid them," Robert shook his head with a wry smile, "but a couple of days ago I was out in the forest cutting down some timber when a sudden rain came up. When I sought cover, I was fortunate enough to find a stone outcropping, a ledge of sorts, big enough for me to crawl in under, and I fell asleep waiting for the rain to stop. When I woke up, I realized that I'd slept without dreaming so I've been going back there to get some rest."

"A cave?"

"Not really big enough or deep enough to be a cave, but it affords me cover and I sleep without dreams."

"Have you told anyone else here in Stillmoor?"

"No," he sighed, "but I've thought about it. I just can't see how such a small place could help everyone. There's barely enough room for me."

"Interesting," I murmured, wondering how it was possible the stone could be protection from nightmares. Promising myself to ask Declan if he had an answer, I returned my attention to the lumberman. "Can you direct us to where we can get food and maybe a place to bed down for the night?"

"On down this road a way," he pointed. "It's a big place on the left. There are several hitching posts out front, and the doors should be open at this hour. So far, the Bartons have been able to keep functioning, to keep the place open, feeding travelers and offering lodging. Don't know how much longer they'll be able to do so, but their place is just down that way."

"Thank you for your help, Robert," Abra bowed slightly, "and good luck in your endeavors."

"Nice to meet you," the young man replied, "and nice to meet you as well, Falcon."

"Thank you," I managed to hold off a blush, "and farewell, Robert."

Pulling on Aeon's reins, I followed the warlock as he moved toward the inn down the road. Lothar trotted along beside me, unusually calm for the puppy.

As we moved into the shadows of taller buildings along the road, I became aware of movement above us. The sky overhead was still blue, but I could tell the sun was beginning to go down, and as it did what circled above Stillmoor became visible. Pale, thin, wraith-like forms swirled and bobbed in the air. Silent, but with what appeared to be mouths opened wide in rictus screams, the whisps moved as if driven by some unseen force. I shuddered as I watched the phantoms move, finally forcing myself to drop my gaze and focus on the road ahead. Soon the scent of baked bread and meat wafted to us so we picked up our pace.

As Robert had said, the doors to the inn were open and the tantalizing smell of food and drink greeted us as we tethered the horses to the posts before the building.

"You think it's all right if Lothar comes in with us?" I queried Abra as I removed my cloak, shook out its length, and draped it across Aeon's saddle.

"I should think not," he responded, adding, "unless, that is, he is not visible to anyone."

"What do you mean?"

"Put a spell of invisibility on the beast," the warlock shrugged nonchalantly, "if you want to take him in with us, otherwise, command him to stay out here with the horses."

"A spell of invisibility?" I gaped. I'd been taught such a spell, but only for use on myself. That I might be able to project the energy onto Lothar, rendering him unseeable, had not even crossed my mind. "Um, should I do that? Or will you?"

With a heavy sigh, and an inscrutable glance at me, Abra approached the puppy, bent down to take the animal's head in his hands, and peered deeply into his eyes. He murmured some words I found unrecognizable, nodded, and rose.

"There, it's done. If he behaves himself no one else shall see him."

"What do you mean?"

"So long as he remains calm and quiet, which I instructed him to do, the spell will remain intact and no one will notice him. If he gets excited, starts running and jumping about, the energy I've cloaked him in will break apart and everyone else will see him as you and I do now."

"Ah, I see," I nodded. "Thank you. Let's go eat!"

Though the inn was open to travelers seeking food, we were informed by the owners, Mr. and Mrs. Barton, that no rooms were available. Disappointed at the thought of not having access to comfy warm beds, we were at least treated to abundant food and drink. Mrs. Barton, a heavy-set woman with gray hair braided and pinned upon her head, led us into the main room where she seated us at a wooden table with two benches. Abra requested tankards of ale for the two of us, and when offered stew and bread, he heartily agreed. As an afterthought I asked for a cup of milk, and when it arrived, once Mrs. Barton had shuffled off to the kitchen again, I put it down on the floor near my foot so Lothar could have it. Though Abra's eyebrow shot up in question, he said nothing, and the puppy lapped up the milk quietly before stretching out for a nap beneath my bench. When our hostess returned with a tray, upon which rested two tankards of ale, two large bowls of stew, and a basket of warm bread, she placed everything carefully on the table and asked if there was anything else we needed.

"My good woman," Abra responded as he lifted a wooden ladle to scoop up some stew, "if you've truly no rooms available for the night, might you direct us to where we could find lodgings? Surely this is not the only inn in all of Stillmoor!"

"You're right," the woman nodded as she tucked the empty tray beneath one arm, "this is not the only inn."

"Though I'm sure it's by far the nicest," my companion interjected.

Mrs. Barton paused to look at Abra before casting her eyes toward me. Something in her expression shifted slightly. She looked once more at Abra.

"Well, if it's just the two of you, and if you promise to tell no one," She sighed, "I guess I can find a room for you, that is if you don't mind sharing."

I shrugged when the warlock looked at me questioningly. He nodded as he turned back to Mrs. Barton, "That would be most kind, Madam. We'll be happy to share accommodations tonight. If you'd be so kind as to direct us to the nearest livery stable, we'll see to our horses as soon as we've finished eating."

"No need for that," she smiled as she brushed an errant wisp of hair behind her ear. "We've a stable out back. Your horses will be safe and well cared for there. I'll have my man take them around and bring your things in while you're eating."

"Wonderful," Abra smiled. "That is most kind. And might I add that this food is delicious. I don't know when I've tasted better fare."

"You're welcome," she beamed, a slight blush rising to her ample cheeks. "I'll see to it. You two enjoy your food!"

As Mrs. Barton returned to the kitchen, I took a bite of the stew as I pulled a chunk of bread from the loaf, looking at Abra suspiciously.

"What?" He blinked, feigning innocence.

"Was that a spell you cast that made her so suddenly hospitable?"

"Spell?" With a wink, the warlock spooned stew into his mouth, clearly dismissing my question. He too pulled bread from the loaf to dip it into the hot broth in his bowl.

Chapter 23

The night in the inn had been quiet and restful, for the most part. The room Mrs. Barton put us in was large and clean. It afforded us two good-sized beds, a fireplace, and a table between two chairs, so it was comfortably appointed. Lothar curled up beside me once I had crawled beneath the covers, and Abra blew out the candle the hostess had left burning on a table between the beds. We both settled in, listening to the embers pop in the hearth, and exchanged a few pleasantries before the warlock rolled over to sleep. Sometime deep in the night I heard crying, cross words uttered, something banged, then the quiet returned and I slipped back to sleep.

"Good morning, Falcon," Abra, up, dressed, washed, and carrying two mugs on a tray, stepped into the room with a flourish. "I trust you slept well?"

"Um, I guess," I muttered, rubbing the sleep from my eyes while trying to fend Lothar's kisses off. "I heard something in the night."

"Yes, as did I," he nodded as he put the tray on the table. "Apparently another lodger's child experienced a nightmare last night. Shall I take Lothar out for his morning exercise?"

"His," I hesitated, but continued when I realized his meaning, "oh, sure. Yes, please, if you would. I'll dress and get my gear together so we can get something to eat before we leave."

"Of course! I've already spoken to our hostess who assures me we'll have plenty to eat and take with us when we go. Oh, and I have a surprise for you!"

"A surprise? For me?" Tossing the blankets from my legs, I swung my feet off the bed to rise. The wooden floors were smooth and surprisingly warm, though the fire in the hearth had long since gone out.

"Have some hot tea," Abra smiled before taking a drink from his mug. "You can join me in the dining room when you're ready. I've already packed my gear and have it downstairs. Mr. Barton is busy saddling Whisper and as soon as your gear is ready, he'll do the same to Aeon if you're good with that."

"Of course," I nodded, picking up one of my packs from the floor beside the bed. As I shook out fresh clothing, the warlock left the room, mug in hand, with Lothar on his heels. Taking a sip of hot tea, I propped myself on the edge of the bed before setting the mug down to don my stockings and dark breeches. I pulled my light blue linen tunic over my head, tied the laces at the neck, and secured the sapphire sash around my waist. Downing another sip of tea, I fastened ThornSting's scabbard on my hip before sliding the blade into its sheath. I gave my hair a cursory brushing and pulled it back on the nape of my neck, securing it with a satin ribbon the felinetrix had given me. Tossing the brush into my saddle bag, I put my worn clothing in, pulled the flap over and secured it with a leather thong. With a final glance around the room, I finished the tea before putting the empty mug on the tray and grabbing my gear. When I stepped into the hallway, I was greeted by the scent of smoked meat and baked bread. I made my way downstairs quickly, sudden hunger causing my stomach to growl in anticipation.

The dining room was crowded. I did not see Abra at first, but when I stepped into the room the men seated at the center-most table stood to look at me. The warlock rose and turned to greet me with a smile.

"Ah, there she is," he beamed. "Good morning, Falcon. As you can see, we've been joined by the king's guardsmen."

"So, I see," I stammered, stunned at the sight of the men we had rescued from the torocs. Glancing from one guard to the next as I dropped my gear to the floor beside the table, I could see they had all suffered injuries, some more severe than others. When my eyes met those of Captain Durand, I was surprised by what I found there. Despite the bruised and swollen left eye, the expression on his face was clearly one of relief. "I see you men are in need of my services. What ever happened to you?"

"We had a run-in with some torocs," Lieutenant De Groot offered with a sheepish grimace, bowing politely. "And yes, we could use your help."

Unable to tear my eyes away from Captain Durand, I watched as he rose stiffly and slowly to his feet, the last of the men to do so. Even from where I stood, I could tell his injuries were quite painful.

"Falcon," Abra approached me, slipping one arm around my shoulders, "do you think you could see your way clear to help these fine gentlemen?"

With a nod I replied, "Of course, Abra. But we'll need a room with a bit of privacy. The dining room is no place to treat wounds."

"Of course, of course," he smiled. "I've spoken to the proprietor and I'm told there's a small storage larder just off the kitchen. He assures me that it's clean and big enough for you to treat your patients, albeit one at a time."

"Very well," with a nod, I picked up my saddlebags, one of which held my healing materials, and slipped them over my forearm. "I'll take Captain Durand first, as it appears he's currently in the most pain. Abra, please keep an eye on Lothar for me. Oh, and save me some food, please. I'm starving!"

"The room is just over that way," my warlock companion nodded toward a narrow hallway, "and I believe Mrs. Barton may be nearby. She'll show you, I'm sure. And yes, your animal will be safe with me."

"Come, sir," I took the wounded man's elbow gently to help guide him, "let's get those wounds tended to."

Captain Durand groaned softly, but he made no comment as I moved him along slowly, as carefully as I could. The proprietor's wife looked up from where she was putting food on a large tray. She nodded at us, turned, crossed a corridor, and opened a door. Ushering the two of us into the storage room, she handed me a bright lantern by which I could work.

"I hope this will meet your needs," she offered. "And you can move some of those barrels aside to let light in from the window on the far wall if you need to, so long as you move them back when you're done."

"Thank you," I muttered, moving the injured soldier past the woman, easing him down to sit on a stack of wooden crates. "I'm sure this will be fine."

"I put a bowl of clean water and some cloths there at your friend's directions," she added as she stepped out into the hallway, closing the door firmly behind her.

"Excellent!" With a silent 'thank you' to the warlock for his thoughtfulness, I whispered, "Let's see what magic I can do!"

"Thank you for this," Captain Durand winced as he moved to get more comfortable on the crates. "I do appreciate it."

"Shall I see to your eye first?"

"Never mind the eye," he shook his head. "It's fine. I've had worse."

"I might be able to take some of the pain and swelling away," I suggested, "that is if you'll let me."

"If you insist," he shrugged, wincing as I drew near him.

When I cupped my left hand over his injured eye, he gasped, suddenly straightening.

"No! No, don't touch me," he snapped, pulling away from my touch. "The heat in your hand makes my eye feel worse. Just, just leave it be."

"Very well," feeling disappointed that I had been unable to help, I sighed, "I won't touch it again. But I will give you a cool, damp cloth to hold on it. That should relieve the pain and take down the swelling."

"Fine," he nodded, looking relieved.

I dipped a clean cloth into the basin, wrung out the excess water, and carefully folded it into a small square. As I handed it to him, I added, "Before you use this, take off your shirt. I can tell by the way you move there's some damage there. Let me take a look at you."

While the guardsman gingerly pulled the tunic off over his head, I removed a pouch of herbs from my bag and shook some out into the basin water. I stirred the liquid with the tip of my index finger, charging it with healing energy, activating the oils in the dried flakes. A soft light appeared to trail through the water from my finger so I stirred and stirred until the whole bowl glowed softly. Again, I dipped one of the cloths into the basin, lifting it and wringing out the excess liquid as I turned to Captain Durand.

It was all I could do to keep from gasping when I saw the wounded man's chest. The first thing I noticed was how well-muscled and well-proportioned he was. His shoulders were broad, chest smooth and devoid of hair, arms muscular and sinewy. But my attention was quickly drawn to the angry bruise covering the left side of his ribcage, spreading from beneath his arm to where the waist of his pants rode around his middle.

"I can see why you're in pain," I nodded as I neared the injury, looking at the pattern of blood movement to discern the impact point. "Ah, there it is!" With the palm of my left hand, I covered the source of the wound, feeling flesh, bone, and fluid. "You have a broken rib, maybe two."

"Yes," he drew in a sharp breath, "you're right." Despite his discomfort, he managed to keep the cool cloth pressed to his injured eye.

"Hold still, just breathe. I'll be careful."

As Deacon had taught me, I pulled the trauma from the captain's body with my left palm. The energy was angry, jagged, unbalanced and throbbing. Once I had settled the area, I placed my right hand over his ribs, slowly mending the tissue. I could feel the swelling going down, the blood flow returning to normal, the flesh healing. Even in the dim light of the storage room I could see a dark stain spreading along Captain Durand's waist and down his hip, and with a start I stepped back.

"Can you stand?"

"I," he looked up, somewhat startled, "I can." With that he struggled to his feet, moaning slightly at the exertion.

"The swelling under your ribs had shut off the bleeding," I explained, pointing to the blood stain growing bigger on his pants, "and now that the swelling's gone down the wound beneath it is bleeding freely. We need to stanch the flow. Please, pull down the top of your breeches."

Crossing the room as the captain followed my instructions, I gathered the ingredients I knew would stop the bleeding. From my bag I selected dried mushroom powder, in case there was poison involved, green moss to draw infection, honey to hasten the healing, and spider webs for sealing. As I chose a cloth most likely to be the size I needed, a rap on the door drew my attention.

"Yes?"

"Your friend said you might need this," Mrs. Barton opened the door with one hand, offering a steaming kettle of water with the other. As she stepped hesitantly into the room, she glanced at Captain Durand, her eyes drawn to where he was moving the waist of his breeches down to expose his wounded hip. "Oh," she gasped, averting her eyes quickly, "I'll leave you to your work."

Carefully taking the steaming kettle from our hostess, I poured hot water into the basin and tossed the cloth back before putting the kettle on a short stack of folded fabric atop a crate. The door closed solidly as Mrs. Barton left the room. Gingerly stirring the cloth around in the water, I withdrew it with two fingers to let it drain to cool enough to twist the excess water from the cloth. Keeping my eyes down, I turned back to Captain Durand and moved close enough to attend his wound.

Two jagged gashes ran diagonally along the man's side, just above his hip bone. Of the two, the center wound was the deepest and was bleeding the most.

"This will hurt," I warned him, looking up into his eyes. "Ready?"

"Do it," he muttered, drawing a deep breath to steel himself.

With firm pressure, I put the cloth against the wound. I could feel the man fighting his instinct to step back to escape the pain, but he managed to remain still. My left palm on his chest for balance, I cupped the cloth in my right hand on his side, waiting to sense how the wound would respond. I could not help but notice how warm and firm his chest was, how smooth the skin beneath my hand was, how strong and well defined his muscles were.

'What are you thinking, Falcon?' I chastised myself silently for the thoughts running through my mind. *'Keep your focus!'*

"How is it you were wounded by torocs?" Though it was really none of my business, I thought to divert his attention from his pain with meaningless conversation and if it distracted me from those troubling thoughts so much the better.

"It happened," he answered through clinched teeth.

"Ah," I murmured with a nod, as his reluctance to discuss the matter was understandable.

Suddenly he grabbed my hand on his chest and squeezed my fingers. I gasped.

"You are a seer, yes?" Looking deeply into my eyes, his words shot through me as surely as any arrow. "You know what happened."

"Ambush," was all I managed to whisper before his intensity brought me up short.

"Yes." He responded tersely.

As I had still not figured out how it was the monsters had managed to capture the king's guards, I was honestly curious. "I was given to understand that torocs aren't smart enough to plan and execute an ambush."

"It," he seethed, pain still clear in his breathing and facial expression, "happened. I don't know how, but it happened." Though his voice softened as he spoke, he did not release my hand.

"I'm sorry," I offered.

"What have you to be sorry for?"

"I just mean," I struggled for an answer, myself, as I looked into his eyes, keenly aware of how close we stood. "I meant, well, I just meant that I'm sorry you and your men were injured. That's all."

"Can you see how it happened?" A light of sudden hope appeared in his eyes, though the left was open barely enough to be seen, as he released my hand. "Can you use whatever power it is you have to see how we were taken? I was there and yet for the life of me I cannot recall."

"I can tell you this," with a shrug I nodded. "There was magic involved. The entity gathering the torocs and likely other such creatures is also directing them, aiding them in their actions. What I can't tell you is what this being ultimately intends. I can't tell if it's a witch, a wizard, or some other magic wielder and I can't for the life of me figure out its plans."

"So, this being cast a spell? This is why we were unable to protect ourselves and why we have no memories of the attack?"

"Yes."

"On the one hand," he admitted with a shrug, "I'm relieved that it was not some weakness or mistake that resulted in our being ambushed, but on the other, I'm angry that someone, anyone, could have such power. Have we no recourse at all?"

"Oh, this is much better," I glanced down at the cloth in my hand, noticing the bleeding had slowed. When I looked back up, I found Captain Durand's eyes closed, his face tensed in pain. At my words, he released a breath he had been holding and opened his eyes. He looked down at me, eyes full of emotion, as if he was seeing me for the very first time.

For just a moment, the vision I had experienced the previous night swam into my awareness. I noticed the height of the man before me, how near I was to his chest and lips. A rush of energy, at the recognition and certainty, shook me to the core. My heart began to race in my chest, a terrified rabbit trapped in the cage of my ribs. Heat rushed up my neck, my ears rang, my mouth suddenly went dry. When he bent down to put his lips on mine, the world receded. There was nothing else, no one else, in existence. He put one hand on my back and part of me smiled in delight. But the little voice in my head was screaming a warning.

'What's this? What does this mean? He doesn't even like you. Why is he kissing you? In fact, why are you kissing him? Have you lost your mind? Step back! Get away from him!'

When at last Captain Durand released me, I was left reeling, feeling foolish and confused. He looked at me, surprise etched clearly on his face, blinking repeatedly, mostly with his right eye, before a shield came down behind his eyes. The stony soldier I had first met at May Perry's had returned.

Grateful for any distraction to break the tension, I returned my focus to his side as I removed the cloth from his wound. Peering at the fabric closely, I held it out to show him.

"Look, see? The bleeding is much less," I explained, relieved that the room was so dimly lit he could not see me blush. "I can clean it and bandage it now. You'll be fine."

"It will heal?" He raised an eyebrow at me.

"Yes, it will. I've medicinal ingredients to speed its healing and ward off any infections. And when I'm done with you, I'll smudge you to disperse any residual toroc-borne magic. You'll heal."

"And my men," he interjected, "you'll smudge them all too?"

"Yes, of course," with a nod I assured him, "I'll smudge them all, whether they're injured or not."

"Thank you," he sighed, as I began to sprinkle the dried powdered mushroom onto the moist green moss. "What's that?"

"Just a poultice," I dismissed his question, scooping honey from the small jar the felinetrix had given me. "Now hold still." Smoothing the glob of honey on his most serious wound, I placed the moss on it before adding a wad of clean spiders' web. With my left hand I held the medicinals firmly against his wound, while with my right hand I covered it with a folded cloth bandage and began to wrap lengths of cloth around his middle to secure my work. "You'll have to keep this on for three days and nights. As long as the bleeding doesn't start again, this will help you heal nicely."

"We must get to Ayndor," the captain offered, "and we can have no delay."

"Just ride easy," I nodded, "and take a rest when you can."

"Thank you."

"You're welcome," I replied, ripping the end of the cloth length-wise to tie it off. "You can put your shirt back on. I'll light the sage bundle."

"Oh," he hesitated, "yes."

Once he had pulled his tunic over his head and gingerly put his arms into the sleeves, he stood still while I wafted sage smoke around him. I started at his left side, moving the burning bundle of sage up and down, up, and down, as I circled his body. When I was satisfied there was no residual magic clinging to him, I laid the sage on the edge of a crate, burning end out. I let him know I was done and he could send in the next injured man, relieved when he nodded smartly but did not speak of the kiss.

As Captain Durand left the store room, I moved a few barrels aside on the far wall, opened the window, and tossed the used and bloody water outside. I worked silently, preparing for the next wounded man while considering what I had just experienced, marveling over the awareness that it was the captain who had been in my vision. The kiss had left me confused and feeling off-kilter. Though it had been pleasant, even wonderful, I could not understand why he had kissed me. It made no sense. I was sure my initial impression of Captain Durand was correct and that he had no patience or regard for me so I wondered what had changed. Part of me was flattered at the notion that a man such as he would even notice me, while another part was resentful at his earlier dismissive attitude and his obvious opinion that I was of little use. But again, something must have changed in me, I realized, as the memory of his kiss left me giddy and longing for more.

"Well, maybe your healing ability put a dent in his attitude," I muttered to myself as I poured fresh hot water into the basin. When the door opened slowly, I began humming a mindless tune to cover the fact that I had been talking to myself. "Come in, come in, I'll be right with you."

One by one, the members of the king's guardsmen came in for treatment. Captain Durand had been the most severely injured, though Lieutenant De Groot had a nasty laceration across the back of his sword hand. I cleaned the wound as thoroughly and carefully as I dared before applying a drawing agent in case of infection. As I wrapped a bandage around his hand, I warned him to be careful, to avoid getting the dressing wet or bumping the wound.

"He talks about you, you know?" He looked up, grinning at me shyly.

"Excuse me? Who talks about me?"

"I probably shouldn't say," he shrugged. "Don't mind me. I think I got my head banged up."

"Really?" Releasing the bandaged hand, I began to inspect De Groot's head, touching it gently with my fingertips looking for bumps or lacerations. "I don't feel any injury."

"I'm fine," he insisted, shaking his head as he rose to his feet. "I don't need any…"

"Are you sure you're well?"

"Yes, Ma'am. I'm well. I'll, um, I'll send in the next man." Stuttering, obviously uneasy suddenly, Lieutenant De Groot threw me a salute with his bandaged hand before he hurried away, the door banging loudly in his wake.

Chapter 24

Once King Rowan's guardsmen were all treated, I tidied up the store room, re-stacked the barrels in front of the window, finally carrying the lantern and my gear into the hallway. Mrs. Barton hurried by, an empty tray tucked beneath one arm, and accepted the lantern from me.

"You go on out to the table, Miss," she nodded emphatically, "and I'll bring some food out straight away. You must be half starved by now!"

"Thank you, Ma'am," I chuckled, "and I surely am!"

The men were all seated around the wooden table, talking, eating, and drinking. Beck and another soldier, who had told me his name was Prouse, started to rise as I drew near, but I shook my head and raised a hand.

"Please, don't get up on my account," I insisted. "I'm starving and all I want to do right now is eat."

"Alas, Milady Falcon," Abra pushed up from his chair, "I must get up now, though not on your account."

"What's happening?" Slinging my saddlebags to the floor beside an empty seat, I paused with one hand on the back of the chair. "Abra?"

"As you're now in the safe and capable hands of the king's guards, I must take my leave. I regret to inform you that the king has insisted I return to Castle deBirch."

"How? Why? I mean," I stammered, "must you leave now?"

"Though it grieves me to do so, yes, I must. These fine gentlemen will escort you to Ayndor and I shall see you when you all return to Esling." Bowing deeply, he looked me in the eye, imparting a silent message of assurance. The warlock drew near, put his left hand on the right side of my face, and leaned close to my ear. "I shall keep an eye on you and the situation, my dear," he whispered, quickly kissing me on the cheek.

"The talisman?" I asked, unable to keep my voice from cracking as I swallowed back my emotions.

He simply nodded without further comment, bent down to pat Lothar on the head, and hurried away.

Not quite sure what to do or say next, I started to pull my chair out to sit down but found Lieutenant De Groot stepping in to do so. Blushing furiously, feeling completely out of my element, I sat down at the table and waited to eat. Though only moments before I had been famished, I now found I had no appetite at all and in fact, the mere thought of food turned my stomach. But when Mrs. Barton brought out a tray of warm food and cold drink, I paused, inspecting the fare. A pitcher of milk stood beside an empty stone mug and a plate of warm biscuits. There was a bowl of honey, still oozing from the comb, next to a crock of sweet cream butter, and a pile of perfectly browned link sausages on a platter. Steam rose from a teapot perched beside an empty cup while a box of loose-leaf tea rested beside an empty tea ball. I knew there was a long day of journeying ahead, so I forced myself to slather butter and honey on a biscuit. As I chewed the warm morsel, I realized the food was quite tasty and I helped myself to some fresh milk as my hunger returned. The men sitting at the table with me, I noticed, kept watching me eat, but would avert their eyes when I looked up at them. As much as I wanted to take my time and enjoy my food, I realized they had been there far longer than I and were likely anxious to be on the road and moving toward Ayndor. I drained the milk and finished the biscuits our hostess had brought, finally tossing a scrap of sausage to Lothar before shoving my chair away from the table. As I rose from my seat, the guardsmen stood in unison while Mrs. Barton bustled in from the kitchen, towel in hand.

"Your friend has taken care of the charges," she nodded pointedly, "including the room, the food, and stable lodging for your horses. Mr. Barton has your mount all ready to go."

"Thank you so much," I smiled, realizing that I too was happy to be resuming the journey.

As a group, we carefully moved between the dining tables and chairs, some occupied, some empty, through the door beyond. Morning sunlight washed the street, making me blink at the harsh brightness. As I started toward where Aeon stood tethered to a hitching post, Captain Durand cleared his throat.

"Lady Falcon Rose," he began, "as we were originally charged only with seeing you safely to Castle deBirch, you were never properly introduced to my men. However, as we are to be traveling together for some time, it seems only right to do so now."

"Oh," I blinked, surprised at myself for not really being aware of the matter, "yes. Of course!"

"You know Lieutenant Jan De Groot," he indicated the soldier standing to his right, "and this is Sergeant Gilbert Beck. This is Simon Keller, René Martin, and Edgar Prouse. Gentlemen, this is Lady Falcon Rose, daughter of one of my predecessors, Arne Rose. The king has charged her with helping us deliver his fiancé and her family to Esling."

One by one, as the men were introduced, they bowed slightly standing politely silent while the captain finished speaking. When it was clear their leader was done, one of the men, Keller, I think it was, spoke up.

"And what should we call you, My Lady?" Eyes bright blue and sparkling with good humor, Simon Keller was ruddy complected with a strong jaw fringed with but a scruff of beard. He wore his copper brown hair pulled back from his forehead, secured on the back of his head with a leather braided cord.

"I would prefer to be called Falcon," I admitted honestly, "but if you're not comfortable with that you may call me Lady Rose, I suppose."

"As you wish," the soldier replied.

"And, this is my friend Lothar," nodding toward where the puppy had stopped to sniff the ground near the hitching post. The familiar screech of the raven overhead assured me that my feathered guide was still nearby. Pointing at the dark speck barely visible in the blue sky I added, "And that's Vesta, Cor's friend, and my raven guide. With her help I made it this far."

"Cor?" Captain Durand cocked his head, "Oh yes, Cornelius Welkin, the wizard."

"Just so we set off on the right foot, let me explain," I offered. "When my parents were murdered, my father, before he died, sent me off to Duhne to live with my aunt. I became ill and lost my way on the journey and it was the

Elemental Wizard, Cornelius Welkin, who found me and took me in. When we later learned my aunt had died, he opened his home and his heart to me and raised me as his own child. He and the other wizards trained me in their ways and Deacon helped teach me healing. Vesta is Cor's raven friend and she's been kind enough to guide me."

"That's quite a tale," Lieutenant De Groot replied, the sympathy in his voice and expression clear.

"Yes, well," the captain interrupted, "as the morning is moving on and we have far to go, let's saddle up!"

"Lothar," I called to the puppy. He stopped his investigating to look at me briefly before taking off down the road at a trot. Clearly, he had no desire to ride so early in the day, so I secured my gear on the back of Aeon's saddle and gathered her reins. Captain Durand and Lieutenant De Groot mounted their horses before moving into formation on the road. I swung myself up onto Aeon's back and urged her ahead. To my surprise, Simon Keller took up the position beside me while the other guardsmen fell into place behind us. It felt strange indeed to be traveling in such a phalanx of soldiers, but I had to admit it was nice to be on the road in the company of others. As we rode out of Stillmoor, I heard the steady, distant thwack of the axe as it bit into wood and knew Robert Allen was back at work.

The king's guards and I rode steadily west, the sun on our backs casting long shadows before us. Though it was near mid-day by the time we left the village, the air was still cool and fresh. Lothar seemed content to run along with us, often disappearing into a stand of trees or over a distant rise, only to reappear and come running toward us. It seemed he was developing some sort of game in that puppy mind of his, obviously having fun, and part of the play was to come back and check on us, or at least check on me, before setting off again. The men behind me chatted from time to time, Captain Durand and Lieutenant De Groot exchanged words, but mostly we rode in silence. My thoughts ceaselessly returned to the store room and the kiss Captain Durand had given me. I found it both pleasant and confusing, and wondered if every girl's first kiss had that effect on them.

Glancing up, I noticed Vesta wheeling in the sky and as I watched Cor's familiar voice came to me.

'Falcon,' he spoke kindly, *'I see you now travel with King Rowan's guards.'*

'Yes. We just left Stillmoor and are heading towards Ayndor.'

'What of your warlock friend, Abra?'

'You know him, here one minute gone the next! He claims the king called him back to Esling.'

'I see!' The wizard's voice ceased before rising again from the silence, *'Falcon, we have news. There is a disturbance ahead of you. The other wizards and I can sense it, feel it, but we cannot determine exactly what it is yet.'*

'Disturbance? What does that mean?'

'We do not yet know, lass. But you need to be alert. Keep your senses keen and be ready to react. Whatever lies ahead of you is not natural.'

'Magic? Evil magic?'

'There is no such thing as evil magic, you well know. But it may be magic designed to do harm.'

'That's a rather fine line, isn't it?'

'Touché, Falcon,' came the kindly wizard's chuckle. *'Let me say this, an enemy lies ahead, though we cannot yet tell if it is an enemy of yours, the king's, or the entire country of Esling's. But be warned. Please take care.'*

'Of course, Cor. And since I'm now traveling with men who have been to Ayndor before, I don't really need Vesta's services. You can call her back if you like.'

'Very well. I will do that. I shall let you know as soon as we learn anything more. In the meantime, take care and travel safe!'

'Thank you, Cor!'

Almost as soon as the silent communication with the wizard ceased, the raven above gave one sharp screech before flying back toward the east.

"Seems your feathered friend just left you," Simon Keller, riding a massive bay Ardennaise with dark mane and hoof fringe, broke the silence left in the bird's void.

"Yes," I nodded, "she probably figured out that I'm riding now with humans who know where they're going. I expect she's heading back to Corhaven."

"You were really raised by a wizard?" He grinned.

"I was," I chuckled, "as strange as that may sound."

Before the conversation could get too detailed and curiosity could turn to inquisition, I turned my attention away from the rider beside me. A strange sound came from somewhere ahead on the road. I could not determine what it was, but it was low, irregular, and heavy sounding. I wondered if it was the disturbance Cor had warned me about.

"Captain Durand!" I called out, trying to sound less concerned or alarmed than I felt.

"Whoa!" He drew his horse to a halt and turned in the saddle. "Yes, Lady Falcon?"

"Just wondering if we'll be stopping to rest the horses soon."

"Have you a need to stop?"

"I'm just feeling a little slipping in my saddle," I fibbed, only because I wanted to speak to him privately and it seemed the prudent course to take. "I'd like to check it and make sure it's cinched before it causes Aeon discomfort or a sore."

"Very well," he nodded, "there's a bend in the road just ahead, beyond that is a stand of trees where we can find shade. And if there's been sufficient rain in this area there should be a small stream nearby. We can dismount and water the horses while you check your saddle."

"Thank you!"

We soon rounded the bend in the road, just as the captain had said, and a copse of trees growing on the northern side of the track cast long shadows toward us as we drew near. The stream that meandered through the woods was shallow and wide, but it was there, and it did offer the horses a drink.

"You men take a break," Lieutenant De Groot gave the command, "and water your horses. Walk around and stretch your legs for a bit, but we'll not be here long."

I swung down from Aeon's back, keeping her reins in my hand, waiting for Captain Durand to carefully dismount. He moved stiffly and gingerly, barely containing a grimace as he touched the ground.

"May I talk to you privately for a moment?" I moved Aeon up alongside the captain's steed. "It won't take long."

"Of course, Lady Falcon," he nodded succinctly before turning his attention to his lieutenant. "De Groot, keep an eye on things."

"Yes, sir!" De Groot snapped a salute in response before leading his horse off the road toward the shallow stream.

"Now," Durand turned back to me, "what can I do for you?"

"First," I bit the inside of my lip as I wrestled with how to broach the subject, lowering my voice to above a whisper, "I've always had keen hearing and I'm hearing something disturbing ahead on the road. I don't know what it is, but it's there. Can you hear it?"

The captain looked at me skeptically for a moment, but closed his eyes as he drew a deep breath. Clearly, he was listening intently. His expression remained unchanged for a moment. Gasping slightly, startled, his eyes opened wide in surprise as he regarded me soberly.

"What is it?"

"I don't know," I murmured. "I truly don't know."

"What else?"

"I don't want to make a fuss over you in front of your men," with my voice still barely above a whisper, I explained, "but I'd like to check the dressing on your wound."

"Why the special concern over me? Are you going to check everyone's injuries?"

"Your wounds are the deepest," I retorted, "and the most dangerous. In fact, your wounds are those most likely to kill a man. I just need to make sure the bleeding hasn't increased, or even better, that it's stopped completely. Just lift your shirt and I'll take a quick look."

Turning slightly so his back was to where his men were walking around and stretching, the captain lifted the tail of his tunic and looked away as I examined the dressing. I was pleased to discover that the bleeding had slowed considerably and the blood on the bandage was starting to dry.

"How does it feel?"

"It hurts," he looked down at me, a slight grimace on his lips, "but it feels better. Feels tight and sometimes the pain's sharp and stabbing, but it's bearable."

"Excellent," I replied as I untied, tightened, and re-tied the bandage. "That means the healing's commenced. The bandage must be kept taut against the wound to hold the healing compress in place, so if you feel it stretching or becoming loose, let me know."

"I will," he nodded, hissing slightly as I cinched the fabric tighter around his middle. "And about the sound coming from the road ahead, do you have any suggestions what we should do?"

"This road is moving pretty much due west, isn't it?" I asked feigning ignorance, though I knew darn well that it was.

"Yes."

"As Ayndor lies to the southwest, maybe we should leave the road and travel more toward the south for a while," I shrugged. "Perhaps we can skirt whatever it is that's making that sound."

"Seems like a good idea," he responded, looking me straight in the eye. "Thank you, Lady Falcon." Once again, only for a moment, the light in his eyes softened. I felt like I was seeing beneath his gruff exterior and the heat of a blush rode up my neck, burning my cheeks as it reached my face. Suddenly his expression returned to stone as the soldier replaced the man.

Though he did not explain if his thank you was for my healing treatment and care or if it was for alerting him to whatever might be troubling the road ahead, I simply nodded without comment, pretending to examine Aeon's saddle girth. Captain Durand led his massive white stallion off the road to the stream joining his men beneath the shady trees.

Lieutenant De Groot, walking up beside me as I inspected Aeon's saddle, cleared his throat as he approached.

"Lady Falcon," he bowed politely, "I was just wondering if this hand of mine is supposed to be feeling wet and itchy. It didn't feel this way when you first bandaged it."

"It should not," I raised an eyebrow as I reached for his wounded hand. "Let me take a look."

The wound beneath the bandage was still raw and angry-looking. The cloth against the injury, though not completely saturated with blood and gore, was freshly damp. It looked like he might have accidently bumped the wound and started the bleeding anew.

"Hold on a minute," I offered as I stepped away beneath the trees, searching the ground for just the right thing. In a moment I found what I was looking for, picked it up from atop a bunch of fallen leaves, and blew the dust and dried bark from it. When I returned to Lieutenant De Groot, I gently took his wounded hand in my left hand, slipping the stick I had found beneath the outer bands of cloth. "Now, whenever you feel your wound itching or feeling wet," I instructed, "twist this twig to tighten the fabric. Just keep it snug, don't over-tighten it. Hold the twig twisted in the bandage for as long as you can manage without discomfort. Understand?"

"Yes, Ma'am," he smiled, gently moving the twig around, end for end. "Does it matter which direction I turn it?"

"No, that doesn't matter." Shaking my head slightly, I released his hand, "And I'll check your wound when we make camp. I may have to change your dressing again, but we'll see this evening."

Still mesmerized by the make-shift tourniquet I had created, the lieutenant offered as he started back toward where his horse stood, "Thank you, Lady Falcon."

Satisfied that I had pretended to deal with Aeon's saddle long enough, I gathered her reins, drawing her to the stream where some of the other horses had already drank their fill. Lothar came trotting along the stream, panting, and dripping water from his muzzle, and when he came near enough, I bent over and picked him up in my arms. It was clear he was tired.

"Come on, you," I cooed as I scratched beneath his ears. "You get to ride with me now."

Captain Durand called everyone to attention and we were soon moving our horses back to the road. I mounted my mare before settling Lothar before me. Growing warm in the sun, I removed my cloak to lay it behind my mount's saddle before rolling the sleeves of my tunic up to my elbows.

"Let's go!" The captain commanded as we all fell into place once more. Just past the stand of trees, the captain and lieutenant turned their horses to the right so we all followed and left the road behind. Ahead lay wide open fields, some harvested of crops, others covered with scrub grass. Our journey would be no easier off the well-traveled road, but at least the sound of the disturbance ahead had disappeared.

Chapter 25

As the day wore on, the clouds that appeared in the sky grew heavier and darker the farther south we rode. The air took on a chill so I removed my cloak from the back of Aeon's saddle and wrapped it around my shoulders. A dull throbbing over my left eye warned me that a storm was moving in, though I held my tongue and did not warn the others. I was not sure what they believed a witch might be, what powers they supposed one might have, or whether they thought me trustworthy or merely strange, but I did not want to give them cause to fear me. When the sky grew darker and the chill wind picked up, Captain Durand drew us all to a halt and directed us to keep an eye open for shelter. Apparently, he too felt bad weather was ahead. The land had gone from rough, dry, rocky terrain to rolling hills and gentle slopes. Though the grass that covered the hills was now autumn brown, I could imagine what the place must look like in the spring when everything was green and glorious. Tall, leafy trees had given way to their coniferous relatives and clusters of pines appeared here and there alongside ancient, gnarled cedar trees. Rising in the stirrups, I peered out over the land, searching for any sign of shelter. Ahead, and off a bit to the left, I saw sheep grazing in a small enclosure, giving me hope that their shepherd might be somewhere nearby.

"Captain," I called out, pointing toward where the animals grazed, "there's a herd of sheep! Hopefully, there's someone nearby. Maybe the shepherd's house is close and he will let us shelter in his barn."

"Let us make haste," he nodded in response as he heeled his stallion smartly in the flanks. The startled beast let out a snort, taking to its hooves in the direction of the enclosure. Everyone else took the captain's words as command and quickly spurred their horses on. There was no more riding in formation; it was every man for himself, I noticed, chuckling as I followed.

By the time we reached the enclosure, the sound of the horses' thundering hooves had driven the sheep away. The small herd ran bleating, scattering in their panic to escape. We drew our horses to a halt, dismounted, and looked around. I saw no shepherd in attendance, but there was a slate roof peeking from between the tops of a stand of cedars in the distance.

"Look at that," Lieutenant De Groot had apparently seen the structure's roof at the same time I did and he pointed at it in excitement. "Whatever it is, it's one big building!"

"Come," Captain Durand commanded, "let's go see what the place is."

We led our horses around the sheep's' enclosure, weaving between the trees and brambles surrounding it. I released Lothar to the ground, and he quickly trotted off to relieve himself before commencing his investigation of the area. We moved up a small rise, gathering at the crest of the hill, mesmerized at what lay before us. The stone structure towered over the land. Arched windows devoid of glass indicated there were at least three floors within the massive building, and a wide arched doorway stood atop two broad stone steps. Weeds grew in the yard surrounding the place, vines climbed the stone edifice, and saplings clustered near the foundation.

"What is this place?" I whispered in awe.

"Look," René pointed at the words etched in stone beside the door, "it says Abbaye du Corbeau Noir. It's an abbey!"

"Or, it was once an abbey," Captain Durand responded as he handed his horse's reins to his lieutenant. Beside the arched doorway a bell with a rope tied to its base was mounted against the stone. The captain unwound the frayed and crumbling rope from a wrought iron hook and gave it a sharp pull. The massive bell clanged loudly, shattering the silence surrounding the abbey, but there was no response from within the building. After a moment's pause, he gave the rope repeated pulls, causing the bell clapper to bang again and again against the heavy bell cup, but again no answer came, no one answered the door or came running in from an adjacent field.

"It looks to have been abandoned," Lieutenant De Groot stepped back to look up at the towering abbey. "Who knows how long the place has been empty?"

"If it's empty," I dared to interject, "do you think it's safe for us to shelter here, I mean, at least until the storm passes?"

"Let's look around and see how safe it is," the captain responded. "De Groot, you are with me. Beck, you and the others look around the premises. See if there is a barn or stable for the horses. We may have to stay there ourselves if we can't find a way into the abbey, or if it looks too dangerous inside."

"Yes, sir!" Beck threw Durand a smart salute.

"Lady Falcon, you may come with us if you like."

"Thank you, Captain," I glanced around at the tall grass, looking for a sign of Lothar, "but you go ahead. I'll find Lothar and have a look around."

Without further comment, the lieutenant walked up the steps and tried to open the two heavy, wooden doors. Either the handles were rusted shut or there was a latch on the inside, because even when he threw his weight against the wood there was no movement. Clearly, the two would have to find another way into the abbey. As they set off in search of an entrance, I led Aeon through the tall grass, calling to the puppy.

"Lothar," I clapped my hands as I called to get his attention, "Lothar, come!"

The weeds off to my left rustled briskly as the puppy barreled through the growth. He trotted to me, panting, tongue lolling, covered in weed seeds.

"You silly thing," I sighed, digging my hand into my saddle bag. I pulled out his bowl and filled it from my water skin. "Here, you look thirsty. Drink up. You and I have to go explore the abbey."

As Lothar lapped up the water, I pulled my mare to where a young olive tree stood near the remains of a gate hanging crookedly between two posts. I tethered Aeon loosely to graze, before opening the gate carefully so it would not fall off in my hands. Within the low-walled rectangle weeds and vines choked out what must have once been a tidy and productive garden. Crushed stone peeked out of the undergrowth, suggesting there had been gravel paths between growing patches and a short stone well stood barely visible near the far end of the garden. Shaking my head at what sorry condition the place was in, I headed back to where Lothar had finished his drink and was now scratching his ear with one foot.

"Come on, Lothar," I called to him as I shook any residual moisture from his bowl before folding it up. "Let me put this away." Tucking the bowl back into the saddle bag, I turned to scoop the puppy up into my arms. Scratching his ears and picking weed seeds from his fur, I paused to take in the view of the abandoned abbey. Besides nature trying to reclaim it by swallowing it up in vines and weeds, the place did not look bad. Most of the stone walls still appeared upright and intact. The roof was missing some slate tiles here and there, and moss was growing thick beneath the eaves, but there were no other obvious signs of decay readily visible. The men, I noticed, had all departed with their horses in-tow. I stood before the abbey feeling very small and very alone.

"Well, it looks like you and me, buddy," I cooed to the puppy in my arms. "Let's go look around."

I knew the doors were locked, but beyond the entrance and beneath the row of arched windows, there was a short stone bench, where I guessed the nuns had once sat in silent prayer, and it appeared to be just the proper height for my purposes. Left hand on ThornSting's hilt, puppy cradled in the crook of my right arm, I stepped up on the bench, grateful that it was solid and offered no wobbling. The distance between the stone seat and the window was a bit greater than I had first thought, but I was determined so I took a deep breath, tightened my hold on Lothar, and leapt through the arched opening. To my relief, I landed easily on a smooth stone floor in what must have once been a corridor between the outside world and the courtyard labyrinth within. The arched windows in the outer wall were duplicated on the inside of the hallway and through the carved stone openings I could see statues covered in vines and moss, the inner courtyard having no protection from nature. Wind from the approaching storm whistled through the abbey, swirling dried leaves and dust along the smooth stone floor. Determined to find a place to shelter, if one still existed in Abbaye du Corbeau Noir, I turned to the right and made my way down the long corridor to where two doors stood closed, one in the wall straight ahead and one to the left. The oaken door ahead stood slightly ajar, so I pushed against it only to find it unyielding. Putting my shoulder against the wood, I shoved my weight into it and finally the heavy door squealed open.

The small chapel I found was cold and austere. Seven rows of dark simple pews marched on either side of a center aisle. The massive stone altar at the far end stood empty, the plinths on either side behind it held statues so old, worn, and entangled in vines they were unrecognizable. The column of stones on one side of the dais was hollow and empty, but I knew it had once held a bowl of holy water. My footsteps echoed loudly on the stone floors, disturbing a silence that must have settled over the place before I was born. The two arched windows in the room were protected by stained glass, though the panes were so heavily covered in grime I could not discern the images intended. Looking for a door to exit the chapel, I heard the wind outside moaning and changing its tone. Lothar squirmed uneasily in my arms.

"Let's go find the others," I murmured slightly above a whisper. "This place is spooky!"

What at first glance I took for a corner behind and to the left of the altar turned out to be a narrow set of steps. Though there was no light to see by, the walls were so close and the steps so perfectly spaced as to make it easy to climb. Soon I found myself on the second floor of the abbey. Doorless chambers stood along both sides of the wide center corridor and when I stepped into one room, I discovered it had a stone ledge against one wall and a small stone rectangle on the floor near the opposite wall. As I stood there in the near dark, wondering what the chamber might have been used for and by whom, a spectral entity walked silently past me, arms holding what looked like a bundle of fabric. As I watched, the ghostly woman unfolded what must have been a blanket, shook it out, and prepared the stone ledge as a bed. She turned, approached the stone rectangle near the wall, and knelt, bowing her head before disappearing. The thought of sleeping on a stone bed and kneeling on a stone to pray made me wonder at the amount of devotion such women must have had, and made me relieved that such had not been my lot in life. As I stepped back into the wide corridor, I noticed there were many spectral entities moving about, disappearing into a chamber, or appearing from one, though all were silent and none especially well-defined.

'For an abandoned abbey,' the little voice in my head marveled, *'this place is busy!'*

Lothar trembled in my arms, apparently somehow aware of what I was seeing, so I snuggled him closer as I made my way toward the end of the corridor. A wide stone stairway, off to the right, led back downstairs while a similar one leading off to the left appeared to go up to the third floor. As dismal as the second-floor was, I had no desire to investigate the one above, and quickly descended the stairs on the right. I heard voices as I neared the ground floor, and was relieved to find Captain Durand and Lieutenant De Groot standing near a huge hearth in what must have once been a large dining hall. They stopped talking when they heard me coming down the stone steps and both stood looking at me expectantly.

"How did you find a way in?" Captain Durand eyed me suspiciously.

"Jumped in a window," I shrugged, "and you?"

"We came around the back and entered through the kitchen. There is no door there anymore," he replied.

"Interesting place, isn't it?" Releasing Lothar to the floor, I rubbed my hands together as the air in the room was chilly. A breeze from outside carried the scent of rain. "Shall we shelter here until the storm passes?"

"That's probably best." He nodded as he turned to De Groot, "Lieutenant, take the men and gather what wood you can find for a fire. If anyone is uncomfortable sleeping here for the night they can stay in the stable with the horses."

"Yes, sir!" De Groot saluted, turned, and strode away, disappearing through a doorway I thought most likely leading to the kitchen.

"Who would be uncomfortable sleeping here?"

"A couple of the men are," pausing to select his words carefully, the captain took a deep breath, "religious, perhaps even a bit superstitious, and I doubt they will want to sleep here. Oh, they would if I made it an order, of course, but I try to be mindful of their beliefs when I can."

"That's kind of you," I quipped, inspecting the huge fireplace behind him. "You think it's safe to light a fire in this thing?"

"I looked," he answered, "and I saw a patch of sky up the chimney, so it should be safe. Under the circumstances, I think we should all bed down here in this room tonight. I don't want anyone separated."

"I agree." With a smile I added, "and I think I'll go get Aeon and my gear. I take it someone found a stable behind the building?"

"Yes," Captain Durand offered, "just go around the west end of the abbey and you will see the outbuildings beyond. The stable's not far from the well which stands very near the kitchen entrance."

"Excellent," I replied. Calling Lothar as I made my way through the remains of what was once the kitchen, I stepped outside into a light rain. With the wind whipping around between the abbey and the buildings nearby, I ducked my head as I raced the length of the building, around the corner, and to where the mare stood grazing, oblivious to the weather. Lothar ran with me, not really barking or even yipping, but making an odd guttural sound, the meaning of which was beyond me. I grabbed Aeon's reins, turned her around, and pulled her toward the stable, hastening from a brisk walk to a trot as the rain increased.

Once I got my mare into the shelter of what had once been a fine stable, I relieved her of her tack. At the same time René Martin and Edgar Prouse took care of the other horses. They were chatting between themselves so I did not bother them as I tucked my bedroll under my arm, tossed the saddle bags over one shoulder, and grabbed my water skin. With Lothar bouncing happily around my legs, I ran across the open yard in the increasing downpour. Rain damp and out of breath, I bounded into the kitchen, wet boots skidding on the stone floor.

I discovered two heavily carved candle plinths against the wall and though moving either of them was out of the question, I was able to reach up and remove the thick candles resting on them. The wax was ugly and misshapen from years of heat, cold, and neglect, but the wicks were intact so I assumed they would serve my purposes. I wiped spiderwebs from them and blew a layer of dust and grime from around the wicks, finally placing them both on a stone shelf against the wall. A shallow basin stood on a small table beneath two windows whose panes were still miraculously intact, so I picked it up, turned it over, and shook dust and collected dried leaves and twigs from it. It was doubtful I could draw fresh water from the well near the kitchen door, but at least I could use the contents of my water skin and the basin. I carefully withdrew my bundle of healing materials from my saddle bag and placed it beside the empty basin, before heading into the next room with Lothar at my heels.

The captain and his men had already started a fire in the hearth and they were setting up a makeshift camp in the cavernous dining hall. Captain Durand suggested I bed down nearest the fireplace, and as I was too tired to argue, I tossed my gear onto the stone floor. For a while I stood near the fire warming and drying my hands. Lothar, having shaken the rain from his thick coat, wandered from man to man, investigating what each was doing as well as what possessions they had with them. None of them seemed to mind the puppy's presence or his curiosity. As I began to unfurl my bedroll, I glanced around, noticing that there were only five of us in the place.

"So, I see we are but five here," I looked around, trying to put names to the two soldiers absent.

"Yes," Captain Durand nodded, "Martin and Prouse are bedding down in the stable."

"I saw they were tending to the horses." I pried gently, not wishing to offend anyone, "They're sleeping in the stable because of their beliefs?"

"Indeed," he replied succinctly.

"And it's never a bad idea to have someone guard the mounts," Lieutenant De Groot interjected with a grin. "I'm starving. Shall we pool our resources?" With that he upended a leather pouch releasing cloth-covered bundles to the floor.

"Before it gets too dark outside," I interjected, "and while I still have a bit of daylight to work in, I'd like to check injuries and change dressings before we settle in for the night. Lieutenant De Groot, how is that wound of yours?"

"It's better," he displayed the bandaged hand, twig tourniquet twisted securely across the back. "I've kept the bandage tight and it hasn't felt wet again since you gave me the stick."

"That's good," I nodded, "but I would like to unwrap it, clean it again and redress it. That way it will heal faster if you can keep it dry."

"Yes, Ma'am," agreeing, he added, "where do you want me?"

"I found candles in the kitchen and a basin I can use to wet cloth in, so let's go in there. Everyone else can start eating. Once I see to your injuries you can join them," I explained as I led the lieutenant into the kitchen. "Lothar, you stay here and I'll be right back!"

I could have caused the candle wicks to flame, using the energy Eban Kendall had taught me, but decided that might make the men uneasy. So instead, I hurried back to the hearth, found a twig on the stone floor, and held it to the fire until the end caught flame. Cupping my hand protectively around the small fire on the tip of the twig, I walked as fast as I dared back into the kitchen to light the candles, one after the other. Between what was left of the day beyond the grime-covered window panes and the candlelight, I got a good look at the lieutenant's wound once I unwound the fabric bandage. Pouring water from my leather water skin onto a clean, dry square of cloth, I washed the deep, ugly-looking gashes on the back of his hand, being as careful as I could not to cause him pain or additional injury.

"You have a lovely touch, Ma'am," De Groot smiled sweetly as he watched me clean his bloodied hand.

"Thank you, Lieutenant," I replied. "I'm going to put some fresh healing agents on your wound and wrap it in clean bandages. Hopefully this will keep your hand protected and healing until we reach Ayndor where I can get additional supplies and have a better place to treat you."

"Thank you," he responded with an understanding nod.

Once the man's hand was properly washed, herbal ointment applied, and a fresh clean bandage was applied, I tucked the used stick back under the cloth bindings. I told him to use it if he needed to, but added that it would be better if it was no longer necessary. He saluted me politely, examining the new bandage and idly touching the stick as he left the kitchen. As I stepped outside the open kitchen door and tossed the used water from the basin to the ground, I heard footsteps behind me. I turned to see Captain Durand enter the kitchen.

"Captain Durand," I murmured, bowing slightly, holding the empty basin. Suddenly self-conscious, I set about preparing what I would need to treat his wounds.

"Falcon Rose," he began, "I would like to thank you for treating my men and me. I know I might not have always been very…"

"You're welcome," I interrupted him, not wanting to get personal. "I'm a healer, after all. It's what I do. Now, please take off your shirt and let me see your wounds."

Once more I dampened a clean cloth with water over the empty basin, mesmerized by the sight of the captain taking his shirt off over his head reflected in the glass windows before me. Again, I was suddenly keenly aware of the muscles in his arms and how smooth, broad, and strong his chest looked. His dark hair, damp from the rain, hung in loose curls across his now bare shoulders, and when he looked up to notice me watching him in the window, he grinned mischievously.

"Here now," I began as I squeezed the excess water from the cloth in my hand, turning around only to find him standing right before me, "I…" Startled at how quickly and silently he moved, my thoughts and words scattered.

"Are you a witch?" He whispered, peering deeply into my eyes, "I must know. Are you?"

"I am a…" confused, completely taken aback, I could only stare into those beautifully intense blue eyes, the one injured not fully open. His injury, I noticed, did not mar his good looks. In fact, if anything, the bruised and swollen eye gave him an air of rugged strength and I suddenly could not remember what he looked like without it. I struggled to think rationally, to come up with an answer to his question, to keep myself protected. Caught off-guard, I felt unprepared, completely vulnerable, and thoroughly shaken.

"I am," I started once more to answer, the words dying on my tongue.

Everything moved in slow motion, as he put his hands on my upper arms and drew me to him. When his lips, slightly parted, soft, and warm, touched mine the world went silent. His breath brushed my cheek. I became keenly aware of my own heartbeat, and beyond that, the beating of his heart near mine. My hands touched his chest as he drew me closer, his kiss intensifying, lips parting, tongue seeking mine. Part of me wanted to melt into him, to disappear completely into his energy and never come back, but another part was angry, suspicious, and ready to race away from him the moment I could escape. Briefly, he drew back, looking into my eyes before again putting his lips on mine, more deeply seeking, more hungrily wanting. At last, he released me as he stepped away, still looking at me intensely.

"Have you bewitched me?"

"Have I what?" I exclaimed in surprise. In that instant I realized that it had never even crossed my mind to do such a thing. The wizards had taught me much about manipulating energy and using magic, and I knew well how to enchant or bewitch a man, but the captain's apparent instant dislike of me had colored my opinion of him. Before he first kissed me, I had never looked at him as other than an adversary. The initial kiss may have softened my view of the man, but I had considered that an aberration. It had unnerved and confused me, but I had never imagined that it might happen again or that I could cast a spell over him to capture his attention as well as his heart.

"You heard me, woman. Have you bewitched me?"

"I assure you," I shook my head, laughing softly, "I have done no such thing, sir!"

"I have never wanted to kiss a woman the way I want to kiss you," he admitted. "Surely, this is some spell you've cast."

"I have cast no spell. I'm sure you have kissed plenty of women in your time," I chided, desperately trying to steer the conversation away from me being a witch.

"I have, sure enough, but not like that. I've had women," he continued, "but I don't want you the way I wanted them."

"Thank you," I responded, making a face at him. "How should I take that?"

"I do not know, don't you see? I don't know! That is why I thought maybe you had cast a spell on me, or maybe on you. I do not know how such things work."

"No, there is no spell," I insisted, "now let me tend to your wound. I can see from here you've bled some more on the dressing. Time for fresh healing salves and clean bandages."

"Yes, of course," he drew a deep breath as I removed the sticky, blood-stained fabric from the wound above his hip. "I am sorry, Falcon Rose. I hope I didn't offend you. I don't know what came over me."

"You did not offend me, Captain Durand," I smiled gently, intentionally not looking up from my work.

"Alexander, when we're alone," he replied.

"Very well, you didn't offend me, Alexander," I offered, smile growing slightly at how ridiculous the conversation suddenly seemed. "Let me get this taken care of so you can go get some food. You need to eat to heal."

"Thank you," was all he said, but I could feel the weight of his gaze on me as I worked on his wounds. I had the certain feeling that, were I to look up into those deep blue eyes again, his lips would be right there, ready to slip smoothly and insistently into another kiss. Part of me wanted nothing more than to do so, to surrender to another kiss, but another part burned with embarrassment, felt ridiculously young and inexperienced, and wanted only to be away from Alexander Durand.

Once the captain's wounds were cleaned and dressed, his bruised and swollen eye washed with a cool, clean cloth, he pulled a fresh tunic down over his head before returning to the dining hall. I had but a few moments to pull myself together and prepare for the next wounded man, and I was just tossing the stained water from the basin out the kitchen door when Beck came into the kitchen.

Eventually, we ended up sitting cross-legged on the floor before the hearth, the roaring fire warming the room nicely despite the glassless arched windows in the far wall. I had tossed much of my food supplies onto the floor in the center of our group and we all helped ourselves to the bounty. Lothar was given scraps of meat and cheese, which he seemed to thoroughly enjoy. I poured him a drink from my water skin before he settled down to rest in the open door between the dining room and the kitchen. It felt a bit strange to have the puppy so nearby yet so far away, but he had apparently decided it was his job to protect us as we slept.

We chatted briefly about our various journeys, how much farther we had to go before reaching Ayndor, and how long and unpleasant the journey back to Esling might be. The men were polite, friendly even, but I could not help but feel a bit uncomfortable being so outnumbered and not really knowing anyone. When the wind outside rose and the rain became an incessant roar, I curled up on my side, drew my blanket up over me and tucked it beneath my chin. Though I was desperately tired and wanted to sleep, I was worried that I might have a nightmare and wake up screaming amidst soldiers who would think me weak, a silly woman. Eventually, I felt my eyelids growing heavy, my breathing grew deep and steady. As I slipped off to sleep, I heard a gentle snore from across the room, reminding me of Corhaven and the comforting sound of my beloved wizard sleeping in the room next to mine. I sighed softly as my eyes closed.

Chapter 26

Rushing down a long, stone-walled corridor, I could feel the weight of my cloak on my shoulders, the gentle rustle of its length flapping behind me as I moved. ThornSting's scabbard bounced along my left leg and its pommel rested comfortably beneath my left hand. I did not know where I was or where I was going, but I felt an urgency to be somewhere. Torches along the walls emitted swirls of heavy, oily dark smoke, their light struggling against the darkness. Woven rugs covered the stone floor, though in the meager light I could discern neither color nor pattern. Ahead, on both the right and left side of the corridor, doors stood open so I glanced into the rooms as I hurried past.

'Falcon Rose,' a feminine voice swirled around me, *'you must hurry!'*

'Hurry where, and why? Who are you? Where are you? Where am I?'

'Falcon, you must hurry!' The melodic voice rose and fell, familiar, yet I could not quite recognize it.

'Who are you?'

'Falcon, my brother's intended is in danger. You must hurry to Ayndor now!'

At that, I finally realized the voice was that of King Rowan's sister, Princess Laurell. But I also knew well that the princess had perished years earlier even as her once-captive brother was returned to Esling.

'Princess Laurell,' I called softly, hoping that she might return so I could see her and speak to her, *'where are you? Where am I?'*

'I'm here,' Came the reply as she appeared before me, looking as she had the last time I had seen her. I had aged, but the princess was still as young and lovely as she had been, though her ephemeral image shifted as she struggled to remain visible. *'You and Rowan's men need to reach Ayndor as soon as you can. My brother's fiancé is in grave danger.'*

'How?' My thoughts were so scattered that I could barely get the word out.

'That I cannot say,' The ghostly apparition shook her head slowly as her image grew paler, *'but you need to help her. Help her, Falcon!'* Laurell's image shifted and though what I saw was still a young female, probably close to the same age the princess had been when she was killed, it was no longer the king's sister before me. Though the second girl's features were similar to those of the princess, it was clearly someone else. *'Hurry!'* The young woman pleaded as her image disappeared.

The snapping of an ember showering out of the hearth brought me instantly awake. I threw back my blankets as I sat up. To my surprise, everyone else was awake and standing, looking around, swords drawn.

"What's happening?" I whispered, my voice raspy and thick from sleeping.

"Shhh," Captain Durand, who was standing nearest to where I sat, replied, index finger before his pursed lips. "We are not alone here. Listen!"

As I stood up and fastened my scabbard belt around my waist, I strained to hear anything. Lothar's nails click, click, clicked as he crossed the stone floor to stand beside me. Durand stood silently, face turned upward, shifting his weight slowly from left foot to right and back, as if expecting an attack at any moment. Suddenly, I heard it. Low, murmuring voices echoed from the floor above where we slept. Strange chanting rose and fell. Chains jangled in the distance. Footsteps overhead moved from one end of the building to the other, soon after coming down the stone staircase before disappearing.

"What is that?" I could not help but gasp.

"There's no one there," Lieutenant De Groot announced as he and Simon Keller came in from the adjacent chapel. "We've searched the abbey from top to bottom and found nothing."

"So, the noise is just..." I faltered, neither willing nor ready to finish the statement. I knew well what the sound we heard was, who had made it, and when, but I was not about to admit that to anyone.

"Just noise," the captain nodded, "but the sun's almost up so we might as well get moving. We can stop later for food and water. Right now, I just want to be away from this place."

"Yes, sir!" De Groot and the other men responded in unison. Had I been quick enough I would have happily joined them, for there was nothing I wanted more than to be out of the abbey and back on the road. The dream I'd had of Princess Laurell was still clear and vivid in my mind and her words laid heavy on my heart. I knew we had to reach Ayndor as soon as we could.

Lothar was uneasy, perhaps sensing the discomfort of the humans around him, and trotted along beside me as I carried my gear through the empty kitchen. The storm had moved on during the night, leaving deep puddles across the yard between the abbey and the stable as well as downed branches and twigs from the surrounding trees. I stepped around the standing water, trying to keep my boots as dry as possible, following the guardsmen into the stable. The horses stood unattended, saddles and gear hung properly on the wooden slats separating the stalls.

"Where is everyone?" I gasped, searching the deep shadows within for any sign of Martin and Prouse.

"Martin! Prouse! Where are you?" Captain Durand called loudly, turning this way and that also in search of the men.

"Their horses are still here, Sir," De Groot observed. "They wouldn't have just wandered off on foot."

"René Martin!" The captain called again, "Edgar Prouse!"

There was no response from the soldiers, only the distant call of a songbird greeting the morning and the gentle nickering of one of the horses as it awaited attention.

"What do we do? We can't just go off and leave them," I shook my head in dismay, "but we really need to get to Ayndor."

"Keller, Beck," Captain Durand commanded, "you two saddle up the horses and prepare them for the journey. We will go look around the area and see if we can find any sign of the men. Falcon Rose, you may do whatever you will, either stay with the men or come with De Groot and me."

"I'll come with you," I replied without hesitation. As I turned and started out of the stable with the two men beside me, I noticed something and drew up short. "Wait a minute. Wait."

"What is it?" Captain Durand looked at me impatiently.

"Look at our tracks in the grass," I pointed to the shimmering line of flattened wet summer-brown blades running from the abbey to the stable. "Look at how the wet grass is laying down. If Martin and Prouse came out of the stables during the night, their tracks should be visible. I see no tracks at all!"

"Is there another way out of the stable?" De Groot scratched his head, peering back into the shadows where even now Beck and Keller were saddling the horses.

"No other door, Sir," Keller answered, having overheard our conversation, "but there is a ladder against the back wall. Must lead to a hayloft or some other storage room above."

"Is it possible?" I gaped, "Could your men be asleep up there?"

"No, they'd have heard me calling," Durand snapped, turning on his heel before striding purposefully toward the back of the stable. Without another word, he climbed the makeshift ladder nailed to the stable wall, disappearing into the rafters overhead. Four footsteps echoed clearly above before he called out that the place was empty. As he climbed back down the ladder, ruby cloak drawn over one shoulder to ease the maneuver, he announced again that the loft was empty.

"Nothing but dust and cobwebs," he explained as he brushed his hands off on his trousers, "and a few broken pieces of equipment. The men are not there."

"Well, if they're not there," I reasoned aloud, "and there is no sign of them walking through the wet grass, where else could they be? Their horses are still here so they had to leave on foot."

"Torocs?" De Groot interjected.

"They would have had to come through the wet grass too," Durand shrugged, "and they'd have taken the horses as well as the men."

"Yes, that's right," the lieutenant nodded.

"So, what now?"

"We saddle up, load our gear, and leave this place,' the captain commanded. "We take the horses with us. I am not leaving them behind. If Martin and Prouse are still alive they will find their way to Ayndor. They are strong, capable men."

"You're taking their horses?" I exclaimed.

"If it were your horse," he looked at me earnestly, "would you want her left here? What if you couldn't make it back? What if you were killed?

Would you want your animal left here to starve or be stolen or attacked by heaven-only-knows what?"

"Oh," embarrassed that I had not thought of such things, I hesitated, "I guess, well, of course not. We can't leave them here. You are right." Promising myself to think before speaking again, I turned away from the open yard and moved through the shadows to the stall where Aeon stood.

Quickly, we saddled our horses and mounted up. The captain gave the command to move out. He and De Groot took the lead so I let Aeon fall in behind them. Beck and Keller brought up the rear as we made our way around the abandoned abbey, past the enclosure where the sheep were grazing, moving on toward the south. Keller led the horses belonging to the missing men, both saddled and bearing their masters' gear. Lothar ran along with us, happy to be racing ahead to investigate something, eventually trotting along beside us when we caught up with him. We rode in silence. Apparently, no one felt conversation appropriate as we each dealt with the loss of Martin and Prouse in our own way. As the land before us widened, the rolling hills opened, our formation fell apart and we rode in a group rather than a line. I kept an eye on Lothar, sniffing around here and there, until he began trotting along beside Aeon. Staring up at me with eyes full of pleading, he was clearly letting me know he was tired and wanted to ride with me. I drew the mare to a halt, leapt easily to the ground, and picked him up in my arms.

"Whoa!" Captain Durand called out as he raised his hand in that familiar gesture. Turning around in the saddle, he looked at me pointedly as I climbed once more onto Aeon's back, but he made no further comment. Apparently, it was enough to let me know that I had made everyone stop, even if only briefly, to deal with my four-legged companion. Turning around, and with a snap of his stallion's reins, he led the group onward.

"Don't worry about him," I murmured to the panting puppy in my arms. "I'll always stop for you!" The warmth, weight, and soft fur of the animal was comforting and I had not known how badly I needed that comfort until I had him in my arms. I gently rubbed the soft fur of his ears and scratched under his chin.

Bringing up the rear of the group, I realized, offered me a freedom I had not had before, and an idea popped into my head. Before I silently contacted my beloved guardian, I dropped a gentle 'cloaking' energy over myself, the puppy, and my mount. If anyone looked, they would see us well enough, but our images would be softened to the naked eye and we would not attract attention. I settled Lothar in front of me, with one hand on his back.

'Cor, I need your help!'

'Of course! What is it, Falcon?' Came the response, his voice warm and familiar.

'Two of the king's guards disappeared overnight. We sheltered in an abandoned abbey and the two men, René Martin and Edgar Prouse, slept in the stable. Their gear and horses were there this morning, but there was no sign of them. I need to find out what happened.'

'How can I help, my dear?'

'I want to go in search of them, as I did for Princess Laurell and Prince Rowan when he was captive. I need you to guide me with your words as you did then.'

'Of course! You wish to do this now?'

'I've dimmed myself so none of the men I'm traveling with will notice,' I explained. *'Aeon is following the other horses so it should be safe. Lothar's beneath my hand, but I am not wearing my father's brooch as I did then. Will that matter?'*

'No child,' he answered softly, *'that brooch simply made the connection between you and the deBirch family. The guards have no such connection so you will be searching for them using a different technique. I will guide you. Are you ready?'*

'Ready!'

Taking a deep, cleansing breath, I closed my eyes, focusing on the steady movement of Aeon's hooves, her strong shoulders moving up and back, the sensation of her head bobbing as she moved.

'Falcon,' Cor intoned, his voice taking on a different timbre, *'I am going to ask you a series of questions now. Will you answer if you can and if you know the truth?'*

My thoughts already spinning, I replied, *'Yes, Cor. I will answer if I can and if I know the truth. Ask what you will.'*

'Are René Martin and Edgar Prouse alive?' The wizard asked evenly.

Weighing the question before sending it out in all directions, I searched for the truth.

'No.'

'They are dead?'

'No, not dead.' I murmured.

'But they're not alive…'

'René Martin and Edgar Prouse exist no longer, but they are neither dead nor alive.'

'What does that mean, Falcon? What are you seeing?'

'Darkness,' was all I could utter as a winged shadow appeared from out of nowhere. Suddenly, I knew what Martin and Prouse had experienced, though I was unable to find the words.

'Darkness.' Cor responded before adding, *'Do you mean night? The darkness of night?'*

'No,' I struggled to grasp the right words to convey what the soldiers had seen and felt. *'Not night. Darkness. Dark, dark. Hungry dark. Hungry darkness. Swallowed up. Eaten by darkness. Eaten by the hungry darkness.'*

'The men were…' my beloved wizard's voice cracked as it failed.

'They were eaten by the hungry darkness.'

'Falcon! Come back! Wake up. Draw yourself back. Falcon!' Cor's voice was raised in alarm, a touch of panic made his words stronger and louder.

'Cor!' I replied silently, eyes opening, thoughts settling as I looked around at where we were going. The four soldiers rode at a comfortable distance ahead of me, apparently unaware of what I had been doing. Aeon continued her steady pace, my hand on her rein offering slight pressure to keep her from increasing her gait. *'I'm all right now, Cor. I am back.'*

'Do you recall what you said or what you saw?'

'Not entirely,' I admitted, *'but we are not going to find the missing men, are we?'*

'No child, you will not. You said that they were eaten by the hungry darkness.'

'What does that mean?'

'I am sure I do not know, lass. But I expect that in time you will know that answer too.'

'Thank you, Cor,' I responded, suddenly feeling both relieved and sad for the guards, their families, and friends. *'Any more information about what is going on? Any help from the other wizards? Any word?'*

'Only that whoever is stirring this power is very dangerous,' he paused, *'and we shall all be needed to stop the storm that's brewing.'*

'We are nearing Ayndor, and I hope to be collecting the king's fiancé and her family and coming back to Esling as quickly as possible. I miss you and the others.' A sudden rush of loneliness and longing washed over me. Tears welled in my eyes. I craved a hug like I had never wanted one before.

'We miss you too, Falcon.' The wizard's words touched my heart, wrapping around my shoulders like a warm, heavy cloak. *'I am sorry about the loss of your friends. You take care and travel safe, my dear.'*

The feeling of warmth lifted, the wizard's energy withdrew, and I rode along astride my beautiful black mare, puppy beneath my hand and weight on my mind. I knew Martin and Prouse were no more, but how could I explain that to Captain Durand and the others? And even if I did, how could I explain that they were neither dead nor alive, that their bodies would never be found or recovered for proper burials. Suddenly I regretted my actions, wishing I had not searched for the missing men.

"Maybe not knowing," I murmured to the sleeping puppy under my hand, "is sometimes better. How do I know and not tell anyone?" Glancing ahead, seeing Simon Keller leading the riderless horses, beasts whose owners they would never again see in this world, almost brought tears to my eyes. I slowly shook my head at the realization that keeping such information to myself was not going to be easy.

Lothar lifted his head to yawn languidly, showing his sharp white teeth and long pink tongue. He looked at me curiously.

"It's fine," smiling softly, I whispered, "I didn't really expect you to answer."

With that, I dropped the energy cloak I had been protecting us with, bumped Aeon gently in the flanks, and hastened to catch up with the others.

As I drew abreast of the guards, I realized I'd lost track of time. Had I been riding along, 'searching' for the missing men for mere moments, or had half the day lumbered past? The sky was steel gray, covered in clouds, and offered me not even a guess as to the time of day. I was just about to ask how far we might be from Ayndor when Captain Durand singled out Simon Keller to ride ahead to see how much further our destination lay.

"Scout Ayndor and return," he commanded. "If we can arrive well before sundown we will do so today. If the sun will have set by the time we get there, we will wait until morning."

"Aye, sir!" Keller snapped a salute, handed the rope by which he led the missing men's horses to Beck, turned, and spurred his mount.

We four simply sat astride our horses and watched the soldier disappear, before the captain ordered us to dismount and take a break. I was tempted to ask why we had to wait until daylight to enter Ayndor if we arrived after dark, but decided that would be tantamount to questioning the captain's authority, so I swung down from the saddle without comment. Releasing Lothar to the ground, I stretched my arms over my head as I looked at our surroundings. The terrain had certainly changed as we had traveled. The rolling hills had gone from grass-covered to mostly dry, weed-scattered, pebble-strewn dust. In the distance and off to our right, majestic, snow-capped mountains rose high into the steely cloud-covered sky, but ahead lay only a few foothills replete with tall weeds and scraggly bushes. Scattered stones rose from the ground, some only big enough to trip over, others large enough to rest comfortably on and it was the latter upon which we agreed to eat. The horses were allowed to graze on what meager tufts of grass they could find as we dug into our provisions. Lothar ran around relieving himself on anything that did not move. Finally, he returned to me, eyes full of pleading, tongue lolling. I tossed him some dried meat and scraps of bread that were so hard and dry they would probably have hurt my teeth had I tried to eat them. The puppy's sharp little fangs had no trouble at all making quick work of the crusts and he eagerly swallowed as he looked at me for more.

By the time we had eaten, cleared and re-packed our supplies, the clouds in the sky had begun to break apart and patches of blue led me to believe it was mid-afternoon. If we were to make it to Ayndor, Simon Keller would have to be returning to us soon. I wasn't sure how I felt about spending another night on the road, but I realized I was not looking forward to reaching Ayndor either. I had gathered Aeon's reins and was about to put my foot in the stirrup when I heard the thundering of approaching horse hooves. I looked up just in time to see Simon Keller racing toward us, his cheeks red, face flushed, a relieved smile on his lips.

"Sir!" He reined his horse to a sliding stop, adding between gasps, "Ayndor lies just ahead. We should reach it easily before sundown."

"Excellent!" Captain Durand responded as he mounted his stallion. "Get yourself a drink, Keller, and take a short break. We will go on and you can catch up."

"Yes, sir!" Keller smiled as he leapt from the saddle. "Aye sir!"

Chapter 27

As we rode through the outer gates of Ayndor we were greeted by large crowds of people, some obviously happy to see us, others scowling outright. It seemed a reasonable assumption that Keller had alerted the guards of our impending arrival and the king, in turn, had made an appearance before his people to announce it. Captain Durand had directed us all to don our ruby cloaks, identifying us as emissaries of Esling, and Beck had unfurled a royal flag on a short pole which he seated into a mounting on his saddle. Beck led the way, Durand and De Groot followed side by side. Keller and I brought up the rear with Keller once more leading the unmanned horses. The crowd seemed polite, but there was no celebration, no cheering or clapping, no one waved or called out to us.

"I guess they are not very happy to see us," I confided in Simon, who, though he had caught up with us easily, still looked a bit winded from his ride.

"We are taking away their princess," he smiled wryly, "and their royal family, at least for a time. I'm sure the king has announced to his people that he and his daughters will be going to Esling for the wedding, and the bride will not return."

"Oh," nodding, I muttered, "I hadn't really thought of it like that."

King Radolph's guards, who had been waiting just outside the city walls, escorted us through the crowd gathered in the outer court, past the barbican, and through the inner gate to the royal courtyard. At their leader's command, we came to a halt and dismounted, handing our horses' reins to the stable hands who had appeared silently, ready to serve us. Lothar remained in the crook of my left arm, safely hidden beneath the folds of the ruby cloak, as I was not sure how anyone would react to the puppy's presence. To my surprise, as we passed through the arched double doors to enter the wide stone corridor, we were not asked to remove our weapons, so ThornSting's weight hung reassuringly on my hip, the tip of the scabbard touching lightly on my left calf as I walked. Captain Durand led our group while Lieutenant De Groot and Simon Keller walked on either side of me. Beck followed closely behind us as the king's guards escorted us down the wide hall and around the corner. The Grand Hall opened to us with a flair of horns announcing our arrival. I was a bit taken aback by the fanfare and I could feel Lothar tremble in my arms. Beneath the cover of the cloak, I petted him reassuringly as we were led down a wide aisle covered in a gold and blue woven tapestry rug. Large, black wrought-iron chandeliers hung from the high, vaulted ceiling, their thick column candles casting pools of yellow light on the polished stone floor below. Wrought-iron torches burned in sconces on the walls, and though the room was vast and tall arched windows were open to the outside, the air was warm and pungent with the smoke of burning incense. On the dais at the end of the aisle, the king of Ayndor sat on his elaborately carved and ornately decorated throne. Smaller thrones, one on either side, were similarly appointed though more delicate and upon them sat the princesses. King Radolph of Ayndor was resplendent in robes of royal blue and gold, a heavy gold crown adorned with sapphires, diamonds, and rubies resting atop his black and silver hair. His long beard, neatly trimmed and brushed silky smooth lay upon his chest, and his dark eyes shone with intelligence. At first, he merely looked at us, one after the other. Finally, he smiled broadly, white teeth gleaming against the chestnut tone of his skin.

"Welcome to Ayndor," the king greeted us at length, as protocol dictated he address us first.

"Your Highness," Captain Durand bowed deeply in response, "I am Captain Alexander Durand of King Rowan of Esling's royal guard. My men and I are here to escort you and your daughters to Castle deBirch." Durand rose to stand at attention.

"Captain Durand," King Radolph replied, "you are most welcome here. I assure you that my daughters and I will be ready to accompany you and your men to Esling as soon as possible."

"Your Highness," the captain bowed again.

"But I see it is not just you and your men who have been sent to escort us," the king added, "as you seem to have a female with you. I was unaware King Rowan intended to send a woman."

"Your Highness, this is Lady Falcon Rose," Captain Durand introduced me, urging me forward with the wave of one hand. "Lady Falcon Rose is a member of the Order of Healers as well as a trusted friend and confidante of King Rowan's."

At the captain's words I hesitated, tumbling what he had said over in my mind as I tried to follow proper protocol and bow correctly. My body went through the motions as the little voice in my head marveled, *'Trusted friend and confidante of the king's? Where and when did this happen and why wasn't I informed? Could King Rowan have instructed the captain to introduce me in that way? Was that likely? Can I keep considering this matter and not make a social blunder? Time to pay attention, Falcon. You can wonder about this later!'*

"Your Highness," I bowed as I had seen Captain Durand do, also rising to stand at attention. "I am Lady Falcon Rose and I am honored to be escorting you and the princesses to Esling. I am at your service."

"Lady Falcon Rose," King Radolph said my name as if considering its worth, "this is my daughter, King Rowan's intended, Princess Merilda." He gestured at the young woman seated on the throne to his left. Golden blond hair shining and braided, the king's fiancé wore robes of white and gold, and upon her brow rested a delicately fashioned crown of golden leaves with pale blue gems creating flowers. Merilda's ivory skin was smooth, her cheekbones high and well-defined, and her full lips were stained soft crimson. She regarded me with thickly lashed deep blue eyes, nodding slightly in acknowledgment.

"And this is my youngest daughter," the king continued, gesturing toward the young woman seated on the throne to his right, "Princess Eleanora." The young woman on the throne smiled up at me, not at all as reserved or shy as her older sister. Princess Eleanora was a raven-haired, green-eyed beauty, with skin obviously kissed by the sun. She wore robes of gold and silver, and the golden coronet upon her brow sparkled with emeralds and rubies. A delicate gold chain around her neck disappeared into her decolletage. When her lively green eyes met mine, a shiver shot through me, for her expression was one of haughty challenge. There was no reason for this young woman to look at me as she did, but it was clear she was not the delicate flower her older sister seemed to be. Princess Eleanora neither nodded at me nor did she speak, she just beamed that smile before turning her eyes to the men, Captain Durand especially. For a moment, as I looked at the princesses, I felt plain, average-looking, unfeminine, and graceless. The young women were both so lovely, so elegantly dressed with their hair so nicely brushed and styled. And, perhaps more importantly to me, they looked like they belonged doing what they were doing. They looked trained and groomed for their positions, and they looked comfortable, at ease. The murder of my parents had ripped away any sense of comfort I had ever known, and any future filled with normal aspirations or achievements had been stolen that night. As I watched Princess Eleanora coquettishly bat her eyes at Captain Durand, smile, and move her gaze to Lieutenant De Groot, I realized that I was jealous. I saw how the men looked at the beautiful young women. There was a mixture of admiration, appreciation, and awe in their eyes as they beheld the princesses. The only looks I had ever attracted were those of suspicion, doubt, and maybe even pity. For a moment, I wanted desperately to be someone else and somewhere else. Suddenly, Princess Merilda raised those deep blue eyes to look at me and I remembered myself. Something in her eyes, a searching or pleading, brought me back to all I had learned, all I had become, and I remembered that I had no desire to play games with feminine wiles. Blushing, I glanced back at Princess Eleanora to find her staring at me, more specifically staring at the front of my cloak beneath which Lothar remained hidden. It was as if she could see right through the fabric and for one horrific moment, I thought she would say something, ask to see what I had beneath my cloak, or alert her father that I had an animal in my arms, but she merely smiled slyly, green eyes twinkling, as she turned her attention back to Captain Durand. In a moment of gut-wrenching clarity, I realized I did not like her looking at the captain that way. Of course, I knew I had no right to feel that way. He certainly wasn't anything to me despite the kisses we had shared, yet that pang of jealousy was too keen to ignore.

"You men may bunk in the guard house with my troops," King Radolph announced, "and you, Lady Falcon Rose, will share quarters with the girls' ladies in waiting, if that is agreeable. I have begun preparations for the journey and we should be able to depart Ayndor in two days' time."

"Yes, Your Highness," Captain Durand replied before I could even respond. "Thank you, Your Highness."

Tearing my gaze away from the royal family, I gathered my thoughts and took a deep breath. The emotions I had just experienced, so intense and in such a short amount of time, left me feeling confused and unbalanced. My inner voice assured me that it was just silliness and that it would never happen again, so I put a smile on my face to politely greet the lady in waiting who presented herself to me even as the men walked down the carpeted aisle following one of King Radolph's aides.

"I am Sofia," the young woman bowed her head, her white linen cap shining bright and crisp in the candlelight of the Grand Hall. "I am happy to attend to your needs and I'll show you where you can be comfortable. Please, follow me."

With that, the lady in waiting led me down the tapestry-rugged aisle, through the double doors, and into the wide corridor beyond. To my delight, we walked out into the inner courtyard where marble benches lined wide walks and lush, beautiful plants grew in profusion.

"Um," I cleared my throat to get Sofia's attention, not sure what her reaction to what I was about to say might be, "if we could take a moment. You see, I have this friend here." At that I drew back the side of my cloak, revealing a calm but curious Lothar peering up at the young woman.

"Oh!" She gaped, hands flying to her cheeks. "Oh my, not here. Don't put it down here. Come. Follow me!"

Turning on her heels, Sofia rushed us along the edge of the courtyard, and through a narrow gap between two buildings. She hurried us around the perimeter of a vegetable garden beside an outer stone building with a low roof and open arched windows. The smell of fresh bread baking wafted from the open door and I realized it was the bakery that served the castle. I knew we must be on the backside of the palace where all the mundane yet integral services worked to support the royal family and the city at large.

"Come," Sofia called once more as she stepped beneath a vine-covered trellis. Following the young woman, I found myself outside the castle grounds, in a meadow strewn with fruit trees and wild brambles. "You can let your friend go here. It can run freely and safely."

"I'm happy to stay with you, as the king suggested," I shrugged as I released Lothar to the grass, "but if Lothar can't stay with me, I'd prefer to stay in the stable where I could be with him."

"Our quarters, those of us who serve the princesses," she explained, "are just there, beside the kitchen. I'll let the other women know about Lothar, is it? If they have no objections, he can stay with us. We are very near the back of the castle so no one needs to know about him, but you must not let the royal family know he is within the castle walls."

"They wouldn't take kindly to his presence?" I gaped.

"Perhaps they would not mind at all," she admitted, "but one never knows. It's best if they know nothing of your friend until we're on the road to Esling."

"You're coming with us?"

"Unless Princess Merilda changes her mind and chooses another attendant." Nodding, she added, "I am very much looking forward to the journey and to seeing your beautiful country. May I pet your friend?"

By that time, Lothar had relieved himself and raced in huge, joyous circles around the meadow. He had flushed out a rabbit and run it into the ground, pawing at the earth where the terrified creature had disappeared, whimpering his disappointment. Trotting back to where we stood talking, he presented us with a crooked stick he had picked up from the grass, changed his mind, and took it back to gnaw on one end.

"Of course," I nodded encouragement. "He's usually quite friendly!"

After the lady in waiting crouched down and petted Lothar, cooing to him and telling him what a good boy he was, she rose with a smile, wiping her hands on the fabric of her generous skirt.

"I'm going to go talk to the other women," she assured me, "to make sure they're all right with him staying with us, but I don't think anyone will object. He might be a pleasant diversion. If anyone is likely to take exception, it would be Lady Valeria. She is the eldest of us and she is not well. Sometimes her health affects her disposition, the poor thing. Pain makes her unpleasant from time to time, but I will ask politely. You stay here and enjoy the air. I will return anon!"

Standing in the meadow, looking at the lovely trees, grasses, and what appeared to be a lake twinkling in the setting sun in the distance, I could not help but wonder where the men were and what they might be doing. I felt strangely bereft at being separated from them, I realized, and in some odd way I missed being with them.

"Come, Lady Falcon Rose," Sofia appeared beneath the vine-covered trellis, waving at me, "everyone's agreed! Lady Valeria wants to meet you, and Lothar too!"

Scooping Lothar up in my arms, I trotted across the meadow to where Sofia stood waiting. She was obviously happy and relieved, and she turned to escort me quickly through the grounds at the back of the castle and into the kitchen. The heat from four burning hearths was heavy in the room, despite the door standing open and leaded glass windows canted out to the fresh air. Exotic spices perfumed the room, making my mouth water despite not knowing exactly what it was that was being prepared. I realized, as we hurried through the throng of cooks and maids, that I was hungry and very much looking forward to supper.

"Lady Valeria," Sofia announced, as she led me into a nicely appointed room, "this is our guest, Lady Falcon Rose." With six perfectly tidied beds, two small desks upon which rested candlesticks not currently lit, and several upholstered chairs, it was clearly a place created for and used by women. Fresh flowers in a blue ceramic vase stood on a wide sill beneath a leaded glass window and nearby, rocking in a chair, sat a woman of indeterminate age. Her hair was covered with a crisp white linen cap, similar to the one Sofia wore, and her dress was an elegant dark blue with a collar trimmed in delicate white lace. Her skin was smooth and porcelain, eyes dark and clear, but she did not smile, nor did she greet me. Instead, she merely looked me up and down, nodding silently.

"You can put Lothar down now," my escort suggested. "Lady Valeria has said it's permitted."

"Very well," I sighed, reluctantly putting the puppy down on the floor. "Greetings Lady Valeria. I am Falcon Rose and I'm pleased to meet you."

At first, I did not think the woman was going to respond, but at length she drew a deep breath and placed her hands tidily in her lap, "I too am pleased to meet you, Falcon Rose. You must forgive me if I do not rise to greet you properly. You see, I have an injury on my foot that will not heal and it often pains me to walk. I should not be surprised if I'm let go from service soon, in fact, as I am no longer as helpful as I once was."

"Begging your pardon, Ma'am," I smiled gently, "I don't know if you're aware of it, but I am a member of the Order of Healers. I would be happy to examine your injury and treat it if I can."

"Is this true?" The woman looked pointedly at Sofia, who nodded silently in response. "Very well, Lady Falcon Rose. I doubt there is anything that can be done, but you may have a look. Those who claim to be healers in Ayndor have tried to heal the wound, but they have been unable. It did almost disappear once before it returned even bigger and more painful."

"I'll need my gear," I turned to Sofia, "and fresh clean water."

"I'll see to it right away," she curtsied as she glanced at Lady Valeria, "and I will hurry back."

"In the meantime," the woman in the rocking chair interjected, "you may come sit with me, Falcon Rose. Tell me of yourself, what you do in your country, and how your journey here has gone. Regale me with your tale!" She indicated an empty chair in the corner of the room, not far from where she sat rocking, and I nodded as I took a seat. As I drew nearer, I noticed that she was not all that much older than Sofia or myself, though tiny wrinkles at the corners of her eyes and lips indicated she had been suffering pain and discomfort for some time. She was shorter than me, a bit broader through the shoulders and thicker through the torso, but certainly not heavy or unattractive. As we spoke, I told her of my parents, how my father was a brave and noble servant of King Stephen's, King Rowan's father, and how my mother was a much sought-after healer. Skimming over the details of their deaths, I explained how I had been found and raised by Cor and the other Elemental Wizards, how I had been charged with and honored to rescue the prince of Esling and return him to take the throne on his father's demise. She asked questions from time to time, and I found her to be a kind and intelligent companion. By the time Sofia returned with my saddlebags and my other belongings, I was just reaching the point in my story where King Rowan had dispatched me to help escort his fiancé and her family to Esling.

I examined Lady Valeria's ankle as I continued my tale, gently turning the swollen, discolored appendage as I spoke. Trying not to show expression or alarm as I talked, I could not help but be taken aback by the size and condition of the injury. The flesh of the woman's left ankle appeared raised, angry red, and full of heat. The wound itself was obviously full of infection and the used bandage I removed from it was stained with blood and gore. A pungent odor rose from the area causing me to grimace slightly as I had Sofia carry the basin of water she had procured to where I knelt.

"Please ask someone in the kitchen to bring me some hot water," I smiled at the young lady in waiting, "and if they have clean cloths I may need more."

"Yes, Ma'am," she nodded succinctly as she hurried from the room.

Lothar, having investigated most everything in the room, had taken up a position on the other side of Lady Valeria's rocking chair, and as he slept curled up, she sometimes dropped her hand to pet him gently.

"Do you know how you came to have this wound?" Looking up into her concerned eyes, I asked Lady Valeria.

"I do not," she shook her head slowly. "It just appeared one morning. At first, it was just a bit swollen and had a red center, but it seemed to get worse and became painful. The king had his healer look at it, and he treated it with some ointment. It did seem to get better and I thought it was going to heal, but it did not. In fact, it began to get bigger and the skin ruptured. What came out was nasty looking and smelling and I hoped, once gone, that would be the end of it. But, as you can see, it's never fully healed."

"I see," I nodded, realizing what it was I was looking at. "Well, I believe that this is an insect bite and it must be lanced. The reason it's never healed is because the creature who bit you also deposited its eggs in the wound. After a time, probably more than a fortnight, the eggs hatch and begin to feast on your flesh, eventually depositing their own eggs."

"So, if something's not done soon…" The startled woman rushed to the obvious conclusion.

"Well, maybe not soon," I shrugged, "but yes, eventually the bite would cause your death. But do not worry. I know what to do and how to do it. I have the tools and the training. I promise you will be right as rain."

"Thank you," she sighed, closing her eyes as she drew a deep breath, "so it's best if you do your work right away."

"Yes, Ma'am," nodding, I turned to Sofia who had just entered the room carrying a steaming kettle in one hand and a stack of folded cloths in the other. "I'll need your assistance, Sofia!"

After some quick organizing of my supplies, laying out herbs and ointments, bandages, and cloths for wiping, I washed the small, oh-so-sharp, blade Deacon had given me during my training as Healer. I had only ever used it in practice before, but it fit perfectly in my hand, was well balanced, and seemed eager to do its job. I gave Lady Valeria a sip of elixir Cor and Deacon had taught me to make, giving it a few moments to work until I felt her relax. Sofia brought a wooden stool from across the room and I placed a few cloths on it before propping Lady Valeria's foot upon it. By this time the sun had begun its descent in the western sky and though there was still some light shining through the window, it was not enough to serve me, so I directed Sofia to light the candle on the desk and hold it while I worked.

Once everything was in order, I whispered a little prayer to the powers that be that they might guide my hand and help in my healing work, I gently sliced an incision across the top of the swollen injury. Immediately blood and black viscus liquid oozed from the wound. I did as I was taught, coaxing as much dead tissue from the area as I could, opening the wound further and deeper until I found that which I sought. Deep inside the fevered and angry flesh lay a kernel of black, probably no bigger than a pea, but it had small tentacles reaching out to the surrounding tissue and I knew immediately that they were supplying nourishment to the eggs inside. Cutting swiftly and surely, I sliced through the sac's arms to lift it from the wound. Sofia, holding the candle beside me, offered me an empty dish and when I deposited the egg sac in it, she quickly took it away. I stuffed cloth in the wound to stanch the bleeding, but I knew it would take more than that to heal. Taking the candle from my assistant's hand, I heated the tip of my cutting blade in the flame until it changed from black to red. Firmly, I touched the searing metal to Lady Valeria's open wound. She screamed, in pain and surprise no doubt, but quieted as I removed the blade and poured cool water over the cauterized wound. With a sigh, she relaxed and closed her eyes as I applied healing ointment to her ankle and bandaged it properly. Whether the woman had fainted or was merely sleeping, I could not be sure, but her breathing was deep and steady. I cleaned up the area, put my things away, and followed Sofia out of the room. Lothar, apparently tired and content, remained curled up on the floor beside the sleeping woman's rocking chair.

"Let's get some supper," Sofia whispered as we moved into the hallway.

"Yes, please," I smiled in anticipation. "I am quite hungry!"

Chapter 28

In two days' time, as the king had promised, the caravan was loaded and ready to leave Ayndor. The first wagon was filled with crates, chests, and barrels as well as stacks of folded cloth items. A second wagon was loaded with food and supplies for the journey. Come sunrise on the morning of our third day in the city, a team of four magnificent white horses pulled an elaborately appointed coach into the courtyard and we watched, standing at attention, as the king and both princesses climbed aboard. The coach door was closed by a footman who climbed up on a shelf-type seat on the back before the driver snapped the reins. With a groan, the heavy wheels moved slowly forward as the driver turned the vehicle toward the outer court. Those in service to the royal family who would be sharing the journey waited patiently for the coach to disappear, following on foot or on horseback. King Rowan's guards and I walked from the inner courtyard to the outer where our horses waited, fully saddled and ready to go. Lothar, having run and romped in the meadow before eating, and getting as much attention from the princesses' ladies in waiting as he could, now rested comfortably in the crook of my arm beneath my ruby cloak. With the help of the maids, I had been able to keep the puppy concealed from the royal family and was relieved to be away from the castle and on the road.

Once everyone was outside the outer courtyard, King Rowan's men and I took the lead, followed by four of King Radolph's guards, and the royal coach. The two supply wagons followed, and, to my relief, the servants of the king and the princesses rode on horseback behind them. The remainder of the royal guards, five of them from what I could see from my position toward the head of the caravan, brought up the rear behind a string of unsaddled horses. Whether those unmanned horses were intended for the royals to ride or as a gift for the house of deBirch, I could only guess, but that everyone traveling was either riding in a vehicle or on horseback meant we would make better time than if some were walking. I knew that it was not unusual for servants to walk on such journeys, sometimes bearing heavy loads, so I was delighted that we would not be slowed down by those on foot.

Well before the sun had reached the mid-point in the heavens, the royal family had sent word through the ranks that they required a respite from journeying. Any hope I had of making the trek from Ayndor to Esling a quick and easy one was dashed, and it was with some dismay and regret that we called the caravan to a halt. The curtains on the royal coach's windows were dutifully opened by maids, the footman jumped down from his perch to open the door, and the king stepped down into the summer dry grass wearing elaborately woven satin shoes. Watching from astride my mare's back, I could only shake my head at the sight of the king, resplendent in pale robes, and the princesses, both wearing gowns of cream-colored linen. Chairs were set up for the trio beneath a huge leaf-shaped shade held by a servant, once they were seated, they were offered drinks, fruit, and other delicacies. I looked at Captain Durand, who seemed nearly as dismayed as I felt, and shrugged.

"Looks like we might as well dismount and stretch our legs," I observed, "as who knows how long we'll be here."

"Indeed," he groaned as he swung down from the saddle.

Once down from my mare's back, I released Lothar to the ground and let him get some exercise, tossing a stick I had found just to keep him entertained and away from the royal family. Those of us in King Rowan's guard stayed close to the front of the caravan, as it was clear we were not needed to protect Radolph and his daughters. The guards from Ayndor seemed sufficient to the task, so we were free to relax and wander a bit. We had not gone so far from the city as to see much change in the landscape, but I could see the snowcapped mountaintops in the distance. After having a drink from my water skin, checking on Captain Durand's bandages and Lieutenant De Groot's hand, I had run out of things to do and even Lothar had grown weary of playing fetch. Finally, the king stood with his daughters and the three disappeared back into the carriage. The servant with the leaf-shaped shade turned to make his way to the wagon where he deposited the thing before joining the others. The footman set about preparing the coach while another servant wearing a bright blue tunic and black pants approached those of us watching the proceedings about to mount our horses.

"I beg your pardon," the young man bowed, hands pressed together as if in prayer, "but I am to inform you that His Highness wishes to call a halt to the day's journey long enough before sundown that his servants will have sufficient time to erect the royal tents. His Highness and the princesses will be retiring to their private quarters before the sun sets and they will dine within."

"Very well," Captain Durand nodded, "it will be as the king wishes."

"Thank you, sir," the servant bowed again, "thank you very much, sir."

Once the young man had disappeared back along the entourage, I gathered Aeon's reins, picked Lothar up, and mounted the mare. Captain Durand favored me with a wry smile before glancing at Lieutenant De Groot, "We've got our orders!"

Out of curiosity, and perhaps a bit of boredom, I took to leaving the cadre of guards to ride back along the caravan and visit with Sofia and the other servants. Though I gently probed for information about the princesses, their natures, and demeanors, I got only the vaguest of responses. I could not tell if those who served them were being loyal and protective of their mistresses or if they were in fear of the young women. Eventually, I stopped enquiring or even referring to the royal family and instead we spoke of the food, the weather, and the customs of Ayndor. To my surprise I noticed several children among the servants, six of them to be exact. Four little girls and two little boys rode sharing saddles with adults and when I asked about them Sofia gave me a strange look.

"Her Highness, Princess Merilda, insists on having them around," the lady in waiting said with a shrug.

"Servants in training, are they?" I chuckled for the children looked much too young to be in service.

"Mostly they're given small tasks to complete. We are charged with caring for them, watching over them, making sure they are fed, kept clean, dressed, and safe."

"Is the princess so fond of children?" Shaking my head in dismay, I could not see any reason for the toddlers' presence, unless Princess Merilda simply adored them and wanted some about to entertain and perhaps cheer her. Of course, I reasoned silently, as she was soon to be the wife of King Rowan, she would be fond of children, for she would be charged with producing an heir for the royal line.

"She is not," Sofia answered pointedly, but would offer no further explanation.

"Who are the children? Where do they come from? Where are their parents?"

"The children were collected from various farms surrounding the city," she sighed, dropping her voice to barely above a whisper. "Their parents were paid handsomely, so it's told, and were promised their children would be afforded every luxury and comfort."

"Are they not?"

"What comfort is there being taken away from your home, your mother's love, and your father's protection? They are well fed and afforded shelter and such, but treated more like..." the young maid's words trailed off.

"Pets!" I finished her thought, my own voice lowered.

"Yes," she nodded.

We rode on in silence for a while, until I excused myself and spurred my mount to catch up to King Rowan's guards. The men made no comment when I joined them, and as I had much on my mind to think about, I was relieved at the silence.

As instructed, well before sundown the caravan was drawn to a halt on a level piece of ground and immediately the royal servants set about putting up amazingly grand tents beneath which the king and his daughters would shelter. The royal family remained inside the coach, door and windows open to the fresh air, until the tents were erected and they filed silently inside. We of King Rowan's guards set up camp near the lead of the caravan, building a fire from gathered tree branches and twigs, putting our things on the ground. We removed the gear from our horses, tethering them loosely, and prepared to use the saddles as pillows. As we were digging for provisions through our respective bags, Sofia and two other servants came bearing food from King

Radolph. The aroma of the royal fare had reached us well before we were prepared to eat, but we never dared hope that what succulent delicacies the king and princesses were having might be shared with us. A platter heaped with meat and vegetables, glistening in sauce, and smelling of spices I did not know was given to us, as well as several loaves of oddly shaped and equally strange colored bread. The maids offered to bring us water, wine, or other drink, but we declined as we had plenty in our water skins and were thankful enough just for the food. Sofia suggested we eat at our leisure, adding that she would return for the platters before the lights inside the tent were doused.

"Once the lights go out," she confided, "everyone goes to sleep. No noise must disturb the king."

With that ominous word, she turned and hurried back to where the servants were working behind the royal tent. To my amazement, the food was delicious and there was plenty for everyone. Whether we were being watched as we ate or it was just coincidence, as soon as the platters were empty the maids appeared to spirit them away through the gathering darkness. Lieutenant De Groot spread his bedroll on the far side of the fire and Beck put his things down beside it. Simon Keller put his gear not too far, nor too near, to the right of where I had made my bed, and Captain Durand settled to my left. The men spoke softly among themselves for a bit as the stars began to twinkle in the sky. Suddenly the whole camp went dark as the lights inside the royal tent were doused. The night was strangely quiet, the silence broken only by the gentle swishing of a horse's tail, a cricket's chirp, or a distant owl's hoot. I drew my blanket up to my chin as I laid back against my saddle. Lothar, who had enjoyed visiting with most everyone in the caravan, except for the royals of course, had shared our food and enjoyed a drink from his bowl before stretching out beside me on my blanket. Rolling onto my right side, I closed my eyes to listen to the night, hoping sleep would come quickly and quietly.

Golden sun surrounded Corhaven as I stepped outside, empty wicker basket hanging on my wrist. The air was cool and moist, smelling of deep earth, thick moss, and decaying leaves. Songbirds called and answered from the branches in the trees surrounding the cottage and somewhere nearby a bullfrog bellowed its greeting. Blade in hand, I stepped down from the stoop into the dew-kissed grass, heading to the woods to harvest wild lavender, nettle, and feverwort. Mara appeared from around the corner of the house, shining in white robes, the shock of silver in her hair glowing in the early morning sun

"Child, dear child, where have you been?" She murmured as she slipped one arm around my shoulders. "Child, sweet child, have you been well? Child, my child, come walk with me. Child, lost child, do follow me."

The felinetrix's words confused me. She asked questions but gave me no time to answer. She kept calling me 'child' over and over. The rhythm and sing-song tones sounded familiar, but I could not quite figure out why. In fact, I couldn't understand what was going on as I struggled to escape her embrace, but she held me firm and continued to talk nonsense.

My eyelids fluttered open as the words I was hearing finally broke the spell of my dream. A distant voice, low but female, was singing, or maybe it was chanting. The little voice in my head giggled in relief, *That is what you were hearing in your dream! It wasn't Mara talking nonsense, it was this person speaking, or singing, or whatever she is doing.*

"And just what IS she doing," I hissed under my breath as I sat up to toss my blanket aside. Lothar, it appeared, had scooted away from where I lay and was now snuggled up beside Simon Keller. A momentary twinge of betrayal stole through me as I considered how easily my four-legged companion had abandoned me for another. Just as quickly I chided myself for the thought, as surely even dogs dreamed and moved in their sleep and could not be held accountable for what they did in that state. When the sleepy pup raised his head to give me an inquisitive look, I silently shook my head, put my hand up, and mouthed 'No, stay!' Satisfied, he laid his muzzle back on his paws and closed his eyes. As I looked around the camp, I noticed that everyone else was asleep, well, everyone but whoever was doing the chanting. The soldiers around the fire slept silently and still. The horses tethered loosely in the distance dozed unmoving and quiet. King Radolph's tent stood silhouette against the sky, a darkness deeper than night. Silence had settled over everything, but I knew it was an unnatural silence. I rose quietly from my bed, careful not to step on ThornSting's scabbard lying beside my blanket,

I tiptoed toward where I thought the source of the chanting was. Two of the king's men, guards ostensibly, stood leaning on their halberds, sleeping silently while standing upright. I rounded the backside of the royal tent to find all the servants asleep on the ground, their bodies covered in blankets pulled up over their heads. The children, I noticed, slept on cloth pallets on the ground beneath the wagons, and none of them snored, sniffed, or even moaned in their sleep. For a moment I felt like I was standing amidst a battlefield of corpses, but the feeling shattered suddenly when the voice resumed. The chanting, I realized, was coming from within the elaborate tent that sheltered the royal family. A soft light glowed from beneath the edge of the fabric and peeked from the folds where the panels met. Clearly, someone was awake and busy!

I tiptoed to the corner of the king's tent where the pleated fabric had separated and listened, one ear pressed to the gap. The words I heard were in no recognizable language. The woman spat them out like bitter seeds or rotten fruit. Whatever she was saying, it was surely nothing good and I shuddered at her vehemence. Slipping my fingers around one edge of the fabric, I peered into the tent, surprised to see that it had apparently been sectioned off inside. The area the young woman before me knelt in could be no more than a third of the total size of the royal tent. The glow within was soft and seemed to come from no one source. The young woman on the pile of pillows on the ground was facing away from where I stood, but I recognized the long, golden, lustrous hair of Princess Merilda immediately. She rocked forward and back on her knees and heels, her body keeping time with her chanting, her hands flowing over a mound of dark fabric.

"Oomay keeinsa, doothla va myinga," was what it sounded as if she was saying. Over and over again she chanted the words, their pronunciation shifting slightly, making it impossible for me to even find a pattern. I marveled that everyone in the entire camp could be sleeping as Princess Merilda chanted and moved, however quietly. Surely I could not be the only one who heard it. I could not possibly be the only person roused by the sound. Just as I was about to turn around and make my way back to my bed, one of the sleeping children beneath the wagon began to whimper. A second child cried out in the darkness. When the third little one screamed, everyone woke at once, leaving me frozen beside the royal tent, afraid to move lest I be discovered yet afraid to remain. My heart was slamming against my ribcage as I began to step back, away from the tent.

Suddenly a strong arm slid around my middle, a hand clamped to my mouth, and I was lifted off my feet.

"For Gods' sake, woman," Captain Durand's voice was harsh and low, "what are you doing here? Trying to get yourself killed, are you? Come, let us be gone from here!"

Though I was relieved that it was Alexander who discovered me, and not one of King Radolph's men, I was also infuriated at how he had grabbed me and carted me off like I was a mere trifling. He ran across the ground between the royal tent and our camp carrying me as if I were a child about to be reprimanded. His arm around my middle hurt my ribs with every hurried step he took, and the hand over my mouth made it hard for me to breathe. Had I not been so startled, I would have fought him like a demon, but the children's cries and screams had brought both servants and guards awake and set them in motion. The entire camp was stirring by the time the captain finally set me down near where my bedroll lay in a wrinkled mess.

As Captain Durand, hands on his hips and anger in his eyes, spun me around I became aware of two things simultaneously. First, the other men, De Groot, Beck, and Keller, were all standing there with gentle, knowing smiles on their faces, and secondly, Durand had carried me on his uninjured side but it was more than likely he had strained and broken open the wound I had mended. In that moment I was as angry as I had ever been and I met his fury in equal measure.

"What were you doing there?" He snarled, his energy clearly indicating he could barely keep his voice down and really wanted to roar at me.

"I could ask you the same thing!" I snapped back, "What are you thinking picking me up and carrying me like that! You've probably re-opened your wound. Are you mad? And what were you doing sneaking up on me like that anyway? Did you hear the chanting too?"

"What chanting? I heard no chanting. I woke up to find your bedroll empty so I went looking for you," he shook his head, "only to find you spying at the royal family's tent. Are you trying to get yourself beheaded?"

Torn between defending myself and investigating what was happening with the children, I raised my hands and lowered my head.

"Not now," I whispered, looking up into those deep blue eyes I noticed the injured one was healing nicely. There was very little swelling remaining and the bruise around it was neither as large nor as dark as it had once been.

"What do you mean, not now? I want an answer, Lady Falcon Rose, and I want it now!"

"I've got to find out what's happening over there with the servants and those children," snapping my fingers as if I had suddenly remembered something important, I turned and strode once more toward the royals' tent, keenly aware of the angry captain's footsteps close behind me.

Princess Merilda was just stepping out from between the cloth panels when I turned the corner on the back side of the tent. In her hands she carried the dark cloth she'd had before her when I saw her kneeling within. She hurried across the camp to the wagon beneath which the small children lay crying and screaming. As a servant knelt to pick up and comfort one of the toddlers, the princess shook her head as she stepped in, "No, no. Do not touch the children. Do not awaken them. They need their rest. They must sleep!"

"But, your highness," the young maid started to protest but stepped back as Merilda elbowed her away.

Without another word, the princess knelt beside the wagon and draped the blanket she had in her hands over the children. Instantly the toddlers were quiet. Even from where I stood, I could see that the children still slept, but they did not do so easily. Their little arms and legs still quivered and moved; they tossed and turned; some fisted their tiny hands. It was indeed a strange sight to see such little ones obviously in torment yet unable to cry out or make noise. To my amazement, the little boy who slept nearest the wagon wheel smacked his fist against the wood a couple of times but there was no noise.

"Sleep little sweet one," Prince Merilda sang softly, "sleep as you may. Dreams now will steal you 'til break of day. Slumber so sweetly, innocent child, dream baby sweetly, so meek and mild."

The servants, I noticed, stood silently, not daring to move, though I knew they wanted nothing more than to rush to the children, scoop them up into caring arms, and comfort them. But the scene seemed to freeze as I stood watching. Princess Merilda, apparently satisfied that the children would remain quiet and not disturb her father and sister, stood, and straightened her robes. She tossed the length of her long golden braid back over her shoulder as she addressed the servants.

"That will be all now," she commanded. "Everyone, return to your slumber. The children are resting. There will be no more noise!"

Having made her wishes clearly known, she turned on her heel, strode across the dry-grass covered ground, and disappeared back into her tent. I stood there blinking in disbelief. The enormity of what I had just witnessed hit me like nothing I had ever imagined before and I found myself unable to think, barely able to remember to breathe. I felt heat and a presence behind me and was finally able to turn around, only to find myself looking into the tunic-covered chest of Captain Durand. Suddenly, I realized my right hand was itching, tingling, and vibrating. I knew my emotions were high and my body needed to discharge them so I had little choice but to heal Alexander's wound. Silently, I slipped my hand beneath his tunic to press my palm gently over the bandage on his side. He gasped slightly, startled by my touch, but he must have realized what I was doing, for he did not fight me or try to move away. As the tingling in my hand intensified, the heat grew, and at length I could feel his tissues knitting, his skin mending. Without realizing what I was doing, I slipped my left hand beneath his shirt and placed it on the left side of his waist. His skin was warm and smooth and it felt balanced and natural to touch him in that manner, though the tiny voice in my head was screaming that I must be mad for he would surely be thinking I was enticing him into another kiss or even more. But the moment both hands were on either side of his waist I felt the energy shoot through him from one palm to the other. My hands, it seemed, knew what they were doing and I could feel the healing speeding up. He must have felt it too, because he drew in a deep breath, arched his shoulders back, and put his hands on my shoulders. There we stood in the darkness, oddly entwined, neither moving nor speaking. We would have surely been a strange sight, had anyone come upon us, but no one did and at length I dropped my hands and stepped away from him. Grateful for the cover of night, and the deeper shadow of the tent behind us, I was relieved that he could not see my face, for the flush I felt at having touched him so brazenly must have been obvious. As I turned and walked back toward where we were camped, I assured myself that I was only healing his wounds. My hands had a mind of their own. I was a healer and I was trained to follow my instincts. I was in no way infatuated with Alexander Durand. I had no interest in men or romance, after all. By the time I returned to where the other soldiers awaited our return, Lothar sitting patiently beside Simon Keller's leg, I had myself convinced that Captain Durand meant absolutely nothing to me.

Chapter 29

The next four days and nights passed without incident. There were no more issues with the children waking up screaming or crying, and if Princess Merilda was chanting at night she was doing so more quietly. I did sometimes hear someone mumble or moan in their sleep, sometimes it was nearby, other times behind the king's tent, but it seemed nothing particularly alarming. People sometimes did make noise when they were dreaming, I knew, and what little I heard did not seem to indicate nightmares.

The journey was tedious. With the royal coach and supply wagons lumbering along the hardpacked but uneven road, we seemed to be making very little progress and I grew concerned that we might not reach Esling before the full moon, as King Rowan had hoped. More than once, Captain Durand had approached me with questions regarding why I had been standing outside the king's tent that first night, but I was not prepared to confide my suspicions to him. Down to my core in that truly magical and irrefutable way, I knew that night's events were important. I was certain there were clues in that incident that would lead to a huge revelation, but I was missing something. So, when he asked, I just shook my head and repeated that I thought I had heard something but I was probably mistaken. He never brought up the subject of the healing I had done on him outside King Radolph's tent, nor did I, but within two days of it he was able to remove the bandages from his side. The bruising was still there, but had gone from purple-black to a greenish-yellow. The gashes had mended, but were still puckered and discolored, the skin shiny and tight with the promise of a scar.

Lothar had apparently grown fond of the men of King Rowan's guard and from time to time he would ride with either Simon Keller or Gilbert Beck. He also spent a good deal of time running alongside the caravan, investigating the terrain here and there, and even visiting with the servants at the back of the line. But my furry companion avoided the royal carriage, I noticed, and for that I was grateful. After Sofia warned me about him being loose in front of the castle in the inner courtyard, I could only assume King Radolph and his daughters did not take kindly to dogs and would not appreciate one being in attendance in their journey. Though diplomacy probably would have kept the king's fiancé and her family from doing anything to Lothar, I did not like the idea of them even noticing him, so it was good he stayed away from their coach as well as their tent.

On the fourth night of the journey, as we made our camp ahead of the caravan as usual, I asked Captain Durand about the progress we were making and if it was likely we would reach Esling by full moon.

"Not at this rate," he shook his head with a grimace. "We'd make better time if we could get off the road and cross the open fields, but with the royal coach and those wagons, that's impossible. I don't think the king would appreciate the rough ride."

"That's what I was afraid of," I sighed, "and I wish it were otherwise."

"What do you mean?"

"I don't know," I confessed with a shrug, "but I feel like something not good lies ahead. Ever get that feeling? You know, you can't really say what it is, but something just feels wrong?"

"I'm not a witch!" He grinned with a twinkle in his eye.

"That's not what…"

"I know, I know," he chuckled, "I'm sorry. I know what you mean, and yes, I've had that feeling before. Sometimes it's meant something, other times it didn't, as I recall."

"I hope it means nothing this time," I offered as I spread my blankets, now dust-laden and less than fresh even though I shook them briskly every morning before rolling them back up. "I truly do."

Later that night, as everyone settled down to sleep and the fire upon which we had heated food and drink burned low, I had just closed my eyes to sleep when I was suddenly alert. My heartbeat raced, my skin tingled, and a chill ran up my spine. It took a minute for me to realize what was happening. In the next instant I recognized the familiar dissonance we had encountered before on the way to Ayndor. At that time, we had been able to avoid whatever was creating that noise by leaving the road and crossing the open fields, but recalling the conversation I'd had with the captain, I now understood the feeling of dread I had noticed. There was no way around whatever was on this road, and I could not help the feeling that we were riding into danger. Though I considered waking the captain to alert him to what was ahead, there seemed little point, as there was nothing to be done about it. Lothar, who had been lying some distance away, got up to move closer, finally walking a tight circle twice before curling up next to me. I rested my hand on his back, his soft, warm fur giving me comfort I did not realize I needed.

'*Cor!*' I silently called out as I began to drift off to sleep.

'*Yes, Falcon, my dear,*' came the response in that familiar voice. '*You are correct. The disturbance lies ahead of you.*'

'*What is it?*'

'*It's a vortex.*'

'*What's a vortex? Is that like a portal?*'

'*Yes and no, lass,*' Cor offered. '*Where a portal is a doorway between places and times, a vortex is a force spiraling energy from one aspect to another. It's a fissure.*'

Though I did not know exactly what a fissure was, I disliked the sound of the word and shuddered in response.

'*A fissure, in this case, is a rip in the earth,*' Declan Terrene chimed in. '*There is a gap from which energy is being drawn.*'

'*Is this something that happens a lot? Has it ever happened before? Why does it happen?*' The questions came spilling forth before I could control them and I felt the wizards' chuckle in response.

'*Easy, child,*' Cor resumed the conversation, '*one question at a time. A fissure does happen naturally from time to time, as it's a way for balance to be maintained, but in this case, it is not natural.*'

'*Someone's created this fissure, Falcon,*' Finias Marin added, '*and for a reason.*'

'*I don't understand,*' I cried in silent frustration.

'*Rest, Falcon,*' my beloved Cor spoke calmly, '*and be assured that we wizards are looking into the matter. All will be well, child.*'

Whether it was Cor's reassurance or just weariness that overtook me, I slipped off to sleep with the wizards' voices echoing in my ears and Lothar's warm body beneath my hand.

In the distance, a carriage and two wagons stood above a shimmering mist blanketing the ground. Mala stood beside me as we peered through the portal while Mara, in her feline form, twined around my right ankle. A full moon hung in the sky over the scene we observed, but nothing moved. When the mist rolled and scurried, as if blown by a gentle breeze, mounds on the ground were uncovered, and I recognized them as sleepers beneath their blankets. Sleeping guards stood upright, heads nodding, halberds leaning against their necks. Mala put her arm around my shoulders, and as she did so the meaning of the scene we watched became clear. The mist was erupting from a chasm in the earth some distance from where the caravan had camped, but it easily and quickly stole over the ground. The shimmering fog had everyone in its grasp, all beneath it slept, unable to awaken. As the perspective shifted, I found my own body lying under blankets, there on the ground not far from where Captain Durand slept. Lothar lay with his head on his paws beside me, eyes closed, breathing deeply.

"Watch, Falcon," Mala murmured and as I did, I saw arms and feet moving within the mist. Weapons shimmered in the light of the full moon as they cut through the fog. A deafening roar issued from within the tumult, the dissonance familiar and now identified. Torocs, shadeserpents, dargolems, and more came spilling out of the earth in that shining, shimmering fog, all of them heading for the sleeping caravan. Mala pointed her index finger toward the tent where a soft glow filled one end. As I stood there watching, the scene shifted yet again to where Princess Merilda once more knelt on pillows, chanting, and rocking back and forth on her knees. A pendant, suspended from a silver chain around her neck, glowed oddly green as it softly bounced against her chest when she moved. Her long, elegant hands made strangely fluid motions, though she did not appear to be touching anything, and though her mouth moved, her eyes were open but unseeing.

"Welcome fetch, hie thee home, come ye breath of blood and bone. Welcome boggle, hear my song, welcome flesh of earth and stone," the princess sang softly, in a voice all too familiar.

"Emmeline Caulfield," I gasped at the realization, my thoughts swimming in confusion.

"That's but one of its disguises," Mala nodded.

As I watched, dumbfounded, and nearly overwhelmed, the image of the princess shimmered and there on her knees was the woman I had seen in my dream of the millhouse. Her auburn hair shining in the soft light, green eyes open but seeing nothing.

"I don't understand." Shaking my head, I tried not to whine, "What am I seeing? How is Princess Merilda connected to Emmeline Caulfield?"

"Watch," the felinetrix intoned calmly and as I did so the images shifted yet again. Princess Merilda still knelt and chanted, while the image of Emmeline Caulfield separated from her, wispy and ghostlike. Slowly, a dark shadow rose from behind both images. It towered over them, swallowed them from view, and enveloped the light within the tent. As the scene changed yet once more, the storm of otherworldly beings roiled and rolled closer to the encampment, a dark form rising behind it, seeming to drive it forward. A sudden flash of lightning ripped across the dark sky, the images exploded, and I awoke with a gasp.

Sitting upright, chest heaving and heart pounding, I drew in a calming breath as I looked around me. Lothar still lay nearby, though not as close as he had once been, and the other guards were sleeping quietly. Captain Durand lay on his back, eyes closed, breathing deeply. One hand rested on his chest and his long hair framed his face. Though the light from the crescent new moon was slight, I could clearly see Alexander's features, his strong jaw, high cheekbones, and heavy brows. It was nice just lying there looking at the captain as he slept. I realized in that moment that I felt safe there, in his presence, and surrounded by the other guards. Dreading what might lie ahead, I wished the sun would never rise and the night would not end, as I closed my eyes to drift off into an uneasy sleep.

Before sunrise the men were up, the fire had been stoked, and food and drink were being warmed. As I shook out my blankets and re-packed my gear, I was aware of the sound of the disturbance in the distance, though no one made mention of it. After I had my tea and some sweet biscuits, several of which I shared with Lothar, I put my things in my saddle bags and carried them to where Aeon stood munching on the autumn-dry grass. Captain Durand saddled his stallion nearby. When I was sure no one else was close enough to hear, I cleared my throat to get his attention.

"Captain Durand," I spoke formally in case anyone overheard, "might I have a word with you?"

"Of course, Lady Falcon Rose," he replied as he snugged the cinch on his mount's saddle. Patting the beast on the rump, he secured his saddle bags and walked around Aeon's nose to where I stood working on her gear. "How can I be of service?"

"I'm not sure where to begin, Captain," I admitted, "but you should know that something is not right. I've awakened several times in the night only to find King Radolph's guards asleep at their posts, standing, leaning against their halberds."

"That's," he started, but I quickly interrupted.

"And that's not all. Everyone sleeps. I mean everyone but me, and possibly Lothar. Everyone sleeps when the royal family sleeps. Don't you think that's odd that with this many people in the group everyone is sleeping at the same time?"

"Well, it could be," he shrugged, but I insisted.

"And I don't know if you've noticed, but the noise we heard on the way to Ayndor, that strange feeling, strange... sound we avoided by getting off the road, is back. I began to hear it last night," I explained.

"I had not noticed," he nodded, raising his face to the sky, closing his eyes. "You're right. I hear it. It's faint, must be some ways ahead, but it's there."

"But this time we can't avoid it, can we?"

"Not if it's on or near the road ahead. There's no other way to go. We must continue on this road."

Yes," lowering my voice to a whisper, I confided, "and I don't know that there's anything we can do, at least not right now. Just be aware. We should keep our eyes open for anything unusual, anything possibly a threat."

"Yes, My Lady," he grinned, scoffing at my concern. "By the way, I've noticed your blade, the sword you wear on your hip."

"And?" Perplexed at the sudden change of subject, I stepped back warily.

"Are you any good with it?"

"I can hold my own."

"Don't suppose a witch needs to be very skilled with a sword. Surely you can cast spells and hurl magic so you don't even need to draw your blade," he suppressed a smile, obviously baiting me.

"For your information," I hissed, "I learned how to wield a sword from my father, Captain Arne Rose, long before I had any idea that magic or witches exist in this world. And one day, Captain Durand, I'll prove it to you."

"I look forward to that day, Lady Falcon Rose," he bowed deeply, only to straighten and wink at me before he strode away.

I stood beside my mare, angry, confused, ridiculously intrigued, insulted, and barely able to think. Serious danger ahead and the man saw fit to make light of matters! I was about to go after Captain Durand to tell him what I thought about our conversation, when Lothar came trotting up to me, panting, tongue lolling. As I gave the puppy a drink, everyone else began mounting up while the royal family entered their carriage. I shook the remaining moisture from Lothar's bowl to tuck it into the saddle bag before scooping him up in my arms. Once astride Aeon, I nudged her into formation beside Simon Keller and, when the order was given, the caravan moved forward again.

As we moved slowly along the road which ran mostly north but sometimes meandered east, I had time to think about what I had learned from the wizards as well as what the felinetrix had shown me in a dream. I had to assume it was indeed Mala and Mara and not some nightmare, for her voice was comforting and familiar, and what I saw was beginning to make sense. Suddenly I remembered the wizards had taught me some useful magic, and I decided it was time to make use of what I had learned. Once I made sure Lothar was comfortable, I pulled the hood of my ruby cloak up over my head, and leaned over to touch Simon Keller's hand, which was resting easily on his saddle horn.

"I'm going to close my eyes for a bit," I murmured, "as I didn't sleep well. Don't let me fall out of the saddle or let Aeon wander away, please?"

"Of course, Lady Falcon Rose," he nodded, "I'll be happy to keep an eye on you. Rest your eyes."

"When we're speaking privately you can call me Falcon."

"Yes, Falcon," grinning conspiratorially, "I'll try. Can't say that it feels proper, but I'll try."

"Thank you! Now, don't forget. Don't let my horse wander from formation."

"Yes, Ma'am," he saluted, turning his attention back to the road ahead.

Having my ample hood drawn up over my head, I closed my eyes, took a deep breath, and went in search, comforted by the steady clomp, clomp, clomp of Aeon's hooves. I sent my energy out toward the royal family of Ayndor and through the darkness I saw a light, the color of which I had never seen before. I had done such searches before, and always what I found seemed right and clearly understandable, but what I saw, racing toward me in the ether, was far from clear. As my energy drew near the light, I could make out subtle color differences within it. The aura of yellow was mottled with bilious green and red the color of old blood. Faint traces of purple streaked through the riot and my discomfort grew as I approached it. Still, I had to know, so when I was near enough, I touched the orb with my own energy and suddenly I knew. I did not actually see what had happened to the princess as complete scenes. What I saw, heard, and felt was more like pieces of scenes, as if I had peeked into her past at random moments, but her motivations as well as her actions were clear. Princess Merilda did not want to marry! I caught a brief argument between her and the king, felt her betrayal at being traded off like chattel, sensed her disappointment at being a pawn for a kingdom she had hoped to one day rule. I knew that as a child her father had assured her that one day, she would be queen of Ayndor, and that he loved her much too much to ever let her go marry another man. She would be his prize always, he told her over and over. I felt her sorrow and dismay at her mother's death, saw her anger at the world and realized I had felt the same emotion. Her sister, Eleanora, had been young enough when their mother passed that she did not suffer as Merilda did, and Merilda resented that as well. Anger, fear, sorrow, and betrayal had festered into a fine, powerful hatred. Princess Merilda hid it well, but within that façade of calm raged a burning storm, and that had attracted the attention of a very hungry darkness. The entity had soothed her pain with pretty words. It told her what she wanted to hear, and it promised her help. If she would but let it in, it would see that the world would be as it was intended. It would make sure that SHE would be seated on the throne of Ayndor, that any arranged marriage plans would fall apart, and that she would have everything in the world she had ever dreamed of having. In her pain, she let it in, and it began to devour her, silently, slowly, until what remained was very little. Princess Merilda carried the hungry darkness in her heart, and through her power it was free to wreak havoc on the world. With a gasp, I withdrew from the horrible energy, rocketing my own back into my body.

"Are you well, Lady, I mean, Falcon?" Simon Keller looked at me with concern in his eyes.

"Was I snoring?"

"A little," he laughed, beaming a smile at me. "No, you weren't snoring. You did kind of slump a bit in the saddle and I was afraid I was going to have to catch you to keep you from falling, but you straightened right up. Feel better now?"

"I do, actually, thank you," I nodded, feeling the truth of the words as I spoke them. Suddenly, the memory of what I had experienced touching Princess Merilda's energy came back at me in a rush. The Hungry Darkness I had felt destroy King Rowan's guards, Martin and Prouse, was that very entity now using his fiancé. It intended there to be no royal marriage and it would put Princess Merilda on the throne of Ayndor, but how could that be? King Radolph was strong and healthy, and even if she did not marry King Rowan her father would barter her off to some other power in exchange for allegiance and riches.

In that instant I knew...Princess Merilda intended to murder her father and her sister. She alone would be the royal family of Ayndor. Through her, the Hungry Darkness was sending out nightmares upon which it would feed, gathering power through the fear and terror experienced by the little ones of Esling before affecting the adults. It intended to create chaos and discord. It needed the energy of strife and contention in order to do its work. I stifled a gasp as the realization hit me, it was the Hungry Darkness that had stirred up the torocs, possibly even created the band of robbers riding the countryside.

"Hungry Darkness," I murmured to myself, tasting the words on my tongue, rolling around the images it brought forth. Emmeline Caulfield appeared in my mind, green eyes shining, auburn hair cascading down her shoulders. She was beautiful, and yet she was not. The memory of how she had suddenly appeared skeletal, wizened, and ugly, shook me to my core just before another crowded it out. Z, Emmeline's daughter, had been young, blond, timid, and frightened, with deep blue eyes I suddenly recognized. Z was Merilda and Emmeline Caulfield was the Hungry Darkness! It was using the princess, but she, in her emotional pain, had invited it in and allowed it to take over. Z remained within Merilda, the young girl promised the throne and her parents' love and protection, but that had changed with her mother's untimely demise. Was there enough of the princess remaining to fight the Hungry Darkness? Was there a way to free her and protect both kingdoms from the destruction the entity intended? Suddenly my head hurt, my stomach lurched, and I felt my eyes roll back in my head.

Chapter 30

The ground beneath me rumbled. My head ached, my body felt stiff and sore. My eyes felt heavy and it was only with tremendous effort I was able to open them. Soft light enveloped the room, panels of fabric hung around me. Rich incense wafted through the air, as I struggled to push blankets from atop my prone body.

"Where am I?" I groaned as I tried, without success, to sit up. "What's happened?"

"You are in our tent, Lady Falcon Rose," came the lyrical, feminine voice. I could not see who was speaking, but I recognized it as Princess Eleanora.

"What's wrong with me?" Heat washed over my body, my head throbbed, and a sudden thirst made it almost impossible to speak.

"You are not well," the princess offered as she came into view. In her hands she held a narrow vessel of stone, and as she knelt beside me, I could only pray that it held cool water and was intended for me. "My father's physician has examined you but could find nothing wrong. He suggested perhaps you'd eaten something you shouldn't have or that you'd been bitten by something poisonous, though he could find no bite marks on you."

"Bitten," I whispered, as she slid one cool hand beneath my head and put the vessel to my parched lips.

"Perhaps," she replied. "But he could not say. You've been ill for some time."

Swallowing hard, I struggled away from the vessel and from her hand, "How long?"

"Two days." I could hear the sympathy in her voice. "Everyone has been concerned about you."

"My things," I managed to whisper, "I need my things."

"I'll have a servant fetch your belongings," she smiled as she stood and moved from view.

A gentle breeze blew over me. I heard the soft padding of paws as Lothar moved up beside me, peering down at me with curious eyes, his nose sniffing questioningly. He must have found satisfaction in his examination, for he laid down beside me and quietly rested his head across my middle. I was amazed that the royal family would let him inside their tent, but I realized that I was surprised they had let me inside their tent as well.

"Two days," I marveled, only to suddenly wonder where we were. Once more, I became aware of the rumbling in the earth beneath me and a fear washed over me that we might be near the vortex.

'Cor!'

'There you are, Falcon,' came the wizard's familiar voice. *'We've been very worried about you. Are you well?'*

'No,' suppressing the urge to cry, I admitted silently, *'I'm not well, but I will be. I seem to have lost two days and I think we must be very close to the vortex!'*

'You are correct, lass,' my beloved mentor's words filled me with dread, *'you are indeed camped very near the vortex and it is not safe. The sun is starting to go down and when the night comes,'*

'The Hungry Darkness comes,' I completed his thought. *'And with it comes the army of chaos and destruction. The king and Princess Eleanora are in danger!'*

'You all are in danger,' he warned sternly, *'but rest assured help is on the way. We will stand against the upcoming storm.'*

Before I had a chance to ask anything further, Princess Eleanora and Sofia returned to the tent, the lady in waiting carrying my saddle bags across her forearm. She passed behind the princess to kneel beside me, offering my gear.

"I'm happy to see you awake," she smiled gently. "Can I help you get something from your things?"

"I'm glad you're feeling better," Princess Eleanora announced. "Excuse me." Behind me I heard a tent flap rustle.

"Yes, please, Sofia, I can use your help," I answered. Directing the servant to the healing pouch inside my saddle bag, I had her unwrap the herbal tincture I knew I needed. I had not been bitten, nor had I eaten anything dangerous. The power that had robbed me of two days lay in the hands of Princess Merilda. Somehow, the Hungry Darkness had discovered my awareness of it and had responded by feeding from my energy. I was weakened, but I knew how to heal myself and nothing would stop me. As I managed to sit upright, I drank the tincture Deacon and Cor had shown me how to make. Next, I used the sharp blade to slice into my right hand, bleeding into an empty cup I plucked from my things. Though my body was of this world, my spirit was Aerienesse, and I knew that to heal I must eject all traces of the entity. Unsure of exactly how it managed to feed on me, I could only trust my instincts and hope that whatever traces of the worm-like creatures Abra had once deposited into my body might recognize the entity, collect its influences, and aid me in ridding myself of them. Recalling the many times I had felt the movement beneath my skin, how the things had caused itching and tingling, how Deacon and Cor both had tried to rid me of them, I restored that physical connection with my warlock friend. Suddenly I felt his strength coursing through my veins. A gush of black blood erupted from my hand into the cup. Taking a deep breath, I steadied myself with my left hand. I directed Sofia to bring me bandages and help me with the wound. As she did so, and began to wrap my hand, I realized I was hungry. In fact, I was ravenous.

"When you're done," I whispered, "could I have some food?"

"Of course," she nodded, never taking her eyes from her work, "I'll bring you some food and drink. Perhaps you'd like some water to wash with and some clean clothes?"

"That would be lovely," I sighed, "because I don't think I smell very fresh and I certainly don't feel that way. I'm sure I have some clean clothes in my gear."

"Yes, Ma'am," she smiled, patting my hand gently. "There, that's done. I'll be right back with some water to wash and some food for you."

"Thank you, Sofia," I grinned, marveling at how much better I felt. Though I was still a bit weak and wobbly, my head no longer hurt and my body no longer ached. I had moved the cup of tainted blood out of sight, and thankfully Sofia had forgotten about it. I had use for the contents and I did not want to explain anything to her, or anyone else. My instincts were telling me what to do next and I was relieved and delighted to listen. I put my healing items back in the pouch, returning the pouch to my saddle bag. Inside the second leather pouch, a crisp, clean tunic lay neatly folded over a clean pair of breeches so I sent a silent 'thank you' up to Malamara, who always saw to such details though how she did so I could not imagine. I was about to pull the garments out when Sofia bustled back in carrying a good-sized bowl of water, a cloth, and a towel.

"Here, My Lady Falcon," she smiled as she carefully set the bowl on the ground beside me and handed me the towel. "Do you need help? I can tend to your hair if you like. I care for the princess's hair every day. I'd be happy to serve you as well."

"Let me wash and dress," I replied, "and we'll see. First things first."

"Very well, I'll bring you something to eat," she nodded.

Alone in the royal tent, I carefully moved away from Lothar, pulling my tunic off over my head. With the cloth wetted and wrung in the bowl, I disrobed to wash myself from head to toe. Once clean, I wrapped the towel around my torso, relieved to be refreshed and covered.

Sofia returned, assuring me my food was being prepared, and she insisted on getting my clean clothes from my saddle bag and helping me dress.

"Can you stand or would you prefer to stay seated?"

"I'll stay seated," I sighed in resignation.

"Here," she directed as she shook the folds from my tunic, "just put your arms up over your head and I'll put this on you."

Slipping the shirt over my head, the lady-in-waiting helped me put my arms into the sleeves before pulling it down and removing the towel. I shoved my feet into clean breeches and drew them up my legs as Sofia focused her attention on something atop a small table. Before I could protest, she was releasing my hair from its braid and brushing out its length. She poured oils into her hands, rubbed them together, and drew them through my tresses, distributing the fragrances into my hair before once more brushing and braiding it.

"Thank you, Sofia," I put my hands up, "that's quite enough. You've spent more than enough time on me. I'll be fine."

"I'll go get your food, Lady Falcon," she bowed slightly before disappearing once more.

Soon, the young servant returned with a tray upon which rested a large bowl of cooked vegetables and meat, bread, fruit, and a silver goblet of some dark, aromatic drink. She placed it on a stand near one tent wall, pausing to ask if there was anything else. I assured her that I was sufficiently cared for. After moving to a small fabric-covered stool, I sat down and dug into the delicious fare. Lothar, who had noticed the enticing smell as soon as the food arrived, sat beside me, eyes bright, ears alert, mouth drooling slightly. Sofia left the tent and as soon as she was gone, I retrieved the bowl of blood I had hidden and began my work. I would stop in my ritual to enjoy a spoonful of stew or bite of bread, quickly returning my attention to the spell I was weaving. To the blood I added dirt from the ground beneath my bare feet, as I had yet to don stockings and boots, and I quietly recited the incantation I knew would serve my purpose. From the mud created by the dirt and blood, I fashioned a small body, its head, arms, and legs rudimentary at best, but I knew I required little detail for it to do its job. Once done, I lay the crude fetch on a square of cloth from my bag. Next, I pulled Scorch, my Earth Star, out of my gear and unwrapped it. I let the light from the Earth Star bathe the fetch for a few minutes before wrapping both back up. Scorch went back into the saddle bag, but I tucked the cloth-wrapped fetch beneath my sapphire sash. When Sofia returned for the tray and empty serving dishes, I asked her about returning to my place with King Rowan's guards.

"I do not know, Ma'am," she shook her head warily, "but I shall tell Her Highness Eleanora that you're feeling better and asking. Perhaps she'll come talk to you about it. If she does not, you should stay here."

"Yes, I understand," I sighed, suddenly feeling more like a prisoner than a guest, "protocol and all that. I do hope she'll come in. I'm feeling so much better and I've taken advantage of her generosity as well as the king's. I'm very grateful, but I don't wish to impose on them any more than I have. Please tell her that I've fully recovered and wish to return to my duties."

"I'll do so," she nodded and curtsied. Turning with the tray, she slipped between the overlapping panels of the tent.

"Good evening, Lady Falcon Rose," Princess Merilda pulled a panel of fabric back as she stepped into the room. "I understand you've recovered from your illness. We are all pleased." Though she was addressing me, she stared warily at Lothar, who had curled up on the blankets of the pallet I had been resting on. She looked stricken at the sight of the animal for a moment.

"Thank you, Your Highness," I replied uneasily. The expression on her face did not match the tone of her words, I could clearly see. Though she appeared proper and polite, golden hair falling in loose waves around her shoulders, wearing an elegant gown of deep blue, the fire in those eyes burned bitter and hard. I could tell that she would just as soon I would have perished than recovered. At first glance, she was the lovely Princess Merilda, daughter of the king, betrothed to King Rowan, but below the surface I could see Emmeline Caulfield's energy and the pendant that hung around her neck from a silver chain glowed softly in response. Though the stone had once appeared green to me, it now shown a deep, ugly red. "What a lovely pendant you're wearing."

"Thank you," she touched the stone anxiously, protectively wrapping her hand around it.

"What stone is it you wear? I can't say that I've ever seen such a beautiful color."

"A gift from some foreign kingdom," she answered hesitantly. In those deep blue eyes, I could see a trace of doubt, a hint of unease, and for a moment I saw the pleading I had seen in Z's eyes when she was with Emmeline Caulfield. Just as quickly it was gone. Once more she appeared confident, determined, even haughty. "I don't know what stone it is, as I was not told."

"My apologies, Your Highness," I bowed, "for I did not intend to pry. It's simply so lovely I was curious."

"Yes," she sighed, looking me up and down, "well, it appears you've quite recovered."

"I have, thanks to you and your family. In fact, I'm hoping to excuse myself and return to my duties. I've taken advantage of your hospitality too long as it is."

Princess Merilda opened her mouth to respond, but refrained from comment as her sister and father swept into the room. Princess Eleanora was lovely in a gown of emerald green, her glossy black hair combed back from her forehead, the jeweled circlet of gold on her head gleaming softly. King Radolph wore a black velvet tunic cinched at the waist with a jewel encrusted belt, leggings, and impossibly soft-looking leather boots. His hair, as black as his youngest daughter's, was long, combed smooth, and touched his shoulders. The hair on his chin was neatly trimmed as was his mustache, and in such close quarters I realized he smelled of sandalwood, frankincense, and wood smoke. Suddenly I was uncomfortably aware of the four of us in the small partitioned room of the tent, and I yearned to be away from them, in fresh air, and wide-open spaces. The two princesses discussed the situation as if I were not there, while the king watched silently, his gaze moving from one daughter to the other. Merilda was more than happy to have me gone, but her sister wanted me to remain in the tent until my recovery was assured and there was no risk of relapse. The two bantered back and forth for a bit, only pausing when His Highness King Radolph interrupted them.

"Lady Falcon Rose," he directed his attention and his words to me, rather than his bickering offspring, "you seem to have recovered from your illness. If you feel strong enough and wish to return to your duties you are welcome to do so. If, however, there is any doubt in your mind, or if you feel the need to remain here you may certainly do that too."

"Your Highness," I bowed, not sure if I should be doing so or curtsying, "I am grateful to you and your family. You've been so kind and generous. But I feel fine now, thank you, and I'm delighted to return to King Rowan's guards."

"Very well," he heaved a sigh, "it shall be so. Merilda, Eleanora, come! Let us leave Lady Falcon Rose to gather her things and depart as she will. We have matters to attend!"

With the king's announcement, the three departed the section of the tent in which I stood without further comment. For a moment, my head spun as I considered all that had just transpired. At that instant, all that was about to happen washed over me and I rushed to gather my things and be gone from the royal tent. I hung my saddle bags over my arm, hoping they were not so dirty as to soil the sleeve of my clean tunic. I gathered up by stockings and boots and called to Lothar. I was just about to step outside when Sofia returned and insisted on escorting me from the royal tent to where King Rowan's guards were encamped. The lady-in-waiting held my elbow, guiding me, making sure I was steady on my feet and would not release me until I was safely among the men. My saddle had been placed at the end of one of my blankets and ThornSting, securely in its scabbard, lay atop my bedding. I was at once both grateful and disturbed, though I could not say why. After a quick bow, Sofia excused herself, darting back along the caravan to see to her duties. I, on the other hand, stood unsteadily, boots and stockings in one hand, saddle bags in the other, waiting for someone to say something. Captain Durand stood mutely blinking at me. Lieutenant De Groot beamed a generous smile, and Beck and Keller both grinned and even blushed. I finally dropped my things and took a deep breath.

"Lady Falcon Rose!" The captain grinned at length, "You're awake! Are you well?"

"I'm improving very quickly, thank you," I admitted, putting my bare feet on my blanket and crossing my ankles to sit down. Lothar licked my cheek before bouncing over to Gilbert Beck to have his ears scratched. "But that's of no matter. What about the sound? Have you determined what it is that lies down the road?"

"I sent Keller scouting ahead, and he has news."

"The news isn't good," Simon sighed, looking at me with concern in his eyes. "That noise is coming from troops of, well, troops of things. There are torocs in this army of evil-looking beings. I guess they're monsters. I don't even know what some of the soldiers heading this way are, but they're all carrying weapons and banging drums, jangling chains, crashing shields together. The noise is deafening and deceiving. They're not quite as close as they sound, but they're coming!"

"And did you see anything else? Anything unusual?" I peered up at him, resisting the urge to lead his answer.

"I," he began, but hesitated, "I, wait! I did see something else. It didn't make sense, what I was seeing so I dismissed it, but there was a dark cloud, like some strange smoke that hung over them, swirled around them. It moved along as they did!"

"That's as I thought it would be," I nodded. "Gentlemen, we need to talk. Please, gather around and take a seat. I can't sit here looking up at you like this. You might want to get a drink, as this may take a while."

As the sun began its inexorable descent in the sky, Beck and Keller tended the fire in the center of our camp while I looked around at where we were. Having lost two days during my illness, I had not been awake for the change in terrain. The land we had been traveling after leaving Ayndor had been mostly open, sometimes rugged, fields. The road itself had been hardpacked dirt, narrow and usually straight, but that had changed. Now there were stands of trees around us, not really a forest, but scattered thickets of mostly pine and cedar trees. Our camp was east of the road and from where I sat, I could see the sun cresting the tops of the trees in the west. Lothar stretched out beside me on my blanket, yawning loudly, and rested his head on his paws. Everyone made themselves comfortable on the ground and ate their supper while we spoke. Having already eaten, I sipped a mug of tea Simon had offered and prepared for me while I explained all I had learned.

The guards listened attentively as I explained that someone did not want the upcoming marriage between King Rowan and Princess Merilda to take place. Though I did not explain how I had come to learn of this, I was aware of the truth of my assertion. I could not admit that it was the princess herself who did not wish to be married, so I carefully skirted around the issue of who that someone might be. With as much conviction as I could muster in my voice, I told them how I believed the royal family was in danger, especially the king and his daughter. To my surprise, the men must have assumed I was referring to the king's fiancé for they did not ask which daughter and I felt no need to say.

"I believe," I admitted, "the person who wants the marriage stopped is also the one who has raised the energy to draw together and direct the army of chaos that lies ahead of us."

"Army of Chaos?" Captain Durand raised an eyebrow, "Is that what it's called?"

"In my mind, it is!" With a chuckle I added, "Not that it has a specific name I'm aware of. That just popped into my head when Keller here described it."

"So, what do we do? How do we face this army?" Lieutenant De Groot interjected.

"How many are there, Keller?"

"Forty, fifty," Simon sighed, shaking his head slowly, "maybe more. They're all well-armed. I don't see how we could defeat them, yet there's no way around them. Could we get away from the road and hide until they've passed?"

"Doubtful," I considered, "as I believe they're coming for King Radolph and his daughter. I can't imagine they'd pass us by no matter how well hidden we are."

"So that leaves us…" Beck spoke up hopefully.

"Not in a good place, that's certain. I'm in hopes that help is on its way and that it gets here in time. For now, I guess we stay here tonight and see what the morning brings us."

"You don't sound very hopeful," Captain Durand looked at me pointedly.

"I'm not without hope," I sighed, wishing fervently that a plan would present itself, that Cor would reach out to me in that silent communication we shared and tell me he had the answer, or that Abra would appear leading a vast army of Aerienesse soldiers.

Chapter 31

Relaxing on my back, head on Aeon's saddle, left hand on Lothar's warm fur as he lay beside me, I opened my eyes to find a veil of fog moving over the camp. Not a normal fog, it shimmered strangely smoky blue as it churned into the area. The mist covered the men sleeping around me before it moved on to swallow the royal tent and the wagons beyond. Everyone slept. There was no sound. The mist even drowned out the noise of the approaching Army of Chaos, but I knew they were still coming. I tried to sit up to alert everyone about the fog and the danger drawing near, but I found I could not move. When I tried to call out, I discovered I could not speak. Though I could feel Lothar's fur beneath my hand, I could not move it. The blanket of fog held me to the earth, motionless and helpless.

Struggling to keep panic at bay, to concentrate, and use my powers to be free, I silently reached out to Cor.

'*Cor! Help me!*' I called with my thoughts, trying to remain calm. '*Cor!*'

As I feared, there was no response. The fog was acting as barrier between the wizard and me. For a moment I thought I might be able to focus on my hand and will it to move enough to reach one of my companions, but my vision was obscured by the fog leaving me unable see anything through it.

'*Focus, Falcon,*' the little voice in my head commanded. '*If this is a spell, your shield is enough to protect you. Breathe and focus!*'

Heaving a deep breath, I did focus. At least, I tried, but nothing seemed to work. Was I awake and bespelled or was I asleep and trapped in a dream?

'*You are Warlock, Falcon,*' The words echoed clearly in my mind. '*You are Warlock!*'

'*Fine, I'm Warlock,*' I thought, as I called out in response, '*Abra! Abra!*'

There was a warm pressure atop my head; suddenly I was free. I sat up with a gasp, heart slamming against my ribs, chest heaving. Blinking repeatedly to clear my thoughts, I found that sitting upright, my head was above the fog. I could see the smoky mist had everyone and everything completely covered. The next thing I knew, I was standing, with no memory of getting up. I observed all that was around me. The army of torocs and other creatures was approaching, marching along the road from the north to intercept us. A heavy dark cloud hung over the ghastly troops, though it did not obscure them from my sight. I had to wake everyone! I had to get the king's guards up, armed, and ready to defend the royal family and themselves! Panic clutched at my throat as I realized how close the danger was and how quickly it was moving. Focusing my attention on waking the men, I rushed to where Captain Durand lay sleeping, grabbed him by the shirt, and tried to shake him awake. He did not respond. I hurried to the sleeping Lieutenant De Groot, then Keller, then Beck only to find that I could wake no one. Though I tried to call out an alert, no noise came from my mouth. Just as I thought to run to the royal tent, I glanced down, only to see my physical body lying there beneath my blankets. My eyes were closed, head turned slightly, and I was breathing deep and steady. The sleeping puppy lay beneath my hand. With every ounce of will I could muster, I mentally called Lothar to wake me, to wake us, to save us.

"Arrrrooooooo…" Lothar leapt to his paws, spun around, and pounced on my chest. The howl shattered the night, breaking the spell of slumber.

Pulled violently back into my body, I shuddered as I sat up, awake, and clutching my amber pendant. Immediately my mind was clear, free of the magic riding in on the fog. Captain Durand coughed as he sat up, blinking in confusion at what he saw around us. In a flash, he was on his feet, calling out orders to the others, sounding the alarm. I got up, grabbed ThornSting's scabbard, and quickly buckled it around my waist.

"Falcon," a familiar voice sounded behind me.

"Abra!" I gasped, as I turned to see the warlock. He stood there calmly, looking as if there was no cause for concern in the world. It was all I could do to keep from running to embrace him in relief.

"It is time, Warlock!" He spoke cryptically, "Time for the talisman. You know what to do with it."

From a wide cloth band around his middle, the warlock drew the double-bladed haladie, its two ruby-colored stones glowing softly in the darkness. The memory of traveling through the portal to retrieve the talisman came clearly to mind, as did Abra's explanation as to why we were there rescuing it. I recalled the two carved serpents on the handle, each holding a stone, and how the talisman had come to life, dripping gore, and smelling foul. For a moment my mind knew only confusion, but when the stones glowed brighter, I recognized them. Suddenly I made the connection.

"I can't kill Princess Merilda!" I gasped at the thought, though it was clear to me that the pendant she wore and the stones on the haladie were the same. "I can't do it!"

"Not the princess," the warlock calmly shook his head. "You must destroy that which she invited in, which has taken her over. Destroy the Hungry Darkness."

"How?"

"Separate it from her," he explained, moving the sharp haladie this way and that through the air. "Once it is away from her body you can destroy it."

"But..."

"The pendant, Falcon," Abra whispered. "The pendant!"

In that moment, I remembered the fearful blue eyes of Z, the deep azure terror I had seen in a flash in Princess Merilda's eyes, and realized what I had seen was the real princess, the young woman she was before she opened herself to the evil entity. I understood that I was to save her, as well as the other royals and everyone else in the caravan.

"Time is of the essence, my dear," the Aerienesse handily tossed me the haladie, its twin blades spinning silently through the air.

Without thought, I reached out and grasped the weapon, my fingers closing easily around the intricately carved bone center.

"Hurry!" He nodded, spurring me to action. As I raced across the ground to King Radolph's tent, I noticed a light appearing in the road. Within the light stood four beings, tall, powerful, and unyielding. It was with sudden joy in my heart that I recognized the Elemental Wizards.

They were standing between the Army of Chaos and the king's caravan. I had no doubt the wizards could protect themselves, but the thought that they might be injured compelled me to move faster. I had to get to Princess Merilda!

As everyone in the camp had awakened to Lothar's howl, soldiers were seizing swords, spears, shields, maces, and any other weapons they could find. The servants too were arming themselves, preparing to fight and possibly perish in service to their king. I had to push my way through the confusion of bleary-eyed, terrified Ayndorians on my way to where the princess was, and when I finally arrived, I yanked back the panel of tent fabric only to find her standing there with a blank look on her face. Before she could blink, move, or react, I clutched the chain around her neck, pulled the pendant from beneath her gown, and cut it free with the haladie. The stone pendant shone bright red for a moment, before going black in my hand. To my dismay, Emmeline Caulfield's image rose from the body of Princess Merilda, its green eyes flashing anger, its cheekbones wickedly sharp and skeletal, its horrible maw of a mouth gaping. As it drew away from the princess and toward me, I spun the haladie end for end, waiting for just the right moment. The once beautiful auburn-haired woman reverted to her horrific true skeletal form, and as it left the security of its host, it finally became vulnerable. In one swift movement, I drove the haladie into the collected evil energy of the Hungry Darkness, as its ruby-colored stones exploded into shimmering light. The carved dark serpents that held the stones rose from the center handle, snapping and snarling, gobbling up the vestiges of the entity's power. Finally, they shrank back into the haladie as it dropped to the ground.

'Well done, Falcon!' Princess Laurell whispered in my ear. I could feel her energy near me, but I could not see her. *'Now, the nightmare blanket!'*

Before Princess Merilda could react, I plucked the dark blanket from the ground beside her. Dashing out to where King Rowan's guards and King Radolph's troops were gathering to weigh into the oncoming fray, I tossed the blanket on the first fire I saw burning and did not linger to watch the flames consume it. Abra approached from our camp, arm raised, hand opened. Knowing instinctively what the gesture implied, I easily tossed him the haladie.

"Solar Sword!" When the warlock called out those two simple words, I knew what to do.

Without hesitation, I willed the Solar Sword into my left hand and ran to the road where the Elemental Wizards were holding the Army of Chaos at bay with what appeared to be a wall of shimmering light. The dark cloud still hung over the top of the approaching army and with a flash of insight I had rarely experienced before, I drew my arm back hurling the Solar Sword into the center of it. The instant the light touched the dark mass it exploded, raining sparks and fire down over everything in the road. The Elemental Wizards and I, as well as the men running up behind me to engage in battle, were shielded by the wall of magic, but on the other side, everything was destruction. A roar, so loud I wanted to clap my hands to my ears, split the sky as the torocs and other creatures raged in fear and pain. When the light from the fires suddenly went out, the Elemental Wizards dropped the magic shield and disappeared. Many of the Army of Chaos fled, their skin and hair on fire, though some remained. The attackers' numbers were greatly diminished, but a few charged toward us, swords drawn, maces swinging. As I drew ThornSting from the scabbard on my hip, I saw King Rowan's guards moving up alongside me and, in a line, we surged forward. Swords slashing and stabbing, shields blocking, spears hurtling through the air, we fought the remnants of the Army of Chaos, killing a dozen or so before the rest threw down their weapons and ran.

"What happened?" As the last of the torocs fled, Lieutenant De Groot exclaimed, "Why did they give up? Why did they run?"

"Only a few truly had the taste for battle," Abra joined us as he surveyed the carnage. He walked past us to pluck the Solar Sword from the road where it had landed. "You see, most were held in thrall by the Hungry Darkness and had no choice but to do what it demanded. Those were the creatures that ran the minute the cloud was dispersed. Only the torocs who are naturally violent but equally mindless remained for the fight, but even they gave up when they saw their fellows killed."

"So, it's over! The Hungry Darkness is no more and the Army of Chaos is disbanded?" I looked at my beloved mentor hopefully.

"Almost, my dear," he nodded soberly, as he returned the Solar Sword to my hand, "almost!"

"What more?" Captain Durand wiped a bead of perspiration from his forehead, turning his gaze to me, as if he thought I knew the answer. I responded with a shrug.

"The vortex must be closed," Abra looked directly at me. "And King Radolph must be apprised of the situation."

"King Radolph!" I gasped at the sudden realization that though I had relieved his daughter of the demon she had allowed to take over her body, I had left the very angry and very volatile young woman who felt he betrayed her unattended. "Dukes and Dragons! The king is in danger!"

At that, I tossed the Solar Sword into the air, where it disappeared silently. I sheathed ThornSting, turned on my heel, and rushed to the royal tent. King Radolph's guards surrounded his canopy and as I reached the entrance, one of the guards pulled the flap open for me, nodding, "You are expected." Pausing to glance over my shoulder, I saw Captain Durand had followed. When I entered the royal tent, he joined me.

King Radolph and Princess Eleanora sat side by side in elaborately carved, straight back chairs. Perhaps not as heavy or detailed as thrones, the furniture seemed appropriately regal despite being light enough to be easily transported. The king looked upset; his brow creased in obvious worry. His daughter, seated to his right, had tears streaking down her cheeks, and she daintily dabbed at them with a linen handkerchief. Both members of the royal family wore dressing gowns beneath their robes, having neither the time nor the inclination to dress in the middle of the night.

"Your Highness," I bowed my head. When I looked up into his eyes, I saw pain and confusion in their depths. "I beg your pardon that I had no time to explain what had happened. Danger was approaching quickly, so I had to deal with Princess Merilda succinctly. I owe you an explanation, Sire."

"Princess Merilda is in the custody of my personal guards," he shook his head with a sigh. "She tried to harm herself with a blade."

"I am so sorry, Your Highness," In sympathy I replied, "She is well?"

"She was stopped before she cut too deeply," He responded.

"I'd like to explain if I might," I beseeched him, "for you see, your daughter was angry and distraught over being forced to marry King Rowan. In her emotional distress, she opened herself to an evil energy that sought to undermine the upcoming nuptials. This being, the Hungry Darkness is what I called it, was, with the help of Princess Merilda's magic, sending nightmares into the dreams of children to feed off their fear. It grew stronger dream by dream, night by night, until even your daughter could not control it. It overtook her and it would not let her go; she could not escape it."

"Continue," King Radolph nodded.

"This evil, the Hungry Darkness, used your daughter and the collective fear of the children to call forth an army of torocs and other creatures. The army was on its way here to kill you and Princess Eleanora, but I was able to remove the Hungry Darkness's talisman from Princess Merilda's person and destroy it so the entity released her. I gather that when she was free of its influence and realized what she had done, or allowed to be done, she could think only of destroying herself. I'm sure she'll never forgive herself."

"She and I had discussed her upcoming marriage to King Rowan," the king mused aloud, "and though she'd not seemed especially pleased at the prospect, she did not refuse or object. I might have reconsidered the union had I known how she felt. Still, she is guilty of using magic and for that she must be punished."

Fearful of showing any reaction at the king's decrying the use of magic, I froze. If the man had any idea just how much magic was surrounding him, affecting his people and his life, I was sure he'd be stunned. Still, I reasoned, I was not one of his subjects and his beliefs and rules did not apply to me. King Rowan knew well I was warlock, that I wielded power others would consider magic, and it was to his service I was oathed.

As her father spoke further about his eldest daughter's wickedness and the marriage that would not take place, I watched the expression on Princess Eleanora's face go from sadness to hopeful anticipation.

"It's you who are in love with King Rowan," I gasped at the truth even as I spoke, startled at my own audacity in saying it aloud, "isn't it, Princess Eleanora?"

Blushing violently, she only lowered her eyes, smiling softly.

"Is this true?" King Radolph asked his daughter.

"Please, Father," she murmured, "another time!"

"Sire, if I might be so bold," I interjected, "what will become of Princess Merilda now?"

"Come morning, my men will escort her back to Ayndor and deliver her into the hands of the sisters of St. Benedict where she will be given the time and opportunity to consider her deeds. She will not be marrying King Rowan."

"I understand, Your Highness," I bowed my head, "and again, I am sorry for all that has happened."

"Thank you, Lady Falcon Rose," he replied. "You may go now."

We were dismissed, and it was with great relief I stepped out of the tent into the now quiet night. Captain Durand joined me and together we just stood there, taking in the fresh air, looking up at the stars and waxing moon in the sky. Suddenly, the enormity of all that had happened washed over me. In a flash, I recalled holding young Brice as he slept for the first time in days. I saw the twins, George and Geoffrey, being able to sleep at the same time. I remembered the horrific scenes of toddlers and small children perishing in gruesome ways. The keen awareness of having been in the presence of the Hungry Darkness, in its Emmeline Caulfield form, as it held Princess Merilda as Z in its thrall in my dream shook me to my very core. Suddenly, the crystalline knowledge that it was all over, that the threat was gone, that all was well nearly brought me to my knees with relief. Tears welled in my eyes. I could not keep a sob from escaping.

"Are you crying?" Captain Durand's voice was filled with surprise.

"No," I muttered, turning my head away, trying desperately to regain my composure.

"Falcon," he insisted, turning me to face him. "You are crying. It's all right."

At that he drew me into an embrace, putting his arms around me while chuckling softly.

"I am not crying!" With weakening will, I protested.

Feeling so safe, so secure, and utterly exhausted, I wept. I wrapped my arms around his waist, leaning my face against his chest to cry. Part of me wanted to be angry at his chuckling, but as it sounded good-natured, I ignored it.

"Of course, you're not crying," he responded, "you're just wetting my shirt."

"I'm sorry," I gasped. Trying to pull away, I found myself held securely against his chest.

"I must confess this is the first time I've held one of my guards while they cried!"

"I'm not one of your," I began, leaving the words unspoken.

How long we stood there in the darkness, him holding me firmly, letting me cry out my emotions, I could not tell, but it felt both a long time and a moment passing all too quickly.

"Two things, My Lady," he offered at length. "First, how did you know Princess Eleanora was in love with King Rowan?"

Shrugging in his arms, I sniffed, "I just saw it in her face. Her expression changed when her father announced that her sister would not be marrying him."

"I see." The captain nodded before adding, "Then there is just one more thing, Falcon Rose."

"What's that?" I pulled back from his embrace to look up at him. Though the night was dark, there was just enough moonlight and starlight to see the deep blue in his eyes.

"Your puppy," he released a rich, hearty laugh, "is a wolf!"

Startled by his words, I began to object, but recalled the sound of Lothar howling into the night, his ululation shattering the spell that held everyone in sleep. In that moment, I realized I had never heard Alexander Durand laugh before, and the sound was like music to me. Unable to resist, I happily joined him, my tears suddenly ceasing, my exhaustion forgotten. As we stood there together, laughing, I impulsively reached up to draw his face to mine, stretched up on my toes, and placed my lips on his. As I had never in my life initiated a kiss, I felt a bit clumsy doing so, but it felt right and he did not object. In fact, he wrapped both arms around me to kiss me back. In his arms, for that moment, the rest of the world spun away.

At last, and all to soon in my mind, the kiss ended. We did not separate, but instead merely stood there, gazing into each other's eyes, brazen in our searching, our seeking. What I saw in Alexander's eyes surprised me beyond measure. There was a softness, an openness, and a vulnerability in those eyes I had only caught glimpses of before, and it affected me deeply. I felt myself willing to look back, having the courage suddenly to allow him to see my own vulnerability, my own yearning. Were we challenging one another as we stood there face to face? Undoubtedly, but neither backed down or turned away. Instead, he favored me with a delicious smile, took my hand in his, and started walking me back to where Abra and the others were cleaning up the remains of the battle.

"Come, Falcon," Alexander grinned, squeezing my hand gently, "you have a vortex to close, whatever that means!"

Chapter 32

Abra stood in the middle of the road, hands on hips, watching the activity around him. Lieutenant De Groot, Beck, and Keller were surveying the area, picking up shards of metal, as well as the weapons the fleeing army had left behind. Some of King Radolph's servants were helping as well, moving the remains of the fallen off to the side of the road. Many of the creatures, it appeared, had been burned and crumbled to ash, but a few gory corpses were left in various stages of decay.

"How went your discussion with King Radolph?" the warlock cocked his head, raising an eyebrow as I approached.

"As well as could be expected, I suppose," I nodded, suddenly aware that Captain Durand was still holding my hand. I could not risk disentangling my fingers and drawing attention to the issue, so I stepped forward slightly to hide our joined hands behind my back.

"Very well, are you ready to close the vortex?"

"As ready as I'll ever be," I shrugged, "but I trust you know what to do and that you'll guide me through it?"

"Of course, my dear," Abra smiled with a twinkle in his eye. "Come, it's just this way. We'll walk."

When Alexander did not release my hand, I turned to look pointedly at him, silently pleading for release. He responded by shaking his head.

"Can Captain Durand come with us?" I called to the departing warlock as he strode away.

"Of course! Bring him along!"

The sky was full of stars and a descending moon, but the night held sway. Abra pulled a staff from beneath his long cloak, lifting it to the sky. Once the moonlight hit the stone on the tip of the staff it shone brightly around us, lighting the way. I hurried to catch up with the warlock, dragging Alexander along with me. We walked along the road for a bit, as Abra moved off to the west, picking his way carefully over the uneven ground. Though he held the staff up so the light fell around us, the weeds and vines that choked the path made seeing where to step impossible, so I had to feel my way along as best I could. We walked away from the road for quite a distance before making our way down a gentle slope. As we started up an incline Abra raised his hand in the air as he drew us to a halt.

"This is it," he announced cryptically.

"This is what?" I gaped, moving up beside him to peer at the top of the incline ahead. "Oh, I see." Stunned at what spun before me, I could only stand there overwhelmed. It took my mind several minutes to understand what my eyes were telling it. "That's a vortex," I whispered in awe.

"It is indeed, Falcon," the warlock replied. "You know how to close it?"

"I, um," I could only mutter, trying to string words together into something that would make sense.

A portal, I knew, was a peaceful thing, very much like a doorway, or an opening to a cave. The vortex appeared to be something entirely different. It was circular like a portal, but there the similarity ended. Inside that outer circle energy spun around and around, colors flashing and changing. The vortex emitted a roar, though from where I stood, I could not understand how that was possible.

"Here, my dear," Abra turned to deposit something solid in my hand.

Tearing my eyes away from the mesmerizing sight at the top of the hill, I looked down to find the talisman, the haladie, once more in my hand.

"What am I to do with this?" I gaped, hoping the serpents on the double-bladed handle wouldn't spring to life, hissing and slithering.

"Use it to close the vortex," he nodded at me, patted me on the shoulder, and gently moved me forward. Alexander released my hand as I started climbing the hill with no idea of what I was doing. I climbed, wishing the warlock had given me his staff or a torch, or even handed me my Earth Star. The light from Abra's staff still shone around me, weakly, but it was not enough for me to see much, so I just focused ahead, keeping my eyes on the vortex.

The wind rose as I grew near my destination. It whipped my hair into my eyes, blinding me painfully. My tunic and trousers flapped against my body. The force tried to push me back down the hill, but I bent into the wind and got as close to the vortex as I dared. The roar I had heard from below was deafening standing so close to the source, and myriad voices were carried on that wind. Whispers, murmurs, moans, muffled voices speaking or calling out, they were all coming from inside the vortex and I could understand none of them. The tips of the haladie in my hand began to glow brightly, the color matching a place on the outer ring of the vortex. Suddenly, I knew I had to slip the blade into that slot to begin the closing process, but before that I had to send something powerful through it to seal it forever. The earthen fetch at my middle vibrated and grew hot. Without question, I withdrew the cloth-covered, roughly fashioned body and hurled it into the vortex. The swirling energy within 'Whooshed' as the fetch disturbed its flow. Glancing down at the talisman in my hand, I realized both ends of the haladie were glowing the same color, and I had no idea which to insert into the slot. Forced to guess, I shoved one end of the haladie into the slot on the outer ring of the vortex. The minute it clicked, the vortex expanded, though the wind diminished.

"Oh, that's not right," I told myself, sure in the knowledge that no one would be able to hear me over the howl of the wind. Withdrawing the talisman, I turned it end for end before reinserting the blade. Instantly, the vortex grew smaller, but the wind grew stronger, the howling louder and higher pitched.

"Now what?" I screamed into the wind, truly at a loss, having no idea what to do.

Everything went silent. The vortex still spun, but the air around me was suddenly still. I felt a presence behind me, a firm pressure on my back, and a hand moved around to where I held the haladie, the black leather vambrace on the wrist and forearm wonderfully familiar. My father's scent wafted around me filling me with strength, comfort, and a sense of security. A warm hand landed on my shoulder and my mother's voice filled my ear.

'You can do this Falcon,' she assured me. 'Your strength is greater than the vortex. Our strength is greater than the vortex.'

Filled with hope and fresh determination, I started to pull the haladie down in the opposite direction of the vortex's spiraling energy. At first it would not budge, but when my father's grip steadied my hand, the outer ring began to move.

"Our strength is greater than you," I screamed into the wind. "Our strength is greater than you! Our strength is greater than you!"

With clarity that I was doing exactly what was needed and that success was at hand, I moved the talisman all the way around the outer edge of the vortex. Once the blade had successfully traversed the entire circle, the spinning energy halted and the wind ceased. The vortex simply *winked* out. I stood there on the hill, haladie in hand, alone and in silence, but my mother's words still echoed in my mind, my father's scent, and the feel of his strong hand around mine were still with me.

"Did you see them?" I bounded down the hill holding the talisman in my right hand, steadying ThornSting's length along my leg with my left hand. My knees were wobbly and I felt weak all over, but I was so elated I could hardly contain my joy.

"See who?" Abra looked up at me in surprise.

"My parents! They were there! They were with me. I wouldn't have known what to do or been strong enough to do it if it wasn't for them. Didn't you see them? They were right there!"

"We couldn't see anything once you drew level with the vortex," Captain Durand replied. "In fact, you disappeared entirely. It looked like you'd stepped into a tunnel."

"I can't believe you didn't see them," I sighed, disappointed that I had experienced such a magical moment with no one to witness or share it with me.

"But the important thing is that you did it, my dear," the warlock offered, grabbing my hand, pumping it up and down firmly in congratulations. "The vortex is now closed."

"Something occurred to me, Abra, and maybe you can explain," furrowing my brow in confusion, I shook my head. "The talisman closed the vortex. You and I went through a portal years ago to another time, the past or the future, to retrieve the talisman so...did this all happen because of us?

If we hadn't gone through the portal and gotten the talisman, would any of this have happened?"

"I understand your confusion, Falcon," he patted my hand as he took the haladie from me. "And I assure you, had you and I not claimed the talisman everything would have happened, but we'd have been powerless to stop it."

"So, us taking the thing through a portal didn't cause the portal to become a vortex?" Though not entirely clear on what was stirring in my mind, I blundered on, sure that eventually I would understand.

"Not entirely," he raised a finger before continuing, "but you see, we claimed the talisman from the future in the past, and perhaps dragging it into the past, this past, might have allowed for some energy misplacement. The Hungry Darkness is what fueled that energy into a vortex and used it to call forth its minions."

"Going into the future, bringing something with us to the past which is now," I shook my head, "just thinking about it makes my head hurt."

"By all means," Abra smiled as he slipped the haladie into the wide cloth belt around his middle, "think no more about it. Let us go back to camp and have some refreshment!"

Part of me wanted to protest, to stand there discussing the matter until I fully understood all that had happened, but another part wanted only to return to the fire, snuggle Lothar, and have a warm drink. Captain Durand slipped his arm around my shoulders, steadying me as we made our way back to camp. If Abra noticed or thought anything of the gesture he refrained from comment, and for that I was grateful.

Lothar came bounding up the road to greet us long before we reached the camp. King Radolph's guards had returned to their posts and his servants had returned to their beds, as the rising sun began to turn the night sky pale gray. My fellow guardsmen had stoked the fire and rose to greet us as we returned. They eagerly awaited explanations. Once Abra had a tankard of ale in his hand, and the captain and I had our beverages, everyone sat down around the fire. Lothar stretched out beside me, resting his muzzle on my leg. The warlock began the story of how he and I had claimed the talisman before he turned the tale over to me. I could not explain how I had learned much of what I knew, so I had to gloss over some of the details or even spin a bit of a yarn to hold the storyline together. But eventually, we explained what had happened to everyone's satisfaction. No one mentioned the missing guardsmen, Martin and Prouse, and I could not bring myself to tell them the Hungry Darkness had swallowed them and that nothing of them would ever be found. There were many questions from the men as to what exactly the Hungry Darkness was and how I came to know about it. I could only credit my time and training with the Elemental Wizards, and when I mentioned them, their voices rang out in my mind.

'*Well done, Falcon Rose,*' Cor's words fell sweetly on my heart, '*I'm so very proud of you. We're all so very proud of you!*'

'*Yes, Falcon,*' Finias Marin's voice was clear and joyful, '*well done! Well done indeed!*'

'*You did an excellent job, my dear,*' Declan Terrene added.

'*Couldn't have done it better, lass,*' Eban Kendall chimed in. '*Congratulations!*'

'*I couldn't have done it without you,*' I responded in my mind. '*Thank you all for your help. We'd not have won the battle had it not been for all of you!*'

'*You're welcome!*' They responded in unison, the connection breaking as I felt them withdraw.

"Well now," Abra drained the remnants of his drink as he patted his stomach, "I suggest we all get as much rest as we can. Sunrise will be upon us shortly and the day ahead may be arduous. Let us retire."

Mumbling some vague disappointments that there would be no more drink, King Rowan's guards made for their respective blankets while I rearranged my saddle bags near Aeon's saddle and unbuckled ThornSting's sheath belt from my hips. I stretched out on my side, one hand beneath my head, the other on Lothar's warm back as I closed my eyes. In the darkness I felt Alexander's hand reach out to touch mine and the thought of scooting over to rest beside him crossed my mind. But I was too tired to move and unwilling to explain to anyone else what I was doing should they awaken to find us so close together. So, I lay on my side, one hand on the puppy, Alexander's hand on mine, and that was how I was when sleep claimed me.

Mala and Mara stood beside me, one on my left, the other on my right. We were walking somewhere, though I realized I did not know where we were going. I was comfortable in the knowledge that the felinetrix, both in female form, knew our destination. When I looked at one then the other, they each favored me with a beautiful smile. We walked, and I simply enjoyed being in their presence, until a light appeared on the horizon. Though our pace did not change the light before us grew larger and larger, much more quickly than it should have. Suddenly we stood before a portal, bright and shining. Mala touched my left shoulder, nodding that I should look into the simmering energy. Mara touched my right shoulder, giving it a gentle, reassuring squeeze. Drawing in a deep breath, I turned to face the portal.

The nemeton spread out beneath me, the towering standing stones casting shadows across the dry ground. Two horses stood off to the left of the place, while the light in the center of the circle rose to expand and illuminate the guardians standing before the stones. I saw myself making my way around the light to look into the pit in the earth where the distressed puppy tried again and again to escape. I watched as Deacon went for the rope tying it around my middle to lower me into the hole. Soon I reappeared, puppy in my arms, as the druid pulled me back up.

As I stood there watching, I wondered why I was being shown the incident. I knew what had happened, my memories of it were clear. Suddenly I noticed a different light shining from between two of the most distant stones. An image was coalescing within the light, and as I watched, aware of my heartbeat picking up speed, it became clear that it was the Goddess herself shimmering in that light. Whiter than white, more crystalline than silver, her energy pulsed gently around her. Eyes the shade of fresh lilacs, hair the color of winter snow, her beauty took my breath away and part of me very much wanted to close my eyes.

'Do you know me child?' She asked softly, her voice full of kindness.

'I know you, yes,' I snapped childishly, unable to refrain. *'You let my parents die horrible deaths! You did nothing to stop it! You could have protected them as they both served you faithfully, but you didn't!'*

Though I expected the beautiful deity to grow angry, possibly even strike out at me in punishment, she did not. She only lowered her eyes and bowed her head as if in sorrow.

'Your anger is understood, though misplaced,' Came a strong male voice. At first, I thought it might be Cor speaking, only to realize the tone was much deeper, more powerful. From between two more of the stones shown a light of brilliant gold. The God himself stepped into the nemeton to stand beside the Goddess.

'So, who should I have been angry with? Who was to blame?'

'You know the answer to that, Falcon,' He replied calmly. *'Though you turned your heart away from us, we never left you. We have always been with you and we will always be with you.'*

'Are you angry now that I snatched away your sacrifice? Is that why you're showing me this?' I pointed at the scene near the edge of the nemeton where Deacon and I were walking back to our horses, the newly freed puppy joyfully bouncing around us.

'Who do you think put Lothar there for you to find?' As the Goddess spoke, I noticed her voice sounded like raindrops dancing off tender leaves. I longed for her to speak further.

'Wait, you mean that you put the wolf in the pit for me to rescue? Why? Why would you do that?' Trying desperately to hold on to my anger and indignation, I countered more forcefully than I'd intended.

'I had to find a way back into your heart, my darling. Lothar is yours, your spirit guide, your animal companion, your champion, and protector. In time, you'll find he walks between worlds and comes and goes as is needed, but for now he is yours.' The Goddess' words fell on me like a soft shower, washing away the pain and anguish I'd fed for years. Part of me still wanted very much to hold onto my anger, as it had shielded me from the depths of utter sadness, but most of me was ready to let it go. And when I thought of the love and adoration I saw in Lothar's eyes, I could only be grateful to the deities for bringing him into my life.

'I do love him,' I admitted, suddenly feeling foolish. *'And I do thank you for him. I suppose I should thank you both for having my parents stand with me to close the vortex, as you must have had a hand in that. I guess I realize now I was never really without them.'*

'Never without them,' The God echoed my words, his golden aura expanding over the scene. He wore a sleeveless robe of shimmering golden

light, his bare arms well-muscled and well defined. His long golden hair was smoothed back from his forehead and a circlet of gold rested beautifully above his piercing eyes. *'And never without us!'*

'Never without you,' I murmured as the scene before me disappeared. Mala and Mara, who had been standing beside me, vanished. I stood alone before the now empty portal, reeling in the newly discovered perspective I'd been given. It was an amazing thing to know such powerful beings were not only aware of my existence, but that they had a hand in my life, and in my world. I was not sure whether to feel elated and reassured, or small and manipulated, but I knew there would be much time to consider such things. Alone, thoughts awhirl, I turned around to walk back the way I had come. As I retraced my steps, I felt others around me, walking along with me, though I could not see anyone. It felt good to be going back, back to Lothar, back to Abra, and back to Alexander. The road disappeared as my thoughts spun out around me.

Chapter 33

We arrived in Esling one day past full moon, and if King Rowan was disappointed or upset with us for being late, we never knew of it. A scout was sent ahead to Castle deBirch to let him know we were arriving, and by the time we entered the city the celebration was underway. The crowd gathered in the open court cheered and waved as we rode by. Flowers were tossed at the royal carriage as Princess Eleanora peeked out through the window to wave at everyone.

King Rowan greeted King Radolph and his daughter on the steps outside the castle. Accepting salutes from his royal guard and myself, he escorted his royal guests inside. Captain Durand spoke in hushed tones with the king's aide before letting us know that we were dismissed with His Highness's thanks and that we would be expected to attend a ceremony at Castle deBirch in one week's time. With dismay touched with disappointment, standing beside Aeon before the empty steps to the castle, I turned, reins in hand, to make my departure. Lothar, walking along beside me, favored me with a look of confused curiosity. I was about to pat his head and assure him all was well when I heard my name called.

"Lady Falcon Rose," the young page, Edward, raced through the ornate double doors of the castle, hurrying down the steps to where I stood, "His Highness wishes to see you. You and Captain Durand as well as Abra are to remain. You are to stay here."

"Well," I blinked in surprise, "I guess we'll stay. Please have Haggerty tend to our mounts, Edward."

The king's aid rejoined us near the steps to escort us inside. We were led to a cozy room where we could relax and enjoy food and drink. As we waited for our audience with the king, we discussed what the matter might be, ranging anywhere from the possibility of a public hanging to a knighthood for the warlock. Eventually, we gave up the game to sip our respective drinks silently. Edward tapped on the door tentatively before entering and requesting Captain Durand follow him. Abra and I were left alone, surprised and slightly offended. We looked helplessly at one another before breaking into gales of laughter. The absurdity of the situation hit us both at the same time, and relief was born on humor.

"Well, I guess we're second- and third-class citizens, respectively," I chuckled, helping myself to a tankard of ale, though I seldom drank the stuff. It was foamy and cool, and it quenched my thirst nicely. A basket of bread and another full of fruit sat on the table near the window so I picked up a roll, sniffed it, and took a bite. The bread was tender, fresh, and still warm.

"Perhaps the king has something to discuss with the captain that pertains to court business and nothing at all to do with us?" Abra shrugged, taking a long draught from his own tankard. "In the meantime, it's not so very bad to be here in this fine room with good food, good drink, and, if I may be so bold, good company!"

"You may indeed be so bold," I nodded as I resumed my seat in an elegant, upholstered chair beside the hearth. Lothar joined me, tail wagging, sniffing my hand in hopes of sharing my bread roll.

"So, what will you do with your wolf now, Falcon Rose?"

"What do you mean? The beast hasn't changed, he's still my friend. He'll remain with me for as long as he wishes to do so."

"And this won't cause a problem in your future? People won't see Lothar as dangerous and a threat? What if he gets hungry and lays waste to an entire herd of sheep?"

"I don't think a wolf capable of laying waste to a herd of sheep would be inclined to remain in the company of a mere mortal like me."

"Don't deceive yourself, Falcon," the warlock grinned as he tossed Lothar a scrap of food, "you are anything but a mere mortal. You are Warlock, you're a healer, and you're a solar witch, any one of those things being particularly marvelous. And on top of that, you're Aerienesse, at least your spirit is."

"What does all that mean?" I countered, "I mean really, in the grand scheme of things, what does any of it mean?"

"It means, my dear, that you're imminently capable of keeping a wolf as a friend. I was just having a spot of fun with you."

"Ah, I see," nodding sagely, or what I hoped would be sagely, I had another drink of ale.

"Speaking of a spot of fun," Abra continued, "I noticed you and the captain have grown close."

Cheeks flaming, ears ringing, I could only gape at my cherished warlock mentor and not respond.

"I think you two make a..."

"A what, Abra? We make a what?"

"A formidable pair," he blinked, clearly having changed the response he'd intended.

"Yes, well," I sniffed, "let's just leave that matter alone, shall we?"

An uneasy silence fell over the room.

"Abra," I asked as something suddenly occurred to me, "I get that the Hungry Darkness was using the image of Emmeline Caulfield, but why? Why did it, I mean she, why did she appear to Jack Adler and help him out? Why did she have Merilda as Z with her? Why did I dream that?"

"I can't say for sure," he responded thoughtfully, "but I suspect it was trying to tap into your power. Though you don't have the fears children do, if the Hungry Darkness could make you fear and feed from it, it would have your power, which is considerable."

"So, it was trying to get to my power," I reasoned aloud.

"Because it was Hungry Darkness. It craved power. It could not resist trying to take yours."

"And the haladie? How is it that was able to destroy the entity?"

"Remember the gentleman we met in Stillmoor? The chap discovered he would not have nightmares if he slept in the small cave he found. I believe that stone was impervious to the Hungry Darkness's power, and it was that type of stone from which the blades of the talisman were crafted."

"And the pendant Princess Merilda wore, the stone in it was the same as the stones on the handle of the haladie."

"Indeed, it was," he nodded exuberantly, "and when you took it from her, you broke any hold the Hungry Darkness had. She had been taken in by the beauty of the pendant, and once she'd accepted it, the entity was able to gain control. But let us be clear, it was her anger, her bitterness, her feelings of betrayal that led to her undoing."

"I understand," I sighed. "Still, if her father had been more understanding, perhaps none of this would have happened."

"One might also suggest that if Princess Merilda had only been more amenable to marriage, more cooperative, and more accepting in her royal duty…"

"Royal duty," echoing his words, I added, "I can't even imagine! Those of us who have no royal blood can only look at such rulers as living in wealth and splendor. We can only see the beauty and abundance they appear to enjoy and have no idea of what it must really be to be born into that world. Merilda was born to duty, even though her mother promised her otherwise. To the king she was little more than chattel, a bartering piece for an allied kingdom. I can't say I blame her for feeling as she did, though her actions could have been disastrous."

"Indeed," he nodded, thoughtfully stroking his beard, "her feelings may have been valid but her actions were so very dangerous. It's fortunate for her that King Rowan sent you on this journey."

"So, what happened to the pendant?"

"Do you not remember?" The warlock blinked, his expression one of clear surprise.

"I remember the stone went black, but beyond that I don't recall."

"When you separated the pendant from the Hungry Darkness's host it severed the connection and the stone died. You must have flung it from the princess as it was recovered near the mouth of the royal tent sometime later. It has no power now, it's lifeless, but if you want it I have it," he explained patiently.

"No thanks," I shook my head, "you can keep it. I want no trace of the Hungry Darkness anywhere near me!"

At that, a rap on the door interrupted our conversation. When the door opened, the young page, Edward, appeared once more.

"If you will both follow me, please," he bowed politely.

"Fine," I replied, happy to be free of the possibly embarrassing conversation likely to follow. Patting the resting Lothar on the head, I told him to be good and stay put in front of the hearth. I adjusted the royal cloak on my shoulders as well as the sapphire blue healer's sash on my waist, before stepping into the hallway behind Edward. Abra drained his tankard, set it down on the table, and joined us in the corridor.

The young page escorted Abra and me to the Grand Hall, bowed, and disappeared down the corridor. As we entered through the soaring arched doorway, we were greeted by a scene of beauty and opulence. Torches burned in wall sconces; elegantly wrought chandeliers overhead cast a warm glow on the glossy marble floor below. Rows of elegantly dressed people stood quietly on either side of a main aisle covered with a richly-woven emerald tapestry runner. On the dais at the end of the aisle King Rowan sat beside Princess Eleanora on similar thrones. King Radolph stood beside his daughter, a protective and reassuring hand on her shoulder. Captain Durand stood at attention with the other guardsmen just below the dais, and as Abra and I entered the room everyone turned to look at us. Feeling the weight of responsibility and a touch of discomfort, I started hesitantly down the aisle, holding the warlock's elbow as I did so.

"Abra, my good friend," the king greeted the warlock warmly, "I thank you for your invaluable help in this matter. As always, your timing and assistance were impeccable!"

"Your Highness," Abra bowed, "it is ever my pleasure to serve."

"Lady Falcon Rose," King Rowan addressed me formally, "it has come to my attention that you have acted with bravery and valor in delivering my fiancé and her father to me."

My mind was busy spinning with his words, but I did notice he referred to Princess Eleanora as his fiancé and mentioned nothing of Princess Merilda.

"I," glancing first at the king, then Captain Durand, then Abra, I realized that I did not know what to say or how to respond. "It was an honor, Your Highness."

"And to that end, it has been suggested that you assume the role of captain of my personal guard," he continued. "What say you?"

Blank! My mind went blank! I heard the king's words, knew basically what they meant, but the repercussions of what he had said staggered me. I looked at Alexander, standing there at attention, but he only looked back with a serious expression on his face.

"Your Highness," I breathed, but barely, "with all due respect, you have a captain of your personal guard and he's a very fine one at that! I would not take that from him."

"It was Captain Durand who suggested you take the position," King Rowan beamed, looking at me before turning to nod at the captain.

"But, but," I realized I was stammering, as I stalled for time to collect my thoughts. I cleared my throat and began, "King Rowan, Your Highness, I am deeply honored by the offer of this post, but I must decline. There was a time, My Lord, that I would have leapt at such an offer, to serve you and the house of deBirch in the same manner my father did, but I have learned that I am not a soldier. I am a healer, and that is my destiny. My sword shall forever be at your service, and I will gladly serve in any manner I can, but I must refuse the position of captain." With that I went down on one knee and bowed my head, as it was protocol. The moments seem to tick by, silence falling over the crowd like a heavy blanket before King Rowan rose and all in attendance stood.

"Lady Falcon Rose," he decreed, "it shall be as you wish. Captain Alexander Durand shall remain the captain of my guard and you are free to return to your duties as healer. I accept once more your offer of service, should the need arise. You may go now with my thanks as well as the thanks of all Esling. Your service shall be rewarded!"

A cheer went up around the room as the king returned to his throne. Abra helped me to my feet, as the ale and the excitement had left me a bit wobbly. Once in the wide corridor outside the Grand Hall, I turned to Abra, smiling giddily.

"Well, that was unexpected," I laughed, overcome with relief. It was only at that moment I realized Captain Durand and his men had followed us out to gather around us. There were words of thanks, congratulations, and well done offered and reciprocated, a few pats on the back and handshakes shared, and everyone insisted on giving me a hug, Alexander stepping back so the others could go first. I embraced the men warmly as Abra looked on, an expression of smug self-satisfaction on his face. At last, the guardsmen feigned duties elsewhere as they moved off down the corridor, leaving me alone with the captain. When it was his turn to hug me, I stiffly accepted his embrace as he briefly wrapped his arms around me.

"Lady Falcon Rose," he stepped back to look me in the eye, "you are the most infuriatingly captivating creature I've ever encountered. You intrigue me, you fascinate me, and for a time I thought surely you had bespelled me."

"Captain Durand, I," I started to protest but he put his index finger against my lips to quiet me.

"And I do not know how," he added, "but I know it was you who brought about our escape from the torocs. I didn't see you, didn't hear you, but I sensed you were there. One moment my men and I were surrounded by the monsters and about to be slain. An instant later the creatures were either dead on the ground around us or they were fleeing in fear for their lives. I know it was you, and I could think of no better captain of the king's guards than one who could defend and protect the kingdom with such power. That's why I suggested to the king that you should be made captain."

"You, you knew?" I gasped, as according to Abra it was impossible that anyone would be aware of us having traveled as we had through the portal. "How's this possible?"

"That I do not know, Falcon," he shook his head, "but I know what I know. And I do not say this lightly, but you have captured me in your spell." Looking deeply into my eyes, his voice lowered to an intimate whisper, he drew nearer.

"I assure you I cast no spell," I started to protest, not knowing where he was headed with the mention of a spell. "And you are the only man for King Rowan's captain of the guard."

"Falcon," he interjected as he took a step closer, "you have captured me, and...."

"And?" I could barely hear my own voice over the pounding of my heart. Alexander was now close enough that he could touch me without reaching.

"And," his eyes pierced my soul as he murmured softly, his lips so near and so inviting, "it would be an honor if you would…"

"If I would?" I whispered a reply, no breath left in me.

"If you would," he continued, the corners of his mouth twitching as the struggled to suppress a smile, "spar with me."

"Spar with me," I murmured, echoing his words. "Wait! You want me to SPAR with you? That's it? You wish to cross swords with me? That's what this is all about? How in the world could…"?

So swiftly that I had no means to counter the move, he slid one arm around my waist to pull me close. Before I could finish my thought or my response, his lips were on mine. My mind fell silent. I waited for the little voice in my head to scream objections, to direct me to flee or cause him bodily harm in order to escape, but it remained still. There in the corridor outside the Grand Hall of Castle deBirch, Captain Alexander Durand held me in his arms, kissing me deeply. Any thoughts of protest scattered. I realized that it was I who had been captured so I joyfully surrendered…for the moment.

Chapter 34

Snow fell softly around me, sparkling on my blue-gray woolen cloak as well as Aeon's ebony ears and mane. The world was silent as we made our way through the heavy drifts, white flakes dancing and swirling around us. Lothar, now barely able to fit on the saddle with me, lay sleeping beneath my cloak, his soft fur warm and dry under my hand. Where I had been and how long I had been gone was of no concern, for my only thought was to see Corhaven and my beloved wizard again.

Finally, the lovely cottage appeared in the distance, nestled comfortably at the edge of the woods, its thatched roof invisible beneath a blanket of fresh snow. So familiar and so inviting, Corhaven was home and I had missed it tremendously. Quickening Aeon's pace, I imagined the blue-eyed, white-haired wizard inside, stoking the fire in the hearth, maybe making a batch of his famous Tomcakes in honor of my arrival. Though I did not remember the words exchanged, I knew I had contacted him using our special silent communication and he was delighted that I would soon return.

Something was wrong, I realized as I neared the cottage. There were no tracks in the fallen snow to indicate anyone had been about, and no smoke rose from the chimney to perfume the air. The windows were dark; the place looked empty. Halting Aeon near the paddock fence, I wrapped her reins around a rail after releasing Lothar to the ground. The young wolf looked excitedly at the fallen snow, dug his nose into a drift, then dropped his shoulder into the stuff. With a chuff, he shoved himself into a snowbank, rolling onto his back, to wriggle in joyous abandon. Leaving the animal to his fun, I crossed the yard to the front door, avoiding the deeper drifts in an effort to keep my boots dry.

Cor should have been at the door to greet me. He knew I was returning and he should have been there, door opened wide, cottage warm and welcoming, but the door was closed. Having never been faced with the situation before, I didn't know whether to knock or just open the door and go in. But the hairs on the back of my neck were standing and the chills running up my spine were not caused by the snow. Something told me that knocking on the door would be to no avail, so I lifted the latch and shoved the heavy wooden door open.

The cottage was cold. There was no fire in the hearth, no candles lit for warmth and illumination. The place smelled of age, dust, and decay. Dried leaves and bits of nut shells lay scattered on the table before the hearth. A black and white cat stole inside, leaving little paw prints in the skiff of snow that blew in behind me. Quickly, I shoved the door closed to lean my back against it, struggling to understand what I was seeing.

When the feline, seemingly oblivious to my presence, leapt up onto the table I saw what it had carried in. The crushed, mangled black feathers, curled claws, and broken black beak jutting from the cat's mouth made it clear the prey had been a raven. My heart sank as I recognized the body of Cor's beloved bird, Vesta.

"Mala," I cried, "or Mara! How could you?"

The cat merely sat down, blinking innocently at me with bright green eyes, and spat the carnage out on the table. As if to taunt me, it set about chewing the head off the bird, crunching and grinding bone and flesh.

"What the devil is going on?" Shaking my head in disbelief, I pushed myself off the door to hurry through the cottage. Surely, there was some clue, some note or other indication to help me determine what was happening. "Cor! Where are you? Cor!"

I went from room to room, hoping beyond hope to find someone or some answer, but the cottage was empty save me and the cat. There came no response to my cries, and when I tried to contact the wizard with my mind, I found only an empty void. In desperation I tried to contact the other wizards, Declan, Finias, and Eban, but none answered. Watching a veil of spider webs waft gently between the ceiling rafters, tears welled in my eyes as I realized how utterly and absolutely alone I felt.

"Abra!" I called out, choking back a sob, "Abra, where are you?"

No answer came from the warlock, but just to the right of the empty hearth, a curtain of energy stirred. Shimmering, growing larger, the portal appeared silently. Apparently disturbed by the energy shift in the room, hissing with hackles raised, the cat snatched up the dead bird, leaping off the table to disappear into one of the other rooms. Mesmerized, I took a step closer to the portal in hopes of seeing what might be within, but my own image, tired and disheveled from my journeys, was all I could see. Long red-blond hair made wavy and curly by the snow, cheeks and forehead pink with chill, my green eyes shone oddly in the rippling reflection of the portal. Disquiet settled on my shoulders as I sensed approaching danger.

"I think it's time I go," I spoke to myself, voice barely above a whisper, wishing I was already away.

One hand on ThornSting's pommel, I turned from my image, determined to leave Corhaven with utmost haste, when a hand shot out of the portal to grab my wrist. Before I could shake the grasp off or try to escape, I was yanked into the portal head-first.

"Noooo…," my cry went with me into the void.

Also by T.S. Mos…

Falcon's Flight

Mystaken

(21st Century Vampire series)

Cat's Tale

Cat's Eyes

Cat's First